Of Sudden Origin

C. Chase Harwood

Of Sudden Origin

ISBN-10: 0692226451
ISBN-13: 978-0692226452

Thank you to my B-Readers, Mom, Leslie, Jane, and many others who don't necessarily seek out genre fiction for the beach. Having the opinions of people who aren't beholden to the genre helps make the work that much stronger. Richard Pine at Inkwell, gets a shout out for timeless and thoughtful advice that has been foundational to making me a more thoughtful writer.

I am most especially grateful to my copy editors, Chance, Peter and Tony. Your insight is invaluable. You keep me from looking the fool.

C. Chase Harwood lives in Los Angeles with his costumer designer wife and their boy/girl twins. When not diligently focusing on family, he works in Hollywood playing in the magical world of TV and Film. Writing tales to stir and thrill the soul is everything in between.

PREFACE

In 1999 professor of anthropology Jeffery A Schwartz of the University of Pittsburgh postulated a solution to the so-called Missing Link. He proposed, that given the poor fossil record for evolutionary graduation, that there were no missing links. He then offered an alternative to the accepted Darwinian model: Rather than life evolving through a slow adaptation to ever changing environmental factors, he suggested that evolution was actually a history of rapid genesis and extinction, with long periods of stasis in between. Schwartz used a growing body of molecular scientific evidence to show that evolution is not a progression of perceptible mutations within species, but rather a series of sudden origins, where new species burst forth upon the scene.

In 2010 Chris Venditti and Andrew Meade at the University of Reading in the UK and Mark Pagel at the Santa Fe Institute, New Mexico, followed up on Schwartz's work, among others, with a paper published in Nature. They concluded that the Darwinian theory of natural selection (whereby, over eons, transformations occur due to subtle changes in environment) made up for only 8% of evolutionary change. While studying rates of speciation in 101 groups of plants, animals, and fungi, they used four different evolutionary models to see which model best fit evolutionary history. They concluded that 78% of evolutionary family trees came into existence via singular, rare events, such as dramatic climate change, heaving mountains, shifting lands and *disease* - to name just a few.

In 2004 engineers and scientists at the University of Texas at Austin and the University of Michigan successfully forced an evolutionary leap: In a process likened to natural selection, they made random alterations in the DNA of E Coli bacterium and then observed the bacterium come up with an entirely new way to make disulfide bonds – the stiffening struts that help give proteins their shape. A critical structural component of healthy proteins, disulfides keep molecules from forming into the broken building blocks of disease, such as Alzheimer's, cystic fibrosis and mad cow. These researchers offered a new alternative to the control of disease – bioengineered evolution.

Creationists have latched on to some of the above to support their own theory - that an intelligent being, an omniscient engineer, controls all of this – completely new creatures simply don't spring forth from the ether; a greater hand is involved. Scientists would of course disagree; pointing out that these new manifestations are but the final result of an immeasurable buildup of genetic mutations – mutations, that when given the right environment, the right set of circumstances, will spring forth as new species.

PART ONE

THE EXODUS IS OVER

Nature encourages no looseness, pardons no errors -
Ralph Waldo Emerson

1 Growing Things

Like most prey animals, the white-tailed deer exits the womb and in moments, struggles to stand. To survive in a world where it is a delicacy on the large predator's list, it must be able to run almost as soon as it hits the ground. In a dense forest in Northern New England, a very odd looking infant who was already on the edge of intellectualizing this, watched with glee as its mother butchered a fawn. In its own way, this baby was a creature born to survive the moment it entered the world. Within the labyrinth of connections in its fast growing brain, there was a new sense, a new skill if you will, that neither dear Mother Earth, nor God if you prefer, had ever experimented with. While its mother, and a few others around her, gorged themselves on the flesh of the still twitching animal, the infant directed Mom to concentrate on the choicest parts. Though its own sharp teeth were just breaking through its gums, and it still preferred her warm milk rather than blood, marrow and muscle, it could nevertheless taste, smell and feel what its mother was eating. Everything that its mother sensed, the baby sensed as well. Its mind was connected through the ether to the others. As such, it directed its mother to eat only the choicest parts. As she gorged herself, it could feel and sense the mild frustration of the other's around it, and it gleefully directed them to chew on the lesser bits.

As it sat on the forest floor, crushing leaves between its tiny fists, the infant got an idea: a part of it already understood humor, and it directed one skinny male to gnaw on a hoof. The child could sense the male's irritation and its sharp pointy ears folded back with amusement while a large smile spread across its healthy pudgy face. It watched its legs kicking with pleasure and it couldn't help but notice how different its legs were from the others around it. This thought, like all its thoughts, immediately transferred to the mother. What was left of its mother's mind thought, *Fucking odd shape. Like the thing I'm gorging on.* The child's legs were hinged like the rear hocks of any four legged animal, only with elongated human feet; like a cat's hindquarters; built for speed.

Driving through ancient New England farmland, Jon Washington listened to the engine of his Jeep sputter with its last sips of fuel. With exhausted eyes, he scanned the old stone walls that broke up the rural landscape and thought, I don't have a clue about growing things. When his truck finally ran out of gas on a dirt road in the middle of a forest in New Hampshire, he looked around the thick wood and decided that he was far enough from civilization to warrant a piss... standing, instead of sitting, a bottle held to his crotch, the doors locked, engine running.

He'd been driving for five days straight; the last of the police and Army checkpoints the only things slowing him down. Atlanta had fallen in early April, and when Charlotte had been compromised, he, like all refugees, kept heading north. He had paused in Atlantic City where another wall had been hastily erected. He could still reach his editors who had bugged out to New York so he settled in to gather more information, report on what he thought could be helpful. A week later, commercial communication in North America fully broke down.

In some ways it had paid off to wait until the last moment to leave; the byways of the nation were now mostly open to him. At first, working north from Florida, he had struggled with the masses, witnessing the worst of the human animal when overcome by fear. It had been so tragically cliche, so Hollywood disaster, disappointing... but so very understandable. The bulk of the population, who were still ambulatory, had run in shear panic; literally driving over each other trying to escape. On the highway to hell that was Interstate 95, the number of victims of mob rule was too many to count. He could only marvel at the way that people became lemmings, the flight instinct taking over any rational thought. If they hadn't run each other over, they'd shot at each other in pointless me-first-isms. Law Enforcement, First Responders and the Military simply couldn't handle the mindless wave - not for lack of a plan, not for lack of trying - many a selfless soldier, firefighter and cop died trying. It was sheer numbers multiplied by abject terror. Nothing frightens a human being more than the idea of being eaten alive. Nothing stirs pure unmitigated panic in a person than the notion of being ripped limb from limb while being eaten alive by other human beings.

Jon pulled the parking brake and climbed out of the 4X4 while grabbing his police baton and shotgun. The two tools had become extensions of his arms since Atlantic City, pilfered from a dead cop's car. His truck was loaded to the gills with other less fortunate people's survival gear; again, being one of the last ones out made for easy pickings.

The air smelled clean. It had rained earlier and the damp pine needles mixed with ozone made the surroundings fresh and sweet. During the entire drive north he kept telling himself he'd have to grow things. The canned and foil-wrapped food he'd scavenged wouldn't last him long.

Hunting was something else all together. Other than the three Fiends in Atlantic City, he'd never shot anything in his life, and that had made him vomit.

As a reporter for the *Atlanta Daily Mail,* Jon Washington had been at the front lines. His ability to get information to the rest of the country was, he thought, the most important thing he could do. Information was critical in keeping the American people safe. Information was the best weapon they had.

When the Everglades containment fencing (also known as the *Everglades Wall*) failed, Jon Washington was there to report that the Army was falling back to the *Lakeland* blockade, giving citizens the time to move north behind the next barrier, officially named *The Orlando Wall.*

Before the Orlando Wall collapsed, Jon was among the first to note, from personal experience, that the infected had somehow gained a foothold on the North side. It was then that the WHO had gotten somewhat of a lock on the disease. It was bacterial in nature, and like the bacteria that causes meningitis, it was capable of passing through the blood-brain barrier; the vicious creature piggybacking on the very white blood cells that the body was sending to destroy it. They determined that it wasn't just spreading from a bite or a breath; it was showing up in municipal drinking water. The consensus was that someone was doing this. It was terrorism and it was national.

When people were suddenly becoming infected in Los Angeles in late March, then Seattle and other big cities, up to that point free of "infected" behavior, it was considered terrorism with weapons of mass destruction.

The disease was dubbed Frontal Negation Dementia by a USAMRIID scientist named Andre Zacharia and shortened to its acronym FND-z. The people gave it another name, one that they could get their heads around, one that made sense given the biblical proportions of its spread; they called it Cain's Disease – Cain: He who slaughtered his brother.

It began with an insatiable thirst that water couldn't quench. At first, many thought it was some kind of rodent poison, but that was quickly dispelled when the victim began to behave as if he'd been drugged with a huge hit of PCP: A person, once fully succumbed to Cain's, has a tenfold threshold for pain; muscles that once seemed fit to only lift a can of food, could now, in a short burst of energy, heave a refrigerator aside, kick down a door or grab a wrist and never let go. *Fiends* (as the infected became known from the phonetic of FND-z) could be anyone, even your grandmother sitting right next to you. At first she's thirsty and then she's begging for water, which offers no remedy as her skin grows hotter and she sweats through her nightgown. Over a period of hours she rants and raves in feverish delusion, her guts twisting in pain, agony building with frightening speed, the helplessness of the observer compounding every moment. Then a sudden calm, usually sleep, even a coma-like state. The fever has broken. Thank God. She can rest. An extra blanket is found. Another cool washcloth applied. Her color returns and her eyes finally open, and... grandma isn't grandma anymore. With eyes and mouth suddenly dripping with desire, she offers a look that can only be described as purest evil. She's still human, but there is nothing human in that look; a smiling rabid wolf occupies the space that was her. Laughing with lust, she attacks. She's as strong as an ape because she feels almost no pain. She'll snap her own bones in the struggle to gorge herself on your blood, to take a bite right out of your face, your neck, your thigh, tearing into your muscles with talon like fingers and literally shredding them off your skeleton. And this won't stop until she's either been shot, stabbed or beaten to death. She's the perfect killing machine, a shark that can't be sated. If you initially survived her attack, it wouldn't be more than twenty-four hours before you became a Fiend as well. A bite, or getting spittle or a splash of blood in the mouth, eye, open wound, even too close a breath and it's all over. Do yourself before it does you.

Jon stopped as he got out of the car and listened. A light breeze rustled the trees, shaking loose the day's rain that pitter-pattered over the soft ground. He could hear a woodpecker in the distance; a good sign. Fiends tended to want to feast on any flesh: bird, reptile, fish or mammal - if it had a heartbeat, it was fair game. Most animals sensed a Fiend well in advance and fled long before they arrived with their grunts and howls, sounding like a mad troop of chimps.

The leather of his motorcycle racing coveralls creaked as he stepped onto a large granite boulder to get his bearings. Feeling relatively secure, he kept his riot helmet off to allow his ears and eyes to work better. The Moto Guzzi rig, while garish in color, did an effective job of warding off bites. The leather, with its thick padding and built in skid plates for motorcycle racing, was just strong enough to give him time to maybe break loose, maybe strike out with the baton, thrust with a knife.

2 Summer Houses

The piss was downright luxuriant as he stood and relieved himself for the first time in several days without a bottle held to his crotch. As far as a good crap, he'd have to take something to help with that. An uncomfortable constipation had taken hold of him and he knew it wouldn't let loose until he could squat and feel invulnerable.

The breeze momentarily picked up, startling him as the higher branches waved back and forth, the forest suddenly filled with noise. He instinctively zipped up and crouched, clutching his shotgun, spinning in a three hundred and sixty degree turn. Seeing himself in the window of the Jeep, hunkered down with the gun, he stopped and chuckled while standing up again.

About one hundred yards off, he spotted the edge of what looked like a lake shimmering through the trees. Grabbing his helmet and locking the Jeep, he marched in the lake's direction. He'd been trying to get to the Canadian Wall when he ran out of gas. As foretold in every modern apocalyptic tale, all the major thoroughfares were teaming with the infected, and blocked with abandoned cars. His only choice was this backwoods escape. He hadn't accounted for just how rural New Hampshire actually was. The last two gas stations he had passed were abandoned, the pumps turned off. He didn't have a clue how to turn them back on. A hoped for gallon of fuel in someone's barn turned out to be pre-mixed with oil for a lawnmower.

His GPS showed him to be shy of the border by a hundred and fifty miles; a long way to hike in rugged country with limited food supplies. A lot nicer to have a steel and glass cage around you. He needed another vehicle. The lake likely meant summerhouses. Summerhouses often meant a summer car. Unfortunately, houses also often meant Fiends.

Damned infected people had plenty of brains left to figure out that most folks just hid in their homes. Of course that was changing now. The Exodus had placed the bulk of the healthy American population behind the Canadian Wall. The infected weren't far behind. The food supply had moved north and so were they.

Jon's grandmother intruded on his thoughts again, interfering with his need to focus, to walk quietly. At first he figured she just had the flu. The flu was raging during the winter and had the same initial symptoms as Cain's or 'The Terror Disease' as the New York Post and The Washington Times had dubbed it. While covering the *Stand* at the Orlando Wall, Jon was able to take a break and visit Granny Kat who had retired to Daytona ten years before. As his last living relative, he doted on her like a spoiled child. She in turn did the same and they worshipped one another in a way often lost as a child passes into adolescence. Granny Kat had cooked a key-lime pie that night, just in time for Jon's arrival. She hugged her grandson and then had to sit down, gulping what she said was her third glass of water in an hour. She was sweating and her pallor had turned gray. Jon escorted her to the couch in her sitting room and put a blanket over her. He got a thermometer and confirmed the fever: one hundred and three.

With what seemed like standard high fever delirium, the fierce fever of Cain's masked the loss of mental clarity. What was really happening was an incredibly rapid digestion of the frontal lobes of the brain and a near re-purposement of its complicated design. Within an hour, Granny Kat no longer recognized her grandson. A couple hours more and she didn't recognize herself. Like the endgame of Alzheimer's, the bacterial assault resulted in the complete destruction of personality. However, unlike the cruel reduction of self that is dementia and its various forms, Cain's left the victim with the most ancient part of the brain intact; the reptilian - the part that harbors fear, anger, the need to survive, lust, and the killer instinct. The highest form of existence, love, was replaced by something wholly unholy. It was irrationally hungry, thrilled with sexual assault, and gained profound pleasure from the kill. The unique virtue that made the human animal humane was lost whole cloth.

When Granny Washington suddenly came off that couch with the strength of a rabid jungle cat–

Jon felt his chest constrict with the memory of it, a combination of intense remorse and subconscious terror. His face had grown flush, he could feel the heat of it, and he realized that he was holding his breath. He exhaled and told himself to pay attention. Losing focus was a fatal mistake. After... after her death... his safety had become less of a worry. Nevertheless, he still had a job to do. Though there was no news desk anymore to send updates to, for his own sanity, he remained a reporter. His work was what saved him from a deep depression, and it was another reason why he was one of the last ones heading out.

He assumed he had been spared from the disease so far because of his near obsession with drinking only bottled water, a sip of which he took now as he walked through the woods. It had become unfashionable to drink bottled water in recent years (the attached carbon footprint having become unacceptable to a society fighting global warming) but Jon still kept the stuff squirreled away in his car for when he was alone. He'd occasionally get a honk and a finger wag from a scolding fellow driver, but most folks left him alone, others tipping their bottles in a toast, sharing a moment of sin.

It was May now. The whole disaster had begun the previous September. Until January, it had remained contained in Florida. When it became clear that Cain's had been released in the water supplies of ten of America's biggest cities, the Federal government actually had a plan C. It involved a massive evacuation to Canada, as well as Puerto Rico and Hawaii. Mexico became a de-facto haven, but the newly finished border fence stopped most escaping American's cold, and at the mercy of a rapidly growing army of Fiends at their backs. Mercy... mercy was a quick death. Mexico (the country now run by a massive drug cartel in all but name) handled its own small northern outbreak with brutal efficiency, quarantining the depth of its first twenty miles of its US border with ruthless death squads. Hawaii and Puerto Rico became victims of an air travel society when, early on, the sick and the healthy alike looked for refuge on those islands. Paradise was lost as the Pacific State and the Caribbean protectorate were sealed off and ultimately abandoned to chaos. As far as Jon knew, it was only the US that had been attacked. His shortwave radio merely told of the economic collapse occurring on the rest of the planet and the concurring bedlam that was its natural consequence. And now there was another twist: He hadn't witnessed it himself, but a few soldiers talked about it. Some kind of mind control. Like the infected could reach out mentally, get in your head and mess with it. None of the men he talked to could really describe it other than to say that it scared the crap out of them worse than a whole charging mob of the marauding berserkers. Jon could only take their word for it. His own experience with infected people had been harrowing enough without the added element of mental telepathy.

A branch snapped under his right foot and he stopped cold, listening for the consequences. He needed to concentrate. His city-boy gait must have sounded like a foraging bear without a care in the world. As he resumed walking, each crack of a stick had him wincing at his clumsiness, his unintended signal of approach. As he got closer to the water, he began to make out the lines of a small house. It had a pitched roof and clear-coated pine siding. It looked to be in good shape — at least from a distance. He stepped onto a dirt driveway that must have wound its way back to the road where his Jeep was parked and paused, looking through the trees. He had a small pair of binoculars on his hip and leaned his shotgun against a tree to allow for a steady view.

There didn't seem to be any movement. No generator, no lights, no smoke. The only sound continued to be the breeze; the woodpecker seemed to have moved on. He moved forward more slowly, really watching his footfalls. As the house became more visible, he could smell what he hoped wasn't there. He'd done a story about slaughterhouses a few years back. The smell of fear and blood is its own unique aroma. He stopped and slid his riot helmet over his head, leaving the visor up so that he could see and hear better.

The windows on the near side of the house looked to be broken in. A rotting, fly infested corpse lay on the ground outside. No way to tell if it was a Fiend or a victim of one, but the fact that the skeleton was mostly intact indicated that it was probably the former. Fiends didn't go after each other; the disease had no reason for assaulting itself. Somehow, the infected recognized the un-infected and only attacked them. Nature nevertheless continued with its egalitarian ways - in this case a parade of insects was slowly reducing the corpse to its component parts.

Jon slowly made his way around the perimeter. The evidence of a last stand was everywhere. The fools inside had watched too many zombie movies and had assumed that they could just board up their windows. The boards had been pried off - no point in trying to break a door down with so many windows to go for. The builder had wanted to take advantage of the view. The lakeside was almost all glass - broken glass now.

After Atlantic City, Jon knew better than to walk inside what seemed like an empty house, at least not without knocking. Lowering the visor to his helmet, he lifted his police baton and whacked it a few times against a tree. If there was a Fiend inside, he could expect it to come charging out any second, howling for a kill... nothing. He waited a beat and then whacked the tree again, just in case it or they were asleep and needed waking... still nothing. He raised his visor and called out, "Hello? Anyone home? Anyone alive?" Lowering his visor, he stepped forward.

Not all Fiends attacked like drug-addled lunatics. Some hid, biding their time. Some knew how to hunt. For some, a primal instinct stayed with them, an animal cunning. These were the truly dangerous ones. They were the alphas that could organize others into a pack of sorts. The Army called them troops, just like chimps. They even kept the understanding of rudimentary tools, mostly in the form of a club or a rock as a projectile, but blades or any sharp instrument could come into play.

He stepped onto the porch, picked up a shard of wood planking and tossed it inside, listening to it rattle across the floor... nothing. He stepped through one of the smashed picture windows. The house was trashed. Overturned furniture and broken glass, books, board games and puzzles, family photos and fishing trophies; all of the trappings of a happy vacation home turned to refuse. The kitchen had a big granite-covered island, behind which the occupants had made their last stand. Their picked-clean bones told the tale of their grizzly end. They were scattered around the room, the evidence of a feeding frenzy.

From a count of skulls, it appeared to be a group of five. At least one was a child. There had also been a dog, a pretty big one from the looks of it. A cautious search of the rest of the house confirmed that they had all died together in the great room. The Fiends had feasted and moved on. But for a few kitchen knives and a golf club, there were no weapons in the house. Someone had fashioned a mace from a bat and some nails, but that was it. They didn't have a prayer.

He inspected the cabinets and found them to be nearly empty of food. There was a myriad of other supplies - flashlights, extra batteries, radio, gas canisters - but not much more than would be expected in a cabin. These people had been caught pretty much flat-footed. The fact that there was no car outside told him that either someone had gotten away or more likely, decided to try their luck elsewhere before the onslaught occurred.

He stepped back outside and walked down to the lake. The house had a small dock with an aluminum rowboat tied to it. As Jon scanned the shoreline, little wavelets made metallic sounds against the hull. About a hundred yards to his right was another house, or what was left of one. It appeared to have burned to the ground. In the middle of the lake was an island. It looked to be about a half mile out. With his binoculars he could make out a small empty dock. If there were any other structures, they were obscured by the trees. He decided to walk up the driveway to see if there might be a car between the house and the road, perhaps an unlucky would-be escapee or maybe the folks in the house parked closer to the road to throw an attacker off the scent. It sounded lame, but he didn't have anything better to do.

3 Infected

The driveway led back to the road. No car except his dead Jeep. In short order he found the driveway for the burned house. From a hundred yards away, he could smell the charcoal crusted timbers. It had been rained on at least once since it burned, and the black pile of timbers let off a wet acidic smell. As he walked, he heard the woodpecker again. It was a reassuring sound; a bird busy at work meant it felt secure. There was a separate garage that remained intact, but the main house's chimney had collapsed onto the driveway, blocking the barn-style door. There was a side door standing ajar. He paused and then took a cautious step forward, peering inside. Eureka, an old mid-nineties Volvo was parked amongst a slew of recreational stuff, a canoe, a small sailboat, rafts, as well as bicycles and other garage items.

He grabbed a small stone and tossed it inside, preparing himself for a charge. Nothing. He lifted his visor, tentatively stepped forward while sniffing the air - must and damp oily wood. He could see that the trusting owners had left the Volvo unlocked. The amount of dust layered on top wasn't encouraging. When he opened the door the dome light didn't come on and he squished up his face in mild frustration. The key was sitting in an ashtray between the seats so he inserted it and gave it a turn - not even a click. Perhaps they'd had taken the battery cables off in order to save it while they were away. A quick check under the hood told him otherwise. With a sigh, he realized that he'd have to hike up to the Jeep, take its battery out, and bring it down to the Volvo.

He stepped back outside and looked at the chimney stones. Two big ones were piled right against the door. He'd need something to pry them with. He'd get a big branch from the many littering the forest floor. He took off his helmet and set it, along with the shotgun, against the wall. He walked around to the back of the garage and right there, not more than thirty yards away, two infected squatted over a carcass. He saw them first, but not by much. They were adolescent males, utterly filthy - blood streaked faces, tattered clothes and tangled, greasy hair. They were struggling with a dead porcupine and so engrossed in their meal that they hadn't heard him walk up - but they saw him now.

Jon found himself stunned, his muscles locked up as though he'd been delivered an electric jolt. His brain said run, but his feet glued themselves to the ground. The Fiend holding the dead animal had both arms sleeved with tattoos. It suddenly jumped up and without dropping its kill, charged at Jon full speed, the other charging right behind. Jon finally unfroze as the tattooed Fiend's bloody maw opened with a horrific scream.

Jon ran. He ran in a straight line right back up the driveway. Out loud he found himself yelling, "Fuck You, Fuck You, Fuck You!" over and over. He didn't dare turn around for fear of stumbling. His police baton banged against his leg, but he wasn't going to try pulling it out of its belt loop and risk a fall. He got to the main road before he realized that he had left his helmet and gun behind - not that he could have done anything about it. He could hear the two Fiends only paces behind him, one letting out another scream, kicking his adrenaline into overdrive. He could see his Jeep in the distance and he angled his way toward it. His mind was rushing to keep up with his fear. The Jeep would just be a death cage, but he had no place else to run. They were gaining on him.

He grabbed the door handle and yanked, only to be stopped by having locked the door earlier. He fumbled for the keys while cursing himself and glancing at the charging monsters. He pressed the unlock button, threw open the door, and dove in while hitting lock again as they slammed up against the truck. They bellowed and punched, spider webbing the driver's glass, one of them using the porcupine carcass for a bloody cudgel. He found himself involuntarily screaming as he tried to get his mind to formulate a plan. He had perhaps seconds and they'd be through.

The Jeep was on a down slope. If he could... He stomped on the clutch, dropped the stick shift into neutral and released the parking brake. The truck started to creep forward. A look outside nearly stopped his heart as he watched one of the bastards pick up a rock and heave. The thing bounced off the driver door just as the truck started to build some momentum. "Come on Come on Come Come on!"

The wheel without power steering was like a turning an old tractor. Another rock, bigger this time, went skipping off the windshield. He was going maybe five miles an hour now, then ten, the Fiends running along side. Steering with all his might, he avoided a tree, kept the thing on track with the road, then the driveway to the burned out house, and now he was out pacing them and he cheered. "Yeah, motherfuckers!"

Then he could see the lake, and the plan was for not. With a sudden sense of defeat, he took his hands off the wheel and watched as the Jeep rolled past the ruined house over a tidy lawn and out onto a dock, ultimately launching itself into the lake. It then promptly began to sink.

The impact buried Jon under a mountain of food, assorted blankets, tents, a camp stove and bottled water. From what he could see, he was submerged under cloudy green water.

Despite the spider webbing, the windows were holding. Then the seals started to leak as the water pressure increased. He had maybe a few minutes and then he'd drown. After all he'd been through this would be a stupid way to die. Still, a part of him wanted to stay in the truck. As he struggled to get out from under the weight of his gear, he really thought about it. It was an absolute horror show up there and from what he could tell, Cain's was winning the war. It was exhausting trying to survive an apocalypse. And who, besides himself, was he surviving for? He had no living relations, no girlfriend, no ex-wife. He'd always lived the life of a loner, happy to go on assignment to other states, other countries, a girl in every port. His primary reason for existence was to pass on information. What was there really to go on for?

On the other hand, he'd made it this far. If he gave up now, what was the point of the hard slog up through the South all the way into New England? He was almost to Canada. He'd be an asshole to throw in the towel now.

Strangely, as cold water came up over his calves, he found himself flashing on the defense plan for Canada. It meant giving up the West but they had drawn the line at Lake Winnipeg. Running north and south from that famous body of water was a system of rivers and smaller waterways that more or less connected the Great Lakes and the Saint Lawrence River with Hudson Bay way up north. For the most part, the infected had lost the skill that is swimming. US and Canadian engineers were working around the clock, digging connections between these waterways in an effort to create a massive moat around Eastern Canada. There were gaps, but those would be plugged with minefields and constant patrols.

In the winter, when much of that water froze, it was going to be a challenge, but maybe not. It was suggested that the infected would be forced to stay in the warmer southern climate or risk freezing to death.

When the water reached his thighs, Jon snapped out of his reverie and considered once more the supposedly easy out that was drowning. Then he laughed at the thought. He'd fight until he was either home free or dead. It sure as hell wasn't going to be by his own hand.

The water pressure would make it impossible for him to open the doors until the cab was full. He managed to get his hand on his police baton and struggled to slip it out of its belt loop. After a few awkward yanks, he got it free, gripped the side handle hard, and rammed the short bottom end into the compromised windshield. A small hole appeared and water shot at him with the pressure of a focused garden hose. He rammed the baton again. The water rushed in with a wallop. Jon found himself swirling in a cloud of gear and glass. Though the surface was only ten feet away, he was completely disoriented. Using the steering wheel, he thrust himself up and out of the truck.

When his face broke the water, the first thing his eyes focused on was the two Fiends, standing at the end of the dock. They screamed with excitement, yet hesitated to jump into the water. Jon looked to his right and saw the dock for the house next door and the rowboat tied to it. With the weight of his leathers pulling him down, he started swimming, the damn infected followed his progress from the shore. Maybe he'd confuse them if he swam under water. When he was twenty feet from the dock, he took three deep breaths and dove.

He still held the police baton along his forearm. It made swimming a bit of a struggle, but he'd be damned if he was going to let it go. He swam under the dock and slowly let himself rise so that he popped up between it and the boat. His lungs were searing, but he forced himself to take the quietest breath he could as he broke the surface. He pulled his knife from the sheath that was tied to his leg, cut the ropes and began to gently push the boat away from the dock. Suddenly, he could hear their feet running across the planking. He kicked away with all his might. They splashed into the water, reaching out and screaming, not really swimming, but achieving a sort of doggie-paddle cum spaz-splash. The tattooed one hurled the porcupine at him, the carcass sailing just past his face. The other got a grip on his leg. Jon kicked the creature in the chest, twisted free and plunged the knife into its shoulder. It howled in anger and pain, giving Jon a couple of yards of distance. The rodent chucker was still sloppily swimming toward him, and Jon used the baton, stunning it with a blow to the head.

Free for a moment, he swam a little more and then tried to pull himself into the boat without swamping it. As he struggled, his legs and arms felt weighted with lead. Then the Fiend with the knife still in his shoulder caught up with him, grabbed his left leg and bit down hard. It hurt like hell and he begged the god of *Scorpion's Titanium-Tanned Racing Armor* to let its product hold up under three hundred pounds per square inch of biting power. He turned, twisted the knife and pulled it out. The monster gnashed and bit at him. This was the most deadly kind of proximity with an infected person and Jon could feel his repulsed and frightened body try to levitate from the water. He jammed his gloved thumb into the Fiend's eye and then drove the knife into its sternum and up into the heart. The blade wasn't coming free this time and he had to let it go. He kicked away from the dying thing as fast as he could, lest he ingest some of the growing blood blooming in the water. The one he had hit was the baton was nowhere to be seen. He had to assume that it had drowned.

With a do or die heave, he pulled himself into the boat, got the oars into the oarlocks and turned the boat toward the burned out house. He had to get his helmet and gun. Then he saw more of them, dozens more running through woods, heading toward the shore. He stopped rowing. The breeze was coming up and it gently pushed him away from land. He looked over his shoulder at the island and pointed the boat there instead. Then his stomach growled. He didn't have a single morsel of food. If he weren't such an optimistic guy, he'd swear he was screwed.

The female Other that led them, stopped short of the shore and just watched. It and the Others with It arrived too late to get the Fresh One that was rowing away.

As though channeled up from the swelling in its belly, a pregnant Other felt its stomach churn, and the sense of frustration from the Others around It entered its mind. The thing that grew inside It was speaking to It again – not speaking, but feeling. Mostly It liked the feeling; the thing in its belly guiding It, helping It track down the Fresh Ones. But when It was hungry, the feeling became very harsh and It even considered cutting out the thing that grew inside.

The one that led them held its own little guiding thing in its arms – that baby Other was asleep. When it was awake, all of the Others around It got the feeling together - the baby Other guiding them.

The pregnant Other could see less panic in the Fresh One's eyes as it moved away in the boat. Another pang of hunger feeling shot up from the thing that grew inside, and It held Its growling belly with fierce frustration. They would watch for a while then the Other that led them would renew the hunt for other Fresh Ones – the infant Other that the one that led them held always knew where to find more Fresh Ones.

When Jon got close to the island's shore he heard a new woodpecker and chuckled, deciding that he wouldn't count on them to raise the alarm in the future. He quietly tied up to the dock and walked up a path, holding his police baton at ready.

In a clearing was small house, a shack really. Its windows seemed intact. The front door was closed. There was a fire pit out front with a bunch of split log benches around it. It appeared to be an overnight camp, a place to come out to, cook hotdogs and tell ghost stories. The fire pit had some old damp ash in it. Tales of lovebirds, poets and profanity users were carved into the benches.

He walked the perimeter of the shack; reminding himself after the garage incident, don't walk into a house without sweeping the outside first. He cursed himself for having let his guard down. His excitement over the car overrode all caution. He told himself he wouldn't do it again.

Sniffing the air, he could smell no evidence of death. After whacking the baton on another tree and getting an echo in response, he walked up to the front door and tried the latch. It opened with a light creak. Inside there were several bunk beds, a potbelly stove, a kitchenette with a slop sink for cleaning fish. There was no food and nothing to eat with. Clearly, the camp was for overnights only. He could sleep in safety, but he wasn't going to fill his stomach. Heck, he didn't have an appetite anyway. The adrenaline rush had taken so much out of him that all he wanted to do was sleep. Snapping himself out of it, he decided he'd better go back out to the dock and make sure one of those infected sons of bitches wasn't a better swimmer. He scanned the water with his binoculars and then the shore. The Fiends had gone - for now.

He found a path that appeared to circle the island. It followed the shore and he was able to scan the mainland as he walked. He noted a surprising lack of other houses around the lake until he reached the opposite side of the island. On the far shore stood a huge mansion. He guessed that this end of the lake was privately owned or at least the eastern shore was.

The sun was getting lower so he finished circumnavigating the island and went back to the cabin. He hadn't gotten any real rest in weeks. The empty cabin called to him like some kind of magic sleep chamber and his eyelids got heavy. For the first time in a long time, he felt relatively safe. He finished off the last of his water, curled up on one of the bunks and was asleep in moments.

4 Breach

Jon woke to the sound of gunfire booming and echoing across the lake. For the first few moments, he couldn't get his bearings. He sat up in the bunk, hit his head on the one above and cursed, reminding himself to *slow down*.

KABOOM! More gunfire, small arms, and then the thunder of a heavy machine gun. His memories transported him to the tank turrets at the Orlando Wall – the machine guns blazing away in unison. At the Orlando Wall, the military had pulled together nearly every piece of fighting equipment left in the continental US. Nothing was going to get across. They'd learned from Everglades about gaps in the line and this time the Fiends were contained. But they weren't. Now, the bulk of that hardware was abandoned in the chaos that followed the exodus to Canada.

He carried a small flashlight on his belt, the one he'd taken off the dead cop. It had a red filter option so he wouldn't screw up his night vision. He turned it on and walked out to the island path. With no Fiends at his door, he was fairly confident that they either continued to drown trying to get to him or they figured out it was hopeless.

Across the water he saw the mansion's perimeter lit up with flood lights, the glow giving a sparkle to an otherwise black lake. Fiends surrounded the perimeter wall while several people on the roof were picking them off. The fifty cal blazed away and half a dozen infected exploded into red pieces of meat.

It was the lights that were the big attraction. Jon shook his head as he watched the display, *idiots.*

At Everglades, Fiends were like moths to light. They just couldn't help coming. The Brass actually recommended the lights at first, better to corral the creatures into kill zones, just like these folks were doing, but when the right flank of the wall was overrun by a million hungry ghouls, they rethought the idea. It was night vision only after that. Jon wished he had a way to signal the fools that they were just inviting thousands more to run through the night to come and eat them. He watched for a while and then got tired of the carnage. He walked back to the cabin and tried as hard as he could to get back to sleep.

The assault went on for hours and he tossed and turned as the barrage continued. A dying Fiend sounded no different from someone who wasn't infected. The screams of pain were only slightly drowned out by the louder screams of rage mixed with steady gunfire. Finally, around three AM, he gave up and walked back out to see what was happening.

He had to decide if he wanted to signal these folks. He had no food and damn if he wasn't out of bottled water too. The chances of the lake being tainted by terrorists were near zero, but on the other hand, several Fiends had died in it. Who was to say that their corpses wouldn't foul the water? A look at the number of infected still assaulting the outer wall confirmed his opinion that the defenders didn't understand their enemy. He decided that for now, it would be better to remain unseen. Then the gunfire got even more intense. The infected had discovered a couple of trees overhanging the wall. They were climbing up and jumping inside as fast as the people on the rooftops could kill them. Like the Army at Everglades, the people in the mansion had badly underestimated the resourcefulness left in a Cain's-addled mind. Jon had written a post about this entitled *The CW Will*

Kill You. Like nearly everyone else in the country, the folks across the water were victims of popular culture, handicapped by conventional wisdom. People equated the infected with the mindless automatons that were cinema zombies. Zombies they most certainly were not.

Suddenly, the gunfire from the roof stopped. The screaming and howling of the Fiends stopped as well. But for a few pops from individual arms from the upper windows, it was eerily silent. Then the defenders on the roof began to scream in protest, yelling, "No," begging for something to stop, and just as suddenly, they shot at each other; in seconds, gunning each other down. Jon was stunned. Then a door opened and an unarmed man stepped out fitfully walking, almost as though he was struggling with himself while walking toward the heavily fortified front gate. Another man stuck his head out the window and yelled at the walker, the echo of his panicked voice carrying across the lake – "Roger! What are you doing?"

Roger hesitated by the fence and then hurky-jerky reached out, flipping a switch. The gate rolled open and he was instantly overcome by vast wave of waiting Fiends.

Jon winced as he saw them charge for the open door. A heavily armed woman stepped into the breach, trying to pull it shut, but it was too late. The Fiends pushed their way through and were met with the sound of hollow gunfire, muffled within the big house.

Madness. Why give up and let them in? Jon's hungry stomach filled with bile as he thought of the fate of those people. The ones who survived the attack, who escaped into another locked room but were nevertheless infected, would be out killing their fellow men by the same time the following night. Everyone else would be eaten alive if they didn't take their own life first.

With the same part of the mind that was reserved for rubbernecking a highway crash, Jon found himself settling in to watch the rest of the show. Within ten minutes, the gunfire became more random and undisciplined. It was mixed with agonizing screams and useless pleas for mercy. Then flames started shooting out of some of the upper story windows.

The shooting diminished to a few pops now and again and he stood and stretched, thinking that it was basically over. Then, out of the randomness, there was a steady organized burst of gunfire. A group of ten heavily armed people came running out of a smashed picture window. Jon found himself smearing a light film of tears from his eyes in order to look again through the binoculars.

As they ran down to the dock, the group stayed tightly formed, keeping up a steady and disciplined hail of fire. The Fiends swarmed them, but they kept on moving. Jon found himself cheering them out loud, like a fan screaming for a running back to get into the end zone.

Five of the ten made it to the waterfront, punching and kicking and then finally getting to the dock. A short tug of war took place when one of them was yanked back and forth between her comrades and the pursing Fiends, her terrified screams rising above all the others. The Fiends won and the four survivors dove off the dock, swimming for their lives.

Jon had a decision to make: As exhibited at the mansion, strength in numbers meant little in terms of self-preservation. When you're alone you don't have to turn and help the one being pulled to the ground. Yet, he'd been alone for a long time. He could use a little human companionship. He pulled out his flashlight and hailed the swimmers. They spotted him and angled for the island. Jon had a sudden desire to take back his signal, but it was too late. He'd see what fortune would bring.

The swimmers came to a halt about thirty feet off shore and dog paddled. One of them called out, "You alone?"

"Yeah, it's safe." (Other than reflexively screaming obscenities, it was the first time he'd spoken out loud to someone in more than a week. His voice almost sounded alien to him.) "There's shelter and the bastards continue to prove that they can't swim for shit."

The group came on, one of them clearly in distress, the man swimming with just one arm. As they waded ashore, Jon stepped in up to his ankles and offered a hand. "I'm Jon. Jon Washington."

"Tom Newman. Guess you saw what happened to us back there."

"Yeah, I saw. I'm sorry."

A thin man and a woman with short cropped dark hair helped a third over some slippery rocks. The third guy was built like a pro wrestler and held his arm while swearing, "Shit! Mother fucking shit! Now what?"

They all seemed to be in their mid to late twenties. Jon couldn't really tell except for the wounded man who looked a little older.

Tom turned to the guy. "You're bit Bob. You might as well be dead."

The woman looked stricken. "What if... I don't know. What if he doesn't come down with it?"

Tom snapped, "Everyone who gets bit comes down with it, Nikki! Everyone. Mark, back me up here."

Mark, the thin man, just nodded.

Nikki balled her fists in frustration. "Well, fuck, Bob! You fucking promised that we'd get through this thing!"

Bob sucked against his teeth in pain. "Thanks for the sympathy, Nik."

Mark said, "What if we just tie him up. You know, watch him overnight. I mean we can't just... We can't shoot Bob."

Jon said, "We tried that a bunch of times in Florida. There was always hope we'd say. Hell, I had to kill my own grandmother with a fire poker when she turned." He realized he was being insensitive and changed his tone. "My point is we got to where everyone decided it was more merciful to let the people do the deed themselves. If they weren't willing... well, the Heavies do that now."

Nikki said, "Who asked you?"

Tom looked at Jon anew, "You were in Florida?"

Bob said, "Um, hello? I'm the one who's bitten here. Obviously I have to end this thing. I'm certainly not going to become one of those fucking mindless things."

"But what if it's not... what if it... what if you're immune? That could happen, right?" asked Nikki, desperation in her voice.

Tom put a hand on the wounded man's shoulder. "What do you want to do, Bob?"

Despite the pain, a look of clarity came across Bob's face. He turned to Nikki and looked into her eyes. "I want this to be the last thing I think about, looking into your eyes and loving you."

She said, "Are you fucking kidding me? You're going to hit me with that cheese? We're Marines, Bob."

"I still love you."

Nikki softened a bit, then said, "Nice of you to mention it when you're dead."

Bob let out a sigh and then shrugged. He looked at the others, "I've read that drowning isn't a bad way to go once the initial panic is passed."

Jon said, "I just had the same thought, a few hours ago." He realized how callous he still sounded and said, "Sorry, that was - It's amazing how this situation seems to take the humanity out of all of us."

Bob continued, "I don't want my girl to see or hear me get shot or strangled. I think drowning is best. Maybe tie a rock to my waist and I jump off your rowboat there, out where it's deeper."

Nikki said, "I'm not your fucking girl, you halfwit. I never said I'd be your girl." Then suddenly her hard face became stricken, "Why the fuck did you have to try and save Mary? That girl was nothing but trouble and you got bitten for it."

Bob shrugged again, "I'm sorry, Nik."

Tom and Mark rowed Bob out a hundred yards or so from the island. Nikki watched until they stopped and then went into the cabin. Jon stood between the cabin and the water's edge regretting inviting these people to his haven. He could just make out Mark and Tom securing a big rock to a line and tying that to Bob's waist. Bob made sure the knot was tight and then let them tie his hands behind his back. Bob stood up, saying something to his friends that Jon couldn't make out. The condemned man glanced back at the island, took a long look at the sky and nodded. His friends tossed the rock and he jumped in after it, disappearing in a blink. Mark and Tom waited for a few minutes and then rowed back to shore, their return journey lit up by the mansion, which was fully engulfed in flames.

As Jon tied the rowboat to the dock, he asked, "I know you guys escaped with just the shirts on your backs, but any chance you got any food?"

Mark opened a pocket on his parachute pants and tossed Jon a food bar. Jon opened it with his teeth and nearly ate the thing in one bite.

"When was the last time you ate, Dude?" asked Tom.

"Day and a half ago. You got another?"

Mark handed him another and then pointed back toward the mansion. "Plenty more of that on our boat over there, if we can get to it. Maybe tomorrow the fuckers will have moved on."

Jon bit into the second bar. "Who thought it was a good idea to shoot the Fiends? You know, attracting them with the lights?"

"The guy that owned the house. It was his setup," said Tom. "He had stockpiled the place with food and ammo - a real survivalist dude. You know the type. He invited anybody in the area to come in, even let in a few stragglers at the end. It was the stragglers who led the Shitfobs to us."

Mark picked up the tale, "They were right behind them. The mansion guy had watched the Army at the Miami Wall on TV. I guess they called it Everglades for some PC reason, something about not wanting to offend Latin Americans. Anyway, they had figured out that the devils were crazy attracted to light and they could mow them down like ducks in a barrel. We figured we'd just do the same thing."

"Ducks on a pond," said Tom. "Fish in a barrel."

"Whatever. Fuck you."

Jon asked, "You didn't watch the follow up I guess. The part where Everglades got overrun? They attracted more of the things than they could handle."

"I guess we missed that part," said Tom. "But this was something different. It wasn't how many of them were out there. Fucking Roger just walked out and opened up the gate. It was like he was in a trance or something."

"Yeah, I saw that," said Jon.

"Suicidal," said Tom. "Pretty much killed us all."

"Well, the whole infected population is heading north, following the healthy," said Jon. "It was only a matter of time before they got to your door. Why didn't you guys head for Canada like everyone else?"

Mark said sarcastically, "Well, Tom. You were one of the 'deciders', why don't you explain to him why we stayed here."

"Eat me, asshole," snarled Tom. "We voted on it." To Jon he said, "We really did have everything we needed for months, maybe even a year. We figured the government had enough trouble on its hands. Why add more refugees to the problem? We thought we could take care of ourselves."

Mark said, "Well we're fucked now."

Tom asked, "Where's Nikki?"

Jon nodded toward the cabin. "She seems like she wants to be alone."

They let Nikki be by herself for a little while, but they all needed sleep. When they opened the cabin door, they found her curled up on one of the bunks.

She said, "I'm almost asleep. Keep it quiet."

5 Shoreside

When dawn broke they could see that the smoldering wreck of a mansion was now abandoned. A scan with the binoculars revealed a few dead bodies. Jon rowed Tom over to the dock and tried to avoid looking at the carnage that had been last night's feast. Tom hopped onto a ski boat, which started right up. They quickly threw the lines off the dock and towed the rowboat back to the island. The ski boat was full of emergency supplies and Jon decided that it was good that he had joined up with these people.

A short while later, the four of them sat around the cold rocks of an unlit campfire eating breakfast. Tom asked, "Why do we have to be in such a hurry? We've got enough food for weeks. Who says the government isn't going to send a force down here. You know, counter attack?"

Nikki said, "I, for one, am not going to play foursome on a little island with you jerks and hoping for a rescue that isn't going to happen."

Jon said, "I have to agree with Nikki, at least on substance."

Mark said, "We've got a better chance of surviving if we stay here than if we put ourselves on some Shitfob infested road." He looked at Jon. "Shitfob means Shit for brains; military speak for the diseased. You're hanging with real honest to goodness US Marines."

"I'm familiar with the term," said Jon.

Nikki scowled at Mark. "You're a washout like the rest of us, Newman. Why don't you just shut it?"

"Food is definitely an issue," said Tom, trying to steer the conversation back. "We could raid the few houses along the shore as needed. There's got to be tons of canned stuff out there. There's also a small town around the next bend. Probably lots of prepackaged food there."

Mark nodded in agreement, "Yeah, we've got plenty of firepower. We can certainly make quick excursions ashore, cover each other, scrounge for what we need and get back. It's easy enough to sit out in the boat and make a careful observation before docking or whatever."

Nikki said, "What part of, *I don't think so,* are you guys not getting?"

"So what? You gonna bug out on your own, Nikki?" asked Tom.

Jon stood and paced, "The roads are tough without a car. Got a few million infected coming this way. If we don't get out now, we probably won't get out."

"Exactly," said Nikki.

"So what makes you the expert, Mr. Washington?" asked Tom.

"I'm not, really. I've just spent a lot of time running from the things. From the Orlando Wall on, I was a reporter assigned to an Army platoon. They're all dead or infected now. I was the only one to get away. We got as far north as Atlantic City before we got overwhelmed."

"Damn," said Mark.

"We were bringing up the rear of the final retreat. It was an all-volunteer force. Everyone knew it was a long shot. I got away in a dead cop's car and promptly shredded the tires going the wrong way through a spiked parking lot exit. It seemed like a thousand of them were chasing me. There was a Jeep with a dead guy pulled out of it, three Fiends busy feeding on him. I ran past them and jumped in, barely got the door closed. I made it here on two tanks of gas then ran dry."

Tom perked up, "Where's the Jeep?"

"Bottom of the lake. Another story. The point is, we hang out and it's only a matter of time before it goes bad. There's too many of them and they're like machines. I know they sleep, but they don't seem to stop, night or day."

"I've seen them sleep. They do sleep," said Mark.

"I guess I'm saying I've got my rowboat. I'll find a way. I'll just ask for a little food, a weapon and some ammo. Nikki, you want to come, that's fine with me."

Nikki said, "That might work."

Tom mulled on it, ignoring Nikki. "I don't think we can do that, Jon. If we're staying, we'll need all the food and weapons we can keep."

"If I stayed I'd be eating the food anyway. Shooting a gun anyway."

"Yeah, but in defense of all of us."

"I gotta agree with Tom on this one," said Mark.

"Oh, fuck you guys," said Nikki. "Two want to go, two want to stay. We split the food and weapons. Simple."

Tom and Mark ate silently. Finally Mark said, "Okay. Maybe it makes sense to git while we still can."

"You're such a pussy," said Tom.

Jon said, "Unless we find a vehicle, we're not going to make it far. I found a Volvo over that way, but the battery is dead. We should cruise the lake, find another house."

They scanned the shore were the burned house was and saw no activity. They gave Jon Bob's pistol, an Army issue 1911 Colt 45, and some ammo. When they were all geared up, they climbed into the boat and slowly cruised across the lake. Jon's helmet and shotgun were the first priority. The aimed for the burned house and as they got close Mark let the boat idle and drift slowly toward the dock. As they passed over it, John could see his Jeep resting down in the murk below.

When it was close enough, Jon stepped off the bow, scanned the woods and walked as fast and as quietly as he could to the garage. His helmet was there, but no shotgun. He was sure he had set the shotgun down next to the helmet. He gave the area a cursory search and then looked back at the boat. Tom stood with his arms out wide with *what the fuck* drawn across his features. The hair on Jon's neck was at full attention, his leg muscles jittering. Frustrated about the gun, but not wanting to spend any more time on this shore, he jogged back to the boat.

"My shotgun's gone."

"Don't know what to say about that," said Tom. "Get in the boat."

Jon climbed back aboard, slipping on his helmet. He immediately felt more secure. The thick padding felt good surrounding his skull.

After a couple of bends they could make out the top of a ham radio tower poking through the trees, then a small house about forty yards inland. They stopped the boat well back from the house's dock and scanned the shore. They could just make out the front end of a minivan poking past the backside of the house.

"Jack-pot, first try," said Mark.

"Looks quiet enough," said Tom.

Jon held his binoculars to his eyes, "Don't count on it."

Tom said, "Okay, let's just sit here for a while and keep watch."

Mark turned off the boat's engine. Small lapping waves and a light breeze slowly pushed it toward the dock.

Jon listened for birds and heard none. "I've also learned, and it doesn't necessarily mean anything, but when there aren't any birds singing, no insects either, it's generally not good."

They all listened. Mark said, "That's definitely unnerving."

Nikki sniffed the air, "I'm smelling something rotten."

Jon looked at the breeze on the water, "The wind's shifted. That's all of the corpses over at the mansion."

Tom reached past Mark and turned the engine back on. "Maybe all of the birds have flown upwind to get away from the stink. It seems quiet enough. I say we dock, listen some more and then check it out."

No one objected so Mark pulled up to the dock, turning the boat around to face outward for a quick getaway. Tom hopped out and tied off. They stood still again and listened.

As the breeze swayed the trees, insects started to hum, thickening up the air with a steady sawing sound.

Tom said, "Bet it was just us keeping 'em quiet. The van keys are probably in the house, hook near a door if we're lucky. Mark and I will do a sweep around the house. Make sure the other side is clear. If there's a back entrance we'll enter there and signal for you to come up, Jon. Nikki, you'll stay at the head of the dock and protect our escape route."

Nikki smiled, "Whatever you say, cowboy."

Tom turned back to her, exasperated. "Look, I know you're combat, but with the recall, I'm still technically your superior so I want your good aim covering us from here. Am I wrong?"

"Murphy's Law says it doesn't matter, but aye aye, Skipper."

"What does that fucking mean?"

"If it's going to go wrong, Tom, it will. Your plan seems fine."

"Well, why didn't you just say that?"

Jon said, "Um, can we do this thing?"

Mark and Tom set off and then split up to walk around each side of the house.

Jon loudly whispered, "Check the van itself. Keys might as likely be there." He dropped the visor down on his riot helmet and snugged up the chinstrap.

Tom and Mark disappeared around the other side of the house. Jon and Nikki could hear them trying the mini-van doors. A minute later, Mark opened the lakeside door from the inside and waved for Jon to come up. Jon walked forward noting that the birds, if there were any, continued to stay silent, but the insects were busy.

When Jon got to the door, Mark pretended to close it in his face like Jon was a salesman, saying, "We don't want any." He chuckled and let Jon step inside. "No car keys so far."

6 Nikki

While she stewed over being ordered around by a dolt like Tom, Nikki wanted a smoke so badly that she felt her gut twist with the craving. She'd had a carton of Camels back at the mansion and now she didn't even have a used butt in her pocket. Crappy time to go cold turkey. Cigarettes... dishonorable discharge – she and the knuckleheads inside, and of course, Bob. They'd all been part of the same supply company. The black market for cigarettes in Sudan was intense, particularly for American brands. Amazing how the cowboy image could still push tobacco. She'd had a successful career as one of the first frontline female shock troops in the US Marines. The supply company had been a disciplinary measure - an incident with a local tribal leader sending her career to the shitter. She'd pulled force security duty, and in the middle of a meeting between her battalion commander and some asshole chief, the smarmy prick had boasted about the literally hundreds of woman and children he'd supposedly raped. She asked the fat bastard, with his thick eyebrows and food stained beard, to stop talking about it. He simply smiled at her and started another story about three little girls and their mother. She then yelled at him to stop, and her commander ordered her to step out of the tent. Just before she was out the door, the chief raised his voice, telling the colonel that he would love to taste Nikki's sweet camouflaged cunny. She didn't hesitate. With what she would later describe as a reflex, she drew her sidearm and shot the pig between the eyes.

As it turned out, the tribal leader had been playing the US, feeding the Marines with bits and pieces of intel while actually delivering massive amounts of critical data to the enemy. It was that twist that kept her out of Leavenworth, and instead, into the supply company. The black market bust was just bad luck. She knew it was going on, but chose to say nothing, look the other way, try to get along with her new platoon. When the contraband turned from cigarettes to heroin and the law was laid down, her silence made her an accomplice. She was washed out along with the jerks now ransacking the house. Hell, she was over it by then anyway. Combat was her thing; delivering port-a-potties to rear echelon pukes was about going nowhere fast.

Crack, she heard a twig snap, somewhere up the hill, deeper into the woods. She felt her skin tingle with energy and her eyes dilated into black saucers as she scanned the trees past her gunsight. Woods were noisy places all by themselves. Trees constantly rained leaves or sap and shed old branches. Birds, squirrels and other animals made all sorts of ruckus during their constant foraging. She listened for a moment longer, but heard nothing unnatural so she slipped back to imagining a cigarette between her lips, the smoke gently flowing out of her nostrils and curling up around her head. God, she needed to get her hands on a pack. Maybe there were some in that house. Then something curious happened: She felt a strange sensation, a buzzing in her head, vague but jumbled images tumbling through her thoughts. She couldn't control them, couldn't stop – God, the smells, tastes – body odor and mossy forest and...blood. She shook her head, losing focus and just as suddenly, it was gone.

"What the fuck?" she whispered to herself, rubbing her eyes, trying to re-focus on her surroundings.

The house was full of flies. Rotten fruit sat on the counter. An unfinished rotting meal for two sat on the dining table. The fridge stood open with more rotting food inside. The smell was overwhelming.

Mark said, "There were skid marks in the driveway. They must have had another car. Bugged out in a hurry."

In one corner there was a desk with a ham radio set, a computer, printer, and a small stereo. The printer had something freshly printed in its tray. It was a news article from Reuters. The headline stated: *New England overwhelmed. Cain's Infection reaches Southern New Hampshire and Vermont.*

Jon flipped the paper around and read, "It's dated May 23rd, three days ago."

Tom came out of the laundry room, "No keys in there." He pushed past Jon and sat at the desk opening drawers.

Mark said, "Cozy place, huh? Too bad we can't just crash here tonight."

Jon said, "Enough talk. I'm surprised we haven't been attacked already."

The three of them started working the cabin over in earnest. The keys had to be somewhere.

Higher up the hill there was movement in the woods. *The One that the Others mostly followed crept forward toward the shelter that the Fresh Ones had gone into. The Fresh ones made lots of noise, which helped mask the Other's approach. Another group of Others approached the Fresh One that kneeled down near the water. There were perhaps thirty Others in all. Some were full and tired from killing and eating the many Fresh Ones who had hid in a different shelter only just this morning. Their hands, hair, faces and tattered clothes were covered in gore.*

The One that led them was perhaps forty-years old. It crawled to a stop at the edge of a rise, some part of Its mind acknowledging the pain in Its knees where the flesh was scraped off. Wearing what was left of a tattered skirt, It had skinned its knees bare as It skidded across gravel and tree roots in the early morning assault. The fat little Fresh One had been trying to crawl under the shelter that the other Fresh Ones were hiding in. While Its companions had attacked the small home from every angle, It stood back and watched as the pudgy little one climbed out a window and crawled for a gap under the foundation. It had screamed with glee as It ran and dove on top of the squealing thing. Its triumphant howl was only dampened when Its mouth clamped itself on the Fresh One's fat little neck. It had laughed through the bubbling hot blood and then tore at the young one's windpipe, ending its screeches.

Watching the new prey in the house below, It signaled for the Others to stop crawling up from behind. It held Its infant close and watched the baby's huge dark eyes zero in on the Fresh One by the water. Then It laid the baby down and sucked in a breath full of the damp leafy ground, feeling the baby send its signal of desire to the Others, the killing fever rising within the group. It was patient. It would wait for the perfect moment to make the assault.

The search was growing frustrating and Jon was getting even more anxious. He could feel the hair on his arms standing up and he started imagining someone watching his every move. It became so intense that his focus started falling to the windows, scanning outside.

Mark was digging in a closet full of games and said, "Hey look - Life. You remember this one? The little cars that go around the board and you do stuff like go to college, get married and add kids until you either retire to the mansion or end up in the poor house?"

Tom ignored this. "I'm beginning to think that whoever took off in the other car had the keys to this one in his pocket."

Suddenly they were startled by the sound of gunfire. A quick glance out the window revealed Nikki on one knee aiming and then pulling the trigger repeatedly.

Jon looked out toward the woods. A couple dozen Fiends were running at the house. "Outside! Now!"

Instead, the two Marines turned toward the uphill windows with the intent to shoot.

Nikki kept up a steady and careful fire as she dropped a Fiend with every other bullet or so. The civilian model M16 was semi-auto, deadly accurate in the right hands. Unfortunately, the NATO 5.56 round didn't provide enough punch to drop them all with certainty. Some were hit and kept running like nothing had happened at all. Then, out of the corner of her eye, she saw more running along the shore right at her. The men inside were going to be cut off. She adjusted her aim to the closer threat and fired until she was out of bullets, ejected the mag and flipped the other one taped to it into the receiver.

Inside the house, Tom racked his shotgun, smashed out a window and sprayed buckshot up the hill. Mark, seeing that they'd left the door wide open, fruitlessly slammed it shut just as a big Fiend, with lots of downhill momentum, smashed it to splinters. Mark was knocked flat to the floor and he screamed in terror and agony as the big one bit into him. Another Fiend was right behind the first – Jesus! It was carrying Jon's shotgun, finger on the trigger –then it tripped, fell to the floor and blew the top of its own head off.

Tom and Jon ran to the lake door, wildly shooting behind themselves. Tom hesitated a moment for his friend, but Jon, while remembering to slam his visor down, shoved the Marine outside.

Jon's Colt packed a wallop. He shot at everything that moved in front of them, but the beasts were everywhere. He could feel them bite and claw at his leathers. Tom, who had no helmet, was brought down by two of them biting into each side of his neck. Blood spurted in great gouts as they swarmed over his body.

Jon managed to get his hand on his baton and, using the long end along his forearm, beat a path to the boat, firing the gun until it ran out of bullets and then using it as a club. He remembered his high school football training and ran with his knees high, keeping the Fiends from being able to snag his ankles. He kicked them off his legs and finally burst through, only to be nearly shot by Nikki, who had stacked up the creatures like cordwood, calmly shooting them one by one.

With her M16 empty again, she yelled while pulling her Berretta 9mm, "Start the boat! I'll keep them back!"

Jon ran past her without hesitation, jumped in the boat and fired it up. Nikki kept up a furious killing zone at the head of the dock and then turned and ran. Jon finished untying the bow as she jumped in, grabbed the steering wheel and slammed the engine into full throttle sending him tumbling to the deck. Fiends poured off the dock in their race to catch the boat and Nikki didn't slow down until she put three hundred yards between them.

Jon pulled off his helmet and knelt retching on the floorboards. "Jesus Christ, that's twice now that it's been that close. Two times in two days." He leaned over the side and threw up.

Nikki coasted a little further and put the boat into neutral. Her hands were uncontrollably shaking and she hugged herself to try to stop it. "They're dead. Mark and Tom are dead. Everyone I know, is dead."

Jon wiped his mouth and stood. He tried to reach out to Nikki but she slapped his arm away, saying, "Get the fuck away from me."

He sat down and caught his breath. He could make out a pack of infected where Tom had fallen. Some used sharp rocks and a female had a big knife. They were all competing to get their mouths on some meat. He could see the monsters fight over slabs of red flapping chunks. He had to look away or risk vomiting again.

He said, "They waited. They laid quietly, by the tens, dozens. Waited until the perfect moment for us to be distracted. I've never seen it quite like that. The fucking things are adapting."

They remained silent for what must have been five minutes, refusing to look back at the shore, letting the light breeze move the boat at a slow sideways drift.

Finally Nikki spoke, "So now what? Going ashore is a death trap. I agree that we've got to get to Canada. I just don't see how."

"First we go back to the island. We calm down and we think. I have to wash my leathers. I'm covered in infected saliva and blood."

7 Skin Of The Teeth

Jon and Nikki took inventory of their supplies. They had enough food for a month, five weeks if they rationed carefully. There were plenty of guns and ammo. There was a camp stove with several canisters of gas, a well fitted-out first-aid kit, several blankets, and much to Jon's happiness, a water filtration device that doubled as a canteen. All he had to do was submerge it, even in muddy water, and it filtered out everything, even viruses. There was a compass as well as a hand-held GPS (though the battery was getting low and there was no way to recharge it). A hand crank radio received a weak signal from one AM station playing a looped emergency public service message. It was garbled and broken with static. Nikki shut it off.

They cleaned and disinfected themselves as best they could, ate a little food and mostly stared at nothing. In the afternoon, they placed everything back aboard the boat in a logical manner. As the evening wore on, they continued to have little discussion and ate a quiet dinner. When darkness fell, they climbed into bunks on opposite sides of the cabin and listened to each other toss and turn until they both nodded off.

Some hours later, Jon was startled awake as Nikki screamed in terror in her sleep. He stepped to her bunk and shook her shoulder until she woke. Her eyes flashed around in the darkness. A nearly full moon shining through a small window offering the only light. She focused on Jon for a brief moment and her breathing eased. Then she closed her eyes and rolled away from him without a word. Jon lay back down and couldn't fall back to sleep. He desperately longed to kick back in his apartment in Atlanta and get lost in The History Channel.

At dawn the sun streamed through the window and woke them both at roughly the same time. Nikki stepped quietly outside first and washed her face at the water's edge. Jon felt stiff as he got out of bed. He wanted coffee. Some of the MREs were breakfast oriented. They had little chemical heaters inside. One held an omelet with hash browns and a French vanilla cappuccino.

"You want breakfast?" he called out.

"In a minute. You should look at this."

Jon stepped outside. The morning mist was just beginning to lift off the lake. On the far shore, the forest was teeming with Fiends. Several turned having noticed his and Nikki's movements. A few let out the screeching howl causing others to stop and look. Pretty soon, the entire shoreline was staring at them and screeching their horrific noise. The sound wave traveled across the water and pushed against their chests. It was like standing in a stadium full of madmen. Then both of their heads filled with a buzzing disorientation. Their senses were overwhelmed as the smells, tastes and sights of other beings flashed through their minds. Nikki gathered enough wits to grab Jon and pull him back out of sight among the trees.

Jon shook his head, suddenly free of the sensation. "What was that? What the hell was that?"

"Don't know. It happened to me yesterday just before we got attacked.

Jon said, "Let's see what the other side looks like."

"Fine, but let's stay in the tree line. I think it's a line of sight thing."

"What's a line of sight thing?"

She pointed at her head. "That. It stopped when we stepped out of sight."

They moved through the trees to the far side of the island, but this time stopped short of stepping out of cover. The mansion side of the lake was the same. An army of Fiends were marching north.

"Well, now we're really stuck," said Nikki as she instinctively stepped further back into cover.

"Maybe it's just a large group passing through. We can certainly wait it out."

"Maybe. I'm hungry." Nikki walked back toward the cabin. Jon watched the shore for a while and then turned back himself.

Inside the cabin Nikki ate in silence. Jon was loath to disturb her need for quiet, but he wanted to try the radio again. He grabbed it while looking at her for permission. She shrugged and he started cranking the handle. The static returned and the same message seemed to be playing. This time they could just make out the words:

"...Government. This is an alert to all citizens remaining within the New England area. The deadline for bombing has been shifted on the East coast due to a change in weather. Typical weather patterns should return in the next twelve to fifteen hours. Chemical bombing will commence at that time on cities and towns with populations greater than ten thousand. If you are incapable of reaching Eastern Canada above the Saint Lawrence River your only option is to stay inside and seal your home completely. Turn off all air conditioning. If you can, create an additional sealed room inside your home. Allied air forces will be dropping extremely lethal nerve and other chemical agents as well as bombing targets of opportunity. Again: Lethal chemical agents will be dropped across the Northeastern United States in twelve to fifteen hours. If you cannot make it to the Canadian safe zone, you must seal your house completely. Some of these agents can remain lethal to touch for as little

as thirty-six hours and as long as several weeks depending on weather. Leaflets will be dropped giving instructions for proper protection from such agents... Six-thirty AM, six hundred and thirty hours. This is an emergency broadcast. This is the United States and Canadian Governments. This is an alert to all citizens remaining within the New England States and Canada south of the Saint Law -"

Jon shut off the radio. Nikki had stopped eating and stared at it. Jon said, "It's hard enough that we have to defend ourselves against millions of highly infectious cannibals. Now our own government is going to bomb us with chemical weapons."

"Sounds like a pretty good solution to me."

"Yeah, if you're in Canada. I thought we signed a treaty getting rid of all of that stuff."

"Guess not." Nikki looked around. "There's no sealing off this leaky old cabin."

"It's not like we're in a populated area of more than ten thousand."

"Tell that to the massive target of opportunity walking on either side of the lake."

Jon nodded, "Okay, so we have to try and outrun those things on the shore. We can take the boat as far north as this lake goes."

"It's about three miles. Ends at a small town."

Then we get a car."

"Or find a house or other building that we can seal."

"I'm not buying that solution. Being locked in a house might as well be the same as standing outside. They find a way to break in. You know that better than anyone."

She started eating again. "Obviously, finding a car is preferable. I'm just pointing out the other logical option. It pays to have the contingencies covered."

Jon bit into his now cold omelet. Despite a reputation for tasting like reconstituted cardboard, even cold his MRE tasted great.

Nikki drove as they cruised up the lake. They kept their heads ducked down with Nikki popping up every moment or so to check on their course. Fiends on both sides screeched and screamed with excitement as they ran along the banks in frenzied pursuit.

Jon yelled over the engine noise, "It looks like we're going to have to move fast. I'm going to break the must haves into two light packs. We'll have to leave the rest."

"The most important thing is ammo. Pack everything we've got."

In minutes a small town appeared at the lake's river mouth. There was a two-story brick building near the harbor entrance. It was the fire and police headquarters. A dozen police and firemen as well as a few citizens were on the roof shooting at the infected below. Several German Shepherds were on the roof with them and the dogs barked and yipped in frustration at not being close enough to kill. The boarded-up doors and windows were under full assault.

The parking lot held several cars, but that left the question of keys. There were also a couple cop cars in a separate fenced off area. Nikki slowed the boat to an idle as they got closer. The people on the building occupied most of the Fiend's attention, but a few started to take notice of them as well. They ducked back down.

Nikki said, "The cop cars will have keys."

"How do you figure?"

"My uncle was a cop. Small town. They always leave the keys in the car. I even took one for a joy ride once."

Jon raised his eyebrows, but said nothing.

"We drive the boat right up to the edge of the lot where they're fenced off. We run like hell, throw the blankets over the barbwire and try to climb over before the fuckers can get us."

"You lived through Sudan with plans like that?"

"You got something better?"

"Nope. All cops just leave the keys in the car. Got it."

Nikki gave him a frustrated look then decided to let it go. They were running out of time. "I'll cruise really close to shore over that way. We'll draw the things away from the fence and then we'll shoot back this way and beach the boat."

"Okay, you run first with the blankets and toss them over the barbwire. I'll be right behind with the backpacks. I've got better body armor, so you go over first."

"Fine."

Nikki, strapped the M-16 over her shoulders, drove about one hundred and fifty yards away from the fence and stopped maybe thirty feet from the shore, engine idling. The Fiends bunched up in droves following them, some falling into the water.

When the fenced area was clear, Nikki gunned the boat and raced the other way. They hit the boat ramp hard, skidding right out of the water and used the last of the momentum to run right off the bow. The Fiends were running too and they were running fast.

Jon flung the backpacks over as Nikki heaved the blankets only to have them land short, uselessly falling to the ground.

"Shit!" She scooped them up and heaved again with the same effect. The fence was too high.

"Fuck it!" Jon started climbing the fence. "I'll lay on it, you climb over me!"

He scrambled to the top and almost fell. The barbed wire pressed painfully into his gut, but the leather held. The Fiends were almost on top of them. Nikki scrambled up the fence, grabbing onto Jon's belt, then shoulders. A Fiend jumped and grabbed Jon's leg. Then another one got a hold. "Awww fuckkker!"

Nikki threw herself over the other side and landed badly, hitting her head. She buckled in a dazed fashion, while Jon clung to the fence for dear life.

"Nikki! Nikki! Jesus! Snap out of it!"

Still dazed, she unholstered the Beretta, stumbled to the fence and fired nearly point blank into the face of one of the creatures holding Jon's legs. He broke free and scrambled over the top, landing on both feet just as a wall of Fiends hit the fence behind them. The chain link bulged and swayed with the buffeting. The people on the roof starting pouring their fire into the mass.

Jon tried the first car door - locked.

Nikki tried the other one - no good. "You gotta be kidding?"

Fiends were starting to climb the fence. Most were getting caught in the barbwire, but a few had figured out Jon's method and were using the trapped bodies of the others to act as a path. The people on the roof kept picking them off, but Jon and Nikki had maybe seconds before they'd be overwhelmed.

Nikki unslung her rifle and was about to use the butt of it on a driver's window when they heard a loud whistle. A cop on the roof held a pack of keys aloft and then he tossed them in an arc toward them. They hit the top of the car and slid into Jon's chest.

"Thanks!" he yelled.

"Good luck!" the cop yelled back.

Jon opened the doors and they both hopped in just as half a dozen monsters made it over the fence. He re-locked the doors and started the engine.

The Fiends were on the car in seconds, pounding the windows and yanking on the doors. Jon floored it toward the entry gate, which without electricity wasn't going to open, but that didn't stop the push-bumper equipped squad car from plowing right through it. With a screech of spinning tires and scraping metal, a dozen infected were trapped and crushed as the car's wheels spun and slipped over the chain link. Then the razor wire wound itself up around the right rear axle, snaring the car as another group of ghouls threw themselves upon it.

Jon slammed the transmission into reverse, sending a cloud of burned rubber smoke into the air and the wire pulled taught again.

"Forward! Go forward!" screamed Nikki.

"No shit!" He shoved the gearshift into drive and smashed the gas pedal into the floorboards. The tires screeched in protest as the car shot forward, dragging razor wire and a section of fencing behind it. The car started to fishtail and came extremely close to spinning into the lake when the piece of fence whipped around a light post and snapped the wire, setting them free.

The street was full of infected. Snarling creatures ricocheted off the bumper and fenders like rag dolls. The volume of bodies slamming against the car was nearly deafening and Nikki and Jon screamed mindlessly, adding their horror to the incredible din. Blood and hair and spit and dirt and pieces of clothing splattered all over the hood, doors, and windows. Then suddenly they were past them. The road ahead was mostly clear and Jon released some of the death grip he'd had on wheel. He sat up, his shoulders un-hunched and he lifted his head to look into the rearview mirror.

Nikki spotted the cop on the roof, waving his radio over his head and she switched on the police scanner.

Immediately a voice came over the other end - "listening...? Folks, this is Officer Frank Gifford. You just escaped with one of our cruisers. You listening? This is Officer Gifford, You folks listening?"

Nikki picked up the mike, "Yes officer, what can we do to help you now?"

"You can keep driving. There's no way to safely come back for us."

"Sir, you know they're bombing bigger towns tonight?"

"We're probably too small, but just in case, we've got a sealed room anyway. Don't worry about us. The bastards aren't getting inside. We're going to stay up here to be sure.

If we see the bombers, we'll get the bastards nice and clustered around us. The important thing is for you folks to keep going north. It's about three hours to Montreal at… What? What is that? What's that buzzing? What is that?" They heard him call out to the others on the roof. "You guys feel that?" Then Gifford took his thumb off the mic. Nikki tried to raise him again, but no luck. The gunfire suddenly stopped.

Jon slumped down in the car so he could just peer out the window and said, "Fuck. Keep your head down."

They sat in stony silence as Jon drove. After ten minutes or so, he wiped the cooling sweat off his face, "We need the GPS, I know I'm driving north but I don't really know where or how to get to the border."

"Well, that's a drag, cuz we left the backpacks back in the parking lot."

Jon sighed and shook his head.

"Maybe there's a map."

"Kind of a basic cop car. Not even one of those computer thingies."

Nikki looked through the glove box and the center console. "Some helpful gear here but no map." She pulled out a fifth of whiskey and held it up with a smirk. "I wonder if anybody gets a DUI in that town."

Jon fumbled with the key fob and unsnapped the other keys. "See if one of these releases that shotgun."

Nikki found the key and unlocked the gun. There were shells in the center console so she loaded it, racked it and made sure the safety was on.

They drove in silence for several miles. Occasionally a Fiend would run out at them like a car-chasing dog, but Jon would just step on the gas and leave it behind.

"This is my second borrowed cop car in a week," said Jon.

"You drive it pretty well."

"Thanks."

8 Northbound

Just outside of the town of Conway they saw a gas station with a bed sheet made into a banner hanging from the price sign: *TAKE WHAT YOU NEED. PUMPS WILL WORK UNTIL THE GENERATOR RUNS OUT. GOD BLESS AMERICA.* A pitched battle had taken place here - dead Fiends and half eaten humans littered the area around the gas pumps. A car had crashed through the front window of the attached convenience store.

Jon slowed down to a crawl, "It wouldn't hurt to top off the tank. Maybe there's a map and some food and water left. I say we risk it."

"Fine. You go in with the shotgun. I'll cover you."

Jon pulled up to the pumps, trying to avoid running over any bodies, and put the cruiser in park, leaving the engine running. He slapped on his helmet and they both stepped out to listen. No birds. No generator. Just a grunting coming from inside the store.

Jon said, "That doesn't sound good." He took the safety off the shotgun.

Nikki shouldered her M16 scanning past the sight into the store. There was another grunt that turned into a moan. "Let's not be heroes. We'll find something farther along."

"I think I see one of those map carousels. We need a map." He kept the shotgun leveled and stepped to the doorway.

The car had smashed through a good portion of the store. The passenger's lifeless body hung through the front windshield. The driver was a woman, still seated, her head pinned against the steering wheel by a heavy looking suitcase that had been launched from the back seat when they smashed to a halt. The blood had only just congealed.

A live male Fiend was trapped between the front bumper and the store's mangled checkout counter. Despite the blood trickling from its mouth and legs twisted into an impossible shape, it feebly growled while trying to reach for Jon.

Nikki stepped up to the smashed window and surveyed the scene. "That's fucked up."

"Shouldn't you be watching the outside?"

"I'm still out here. Just want to make sure the bogeyman doesn't jump you from behind some shelf."

Jon spun a rack of maps mixed with post cards and grabbed a local and a Greater New England one. The food had mostly been picked clean, but there were some bags of snacks still scattered around. The only liquid was Yoo Hoo chocolate drink and a can of Monster energy. He grabbed both.

The sound of an approaching car grabbed their attention. A big Hummer SUV was screaming down the road. The front was covered in gore from running down Fiends. The truck slowed and a rough looking man in bright orange hunting cap yelled from the passenger seat, "You got about sixty-seconds before a wall of them things come running up this road. You need a ride?"

Nikki looked to Jon, "What do you think?"

Jon flipped up his visor and said, "I think we're good with the cop car."

Nikki turned back to the guy, "We're good, thanks."

"Suit yourselves!" The SUV peeled out.

A gathering sound of screaming, gnashing humans could be heard. Nikki turned and looked down the road. It was turning black with a running mass of Fiends.

She said, "We've got twenty-seconds to get in the car."

Jon grabbed what he could carry, stopped for a hidden liter of A&W root beer and ran back to the car, tossing the food in back as he jumped in and put the pedal to the floor just as they were about to be surrounded.

Nikki put her hand on his thigh and squeezed, "Not too fast. We've gotten away. Don't need to run off the road."

Jon took the pressure off the accelerator and looked in the rearview mirror. Most people would stop running if their quarry got away. The infected didn't even slow down.

Nikki opened the New Hampshire map and scanned it. "Okay, we're going to be passing through the White Mountains, Mount Washington and whatnot. We keep taking Route 16 past Gorham to where it hits Route 26. We have to kind of zigzag up to Quebec from there. It looks like there's a border crossing at a village called Canaan. We could try angling over to Interstate 91 instead, but word was..."

"I know how bad the Interstates are. Total carnage. Let's definitely stay with the smaller roads."

They drove in silence for a while, Jon occasionally taking a glance at Nikki. She had a strong jaw line, definitely pretty, short-cropped dark hair, sharp nose with full lips. She felt his gaze but chose not to return it. She'd had men stare at her since she was a young girl, worse when she became a Marine.

Jon said, "I'm from Connecticut originally. Been living in Atlanta since –"

"Listen. It's Washington, right?" she asked without meeting his eyes. "I don't want to be rude, but I'd rather not get to know you more than I do right now. You're a reporter dumb enough to still be on this side of the wall. Maybe I'll hear your story in Canada, but until we get there, you're as good as dead."

Jon offered a condescending smile. "I'm not going to say you're dumb, but you're down here too."

"Very true. No point in getting to know me either."

He shut up and drove. The countryside was magnificent, tall snow capped mountains, thick forests, babbling brooks. He figured he might as well enjoy the scenery. It's not like he was really interested in her story, it was just the trained reporter in him. He couldn't help but ask questions. If he survived this, he would put it all down in a book, a small personal history, from start to finish. Whenever that was. Anyway, she was good looking.

As the miles went by, they'd pass abandoned cars, sometimes piled up enough to create tough obstacle courses. There weren't a lot of dead people though. For the ones who had been stranded, someone else had either given them a lift or they had walked – or maybe they had been dragged off by the infected to be fed upon in the nearby woods.

When they got to the outskirts of Gorham, they steeled themselves for attack and weren't disappointed. By the time they got to the main intersection of town, Fiends seemed to come running out of every building, every front yard.

Jon's feet danced back and forth from gas pedal to brake, swerving around most of them, hitting a few until they broke through the gauntlet on the far side of town. In Berlin they were greeted by a town on fire. At times there was only twenty feet of visibility. Jon turned on the headlights and Nikki flicked the vent to re-circulate the air. Bodies lined the road. A few Fiends crawled on hands and knees gasping. Others stayed low to the ground below most of the smoke where they could continue to feed on corpses.

They had nearly made it out when a lumberjack sized, bloody faced madman charged around a corner and landed on the hood of the car. He held a tire iron and immediately began smashing it against the windshield. Jon and Nikki screamed an involuntary curse.

Jon floored the car, zigzagging back and forth, but the thing held on. The first couple of swings with the tire iron spider webbed the already fractured windshield. The third blow made a hand sized hole. The snarling creature dropped the tire iron and shoved its whole arm inside, grabbing at Jon's throat. It reeked of body odor, blood and feces. Jon ducked and weaved and held his head back as far as he could while still reaching the gas pedal.

Nikki pulled her hunting knife out of the scabbard on her leg.

"Jesus, don't stab it, you'll get infected blood all over us! Lean out the window and shoot it in the head"!

Nikki unbuckled her seatbelt and pulled out the Beretta. She dropped the window and half leaned out of the car. Just then another Fiend launched itself at the side of the car, grabbing her arm, causing her to drop the gun. "Fuck!" It bit down on the sleeve of her jacket, but only got a mouthful of leather, it's hands grabbing and pulling as it held on.

The Fiend on the hood gnashed its teeth while its bulging eyes scanned all over Jon for a place to grab some flesh. Jon suddenly made a hard left and then jerked right, nearly throwing Nikki out of the window. The maneuver threw the windshield grabber's lower body off the left side of the hood allowing Jon to scrape it off along a telephone pole.

Nikki's attacker continued to hold on and she yelled in agony as her arm was bent back while the Fiend dragged along the ground. Jon unholstered his Colt, cocked it while driving with his knees, and slapped it into her flailing left hand. She turned and fired a round point blank into the Fiend's head and it fell away, rolling like a wet rag doll into the gutter. She pulled herself back inside, closed the window, buckling back up.

Jon glanced at her, "You all right? It bite you?"

Nikki opened the glove box, removed a pair of latex examination gloves and slapped them on. She then pulled up her sleeve and checked her arm. "No bite, but the fucking thing nearly pulled my arm out of the socket." She massaged her shoulder and reached back into the glove box, pulling out the whiskey and pouring it on her jacket where the Fiend had bit. She snapped off the gloves, tossed them out the window and then doused her hands with the whiskey as well. She tipped some more down her throat and then offered a swig to Jon. "Man, what I'd do for an LAV right now."

He took a gulp and handed it back. "Lav? Like a toilet?"

"L.A.V. – Like a light armored vehicle."

"Oh. Right." He glanced at her again. "Still, I'd be happy with the toilet– in a high rise condo… in Paris."

She gave a light chuckle.

"Sorry I nearly tossed you."

"I lost my pistol."

"At least you didn't get bit."

"The son-of-a-bitch's claws felt like a vise grip."

"If we stop again, we'll check the trunk. There's usually a lot of gear in a cop car. Maybe there's a vest or something for you. Another gun."

"Let's just not stop."

"That's a good plan too."

The air howled through the hole in the windshield and Jon found himself ducking to his right to keep it from hitting him directly in the face.

Nikki kept her head turned away from him and he could see her try to shrug off a sob.

Jon tried to soften his voice. "It's all right to be freaked. I've seen the toughest soldiers cry like babies during this thing. You okay?"

She turned, wiping snot from her nose with the back of her hand, "Marines aren't soldiers, we're Marines. You one of those dumb question reporters?"

Jon gave her a wry smile and turned back to his driving. "That's the closest call I've had."

"Welcome to the saliva club."

"Thanks. How can I get my membership revoked?"

Nikki tried the AM and FM radio, but could only find static. As they drove into deeper forest, the carnage thinned out and the countryside became peaceful looking again. A beautiful river flowed past them on the right and they both relaxed a little until they noticed the bodies floating along, others tangled in branches or caught on boulders. That's when Jon's hands started shaking. It was just a tremor at first and he shook them out over the steering wheel.

Nikki hardly took notice, her head buried in the map. "There's a town coming up when this road comes to a T. The shortest distance is to break left, but it eventually takes us closer to the Interstate and bigger population centers. If we go right, it takes us into Maine. It's more rural, definitely farther, maybe fewer obstacles though. I vote right."

Jon tried slapping one of his hands on the dashboard.

"What's wrong?"

"Not sure. Nervous tick, I guess."

"Combat shakes. Happens all the time. Better pull over and let me drive while your nervous system sorts itself out."

"Just a moment ago you were having your own mini-meltdown. And what happened to not stopping?"

"I'm fine now. You're exhausted. You might stop us with a tree."

Jon considered this. He was certainly exhausted. "Maybe I'll shut my eyes for a few. If I think about it, I haven't really done anything but run and fight for three months now."

He pulled the car over to the shoulder. "Let's not open the doors."

"Why don't you climb in back. Lay down. See if you can catch a few Z's. You can spell me afterwards. The next town is Errols. One street. We'll be in and out in two minutes. I'll wake you only if I have to."

"Okay. That sounds good. Thanks"

Jon climbed in back and Nikki slid over. He was halfway out by the time she pushed down on the accelerator.

PART TWO

THE SEARCH FOR A CURE

9 Tran

Dr. Robert Tran lay in bed, frustrated that his tiny opportunity to catch up on sleep was once again spoiled by his nagging subconscious. His brain had been tickling the back of his head for days. The researcher for the Centers for Disease Control knew the signs and it kept him awake with annoyed anticipation. The scientist in him suggested that he take a sleeping pill - a sleep-deprived brain being useless for dealing with a national pandemic. The holy-shit-we're-all-going-to-die-a-horrible-death normal human side of him said, "Sleeping pill? Are you nuts? You've almost got it."

A songbird began singing outside the window of his trailer. It was still dark out, but the bird didn't care and then another one joined it. Tran pulled his pillow over his head to block them out. He'd been crashing in this FEMA trailer outside the now Relocated-to-Ottawa CDC headquarters for three months. Ever since Atlanta was overrun, the race against time had taken up residence in a research park in the Ottawa suburbs. Tran was a member of the Bacterial Zoonoses Branch, which was charged among other things with scientific support for CDC's terrorism preparedness and emergency response. In reality his job was (to use the CDC's words) *Pathogen discovery and characterization of unusual bacterial pathogens and novel causes of critical illness and unexplained death*. Currently, the critical illness department was overwhelmed. No one was really sleeping, and to make matters worse, as the now partnered Canadian/American Government declared martial law, a food rationing system had just been brought into effect. Tran's stomach gurgled at the thought and he sat up to get a drink of water while cursing the chirpy birds outside.

The trailer's potable waterlines had been hooked up to an old galvanized pipe system and much to everyone's annoyance there was no filter and no home filters to be had. The result was rusty water. To minimize some of the metal, he held a handkerchief over the glass and let the water slowly filter through - and that's when he had it - the tickle in the back of his head turned into a eureka moment: The birds, the dirty water, the bacteria that riddled the brain of the infected, it all came together like the last successful turn of a Rubik's Cube.

Turning on a light, he threw his glasses on and flipped open his laptop. First he brought up a map of the initial spread of FND-z. For each date that the infection jumped north, it showed a different color swath over the Southern Continental US. Somehow, the disease had overcome every quarantine effort the government, and even panicked but still organized citizens, had set up. Of course, now the thing was a self-perpetuating killing machine, wrecking any computer modeling that showed predictive behavior. In April the population density of infected had reached a tipping point beyond quarantine within the continental US. It was literally the last hope of North America that the final barrier, the Saint Lawrence Wall as it was now called, would hold.

Tran typed into the CDC database and pulled up the data for the migratory behaviors of North American birds. The Zoonoses branch also dealt with the Avian Flu (*if only this pandemic could be so insignificant*), and bird migration was a standard element in the research. He then began clicking on a list of bird species. Each click detailed the migratory patterns of that particular species. After several clicks he stopped on the Tree Swallow. Another click isolated only Tree Swallows migrating from southern Florida: and there it was, the migratory pattern preceded the quarantine breaks by a week at the most.

He highlighted various sentences in the bird's description page: *Songbird white on the bottom, shiny blue-green on top. Outside the breeding season, the birds congregate into enormous flocks. Use many feathers from other birds in their nests built over or immediately adjacent to water. The Tree Swallow winters farther north than any other American swallow, its spring and summer breeding range covers most of the Northern US as well as Canada and Alaska.*

The recurrent sound of bird chirps outside snapped Tran out of his search. He set down the computer and quickly started throwing on some clothes.

With a combination of excitement over his potential solution, to at least part of the puzzle, and a tremendous foreboding, over songbirds no less, Tran barged into the Zoonoses lab with a severe lack of coordination. The lab, actually the entire CDC and its Canadian counterpart, were on a twenty-four hour war footing. Sleep was an afterthought, as was food (until the rationing kicked in and reminded people that they had better eat when they could). Tran crashed into several stools and nearly knocked over some lab equipment as he set down his computer bag and notebooks.

Susan Chancellor and her assistant, Aaron Burnbaum, were standing in front of an electron microscope studying an image of live FND-z bacterium.

Susan said, "Tran. Good, you're here. Even though this nasty bug keeps shape shifting, I think we've finally sequenced its genetic code."

"It's from a bird or bird related," said Tran.

"How did you know?"

"A Tree Swallow to be exact."

"Actually, we believe it's from a variety of chicken. We think Cornish Game Hen. What makes you say Tree Swallow?"

"Because Cornish Game Hens don't migrate."

"Meaning?"

Tran opened his computer and woke it up. He still had the screens up from earlier. "This thing is not some terrorist attack. It's evolution at its best – or worst, depending on how you look at it."

Susan and Aaron moved over to Tran's computer and folded their arms in anticipation.

Tran continued, "We know that this bacterium made it into the human circulatory system via water. COTPER even confirmed this occurrence in municipalities with less regulated pollution controls. You know, like Miami's Biscayne Bay aquifer. On any given day the folks in Miami have no idea where their water is coming from."

"Yes, yes, we know all of this," said Susan.

"People who drank from that aquifer and became ill, were getting their water from wells or other non-protected areas upstream from purification plants."

Aaron said, "You're not telling us anything really new, Tran."

"Just laying the groundwork. Now I want you to look at this map of the disease as it jumped past the containment zones and look at the dates. Now look at this map of the migration patterns of the Tree Swallow, in particular, those tagged in southern Florida. The dates are basically a week apart."

"It's interesting Robert," said Susan, "But we're getting chicken not swallow."

"Bear with me," said Tran. "The Tree Swallow builds its nest, in part, by using the feathers of other birds. In fact they have been known to do aerial combat with each other over falling feathers. What if you're right and it *is* chicken, but what if the bacterium jumped to the Tree Swallow who was stealing the chicken's discarded but contaminated feathers?" Tran felt rather proud of himself as he wrapped up that last sentence.

Susan said, "Hmm, I have to admit I kind of like it. However, it doesn't explain avian/human transference."

"The Tree Swallow nests primarily near to or preferably over fresh water. Birds have to poop. These birds poop in the water. Classic vector-borne to water-borne transference."

Susan gave it some more thought then she nodded to herself. "It makes sense. I'm going to devote your team's energy to it, Tran. Get them in here."

"I think we're going to have to devote everybody to it."

"Why?"

"The Tree Swallow does most of its summer nesting in the Northern states and all of Canada. Based on conjecture only at this point, because this year's migration studies are obviously shot, I'd estimate that they have already arrived in their traditional nesting grounds. I know what you're going to say, the entire population of infection-free Canada is required to boil water, but I guarantee you there are folks in rural areas that are quite sure of the safety of their local, non-municipal water supplies and aren't bothering with the boil order. It's a guess of course, but I think we can assume that the Saint Lawrence Wall will be breached from within, and soon."

Susan and Aaron went cold at the thought.

Director Louis-Gelding was briefed and was quickly convinced that Tran's theory had more than merit. She ran it straight up to the joint chiefs where it was decided that a team of CDC scientists, along with a small platoon of Army Rangers, should be dispatched to Southern Florida with the intent to locate the suspected poultry farm. It was hoped that by finding the original super bug it could then be genetically altered to reduce or preferably eliminate its harmfulness. A vaccine of sorts then might be created that could help a human host fight off the little bastard. Unfortunately, this wasn't going to save tens of millions of Americans who had already been infected. For those poor souls there was no hope. The brain damage was irreversible. Their only salvation rested in a quick death. The armed forces had a plan for that going in high gear. The assault would be the greatest clash of forces in human history. The preparations were enormous, not the least of which was the added burden of repatriating America's massive overseas military forces. The seemingly never ending Overseas Contingency Operation (aka, terrorist whack-a-mole), and the containment of China had become an afterthought in America's fight for life.

Tran, Susan, Aaron and five other CDC scientists packed preassembled gear for field-testing into a van. Until now, no one ever imagined that Florida would be a Hot Zone. All of the scientists had been flown to various South, Central American, African and Southeast Asian countries at one time or another. All the same, the routine was identical: A small amount of personal gear was allowed. Everyone made sure his or her hazmat suit was packed and ready to throw on before touchdown.

The vans pulled up to a small civilian airport, which was now occupied by the US Army. It was abuzz with activity as the scientists stepped out next to two big CH-47D Chinook helicopters. A captain dressed in battle fatigues barked out orders to a platoon of thirty-two Army Rangers, a squad of which was finishing loading a Humvee into one of the Chinooks.

A Bird Colonel, dressed for desk work, directed another squad to start transferring the scientific equipment. The two men walked over to introduce themselves, "Ms. Chancellor? Colonel Gilbert Shaw, director of the flight operations here. This is Captain O'Shea who will be leading the military aspect of your mission."

Susan reached out and shook their hands, "No time to lose, gentlemen. We can talk about the particulars of the mission while en route."

Captain O'Shea spoke with a soft North Carolina accent. "That's fine, Doctor Chancellor, ma'am." He pointed at the nearest helicopter, "If you and your team would board that one from the rear, Sergeant Bullock will get you seated. We should be ready in five." He gave a slight tip of his helmet and went back to work.

Colonel Shaw, with a pained look in his eyes, followed alongside the scientists saying, "This equipment is the best the Army has in this area. Considering the pending re-invasion of the homeland and the myriad of other things we're trying to juggle, we're lucky to gain the use of them. Still, I'm told your mission gets first priority." The man was clearly uncomfortable about giving up the two helicopters.

Susan said, "That's correct, Colonel. First priority."

The colonel offered a retreating smile and waved an arm toward the big aircraft. They were bigger than a city bus and sported dual rotors. "They're designed for in-flight refueling, but unfortunately our tankers are stretched to the limit bringing our troops back from overseas. We've devised another plan. You'll make two stops on your way to Florida. Both are Army airfields and should have plenty of aviation fuel. From the satellite imagery, there does appear to be evidence of infected humans in both locations. As a precaution, both have been targeted with a nerve agent bombing."

Susan stopped them all twenty yards short of the loading ramp, "May I ask what type of nerve agent, Colonel?"

The Colonel mulled over his answer, then decided to just come out with it. The world was going to hell in a hand-basket, who gives a crap about being PC with chemical warfare? "It's Novichok. We have limited supplies for applications such as this."

"That's a Russian product, no?" asked Tran.

The colonel ignored this, saying, "The thing to keep in mind with Novichok is that it's sticky. It leaves an oily residue that can stay on whatever it touches for months. You touch this stuff and you die. Period. Both re-fuelings will require that all personnel wear their chemical warfare suits - hazmat suits in your team's case. Captain O'Shea's troops are an elite fighting force and they are all veterans of overseas action as well as the evacuation. They've all handled a Shitfob or ten, so you are in good hands. You'll of course have to land twice again as you return north. With any luck, you'll remain incident free."

"Now you've jinxed us," said Aaron under his breath.

Rick Decker, a CDC blood analyst, piped in, "How come we don't just take an airplane down to Guantanamo, get our helicopters there?"

The Colonel grimaced, "Gitmo's gone, son. Cuban's overran it last week. No way to take it back now."

Susan started them walking again. "Well, there are only a handful of chicken farms in southern Florida, the most likely culprit is the one industrial size farm that we are targeting. I believe it's called Happyland Farms.

"Known for their Plump Okeechobee Boilers," added Tran.

10 Stratton

Nikki drove without incident across the Maine border; not much – *Leaving New Hampshire – Welcome To Maine-The Way Life Should Be* - and kept going. They passed occasional houses and buildings, everything abandoned.

Knowing her fellow Americans, she was surprised that more people hadn't stayed to make a stand. Then again, when an entire nation passes your doorstep trying to escape a marauding mass of mindless cannibals... and the threat of nerve gas- She had to stop making excuses for her dumb decision to stay. She had been a fool to agree with Bob and the other guys to hold out at the mansion. If she'd insisted on her intuition, as in - this is nuts, let's get the hell out of here.... Heck, if they'd followed orders, she'd be safely behind the Saint Lawrence.

She cursed herself, then shook it off. She knew very well the pointlessness of lamenting spilt milk. The only path was forward. Accept the mess and get on with it. That's what her father would say. Dad, the Sergeant Major of the Marine Corp, the decorated war hero, daredevil of Fallujah, Operation Iraqi Freedom - he'd stopped speaking to her when she'd been dishonorably discharged, well, really before that. She'd heard he was alive and helping coordinate the re-invasion. She wondered if he thought about her.

Jon's snoring changed and she looked over her shoulder to see if he was awake. He turned on his side and pulled his knees up, still asleep.

She looked back down the road, dad invading her thoughts. She'd joined the Corp to find his heart, make him notice. When she was twelve (and just growing breasts of her own) her mom had suddenly contracted breast cancer and died within a month. It had happened so fast. Her dad had barely made it back from combat duty to be there for the end. As soon as mom had been buried, he had gone from the occasional visit while on leave to full time soldier, requesting repeated redeployments in The Long War. For him, his daughter remained a stranger connected by an occasional email and a rare, almost wordless, video chat. He had come back for the Fourth of July when she was sixteen. By then they were strangers. Awkwardly, he tried to insert himself as a disciplinarian in her then chaotically teenage life. It blew up into an inevitable screaming match and he left to go back to his unit before the celebrations began.

She was raised by a series of Marine Corps' Family Child Care providers (her dad picking up the tab and arranging for someone new each time she became "too difficult" for her surrogate parents). For most of them, the financial benefit of caring for a pre-teen with attitude who then grew into a teenager with severe anger and abandonment issues, just wasn't worth it. So she bounced from home to home until she was old enough to enlist herself.

She guessed, no, hoped, that if she joined the Corp she'd get to see him, get close enough to be acknowledged - Daddy's girl following in his footsteps. It didn't work out that way. He had come to watch her graduate from boot camp, but that was it. He called once when word got around of her daring leadership during an assault on a Taliban stronghold in Waziristan, Pakistan. She'd won a bronze star (the trinket had helped when she was facing that possible court-martial for killing the rapist Sudanese chief). Her dad had asked her about the fight and she found herself embellishing what was really just a classic assault on a fortified house. The difference was that her actions had helped save the life of a US Senator's son (a brave soldier who was pinned down and badly wounded). Her dad sniffed out the embellishments and the conversation turned from a pride-filled occasion to his disappointment with her need to lie. That was the last time she'd spoken with him.

She focused on the road and realized that she had drifted into the oncoming lane, not that anything was coming the other way. She glanced over her shoulder and smiled crookedly as a soft snore escaped Jon's lips. She had to admire this reporter guy. He'd stayed behind to tell the tale. It seemed a bit suicidal, but his survival instinct was clearly intact.

They were approaching the Sugarloaf ski resort when Jon woke. He sat up looking dazed. "Wow, was I out. Where are we?"

"Some ski area."

The hill was covered in meadows where in winter they would be covered in ski-happy revelers. A large herd of deer grazed on the face of one of the wider slopes.

Jon wiped the sleep from his eyes. "It's a good sign if deer can relax."

They passed a sign indicating *Flagstaff Lake 1 mile* and just then, a green Subaru wagon came over the rise ahead. Nikki had to swerve into her own lane as the car shot past them going south. The driver had beeped repeatedly, flicked his passing lights on and off and disappeared, tires squealing around a bend. The deer bounded off into the woods.

"What the hell?" Nikki exclaimed.

"We better slow down."

"I'm not sure I want to keep going."

Jon climbed back in front and grabbed the map. "Can we turn around and go another way?"

"It's a lot of lost ground, but yes. Problem is, it takes us to Route 201, a bigger artery."

They passed a house. Nikki saw movement - a flash of a man in an attic window. "You see that? That guy had a radio."

"Didn't see it."

"Mmm, this doesn't feel good."

"So let's stop. Maybe we walk up to that rise. See what we see."

"Let's just take it easy, I'll be ready to flip a bitch. Floor it if we have to."

They went over the rise without incident and houses became thicker as Route 16 became yet another Small Town Main Street. Nikki feathered the gas and the brakes, not wanting to slow down too much and ready to floor it if she had to.

Jon looked at the houses and saw a curtain flutter here and there and then caught the eyes of a child watching them. "This town isn't abandoned. There's people in some of these houses."

They came around the next curve and found themselves in a perfect ambush. The road ahead was blocked by smashed up cars. One car, just moments before, had overturned trying to stop. Its wheels were still spinning. A family was trapped inside, screaming.

Several men wearing assorted hunting and military gear stepped out from behind the cars, armed to the teeth.

Nikki swore, "Fuck. I'm such an asshole!" She slammed on the brakes, put the car in reverse, but had to slam on the brakes again as another group of armed men ran onto the road behind them and laid a telephone pole across it. They were trapped. A man wearing an Army officer's uniform and sporting an M-16 stepped out in front of the others and leveled the gun. "Out of the car. Hands in the air. Fuck around and we shoot you." He nodded to the side of the road where two bodies lay face down, apparently shot execution style.

Some of the men began pulling the people out of the flipped car, using little mercy.

Jon flicked on the cruiser's PA switch and spoke into the mic. "You people are interfering with officers of the law. Hold down your weapons and let us pass."

The guy with the M-16, flanked by a guy wearing sergeant stripes and full battle fatigues stepped up to the driver side of the car. Both Jon and Nikki pointed their weapons toward them. The man spoke evenly, his voice clear through the hole in the windshield, "Major Gerald Deighton, United States Army. You've entered my area of operations."

Jon tried again through the PA so others could hear. "Step back from the car. Put your weapons down. We have urgent business."

"We all have urgent business. Ours is recruiting soldiers for the defense of this town. You are not police officers. You are surrounded. You will pull to the side of the road, step out of the vehicle, leaving your weapons inside. This is not a request. We shoot all deserters."

Jon turned to Nikki, "What do you think?"

"We do as he says. I've met enough of these angry PTSD types to know that it's worthless to argue." She nodded at the dead people. "Clearly they are not fooling around."

The major said, "I can hear you just fine, ma'am, and I don't cotton to the PTSD bullshit. The people of this town are doing their patriotic duty to defend and then take back this country."

Nikki said, "Can you hear me tell my friend here, that you are probably bat shit crazy and have no idea what's coming up that road?"

The sergeant elevated his weapon so it pointed directly at Nikki's face. Deighton said, "There won't be a third request."

Nikki put the car in park and unfastened her seatbelt. She and Jon stepped out, leaving their guns on the seat.

Deighton said, "That's the right attitude. Keep it up and we'll even give you your weapons back."

Jon looked the major in the eye and tried to gauge the level of his sanity. He decided that he and Nikki were probably in big trouble. "Sir, the orders from our government are clear. All citizens are to get their asses up to Canada. The country is to be bombed with chemical weapons."

"I'm well aware of the orders... Mr.?"

"Washington, Jon. I'm an embedded reporter assigned to the Army. My colleague and I have a job to do."

"Perfect, then you can report from right here. The place where America started to take her country back."

"Sir," said Nikki again, loud enough for the couple dozen others nearby. "When we left New Hampshire, we had thousands of infected right behind us. My guess is there are millions of the things heading north. I was with a group of people holed up in an extremely secure mansion with heavy weapons and months of supplies. We were overrun in a few days. I'm the only survivor. I can see a couple of dozen heads here. What army are you planning to stop them with?"

Deighton gave her a good looking over and decided he didn't like what he saw. "We have more showing up by the hour. Most are armed, all want their country back." He turned to the others, "Right people!"

He got cheers from the group.

"Now, we are not on a major route north, the bulk of the enemy will flow, as they have so far, up the main highways. We've given enough ground. It's time to hold some."

Jon said, "Forgive me major. Have you fought these things? They are not insurgents or even suicide bombers. They're voraciously hungry, feel little pain, and have zero emotion left to appeal to. In fact they love killing. They seem to hunt well in packs and there are millions of them. Oh –

and they seem to have some ability to mess with your head."
He nodded at Nikki. "The mansion she is talking about
wasn't breached. They somehow convinced someone to
open the door."

"That might be a stretch," said Nikki. "That was just one
guy losing his cool."

"No. I saw it. It sounds crazy, but it happened."

The major broke in. "We have not yet had the pleasure of
killing any infected humans, but I am very confident in the
town's plans for defense. We are not concerned with the
threat of chemical weapons. We are too small for such a
waste of precious resources. It is the job of the foot soldier to
root out and kill the enemy."

Jon decided to try the honest approach, "Be that as it may,
sir, you have no right to hold us here against our will. We
will not stand and fight with you. If you remain in this place,
you will all be dead or infected in two days or less. I can
guarantee it."

This got some of the other defenders to look around and
mumble private worries and I-told-you-sos.

"SILENCE!" yelled Deighton. He turned back to Jon and
Nikki, "We'll let you stew about whether you want to help
or not with some like minded folks." He turned to two rough
looking soldiers, "Escort our new guests to the alternate
facilities."

11 Southbound

It was Tran's first helicopter ride. He was only two seats away from one of the door gunners and therefore had a decent view outside. He decided that he liked helicopters. It was the oddest sensation to at one moment feel the weight of the huge machine on the ground, the astonishing noise and vibration of the engines ramping up, and in the next, the wheels lifting off the tarmac. Even though his own weight felt the same, strapped as he was into a fold down webbed seat, he nevertheless got the sensation that he was floating. A sense of glee rose up through his chest, filling his throat and he felt his face grow warm with childlike wonder. Then his organs were pushed down as the g-forces changed. He saw the ground sweep past the window as the Chinook banked to the right, finally leveling off for its primary direction of flight. The flat farmland outside fell away and reduced in scale until it became an uncanny representation of a model railroad world. They crossed the Saint Lawrence about thirty minutes later and Northern New York State revealed its vast sea of trees and small bodies of water. To his left he could see the headwaters of Lake Champlain (the backbone of the new wall that would eventually divide a reclaimed New England from the rest of the country). The flight was downright peaceful as the pastoral scenery moved past the windows. As they crossed over the dairy land that surrounded

Plattsburgh, one of the door gunners broke the serenity, yelling out, "Holy fuckin' shit!"

Those who could, looked outside and gasped. Humans, infected humans, slowly moved north in massive packs. Many simply stopped walking and watched the helicopters go by. Some turned around in useless pursuit. A dairy farm had been overrun, and thousands of Fiends gorged themselves on hundreds of defenseless cattle. One corral was nothing but a sea of moving gore as the infected crawled through blood and guts, coating themselves in the ghastly mixture.

Susan turned away and gagged reflexively. "God help us."

"I thought God was off the table for you Susan," said Decker with a sarcastic tone.

Susan's eyelids became hooded as she turned to Decker. "Let's not, shall we, Rick? Your charm is more than enough at the office. We don't need to fill the skies with it too."

The gunner, Casper Rodriguez, Ghost to his fellow Rangers, turned to both of them. "You better hope that God isn't off the table." The soldier had been thinking about God a lot lately. His entire family had holed up at their ranch in Colorado. The big house on two thousand acres had been his ancestral home for ten generations, before the US Cavalry, before Lewis and Clark, before Colorado was Colorado. Seeing the slaughter below made his stomach tighten with the thought of his familia's horrible end. With the exception of himself and his brother, who was serving with the Marines in Afghanistan, the whole clan Rodriguez: grandparents, aunts, uncles, cousins, nieces, nephews, brothers and sisters had chosen to make a stand at the ranch. It was naturally fortified at a bend in a river with a cliff behind and the water to the front. The open areas that were left were natural kill zones where an attacker was ultimately forced into one narrow choice. The Rodriguez Ranch had withstood many an assault from Native Americans until it was finally accepted as a part of the landscape in the early

Eighteen-Hundreds. Fires and flood had been nothing to them. Their beef cattle had become world famous for its quality and the cache´ of its ancient Western roots. The Fiends had overwhelmed the Rodriguez' in a matter of hours. Casper's father had called via satellite phone to say good-bye. He could hear the last of the gunfire and the screaming in the background. They were about to be overrun. There were no more bullets. Casper, all the way up in Canada, was filled with more helplessness and rage than he thought he could feel. His mother got on the phone weeping and told him to pray, "Pray every day for our souls, son. Pray that we do not become like them. Pray, pray, pray." Casper promised through tears and gritted teeth. He told his mother how much he loved her, and then a loud crashing sound came through his phone's speaker. His mother screamed in horror and he held the phone away from him. He still heard the children's screams in his dreams. He told himself that God didn't have anything to do with this, that this was the Devil's work.

Though Ghost was on a scientific mission to save humanity, science didn't enter his mind for a minute. When it came to the devils below, this wasn't science, this was the Book of Revelation. Satan was rising.

Corporal Beau Preston, who was sitting next to Aaron Burnbaum asked, "So why a chicken farm in Florida?"

Aaron turned to the beefy Corporal without looking him in the eye. These people naturally intimidated the researcher and he found himself wishing he could just sleep or look through the notes on his laptop. Instead, he spoke up, offering his lecture tone as a buffer. "We have posited that the original bacterium, which caused the FND-z pandemic, was created, probably inadvertently, at a chicken farm."

"Yeah? So why a chicken farm?" Aaron tried to smile through lips bent with conceit, and Preston followed up. "I'd like to know why we stopped our re-invasion training and are instead risking our asses to fly all the way to Florida to hunt chickens."

Aaron looked at the man's eyes for the first time and saw deep intelligence and a look of genuine interest. He chastened himself, slightly, for being narrow-minded.

"Have you heard of meningitis?"

Preston nodded.

Aaron wasn't exactly oblivious about his personality. He could feel his annoyingly pedantic nature unfold from the box that barely contained it. "Bacterial Meningitis is one of the leading causes of death and permanent disability among children. The disabilities may include cerebral palsy, blindness, deafness or seizures. In extreme cases, difficulties with limbs may require amputations. In short, it is caused by certain bacteria, the most common being streptococcus, crossing the blood-brain barrier, or meninges, and interacting with the micro vascular endothelial cells." He paused, "Still with me?" Preston nodded and several other Rangers leaned in to listen. "Large-scale inflammation results, due to the body's own immune response, thereby reducing blood flow to the brain and brain stem. The brain cells are deprived of oxygen and undergo apoptosis."

Aaron glanced at Robert Tran and noted the amused look on the man's face. Tran's amused look always got under Aaron's skin. As far as he was concerned, the researcher had no respect for the broader teachings of science. He continued, "Apoptosis is the word for automated cell death, which of course leads to the complications that I just outlined. Meningitis is highly contagious, and is usually spread through the systems that we all have for mucous formation and delivery. In the case of FND-z, or Cain's Disease, as it has become commonly termed, the frontal lobes of the brain are primarily affected, leaving the more base elements of the organ healthy. We haven't been able to determine the exact nature of the aggressive response that follows, other than the fact that the more primitive parts of the brain seem to compensate for the loss of higher function; what we might describe as the moral judgment that comes with the development of frontal lobes in Homo Sapiens-Sapiens. These more reptilian instincts are instead pushed into some type of overdrive. Also unknown is the cause for the apparently insatiable desire to kill and eat the flesh of living things. There is of course the evolutionary obvious ideal, that the disease spreads itself through the interaction of bodily fluids. But why then eat the victim? Why not just bite?"

Preston said, "We all gotta eat, Doc."

This got a chuckle out of the group.

Aidman, Cowboy Johnston spoke up. "So you're sayin' some chicken farmer started all this shit?"

Un-amused, Aaron sat back in his seat and nodded at Tran, "Robert, why don't you finish?"

Tran smiled and said, "We think so." He raised his voice to be heard better. "It's our hope, everybody, that if we can isolate the bacteria in its original form, we can, through gene therapy, block the molecule that allows it to pass through the brain blood barrier. We have already achieved this with certain bacteria that cause meningitis. We can then create a vaccine with our new designer mutant gene or perhaps even an antidote for those that come into contact with the infected."

Preston asked, "So you can cure people?"

"Not likely a cure. More of a stopgap for those that haven't yet had the bug get into their head. Once FND-z passes the meninges, the brain damage is irreversible, and as we all know, the infection works fast, usually within twenty-four hours, in rare cases within six. However, an antidote delivered early, say within three hours, may stave off the infection and save the victim. A vaccine of course would offer immunity, but would have to be injected before any possible contact with the disease."

Tran observed that everyone was straining to listen now so he continued in an even louder voice, "In regards to the seemingly indiscriminate killing and eating of victims, I suspect that Corporal Preston makes the only logical point. We do, after all, have to eat. Victims of Cain's have more or less lost their cognitive abilities. They can't think to go to the grocery store much less grow and harvest food, and naturally occurring plants are inedible to the untrained eye. The infected are really no different from predator fish that only hunt other fish. The land is filled with warm-blooded animals, including people. Think of them like killer whales or better yet, tiger sharks traveling in pods like killer whales; not terribly cunning, less concerned with self-preservation and interested in eating anything that has a heartbeat." Tran paused for a moment and looked out the window. The countryside had once more returned to tranquility. "It's estimated that out of a population of three hundred and fifty-nine million Americans living in the lower forty-eight, as well as another fifty-million foreign workers and tourists plus thirty-million Western Canadians - one hundred and ten million of that number made it into the Canadian and offshore safe zones. One hundred million are thought to have perished, and at least fifty to sixty-million healthy people, no one really knows, remain inside the US and Western Canada."

Preston said, "They say that the chemical bombings of the big cities today will probably kill seventy-million Deadheads, so that would leave two hundred million human sharks roaming around – give or take."

Tran nodded, "Imagine dumping that many actual sharks into the Caribbean – the food supply would get thin pretty fast."

Cowboy looked at Tran with confusion. "So you're saying this Terror Virus isn't from a terrorist?"

Susan decided to speak up, "I'm afraid gentlemen, as my colleague, Mr. Burnbaum suggested, this horrible pandemic is more than likely homegrown and is simply the result of our own poor understanding of biology, mixed with bad farming practices. Or, to put it more simply, greed has finally killed us all. The farm we are searching for probably misused antibiotic-laden feedstock to fatten their birds and reduce loss to disease. Through the power of evolution, a bacterium was born; one that we can't stop with any known antibiotic and which has the power to render us into demons."

Specialist Jordan Jones yawned and stretched, "Guess this mission has to succeed then." He extended his legs into the aisle and closed his eyes.

Other Rangers followed his example, and but for the throb of the spinning blades above, the cabin grew quiet. It was going to be a long trip. Everyone needed rest.

12 Barbwire

   Nikki and Jon found themselves escorted to a holding area where a dozen or so other people were being kept. It was a fenced-in power sub-station with doubled up razor wire coiled around its top. In one corner was a port-a-potty; opposite that, an open-sided tent with cots set up beneath. Two armed guards milled about at a distance of twenty yards or so. Beyond them a backhoe was digging what appeared to be a wide trench.

  A tall, thin man in his early fifties, wearing a light windbreaker and a Red Sox cap, stepped up to them. "Welcome to Camp Sparky. My name's Will Parker. We know why you're here. We all want to get the hell up to Canada. The commandant out there figures he can hold us until it's too late and then let us fight for our lives."

  Jon and Nikki introduced themselves and Jon asked, "Has anyone in here agreed to take orders, join the major, you know, to at least get out of this cage?"

  "We all have at one point or another. He doesn't buy it, even if we mean it. Nope, you're in here until the onslaught." He was almost oddly cheerful as he said this. Jon thought he smelled a politician.

  They were introduced to the other residents, some friendly, others, not so much. One woman was clearly delusional, trying to show them around the space as though it was a garden on her private estate. An old woman lay on one of the cots. She was mostly still, but kept up a constant dull moan. Jon asked if she was perhaps infected. The others didn't seem to think so. She'd been like that for a couple of days.

Will said, "The two guys she was riding with decided to fall in with Deighton."

"You're just in time for supper," volunteered Patricia Gould, the delusional woman - mid-fifties, obese, but in a strong healthy-looking sort of way.

Will said, "They give us two meals a day. There are a lot of provisions left from when the bulk of the town escaped."

Ingrid, a mousy woman in her early thirties said, "We're safer inside the fenced compound than out in the town."

Jon and Nikki looked at each other and chose to keep their mouths shut. No point in popping that bubble. This fence wouldn't hold back the horde of flesh eaters anymore than the police fence in New Hampshire had. It was a cage filled with live food, beating hearts and gallons of blood.

The sub-station appeared to be very secure. It had of course been designed to keep people out lest they tamper with the town's electrical lifeline, and also served to keep children and morons from electrocuting themselves. At its center were several large transformers. They were fed by thick cables coming out of the adjacent power plant. More cables led away from the transformers up to a long line of high-tension towers spanning the nearby lake and over the horizon. The power plant was a large bunker-like building, that sat squatting by the lakeshore crowned with smoke stacks. It had smooth walls and no windows, just two sets of large double metal doors and a loading dock. Though it wasn't operating, markings on the building indicated that it was natural gas fired. Jon saw movement on the roof. Two men were attaching razor wire to the top edge of the parapet wall. If they thought that Fiends were going to somehow climb up there, they were dumber than he thought. Then again, who really new what the things were capable of? He decided to give the soldiers credit for overkill.

Nikki pointed to another pair of men in Army fatigues working on the far backside of the building. They were placing something on the ground and carefully attaching some kind of cable to it. "Trip wires," she said. "They're placing anti-personnel mines around the building."

Several more men were finishing the installation of a barbed wire fence. Beyond that, mounds of fresh sawdust and bright yellow stumps evidenced the recent clear cutting of the surrounding forest, leaving a two hundred yard killing zone around the whole complex. At its edge the forest was thick and green with new leaves covering a dense, fern laden, mossy floor. The backhoe driver was guarded by a well-armed man who scanned the forest with binoculars and occasionally stomped his feet to keep warm.

The razor wire around the enclosure was doubled in a way that precluded Jon from climbing up and lying across it as he had at the police lot. As prisons go, this was a pretty good one. As he and Nikki circled the wire they found themselves back at the main entrance, as their fellow prisoners lined up for dinner.

A pickup truck with three well-armed guards backed up to the gate. One kept his weapon trained on the prisoners while the other two dropped the tailgate and dragged out a large stockpot full of steaming food. They unlocked the gate and without a word, exchanged the pot for a now empty one handed off by Will.

The stockpot contained a beef stew. Jon guessed it had been in cans only a little earlier. It was hot though, and the first real cooked meal that he'd have in quite some time. His tongue and cheeks swelled with saliva in a painful way as he anticipated the first taste. As the food settled in his stomach, he found that his thinking was becoming clearer and his general perception of his surroundings got brighter.

A woman in her early thirties wearing a goose down coat with a mass of unwashed locks slid over next to Jon and Nikki. She was dragging a pair of crutches with her, leaning them against the table. Her eyes were bright with unspoken words, yet she hesitated, letting her mouth run slack.

Jon said, "Hello."

Nikki nodded to the woman, who finally spoke with a whisper. "I didn't say that I wouldn't cooperate."

A man in blue mechanic's coveralls broke in, "Don't bother with Kathy. She thinks we're just bait."

"I wasn't speaking with you, was I, David Miller?" She turned back to Jon and Nikki. "I volunteered to help Major Deighton, but I've got a bad leg. Skiing accident back in December, when all of this was in Florida."

Jon, not sure how to respond, offered, "I'm sorry."

"My bad leg keeps me from being as useful on the outside as I can be on the inside."

"How's that?" asked Nikki.

"On the inside, I'm bait."

Jon looked at her sideways, "What would be the point of that? The infected need no bait. If they see or smell, or however they can tell that you've got a healthy beating heart, you're lunch."

Nikki piped in, "Maybe he stuck you in here, because he doesn't want an invalid slowing down the construction."

"If that's true," Kathy responded, "then why not let me leave, take my car up to Canada?" She pointed to a line of stakes with orange tape on them that led across the muddy grass surrounding the power plant. "Look where the stakes lead."

They bypassed the cage and continued around the building.

Nikki stood and scanned it more carefully. "This prison is on the outside of the new fence and trench."

Jon stood and looked himself. "Well, that's not good." He looked at two men on the roof of the power plant sighting a big machine gun. "Easier to pick them off if they bunch up around a cage full of us."

Kathy said, "No one listens to me. Maybe they'll listen to you."

David Miller said, "I never thought of it that way."

"Me either," said Will who had been listening in.

Jon asked, "What about some of the other citizens outside? I mean they can't all be for this. Maybe they don't know the plan. Can we appeal to someone? Are any of the guards friendly?"

Will said, "They're the least friendly. If anybody is in on this, it's the guys building up this site and the ones bringing us food and water. There's about fifty or sixty armed people here, but most have nothing to do with us. We're isolated."

They were startled by a gunshot, which was followed by another. A lone male Fiend came running out of the woods and one of the fence builders was on a knee shooting. Then maybe twenty more infected charged out following the first.

Kathy offered an involuntary scream.

The backhoe driver let the tractor idle and stood up to join the rest, shooting with precise three round bursts. Several Fiends made it as far as the trench and the soldiers hollered a rebel yell as they shot down into the hole. On the roof, one soldier yelled at another who simply held onto the fifty-caliber machine gun and stared in horror. The yeller shoved the man aside and cocked the big gun. With ground shaking power, the soldier lit up the last of the charging Fiends, blowing them to pieces all over the freshly cut tree stumps. The whole event lasted less than a minute.

Later, after they'd piled up what they could, a squad went out and doused the remains with gasoline, setting it all alight. The smoke from the burning flesh passed right through the prisoner's cage causing them to cover their faces with their blankets as they gagged and retched.

When the sun started to go down, they could make out the first wave of military aircraft flying overhead from the North. Bombers and fighters stretched out to the horizon. Jon knew vaguely the number of planes that the US combined forces had on the continent. This was far more. NATO aircraft had apparently joined the fight. The soldiers let out a cheer and the prisoners found themselves joining in. The exterminator was visiting New England. Misplaced or not, the prisoners felt some hope for the first time in five months.

13 Touch-and-Go

An hour before the Chinooks were to land in Fort Detrick, Maryland, an F-22 Raptor had flown over and dropped two nerve gas bombs, saturating the landing area in deadly poison. The pilot had seen some Fiend activity on the outskirts of the base, but she ignored them, continuing with her mission to drop two more bombs on the next refueling base at Fort Jackson in South Carolina. She had little fear of injuring any uninfected personnel. Both bases had been thoroughly evacuated during the Exodus. Of course there was always the chance that civilians had taken up refuge (the typical barriers around a military base being quite a deterrent to even a highly determined Fiend), but that wasn't the pilot's job to worry about.

Fort Jackson was located right next to the city of Columbia, which to her astonishment, was still on fire. She marveled at the power of kinetic energy; it's ability to render to dust in a few short moments, that which took decades, centuries to build. As Lieutenant Reese Tilden released the second set of bombs, the dull gray that signaled the approach of dawn gave her a brief moment to observe the ground. A gated and heavily fenced tank depot was completely surrounded by Fiends. There was a small building inside with the words HELP painted in bright white on the roof. Clearly someone or a group of someones had taken refuge inside.

She could radio the information in, but there was little to no chance that these folks would get a rescue. They'd have to wait it out for the re-invasion. Of course that meant that they would be long dead or infected.

Deciding to say to hell with protocol, she banked around for another look, reduced her speed and got lower. Sure enough there were people now standing on top of the roof and waving sheets. Fiends were throwing themselves against the fence, many entangling themselves in the razor wire. She could make out the muzzle flashes of a few weapons coming from the building. Heck, her cannon was all loaded up. No point in wasting good fuel bringing all that depleted uranium back to Canada. She'd have to file an action report, but her gun camera would support her decision. She banked again, armed her weapon and came in low.

The F-22 only carries 480 rounds, giving the M61A2 Vulcan 20mm rotary cannon about 5 seconds of sustained fire. Lieutenant Tilden made two passes, firing her gun for two and a half seconds each. Perhaps fifty Fiends were shredded into hamburger and she was gone, happy that she had at least helped a little. What she couldn't know is that the Vulcan also decimated the fencing, leaving at least two hundred Fiends who had avoided the meat grinder to pour inside.

At least the defenders wouldn't face starvation...

Fort Detrick, Maryland was the center for the US biological weapons program until 1969 when President Richard Nixon signed an executive order outlawing offensive biological weapons research in the United States. After that it became the center for 'defensive' biological weapons research. Tran found it sort of ironic that the place was soaked with nerve agent. The Chinooks took two wide circles over the helipad before landing. There were a few bodies on the outskirts of the fort as well as several on the roof of one building. The people on the roof appeared to be refugees who had picked a bad place to hunker down; their twisted forms covered in their own vomit, told the tale of a grisly end via nerve gas. The other bodies outside the grounds exhibited the same postures, but were more than likely Fiends.

Not a soul on either helicopter felt free from remorse for the refugees. Their mission had killed healthy people. It was horrible. Ghost crossed himself, pulled out a small crucifix from his shirt and kissed it.

Before they landed, Captain O'Shea's voice came over the loudspeakers for both birds. "Okay, people, suit up. We land, the refueling teams do their work, everyone else stays on board. No sightseeing. Gunners keep your eyes peeled."

Both the troopers and the scientists had their chemical suits on in moments. All had been through the drill countless times and it went without a hitch. Several Rangers looked at their civilian counterparts with partial envy. The portability and rigorous construction necessary for the Army JSLIST chemical warfare suit consisted of a relatively comfortable coverall but the M-40 gas mask was a sweaty affair with limited peripheral vision. A person could get quite warm in hot conditions, risking significant dehydration. The scientist's Tychem suits, on the other hand, took in the need for maximum movement and sensory awareness; though big and rubbery, they had large hoods with big face shields and a corresponding breathing mask offering a wide field of view. They were also fluorescent yellow - basically saying to a potential Fiend: Pick me.

The Chinooks landed without incident. Two teams of three soldiers hopped out to retrieve the refueling trucks and begin the fill-up. Other than the ticking of the cooling engines and hustle of the working crew, it was a very quiet place, almost like time stood still. There were no birds, no insects, and no breeze to fill the void. Everything in earshot was either dead or gone, the only steady sound... humans breathing into gas masks. The daylight even seemed different. Though it was gray and overcast, the air seemed to have an extra glow to it. It gave Tran the creeps and he chocked it up to an overactive imagination, maybe the reflective nature of his Tychem suit. He looked across at Susan who smiled and winked at him.

That was just like her to offer reassurance in a moment like this. He had come to love his boss. She was tough but fair. Her willingness to listen to opposing points of view and alter her own in the face of a good argument, was what made her leadership stand out. He was lucky to work for her – not at the moment, doing the most dangerous thing he'd ever done – but in general. He couldn't imagine working for someone better.

After the refuel team hosed and scrubbed their JLIST suits off, the Chinooks wound up and took off again without incident. The relief was palpable as everyone loosened their gear and removed their gas masks. But for small asides and a few raw jokes at infected human's expense, for the next four hours, no one really spoke. The plan was to refuel again at Fort Jackson and hopefully bunk down for the night in one of the fort's bomb shelters. The thinking was that a shelter would be free of any gas contamination and the continued presence of nerve agent spread all over the landing area would keep the possibility of a Fiend assault low. Captain O'Shea had been given word, via the F-22 pilot, that there could be healthy people holed up in one of the vehicle depots, but those were on the opposite side of the fort from where they were landing. His orders were to approach from the city side, refuel, sleep and bug out at dawn. By no means were they to make their presence known to any refugees. The mission was too critical for arguments about rescues.

Ten miles before their next landing, the pilots moved down to treetop level. Fort Jackson shared its eastern side with the city of Columbia. Per the briefing, the metropolis was a smoldering ruin. Major buildings were scorched and blackened while whole suburban neighborhoods were burned to the ground. Thunderclouds were rolling in and already a light mist fell over parts of the city. The late afternoon sunlight that still broke through the clouds filled the streets with smoky shadows. The air was pungent with the chemical concoction of an immolated modern society. The people in the helicopters were grateful to put their gas masks back on. A population of infected seemed to still roam about. Several Fiends came running out of intact houses and gave hopeless chase to the big birds.

When the Chinooks crossed the boundary fence at the edge of the fort, all seemed suddenly peaceful. Supposedly, with the personnel evacuated and therefore no healthy people to hunt down and kill, Fort Jackson was an oasis.

It, and the female It hunted with, watched the big machines fly past the trees in the distance. It was feeling gorged as It sucked marrow out of the picked clean femur that It had just cracked open with the ax that It carried. The female's face and chest were red with fresh blood and that gave It an erection when It looked at her. There were many Others around them. They all fed on the Fresh Ones that had been in the building with the big machines.

A few of the Fresh Ones had climbed inside one of the machines and locked the hatches. Lots of Others stood around it, waiting for them to come out. It knew from experience that the Fresh Ones probably wouldn't. It had waited for five sunsets and sunrises for some Fresh Ones to come out of a locked room until It finally got too hungry and left.

Normally they would fuck after eating like this, Others joining in as well, but the female that It hunted with nodded at the machines flying past the trees. There would be Fresh Ones in there too. So It followed her, along with some Others. It wasn't hungry, but It nevertheless felt a strong compulsion to track the new Fresh Ones down.

Everyone snugged up their chem suits as they came in for the landing. The area was clear of Fiend activity and the troops and scientists leisurely disgorged from the helicopters.

The scientists stretched and looked around while the Rangers quickly broke into squads with orders to set-up and guard the perimeter as the fuel handlers did their work. The base's bomb shelters were located adjacent to the landing pads under a series of earth-covered mounds. Captain O'Shea directed Corporal Cavanaugh's squad to secure one of them and ordered the scientists to follow. When the group reached the first shelter, they all stopped in their tracks. The door wasn't sealed. Five Fiends lay dead outside, their twisted and contorted bodies showing signs of the nerve gas poisoning. The door was covered in bloody handprints. Cavanaugh radioed O'Shea .

The Captain touched his mic, "What do you see Corporal?"

"I see Deadheads, sir, and an open door that they were trying to force."

Susan said to Cavanaugh, "Tell him that there may be survivors holed up inside. Perhaps they opened the door when they didn't hear any more noise from the infected."

"I'll let you tell him yourself." He nodded over her shoulder and they all watched O'Shea and Specialist Melman jog over to their position.

Susan walked quickly toward the officer. Her voice sounded hollow through the Tychem suit. "Captain O'Shea, there could be survivors here."

O'Shea pointed out cameras at the entrance and a periscope sticking out of the top of each mound, "Each of these shelters is equipped with multiple ways to observe the outside, including air quality sensors. If they opened the door, they didn't know how to use these things." He stopped next to Cavanaugh, "You try the door yet?"

"Not yet, sir."

O'Shea turned to the scientists, "CDC stays back one hundred feet. Specialist, standby with them."

The scientists moved back with Melman as Cavanaugh directed private Deeter to gently push the door open. Deeter got it to move about six inches before meeting an obstruction. "Sir, we have at least one body up against the door."

With some effort, two other squad members put their shoulders into it and got the door to open wider.

Private Peabody turned with a crack in his voice, "I count three. One appears to be bitten on the face, sir. All male, all appear to have died by Novichok contact. And, sir… they don't have any clothes on."

"Excuse me?"

"The dead people on the other side of the door are naked."

O'Shea observed that the intercom had been pried out of the wall. Bloody fingerprints told the tale of a frustrated Fiend who must have heard a voice and wanted to get to its owner on the other side of the box. He poked his head inside. The lights were on. A staircase led down deep into the ground. The victims at the top of the stairs were indeed without clothes. They appeared malnourished with markings on their wrists as though they had been manacled.

He yelled down as best he could through his gas mask while two soldiers pointed their weapons down the stairs, "Hello? Do we have survivors down there?"

There was no answer.

They pushed the bodies to make way for the door, while two soldiers continued to cover the stairs.

Susan stepped up to O'Shea. "I assume Captain that you're going to go down to investigate. We can't just ignore survivors if they are right under our feet."

"I thought I asked you to stay back one hundred feet, ma'am."

"I asked you a question, Captain."

"And I'm thinking about the answer."

Susan looked at him expectantly.

"Doctor Chancellor, we have a very specific mission... but I don't have to remind you of that. It's not a humanitarian one."

"Actually, we are on the ultimate humanitarian mission, but that's just semantics. We have a mission as humans to try to guarantee the survival of our species in every way. I'm not suggesting that we take anyone with us and I know there is no possibility of rescue right now, but there may be people down there who need aid and/or medical attention, as well as guidance as to how to best make use of these shelters. Particularly if other healthy people should find refuge here."

O'Shea thought about this for a moment then said, "One of the people on the other side of the door had been bitten in the face. That would suggest to me that there's a pretty good chance that the only people down there are infected people. I cannot and will not risk any of us in an effort to find out. We'll post a guard with the door open. If a healthy person walks out, we know what we've got."

"If a healthy person walks out that door, they are likely to come into contact with nerve agent and die."

O'Shea smiled at Susan, "Then we'll leave a note several steps down. There is no gas in the air, so they will be fine if they see the note and call up."

She thought about this solution and decided it was the best she could negotiate. "All right. I guess that will do." She rejoined her team while the Rangers continued to secure the area.

The light mist that had greeted their landing turned into a heavy rain as a loud clap of thunder shook the ground. With the Chinooks fueled up, Operation Henhouse moved into an unoccupied shelter. Jones' unlucky squad drew the short straw and was left outside to monitor the open shelter and also keep watch for other activity.

The stairs leading down into the bunker were long and narrow. They turned back on themselves repeatedly and descended a couple of hundred feet. Cowboy Johnston took off his gas mask and everyone else followed suit.

Susan commented, "Any voice calling from the surface would have little chance of reaching down here."

Captain O'Shea chose to ignore this.

The final landing opened to a foyer of sorts, which led to another door. They opened this one and a body heat sensor turned on the lights, revealing a large room with several other doors and corridors leading off of it. The main room appeared to be set up as a community lounge and dining area. It had some of the basic comforts of home, but in an efficient military way.

Tran made an aside to Aaron, "No elevators. Must've built this place in the fifties. Before the American's with Disabilities Act."

Aaron, always the contrarian as well as literalist shrugged, "I'm sure there are handicapped-friendly shelters."

14 Prisoners

Maine in late spring/early summer could tease a traveler into thinking it might be a warm day, only to stay cool from dawn 'til dusk. Jon awoke from a fitful, semi-lucid sleep feeling cold and stiff on a threadbare canvas cot. The thin blanket surrounding him was nearly useless. Pulling it up tight around his neck, he was reminded that he'd spent the bulk of the night shivering, neither awake enough to fully acknowledge it nor asleep enough to be free from it. His fellow power station prisoners were in various states of wakefulness, some already up, others still snoozing away. With little to do but languish in steady fear, there wasn't much reason to rise and shine.

He looked over at the cot to his right; the old woman, who had been exhibiting dementia the day before, lay with her mouth agape, her eyes fixed on oblivion. His instinct was to count it a blessing, and he sent a kind thought out to the universe in respect for her soul. He turned over and looked at Nikki who lay on the cot to his left. She was still asleep, her blanket pulled up to her chin. She had curled herself into a fetal position. Her closed eyes and open mouth gave her features a childlike quality. As he admired her sharp cheekbones, he felt an unexpected tug in his heart and his body warmed with increased blood flow. Someone sneezed and she woke. She focused on him briefly and then rolled over on her other side. He could smell fire and slowly sat up to scan the area around him. Will and a few others had a small campfire going, heating a pot of coffee. He hadn't had coffee in weeks. The part of his brain that had long ago become addicted to it flashed awake. He stood up stiffly, kept the blanket wrapped around his shoulders, and shuffled over to the group huddled around the small blaze.

Will said with misplaced cheer, "Good morning, Mr. Washington. Pour you a cup?"

"Thank you." He nodded back toward the cots. "The old woman's dead."

"Yes, we saw that. We'll let the others sleep as long as they can and then we'll alert the guards. Better to let folks enjoy as much slumber as they can get."

A man wearing blue coveralls reached out to Jon and offered his hand. "David Miller, Mr. Washington. Own the Irving Gas in town. I'm familiar with your writing. We kept several papers at my station. I thought your work was really good. Very helpful."

Another man, Loren Haymaker, tall and skinny with a large Adam's apple, nodded at the dead woman, "They like to burn'em quick as possible. Major's afraid the smell, if we let 'em rot, will attract the infected."

Jon said, "Major's an idiot. The infected are coming, rotting bodies or not. Burning them will only send up a smoke signal."

A bookish looking man in tweeds said, "Perhaps, but burning the bodies insures against other infections." He held out a hand. "Mr. Washington, I'm also familiar with your work. I'm Doctor Paul Smith. I'm a professor and doctor of sociology at Bowdoin." He shook Jon's hand. "May I say that your reporting from the front was remarkable? You offered information that the authorities seemed incapable or unwilling to provide. Your stories have, I'm quite certain, saved countless lives and gave the ones whose instinct it was to flee early a chance for survival."

"Thanks. Nice to meet you, Professor."

Smith continued, "I should say that I am somewhat of a reporter as well. I and several of my colleagues from Emerson Medical School in Atlanta took it upon ourselves to study the Cain's phenomenon directly. We felt at the time that we weren't getting all the facts. I mean, who in their right mind believed all of that hype? Cannibalism and whatnot. The hospital had several subjects from which to study. We kept our specimens in cages." He looked at his surroundings. "And I suspect that I will ironically perish in this one... but I digress. If you don't mind my saying, despite the precautions taken by our government and its feeble attempts to educate us, our path of action as a society to the threat of this plague has been remarkably imprudent. It is our continued ignorance that has led us to this preposterous situation, leaning back on our militaristic heels, when the solution is simple enough."

"How is that?"

"Feed them. Feed the infected. As long as we kept them fed, the aggression that the victims showed toward my colleagues and me was reduced considerably. God forbid we do the obvious. As it is, Major Deighton's idiocy is inconsequential. His is just the first wave in a pointless banzai charge to the death. It is a mentality that we cannot seem to outgrow as a society, and it will doom us all."

Jon pondered this statement trying to think of a way to take the man seriously and then finally gave up. "Well, again, thank you for the kind words about my reporting." He turned to Will, "Thanks for the coffee. I think I'll look around and see if I can find the weaknesses in our jail."

"But, Mr. Washington. I haven't finished," called Smith.

Jon waved his arm at the man while keeping his head turned away. The gesture said I hear you but don't want to hear more. He aimed for the port-a-john, left his coffee outside and entered to take care of his morning's full bladder. When he stepped back out, he found Nikki drinking his coffee and waiting her turn.

She handed him the cup and said, "Back out in a sec."

A thick fog was rolling in off the lake and a light breeze blew the mist around, occasionally obscuring the power plant. Nikki stepped back out to find Jon observing the power lines that came down from their towers to the transformers inside the cage.

"How'd you sleep?" he asked.

"As well as you. I expected to be overrun by crazed killers at any moment. Didn't help that that backhoe was running all night. Looks like they finished their trench." Jon took that in and then let his gaze shift back to the power lines. They were an obvious way to climb out. A man could walk on one of the thick cables while holding onto another one above his head. The trouble was, if he managed to make it to the first tower, he had to continue the tightrope walk right over the power plant. If he made it that far, there was a bigger tower and then a long span out over the lake to the next one anchored on a small island. After that the towers continued north as far as the eye could see.

Nikki said, "We wouldn't make it past the top of the cage before getting shot."

Jon finished his coffee. "Maybe in the dark."

"Maybe." Nikki stomped her feet and shivered, "Damn chilly."

Jon found himself unconsciously putting his arm around her shoulders. Nikki gently shrugged him off.

"Sorry. Just trying to get warm."

She stomped her feet again and then leaned into him. "Just for warmth."

She felt good under his arm and he tried to ignore it, tried to stay casual, saying, "Night or not, when they come, and it looks like they're going to get in, we climb out of here. If we get shot, it beats the alternative."

Will stepped over to them rubbing cramps out of his lower back. "We've all talked about that route. You're probably surprised that we haven't just climbed out of here."

Nikki said, "We understand why."

"They shot Bill O'Reilly. He was the first guy they stuck in here. It wasn't but an hour after the electricity finally died before he tried to climb out. Deighton let him make it almost to the tower before he had that son-of-a-bitch sergeant of his shoot him. Quite the marksman, the Sergeant - got him through both his hands. Bill fell to his death. It was sport for Deighton. Most of the rest of us in here now? We're the folks that protested that killing."

Jon asked, "What did O'Reilly do to get in here?"

"He was Deighton's commanding officer. Deighton and the few real soldiers here are mutineers. O'Reilly was trying to evacuate the town per orders. Deighton called him an unpatriotic fool and arrested him for supposed 'dereliction of duty'. Most of the other folks who are working with the major are either local survivalist types, ultra paranoid, or they're just scared and confused. There's people in this town that have never been outside it. Others are just stragglers trying to stay ahead of the onslaught. They got caught up in this and don't want to end up in the cage like us."

"So what did you do in this town, Will?" asked Nikki.

"I'm the mayor."

The trench was U shaped with both ends stopping at the edge of the lake so the power plant would be surrounded with water. Two temporary dams had held the water back until the trench was done. One of the soldiers who had been digging postholes the day before yelled out an all clear and then began to hit part of a dam with a sledgehammer. The water gushed in, filling the trench and making it a moat. Between the moat, the berm, the fence, the minefield and the power plant, Deighton's people had their castle.

Two hours after that, the residents began to move in. The only way to reach the castle was from the lakeside via a few canoes and rowboats. Jon and Nikki had to admit that it was a formidable fortress. They weren't so sure it did much to start *Taking Back America*, but it did create a sense of control in an otherwise chaotic world. Their cage was on the far side of all of this, suddenly separate and out in the open.

The detainees stood in their prison and made eye contact with the new residents as they streamed into the castle. Several people seemed to question why there were people being left outside. One woman could be heard yelling, "But that's Will. That's Will Parker." Before she could say more, she was physically shoved into the windowless building.

So the people in the castle weren't all complicit, but it was obvious that the few didn't have the power to change the many.

Breakfast was a new novelty. Because of the moat, the guards used a cattle ramp taken from a boxcar to get to them, extending it across the water like a drawbridge. The food was more of the same, only just a little bit less. Jon worried that he and Nikki weren't getting enough calories. A few more days on these rations and they wouldn't have the strength to escape anyway. The guards entered and handled the dead woman like a sack of garbage. Heaving her onto the bed of their pick-up. The prisoners were shocked, but no one spoke up in the body's defense.

Late in the day, rain came pouring down in great heavy sheets. The front of the tropical storm that had been washing away the nerve agent down at Fort Jackson now dumped its heavy burden over Northern Maine. The ground became a thin slurry of slippery mud. Then the slurry thickened up and became inches of muck as the hard ground yielded to the building storm. The prisoners huddled under the leaky sideless tent. It was meager shelter against the wind whipped rain. A pool of water gathered on the ground at the center, so everyone sat or lay down miserably with his or her knees tucked up on their cots, their thin blankets pulled around them. When the center of the storm was right on top of them thunder clapped, vibrating their organs while close hits of lighting lifted the finer hair on their heads with static electricity. As the evening progressed, the visibility was reduced to fifty feet as the rain came down even harder, testing the thin canopy's ability to remain upright. When night finally fell, they could see no more than a couple of yards.

15 Bunkers

In the Fort Jackson bomb shelter, the scientists and Rangers had chosen one shower area to wash off any Novichok that might have touched their chem suits, then hung them to dry.

Sergeant Bullock called out, "Okay, people, just like the twenty other shelters in this cluster, this place was supposedly designed to hold fifty. Find a rack, get settled and we'll eat. Preston, your squad is on KP. Cavanaugh, you boys have topside shift at twenty-one-hundred."

Each hallway led to a series of private quarters with beds and basic furnishings. The scientists claimed their own wing. As they each picked a room, Christy Tsue, the team's equipment tech, asked her fellow assistant, Will Warner, "How do you suppose they keep the lights on?"

"Don't know. Maybe a small nuclear plant. Only way to keep the lights and air filters going for the kind of extended stay needed to outlast fallout. Ironic, huh? Nuclear power to save you from nuclear power?"

Tran was still coated in his own drying, salty, sweat as he enjoyed the light feeling of walking without his Tychem suit. Having chosen to eat something first, he was the last to get to the communal bath in their wing. His colleagues were surprisingly chatty as they headed past him to go the dining area. Derrick sniffed at him. "Don't hesitate to jump right into that shower, Dude. Endless hot water."

The water was hot and there were full soap dispensers as well as items like deodorant, combs and razors. The place was set up for occupation at a moment's notice: all of the comforts of home in a cave. Tran wasn't normally a long shower taker, but the freedom from fear mixed with the easing feeling of the hot water kept him in there longer. Heck he had it to himself - might as well enjoy it.

As he hung his head and let the water roll off his shoulders, his thoughts drifted aimlessly as he added the bunker to a mundane catalogue of places he had been: work, work spaces, research, moving from Washington to Ottawa, work, research, work colleagues, and then he found himself remembering a date he'd had in DC the night that the news changed from reports of random acts of violence in Miami Dade, to urgent headlines about a massive wave of violence including acts of cannibalism. At the time, he hadn't had a date in about a year. The girl's name was Kimberly and she was hot. His work was so encompassing that he just didn't think much about dating. It was Susan who had set him up. Kimberly was a grad student of hers at Georgetown, working as Susan's teacher's aide that semester.

He chuckled out loud as he remembered begging off - what had he been thinking? Fortunately, Susan wasn't going to let a little thing like his shyness and an insane work ethic stop her matchmaking. He'd finally relented after she threatened to not let him come to work for a week. Ten weeks of unused vacation time from five years of working with her. "Enough was enough," she insisted.

He had taken Susan's suggestion and made reservations at her favorite restaurant, Citronelle, but just the Lounge - after all, it was only a first date. Kimberly chose to meet him there, he supposed so she could make a quick escape when she realized what a hopeless geek he was. Tran was second generation Vietnamese American and though most of his family's conservative manners and traditions had been usurped by good old American everydayness, he at least got himself there first, managed to find a spot by the fireplace, and stood when the Maître d' guided Kimberly to their table.

She was breathtaking; tall, blond, blue eyed – a Nordic goddess. At first he was certain there had been a mistake, but when the Maître d' asked again, "You are Robert Tran?" He couldn't deny it. So the chair was pulled for Miss Kimberly-sadly-Tran-could-not-remember-her-last-name-Nordic Goddess, who sat with a happy sparkle in her eye.

He didn't remember much of the initial conversation: small, get to know you talk, but that changed when the subject of Florida came up. She was a scientist after all and was the first person to put the idea in his mind that the violence down there was perhaps disease related. Of course he worked for the CDC and she worked for someone who also worked at the CDC, so there might have been a bit of professional bias, but it sort of made sense. She had convinced Susan of the idea, who then okayed Kimberly to fly down to Miami where several hospitals were reporting severe trauma and rather psychotic behavior. It would be considered research for Kimberly's thesis. Anyway, they got that nasty subject out of the way and talked about life instead.

Tran found himself having the best intellectual conversation he'd had in months, no, a year, no, more. The dinner was going really well - really, really well. He was fairly familiar with the biological processes that occurred during sexual attraction and he was occasionally distracted with the pondering of it. Thank God his academic mind shut off when they ordered a second bottle of wine. He wasn't much of a drinker, but she had a third leg hidden somewhere. To his distress, she remained more sober than he, and he found himself getting busted more than once as his eyes drifted down to take in her very fit body. It didn't help that she was wearing a tight sweater. She smiled inwardly at his unintentional undressing and even sat up straighter, which of course jutted her breasts out even more. Tran couldn't be positive, but he was getting the feeling that this woman really liked him and then she confirmed it by thanking Susan out loud for introducing them.

By dessert they were "accidentally" brushing their feet against each other. And the conversation drifted improbably to Victoria Secret models and their hot new line of naughty devil girls; bat wings instead of angels, as they'd once done years before.

They finally ended the meal when the frustrated waiter gave up on subtle hints and made it clear that others were waiting for the table. Tran tipped the poor fellow well and they stepped outside. It was cold and Kimberly leaned into his chest as they waited for a cab. With unconscious ease he put his arms around her waist and held her close. He couldn't be sure, but he thought she might have pressed her buttocks into his crotch a bit. His crotch certainly decided so and he was thankful that the cab pulled up before it started pushing back.

Kimberly invited him to share the cab and he happily hopped in. The driver had seen it a million times before – drunk new couple, gropey, kissey, jeez get a room, not in my cab please, sloppy no, no. They'd started making out the moment they got in the car.

When they arrived at her apartment building she whispered to him an offer to come up. He considered it carefully, decided that he was a gentleman, wanted a second date, wanted more than a second date and was going to do this right so he artfully turned her down. She seemed to be pleased by this choice, but her flushed neck and cheeks betrayed a certain disappointment as well. She would be back in a week from Miami and they would take up where they left off – "well perhaps after having dinner first". But she didn't come back. He never heard from her again. Susan spoke to her once when Kimberly called to confirm her suspicions about infection. By then the thing was already getting out of control.

Though he was deep in a military fallout shelter, in his mind, Tran picked up where the cab left off. Then the fantasy fast forwarded to Kimberly in the shower and he was taking her from behind, his fingers hooked into her hips, her head thrust back in pleasure, those perfect breasts pointing up, begging for attention...

He was just about to climax and let the whole thing go down the drain when he was startled by a clanging noise coming through the plumbing in the wall behind him. He turned off the shower and listened – there it was again, it had a pattern - a person was clearly causing it. He threw his towel around his waist and called out to be certain he was alone... Just him in he room. He pressed his ear to the wet wall. It was faint, but in addition to the clanging, he could hear human voices yelling. Unintelligible; the thick wall muffling the sound to bass tones only. A quick search of the hall outside the bathroom confirmed that the sound was coming from a space beyond the bunker he was in. Still wearing only the towel, he ran down the hall and found Sergeant Bullock.

Captain O'Shea was summoned and a quick listen confirmed that it wasn't a code of any sort, just an attempt to be heard. A few rifle butts on the wall sent a frantic return response.

"Damn," O'Shea said. "This is the bunker that we're covering up top."

"Could we maybe bust through this wall?" asked Corporal Cavanaugh.

O'Shea shook his head, "These places are built to be and stay separate. The whole point of isolating them from one another is so that if one fails the others remain intact. We're talking very thick walls of concrete with tons of rebar."

Susan spoke up, "So we have to go topside and enter via the stairs."

"Ma'am. Again, that's not our mission."

Susan gave O'Shea her best I'm ashamed of you look. "Captain, I insist that you at least use the intercom system to see if they can communicate with us."

"Wouldn't they be doing that already if they could?"

That gave Susan pause. Then she said, "What if they're injured or trapped?"

Bullock said, "Captain, we are more than experienced in clearing a building full of shitfobs. Our casualty rate is very low."

O'Shea said, "We have a mission that doesn't allow for any kind of injury. This bathroom will be made off limits. The science team can use one of the others as necessary, now let's get back to it."

Cavanaugh wasn't one to defy orders, yet he found himself blurting, "But, Sir. If there are healthy people trapped in the next bunker – we can't just eat, get a good night sleep and fly away."

"That's exactly what we'll do. We will make a report about this location and when the invasion gets down here, those people will be rescued. That's the end of the discussion."

Up top, darkness had settled in. The rain was heavy, and without lights, stars or a moon, there wasn't much to see and little for the soldier's night vision goggles to amplify, leaving them mostly blind.

Despite the rain poncho, PFC Pete Pillsbury was miserable. Not being able to see beyond 30 meters of hazy green through his NVGs (which were even further diminished by looking through a gas mask) was making him sweat with nervous energy. He felt clammy and uncomfortable and to make matters worse, he needed to take a leak.

With no maintenance staff at the fort, the late spring grass had grown to waist high in several spots around the landing area. Pillsbury raised his goggles to increase his depth perception and shuffled over to the edge of the landing area. His bladder was racing to beat his fingers as they fumbled with his fly, and he found himself doing a quick little dance to keep from pissing himself. He'd just gotten himself unzipped when his feet were yanked out from under him. He hit the tarmac hard, knocking the wind from his lungs, his helmeted head smacking the ground with a whipping motion. As he gasped for air, his brain swimming with the suddenness of it all, he was yanked into the grass.

The Fiends cut off his yelp with a quick series of stabs. There were three of them, knives and an ax, gleefully stabbing and chopping into his guts and chest. Pillsbury could only gasp as the first bite took away his manhood, the second bite came at his throat as the gas mask was ripped away. His final thought was that the rain must have washed away the Novichok.

PFC Dick Kantor had watched his squad mate walk over to the grass and had looked away to give the man some privacy. The steady rain had masked the sound of Pillsbury falling to the ground. When a minute went by and Pillsbury wasn't walking back, Kantor gave another look and could barely make out the grass moving back and forth. He grimaced at the thought of trying to take a shit in tall wet grass, but he understood the need for privacy. When Kantor was a kid, maybe six, his best friend's mom walked into the bathroom when he was sitting there, trying to go. The woman apologized with a bit of horror on her face, like somehow Kantor had been taking crap on the floor rather than using the john. She had quickly pulled the door shut and not another word was said. Kantor had been embarrassed, but the woman's reaction had actually made him feel dirty. He couldn't use a toilet or even undress in front of anybody after that. In his platoon, he was known as Private Dick.

After another couple of minutes he turned again. The grass was still moving. What was the guy doing, jackin' off? He called out, "Pillboy?", which got Specialist Jones and PFC Copigliani (Copper to everyone else) to look over from their machine gun position with the M240B still pointed at the bunker with the open door.

"What's up Kantor?" asked Jones.

Kantor ignored him and stood to look harder at the grass. "Pillsbury, you sleeping? That's a long shit break."

Jones said, "Keep it down, Private. Let's not wake the neighborhood."

Kantor took a few tentative steps forward, instinctively bringing his HK417 assault rifle closer to a firing position. He felt good about the gun. Their original weapon was the SCAR L, which carried a NATO 5.56X45mm round. It was an amazing weapon, but often as not the 5.56 didn't even slow a Fiend down. You could make five hits and if you didn't get a head or heart shot, it could be right on top of you. The NATO 7.62X51mm seemed to do the trick; though occasionally even after a couple of hits with that a lot of them still kept coming. The Army was severely short on SCAR Hs, the US Special Forces version that also carried the 7.62 round. These HKs were a gift from the British SAS and, therefore, in short supply, which for Kantor, reaffirmed the mission's critical nature.

Ghost Rodriguez and four others were posted on top of the bunkers. Kantor's calls had them turning to see what was up. From up high, they could just make out the shape of dozens of humans crawling forward in the grass. Ghost hit the switch on the series of small spotlights they had set up to flood the perimeter. It was like lighting a beacon for a Fiend charge, but they needed to see what they were up against.

Kantor was about to call out once more when lights came on. His voice froze in his throat as he found himself suddenly standing in front of dozens of charging Fiends. They screamed and howled as one, their highlighted eyes reflecting madness as they ran. He barely got his gun up, firing off a few wild shots before he was overrun, his mask ripped off, his face and his neck shredded by a female in a slip dress.

Jones and Copper got the M240B turned around and fired off a burst of shots, dropping a few ghouls, but had to abandon the position and run.

The bunker housing the rest of the platoon had been resealed as agreed upon until the watch change. There was no time to call and wait for someone to come up and open the door. Jones and Copper had to dash into the open bunker next-door, the one with the dead folks inside, the one that up until a few seconds ago they were guarding against anything coming out.

On top of the mound, Ghost got the Mk 48 turned toward the charging Fiends and lit up the night with it. That's when another group, maybe a hundred or more, started running at them from behind the airfield control building on the other side of the bunker system. The four riflemen with Ghost turned, firing short controlled bursts at the new enemy, whooping and hollering with adrenaline pumped excitement. They might as well have been the 7th cavalry at Little Big Horn; they were going to be quickly overrun. "Bug out!" screamed Ghost and the five men ran down the domed wall of the bunker system toward the charging Fiends in front of them. Their only hope was to join Jones and Copper who continued to shoot from the bunker door.

Jones was on his headset trying to call inside to O'Shea "or anybody!" to let them know what was up. The radio was useless for penetrating God only knew how much concrete and steel.

Copper stepped out and heaved both of his grenades and Jones's as well. The fucking monsters spread out instantly like a twisting school of fish, giving the explosives a wide berth. Clearly they had experience with grenades and the explosions only killed or maimed a few. The rest seemed to get even more stoked up by the violence - running harder - their hunting blood in a lather.

Jones saw Ghost and the boys running along the edge of the mound toward them. The Fiends were almost on all of them. It was going to be close. He and Copper yelled, "Come on, Motherfucker's!" while emptying the drum magazine of the M240 in a blazing storm of light and sound.

Suddenly Ghost and his men stopped dead in their tracks and froze like an invisible hand had grabbed them. They yelped in fear and shook their heads as though trying to get water out of their ears. The Fiends charged right over them. Ghost was tackled, his machine gun skittering across the tarmac. The other four were slammed against the grass and smothered or dragged to the ground right in front of Copper and Jones. Jones made eye contact with Ghost; the man's horror stricken last moment flashing a permanent image into the Specialist's retinal memory. As the Fiends tore apart Ghost, Copper felt his senses burst with something other than himself. He screamed out to no one in particular, "IT'S IN MY HEAD! IT'S IN MY HEAD!"

Jones yanked him inside and slammed the door shut, throwing the dead bolt just as the laughing, howling creatures crashed up against it.

Copper's head cleared and in the pitch black he fearfully clung to Jones. "Something was in my head, bro. What they've been saying 'bout them in your head is true."

The pounding on the heavy steel door was muffled, but it was unnerving nonetheless – and hadn't the lights been on before? Jones said, "Felt it too. Fucked up shit, man."

They each had a small infrared flashlight strapped to their helmets, which offered about fifteen feet of illumination for their NVG's. The staircase quickly fell off into total darkness. Somewhere down below they heard what sounded like sinister laughter. Fiends were known to laugh with pleasure, particularly when playing with prey. Jones and Copper swapped in the last drum of ammo on the M240. They both carried knives, but a swarm of Fiends didn't heed a couple of knives.

16 Fingers On The Fence

David Miller held the camp's only umbrella and flashlight while standing at the perimeter taking a leak. He rested his tired head against the chain link. The man had complained bitterly about the filthy port-a-john and refused to use it for pissing anyway, instead, repeatedly angering everyone by standing in a spot he had designated as his urinal. A quiet woman named Nancy Green who had barely spoken since Jon and Nikki's arrival, watched Miller with mild distaste. Just before she turned her head away she saw a naked foot and another shod in the flashlight's beam on the opposite side of the fence. The feet shifted and Miller yelped as something tried to pull his hair through the fence. He pointed the light in front of him to reveal dozens of cold, wet and voraciously hungry looking Fiends. A middle aged female laughed directly in his face while gripping Miller's hair in a tight fist. Miller howled and used the flashlight to beat against the hand and free himself. Nancy Green felt her body shudder and tears spring out of her eyes.

Miller violently pulled his head away, leaving some of his scalp in the Fiend's claw while the flashlight swept the area in front of him revealing bright animated eyes scanning the enclosure for an entry. The female laughed while licking at the bloody piece of scalp. She gnashed her teeth as she met his gaze, her talon like fingers griping the chain link with fierce strength.

The other prisoners were all crying out in various forms of fright. Jon looked over at the castle, but couldn't make out anything in the dark heavy rain. He ran and grabbed the flashlight from David and pointed along the 180 degrees that was the exposed side of the enclosure. The heaviness of the rain cut down the flashlight's reach, but he could see that they were surrounded. A bright flash of lightning lit the scene like a brief electric blue day - there were hundreds of them, thousands – bodies all the way back to the tree line. They were piling up against one another as they reached the edge of the moat. Some were falling in and struggling, drowning, their fellow predators taking little notice.

The prisoners scrambled over each other, tipping over their cots, splashing through the muck to get farther from the fence, bunching up into the center. The creatures started climbing. The noise of the chain link shaking and rattling should have alerted the soldiers, but the roar of the torrential downpour drove every sound into the ground.

Private Ken Ridley was on watch with Private First Class Jeremy Wilson. They were trying to stay out of the rain under a tarp on the roof of the power plant. It wasn't really working; the rain was coming down so hard that it splashed underneath the tarp anyway.

"What the fuck are we doing up here?" barked Wilson. "Can't see jack."

"FUBAR, huh Wilson?"

"Excuse me?"

"FUBAR. You know, fucked up beyond all reason."

"I know what it means, Cherry. Just don't know why you're saying it."

"Cuzza this shit storm coming down on us."

"This ain't World War Two, bitch, but even if it were, only a soldier gets to talk that talk."

"Huh?"

"You froze, Ridley. Froze up like a scared little girl when them Shitfobs came running cross that field. Fact, I think I saw you go change your underpants when the shit was over. You shit yourself Cherry Bitch?"

"No," Ken said, with weak assurance. He had thought he had though. The first chance he got, he went to the toilet to check his drawers. He'd never been so scared in his life.

"I been over there," said Wilson. "I shot a Haji right in the fucking face my first day on patrol. Watched the back of his head splatter all over the fucking rag heads behind him. Looked just like what happened out there today. Platoon opened up and blew all them sand niggers to bits and pieces. Thought they had the jump on us. Douche bags think they can fuck with the US Army."

Ridley took this in and then said, "I didn't shit myself and I am a soldier."

"Bitch, you're not a soldier 'til you've seen the elephant. You missed it. Too worried about crapping your pants."

"That's not tru--"

"Shut it." For the first time in the conversation, Wilson turned and looked Ridley in the eye. It was so dark that they could barely see each other so Wilson turned on his red filtered flashlight. "I don't like being up here with you Ridley. Not 'cause it's raining like a motherfucker, but because boys who shit themselves in the face of the enemy get their buddies killed."

Ridley stared back at him and finally said, "I'm not your buddy."

"Sure you are, Cherry Bitch. If you're not my buddy, then you're my enemy – and you'll have to watch your back."

Ken kept his mouth shut after that. Deep down, he knew Wilson was right. He'd choked. He'd held onto the fifty-cal like it was some kind of life preserver. He froze and he didn't know why. He had expected it to be like a video game – blowing away zombies – it was nothing like a video game.

A little later the radio squawked. It was Tyler Preston who had volunteered to keep watch down route 16 at the Henderson farm. He'd been having a grand old time calling in: 'The flies er comin to the web', as he described the refugees heading north.

"Motherfucking fuck! Someone got their ears on? Come back?"

Ken picked up the radio. "Go ahead, Tyler."

"Fucking, holy fuck! Coming in the door! Fuck yo –"

The sound of gunfire – a brief handful of shots echoed from a distance, then nothing. Ken's radio howled with static and he twisted the squelch knob to stop it. "Tyler, come in. You've got Private Ridley here. Come in?"

"Whoa, that dude is getting his," said Wilson.

"Maybe the storm - screwing with the atmospherics. He's getting trigger happy?"

"Get real - you heard that same as me. Fuckin' crazy motherfucker's toast."

Then they heard a distant jingle of shaking chain link.

"Hmm, now that's interesting," said Wilson. Throwing his hood over his head, he moved to the edge of the roof and peered out. It was nearly pitch black. His flashlight burned through maybe twenty feet of it. He turned and stomped on a switch that lit up the floodlights lined up across the top of the building. The rain and fog was too dense. In fact the brightness of the lights made things worse, the reflection killing his night vision. He could just barely make out the ghostly image of the power line tower fifty feet away. He stomped on the switch again. Then he heard the chain link again. "Either the fuckers are trying to get out or Deadhead's are comin' in." He turned to Ridley, "Can't see jack. You're going to have to go downstairs and walk over there."

"Okay. But why can't we both go?"

"Cause I know how to fire the fifty, you green panty-waste. Now be a man and get the fuck down there."

Ken's soaking wet boots squeaked on the concrete floor as he crossed through the main room. If he ignored all of the dead power equipment, the place really was like some medieval castle. The new residents had used the big room that night for a banquet, celebrating their new digs. They'd gotten rip-roaring drunk and then crashed on sleeping mats all over the floor. To the private's astonishment, Major Deighton was passed out on some kind of head table with a woman curled up under his arm. He desperately didn't want to wake the man if this was a false alarm. The major's wrath was always brutal. He'd be cleaning the latrine for week if he blew it.

The room was full of loud snoring and he could hear at least two different couples quietly fucking somewhere among the slumbering crowd. Ken couldn't believe his crappy luck as he went through a small entry foyer - pulling watch on this of all nights. He quietly unbolted the steel outer door and stepped outside.

The ground was saturated and he cursed as his right boot sunk into a puddle that was higher than his ankle. He swept the flashlight back and forth close to the ground until he'd found the clearly marked path that led past the mines to the prisoner cage. The cattle ramp/drawbridge completed the castle image in his mind - World goes to shit and somehow we embrace the dark ages. He felt bad for the folks in the cage, and frankly didn't understand the major's mindset on keeping them locked up like that. Why not just let them go if they didn't want to fight? If folks wanted to bug out north, why shouldn't they? It wasn't like they had signed a contract with the Army like he had. Keeping them as bait – well that was breaking the law. The country still needed laws.

As he got closer, he could hear the fence jingling with what could only be the weight of people climbing. He thought, Damn if those folks aren't trying to get out. I sure as shit don't want to have to shoot somebody.

He reached the gate for the barbwire perimeter fence, removed the padlock and swung the gate open. The shaking sound of chain link unnerved him as he stepped up to the cattle ramp and kicked the chock that was holding it up. The cable that held it spun out quickly as the heavy ramp swung down and landed on the opposite side of the moat. He brought his rifle to shoulder height like he'd been trained and stepped out to the ramp's center, keeping the flashlight held along the barrel of his gun. The edge of the beam caught something in the moat. It was a body, no, make that bodies floating face down. Then he saw more struggling in the water. He aimed toward the cage and saw Kathy with her crutches laying on the ground. She was trying to climb one of the transformers in the center. White with fear, she squinted at Ken's light and let out a silent cry. Several Fiends finished crawling over others that were trapped in barbed wire and jumped inside. They raced for Kathy.

Just before his bowels let go for real this time, Ken swept the water around him again. He locked eyes with a Fiend who was using its drowned brethren to pull itself up onto the ramp. Another climbed out of the water on the castle side, blocking his escape. Ken raised his gun and slammed it into the Fiend, knocking it back in the water. The thing pulled the rifle from his hands as it fell. He didn't look back and ran for his life.

As he sprinted, he could feel his shit tumbling down his legs, getting trapped where his pants were tucked into his boots, and he found himself laughing with hysteria at the absurdity of it – the extra weight around his ankles. He knew exactly where to go and charged right past the power plant to the lakeshore. In one quick move, he flipped over one of the canoes and started to launch it. A small part of his mind registered that a few canoes were missing, but that was quickly swept away by his sheer panic. He got a leg in the boat just as the first ghoul came running at him. He swung the heavy flashlight into the monster's neck, crushing its

Adam's apple and dropping the thing to its knees. He shoved off as best he could and paddled with adrenaline-charged strength, pulling quickly away from the shore as more of them crashed into the water.

17 The Floodgate

PFC Wilson watched through the deluge as Ken's flashlight bobbed along back toward the castle. The kid was moving at a pretty good clip. He peered over the side and was astonished to see Ridley run right past the open door. He pointed his own light into the gloom and called down to the useless cherry fucker, but got no response. Three-seconds later, a man in tattered clothes ran past in hot pursuit, then another and another. A fourth looked up and saw Jeremy, and then Jeremy knew he was screwed.

Ken paddled with all his might until he was sure he was over deep water then stopped. The canoe made a graceful crescent-shaped turn back toward shore and he watched the rain-filled sky turn orange from the bright flash of Wilson's fifty-cal. The concussion from the big gun echoed across the lake, vibrating the very seat of his canoe. As he sat without noticing his own filth, he could see dozens of Deadheads backlit on the shore. Then his eyes grew even larger, and he took a sharp breath – they were pouring through the door – the door that he had left open. He heard screams come from within, and the sound of several guns joining the fight. The flash from the fifty joined with the even brighter flashes of tripped anti-personnel mines, which lit up hundreds and hundreds more infected as they poured into the compound. He had opened the gate from hell and let the demons march right through.

Seventeen minutes earlier, when the first Fiend had started to climb the cage, Jon and Nikki hadn't hesitated. They each climbed one of the two dead transformers and tried to pull themselves up using the cable above while walking on the one below. With the rain, the cables might as well have been sheathed in ice, cold hands offering little grip. Nikki quickly slid off her belt and looped it around the cable above her, then wrapped her fists in the ends and pulled the looped section tight. By doing this she was able to pull herself forward, and with a quick release, slide, grab again, and pull herself up. Her feet slipped, but her grip on the belt didn't. Jon tried the same trick and had the same success. It was slow going, but they were making progress. The other prisoners piled up against each other to be next.

Acting as the gatekeeper, Will said, "Quick now. Everybody up. No time to lose."

Miraculously, everyone owned a belt except for Ingrid who had been wearing a dress the day they stuck her in the cage.

Will grabbed a fallen blanket and climbed up to the cables. He twisted the threadbare cloth around the upper one and gave it a tug. He handed the woman his belt. "Use mine, Ingrid. This blanket seems to do the trick." He spoke with a smile in his voice and for Ingrid, it was both remarkable and unsettling.

Kathy was last. She stood upon her crutches and smiled weakly at Will. "Go," she said.

"Kathy," he admonished, panic overtaking his cheerful cadence.

She looked over her shoulder into the gloom. The fencing was alive with grunting humans. "You wouldn't know anything about breaking necks would you, Will? You could kill me quick."

"Try climbing."

He helped her up onto the transformer base and she got her belt around the cable. She pulled herself up a few feet but her legs just didn't have the strength or balance and she slipped and fell back into his arms.

"Here, climb on my back."

She did her best, but her hip made it hard to hold on with her legs. Will tried to climb, but her weight was too much. He simply couldn't pull them both up. She cried out as she loosened her grip. Will begged, "Hold tight!"

"Oh, Will. Oh, God. God, help me." She let go, dropping back to the ground with a thud, losing her wind.

Will looked down, released his belt, and started to climb down for her. "I'm coming. Hang on!"

She got her breath back. "No, you go!"

He hesitated. The pause allowed the sound of the climbing killers to be firmly drilled into their heads.

"Go for God's sake!"

He closed his eyes for a second and then without looking back at her, renewed his climb.

Jon took his eyes off Nikki's back. They were almost to the top of the first tower, and he looked over his shoulder during a lighting flash. In that blink of a moment he counted only Nancy Green, Loren Haymaker, Doctor Smith, David Miller and just barely, Ingrid the mousy woman. He had to assume that the rest were coming. At this point, everyone was on their own.

Beyond this first tower there was a sudden spread in the distance between the cable above and the one they were walking on. The one above was now out of reach, making it impossible to continue in the fashion that Nikki had worked out. At least this tower was within the compound, the base only thirty or so yards from the power plant. As Jon joined Nikki on the tower railings, she panted, "We'll have to climb down. Try to steal a boat." She then began to work her way down the slippery rails. The night was so dark that there was no seeing the ground. They could hear the Fiends though. The chain link fence was singing its own tortured tune.

They were perhaps half way down when there was a slight gentle yelp and tall skinny Loren Haymaker flew past them having slipped on a wet rail. His body hit another rail below them and then spun crazily in the dark until there was a wet thump.

Big Patricia Gould was struggling valiantly to get her heft up the cable while bawling over her plight, her tears quickly swept away in the heavy torrent. Will caught up to her in moments. The angle was simply too much for her, and her feet kept slipping. Will goaded her, "Come on Pat. You're a strong woman. Keep going. Pull yourself up."

Patricia stopped instead and simply shook her head while holding on with a death grip. There was no way for Will to pass her. He had to get her to move. He reared one leg back and gave her a hard kick in the ass. It was like kicking sand. She didn't even flinch. He whispered loudly in her ear, "Patricia Gould, move your ass or you'll kill us both!"

Then both of them felt more than heard a buzzing sound in their heads – sudden disorientation – the sense that the infected were all around them – mud under their feet – grunting humans – strong smells. Patricia involuntarily let go to put her hands over her ears. She turned as she fell. Lightning struck and she locked eyes with Will before landing in a heaving mound of screaming humans. Just as suddenly, Will's head cleared. "What the hell?" The roar from below got him moving again.

Nancy Green was acrophobic. She had climbed up the cable without a second thought - fear of getting eaten alive overcoming any fear of heights, but now she was on the tower within the safety of the compound and she watched one by one as Nikki then Jon, Paul, Ingrid and David worked their way down. She heard rather than saw Loren fall; the sudden intake of breath, the sickening sound of flesh and bone careening off steel girders.

Will reached her, his breath coming in great gasps, "Where are the others?"

She pointed down without looking.

"Got it. Patricia and Kathy aren't coming. I'm last. Go."

"You go ahead, Will. I've got to rest a moment."

"Come on, Nancy. Get going. We've already lost two."

"I'll be right behind you. Just please, let me rest a moment."

"I'll stay with you."

"Will! Go!" she whispered loudly.

"Okay. Please don't wait long. There's no time." Without another word, he began to climb down.

Nancy had decided to stay. She really was tired: tired of being afraid, tired of running, tired of being tired. The survivors below waited a full minute for her, but when the guard had stepped out of the bunker and headed for the cage - nearly walking right past them - they didn't wait another moment. There was no choice but to move on.

When dawn broke over Flagstaff Lake, those Fiends who weren't feasting on or infecting the castle residents - or blowing themselves up by setting off mines - stared up at Nancy Green like ravenous hyenas. Her muscles were all one great cramp as she clung to the frigid steel, the sense of touch having left her fingers and toes hours before.

The rain had tapered off to a light mist and she could see for at least a mile. The infected were everywhere. It was like watching a great migration as hills and valleys became black with tattered, hungry looking, wraiths.

When she finally decided that she couldn't hold on any longer, she pried her fingers from the steel, forced her fingers to painfully bend, and carefully took off her prized Patagonia Jacket. Her daughter Piper had given it to her the previous Christmas, when the world had mostly been as she'd known it – mundane and safe in easy suburbia.

Piper, her son Taylor and her husband Cal were all gone now. At least that's how she thought of them. She couldn't bear the reality that they were just as likely running mad across the countryside killing and eating people.

All three had contracted the infection at the hospital where they'd been sent. Cal had lost control of their mini-van on an icy road just a mile from their Maryland home. Ironically, they were on their way back from a seminar on Cain's survival. Nancy had chosen not to go, she had been feeling under the weather and didn't want to get anyone ill.

The previous morning, the hospital had received a group of sickened train passengers who had arrived from down south somewhere. It turned out that they were carrying the disease. The hospital was a massacre. Her attempts to get there and save her family were thwarted by roadblocks in every direction. Within a day the entire county was a contamination zone. She was evacuated to New York and never saw her family again.

Nancy took another quick glance at the ground below, her stomach twisting over the height, dizziness overtaking her. She spotted something curious among the mass of Fiends below her. A female was holding an infant to her breast. There was something odd looking about the child; it was feeding as any other baby might, the female holding it with care, but…. The female looked up and caught Nancy's eye and then laughed in the horrific way that Fiends do. The child let go of the teat and looked up as well. Nancy's blood ran cold. "Oh my God."

The child's eyes were just as wicked, but they were also huge with big black irises – twice as big as a normal baby. Its overly large ears tapered slightly at the tips and pointed forward at the sound of her voice. Nancy suddenly experienced a sensation like nothing she'd ever felt before: Her mind's eye was filled with the presence of another – like a second conscience communicating to her – it was incomprehensible – a series of images – horrible images, blood and guts and screaming and laughing and crying and then that mother's face down there, close up, looking into her eyes, but not her eyes, and the swell of the mother's teat, and Nancy could taste – she could taste the unique flavor of mother's milk in her mouth. Nancy screamed at this invasion of her mind.

Two wretched looking twin females watched the mother and child. A rudimentary element of their original bond had been retained since their infection and they hadn't separated since. They had been tracking the mother and her newborn for days… *Not fair,* they both thought. *Want the infant Other that finds food better than any of the Others.* They were tired of the hunger and they watched with envy the female Other that held the baby. She always found food first, leaving nothing for them, the little one able to keep them away – *making their heads hurt.* One got a running start, followed quickly by her sister, and snatched the infant off the mother's teat – then running, running through the mass of infected, and escaping up along the edge of the lake.

Nancy shuddered as her thoughts became clear again and she nearly fell while briefly losing her balance. She looked down and vertigo caused her head to swim. A few of the more adventurous Fiends had started to climb the tower. Many watched, but many others joined. In moments, the tower's base was covered in howling, screeching, laughing monsters. Then she spotted another child held in its mother's arms. This one was bigger, long legs for a baby, with long feet. A leg kicked out - long strong muscles. The foot looked jointed like that of a cat's rear paw. The things were breeding, and something was dreadfully wrong. Then she could see the baby-bulges of many females, many others holding newborns. Almost as one, thousands of Fiends and their bizarre offspring turned and looked at her. Nancy gasped as her head buzzed with a crowd's worth of human babble, one voice canceling out another so that what remained was a sea of background noise – all of it carrying the weight of profound malevolence.

The Patagonia jacket was a rugged thing meant for all kinds of weather. It would be strong enough. She looped her belt through one of the sleeves and then tied the other to the railing. Next, she looped the belt to itself, then around her neck.

She looked up to the sky and mountaintops for a clean view of the world, scrubbed of the nightmare that writhed below. She took a deep breath and then smiled with the memory of her family on Christmas morning.

As the body quivered and swung, it was too far away for any to reach. The Fiends quickly lost interest and climbed back down.

PART THREE

TRIBULATION

18 Twisted

Before It had joined the attack on the Fresh Ones that came from the flying machines, It and the female that It hunted with had sat and watched from the tree line, expecting more of the Others to start twisting in agony and vomiting and then dying like the Others that tried when it was still light, before the rain got heavy. But they didn't. It had been hard to see, but they crawled right past those dead Others.

The Fresh Ones carried the sticks that killed in their hands, but there were only a few of them. It knew from previous experience that if It watched where it was pointed, the sticks that killed could be avoided. When lots of the Others charged, It could always dodge its way past the sticks that killed, and take down a Fresh One with a savage bite to the neck or a hack with its ax. The female was even better at this than It was; waiting for Others to be the target of the sticks that killed and running past them as fast as it could.

It and the female had been quietly fucking in the trees and keeping an eye on the Fresh Ones from the flying machines, when the second group of Others began to move forward. It and the female liked to fuck almost as much as they liked to kill and they did it all the time. It noticed that the female was getting round in the belly. Another female had had the same thing happen and a little one of the Others had come out of the hole that felt good to put its piss and fuck organ in. That female had fed the new other from her teat. It liked to watch this and it made It want to fuck the female that it hunted with even more. The new Other, the little one with the sharp teeth, liked to talk to them all in their heads. It almost hurt sometimes when the new Other was in there, inside its head, making It do things against its will; like now, as It and the female were crawling through the grass, following the Others. It feared the twisting death, but that was more than overwhelmed by the power of the new Other. Besides, It was hungry again. It longed for the cries of its victims, tasting their hot blood as it filled Its mouth. There were other creatures that tasted good too and It had enjoyed the big slow ones with the teats hanging under the belly, but there was no excitement in that kill. It was a kill only for sustenance. The best to hunt were the ones that looked like It; the ones that were fresh, the blood rich with salt and iron and that smelled different than the Others that It hunted with.

To It and the Other's frustration, most of the Fresh Ones that were here before these new ones had arrived were gone, or had locked themselves away. It and the female had had to eat grass and leaves to cut the hunger as they migrated in search of more food. Then the new Other had found the Fresh Ones that were hiding in the place with the big machines. The flying machine had made many holes in the fence that was hard to get past, allowing It and the Others to get through. They had a feast, gleefully killing the Fresh Ones inside. When they got to this place where the new Fresh Ones had come from machines in the sky, a handful of Others crawled forward, but for some reason they died in agony in the grass and the rest of the Others held back. When the water fell from the sky it made the dirt come off some of the skin and rags that the Others used to keep warm. The big male Other that they mostly followed, looked at its clean skin and then looked into the wet grass. Making a fundamental connection, it crawled forward into the grass and when it passed one of the Others that had had the twisting death, it crawled faster. The new infant Other had watched this and had made them all follow.

When they reached the edge of the grass, It and the female It hunted with couldn't believe that the Fresh One was going to walk right toward them. Usually the Fresh Ones were very nervous and hard to catch. When this Fresh One stopped and took out its organ for fucking and pissing, they and the Other that they followed, quickly reached up and pulled the Fresh One into the grass. They stabbed and chopped while the female bit the Fresh One's organ off and It drove its teeth into Its favorite spot, relishing the taste and feel of the hot blood spraying in its mouth and on its cheeks. The Fresh One could only let out a terrified and muffled yelp and a moan before the windpipe was crushed and torn open. The Fresh One then kicked briefly, but stiffened up when the female stripped off its leg coverings and bit into its inner thigh. Others grabbed onto the Fresh One as well and they dragged it back from the flat black rock that was at the edge of the grass. The Others tore into the Fresh One with almost silent glee, pulling back the Fresh One's rags and exposing the delicious warm flesh. It felt the Fresh One shudder once and then the life force pulled away; the blood still hot but no longer spurting.

Before, when there were lots of Fresh Ones, the Others would frequently only take a bite. In the place with the giant stone and glass shelters, the Others had so many fresh ones to bite or fuck that It never felt hungry or had that almost painful desire to use its piss and fuck organ. Sometimes the Fresh Ones would turn into Others when they were bitten and the desire to eat them went away. Instead, the new Others joined in the hunt for Fresh ones or if there were no Fresh Ones they ate the other creatures that had the hot blood.

Sometimes, when It wasn't all that hungry, It and the Others played a game with the Fresh Ones, seeing what delicious parts they could eat while keeping the Fresh One from dying. If It waited too long, the Fresh One would become one of the Others and the game would be over. This was better than fucking the female It hunted with or any of the other females or sometimes males that It fucked. Seeing the terror in the Fresh One's faces made It get a huge erection. Sometimes It would get overwhelmed with excitement when it was biting off and eating parts of one of the little Fresh Ones, the newborn and very young. Their flesh tasted the most exquisite and almost melted in the mouth. It loved to listen to their high-pitched screams and squeals, which made It laugh with delight, and It would stroke its pissing and fucking organ until it climaxed.

Robert, Susan and Aaron couldn't agree about whether to confront Captain O'Shea about whoever was banging on the plumbing. It was in Tran's nature to question authority, heck it was his job to question everything, but he understood the reasoning behind the Captain's decision. Aaron had no desire to argue with the Army. As far as he was concerned, if there were folks next door, the dead up top at the open door told the tale. They were probably all Fiends now. Susan was nevertheless adamant that something be done to help, and decided to speak with Sergeant Bullock.

Rick Decker was angry about the whole conversation. For him, the Army was in charge. O'Shea was the voice of the Army. "Susan, I remind you that we are on a singular mission. By what authority are you considering jeopardizing that mission?"

Susan sat back down. "I have a moral authority, Rick."

Decker shook his head, "I'm so fucking tired of tree hugging liberal twits like you. Your lack of proper discipline is a perfect example of the spineless mentality of this society. If we had nuked southern Florida when we had the chance, this thing might have been contained and tens of millions would still be alive. Instead, people like you waffled, whining about the precious and unique ecosystem. And now we find ourselves going back to the start of this thing - when it's probably too late."

The rest of the group stared at Decker, speechless.

Finally Robert spoke up. "Actually, Rick, if my calculations are correct, the Tree Swallow had begun heading north about a month before Everglades became untenable and the nuclear option was discussed."

"Shut up, Tran," spat Decker, "Asshole. Always with the quick answer, you are."

Susan jumped in, "Doctor Decker, what's gotten into you? You will not speak to your colleagues that way and you will show me the proper respect. You are entitled to your opinions, but you will deliver them with the decorum expected of a top scientist with the CDC."

Decker was quiet for a moment and then said, "Tran, you're not an asshole. I'm sorry I called you that. Susan, you *are* a liberal tree hugging twit and you can fire me for saying so." Decker got up from the table and walked away, leaving his leftover dinner for someone else to clean up.

Most of the soldiers had overheard the last part of this exchange and the room had gone silent as it played out. The awkwardness was finally interrupted by Sergeant Bullock. "Right. Preston, it's your squad up top next. Let Jones' boys grab some grub."

Preston and his squad mates began to pull their JLISTs back on, assembling their gear. The rest of the soldiers finished up dinner and got back to cleaning their weapons.

Next door, Jones and Copper sat on the stairs next to the three naked corpses discussing their options. The men were shaken, but determined. They were veterans of other battles with Fiends. They'd seen plenty of their comrades die or worse, turn into one of the goddamn things.

They were hardened to it. They'd been trained to put their softer emotions in a box. They still had work to do.

The laughter below had stopped as quickly as it started. Instead they could hear a distinct banging echoing from below. There was a pattern to it so it probably didn't come from a Fiend. They had whispered various ideas on what could be making it, but finally settled on the only option – it had to be human. The batteries on their NVGs weren't going to last forever. Going back outside was suicide. They decided to go down. Perhaps they hadn't heard the laughter coming from below. Perhaps it had been on the other side of the door behind them. In either event, they needed to find out if there was a working intercom between the bunkers to warn Captain O'Shea.

The walk down was ponderous, each switchback a cause for tension as they rounded into unseen territory. The men's muscles became locked with it and Copper actually had to stop for a moment and massage out a muscle spasm in his right hamstring. The rhythmic pounding they had heard up top had gotten louder and then it stopped. The silence was unnerving now. Each footstep, each brush of fabric as they moved, seemed to echo in the tight space. Copper didn't know it, but he kept holding his breath.

Jones finally pulled off his gas mask, breathed with a bit of trepidation and then brought his lips to Copper's ear, "Breathe, dummy. You'll give yourself a headache or pass out."

Copper pulled off his gas mask as well and they continued.

They finally reached the last turn and Jones signaled for them to stop. The door from the landing to the common room was open. A quick glance revealed knocked over tables and chairs. Jones quietly slipped his hand inside his pocket and pulled out a small penknife. He signaled to Copper what he was going to do, then turned and tossed the penknife into the room. It clicked and clacked across the floor and made a dull thump when it hit a turned over tabletop.

The men braced themselves for assault, the machine gun ready to unload, but there was nothing. The only sound was that of their own breathing. It would have been better to get charged. They could mow anything down that stepped in front of the stairs.

Jones looked toward the ceiling, said a short prayer, and motioned for Copper to follow him. They bent low as they entered the room and quietly crouched behind a table. Jones looked over his shoulder and spotted the light switch panel. He nodded to Copper who duck walked over to it. He paused and they both lifted their NVGs so as not to be blinded when he flicked the switches – nothing - the room remained pitch black - visual abyss. They quickly flipped their NVGs back down to stop the disorientation.

Option two was to use a flashlight. Both men carried small flashlights with super bright krypton bulbs. By turning them on, their NVGs would see the whole room lit up. Trouble was it also made them a perfect target - no question who held the flashlight. Copper signaled that it would be him and he pulled out his light, pointing it at an angle toward the ceiling, going for maximum bounce. He nodded and turned it on.

The room was instantly lit and that's when they saw the dude with two M4 assault rifles standing at the entrance to a bedroom hall.

The man had the guns held out under each arm and he screamed, "Fuck you, Fucking Fucks!" unleashing a hail of bullets in the Ranger's direction.

Both soldiers lay flat on the floor and rolled away from their original positions, Copper turning off the flashlight. Bullets plastered the wall behind them, shattered furniture in front of them, the aim scattered and irregular.

Jones was able to get a slight angle on the assailant, but before he could pull the trigger, the man stopped firing and stepped back into the hall.

"Hey!" yelled Jones. "Were United States Army. We're here to help."

Copper added, "We're not no fucking Fiends, man!"

Something was lobbed into the room from the hall, metal and heavy, skittering across the floor and hitting a chair.

"Grenade!" yelled Jones.

Both men covered their ears, opened their mouths and curled into fetal positions.

The explosion was loud - *really fucking loud.* The Rangers survived the blast but their ears rang out with temporary deafness. Bits of furniture and acoustic tile rained down upon them. The room filled with smoke and dust and they reactively pulled their gas masks to their faces.

Jones sat up with the M240 and pointing it at the hall, expecting the berserker to run out with both guns blazing. But there was nothing; just a mad little laugh and a teasing almost sing song, " *Fuck yououuu."*

In the bunker next door, they all felt more than heard the grenade go off. It was a dull thump, but it was unmistakably explosive.

O'Shea yelled up to Preston's squad still ascending the stairs. "Hold up Squad Three."

Bullock said, "The folks next door are a definitely knocking."

O'Shea pressed the intercom button that was located at the base of the stairs and called outside to Jones, "Specialist Jones?" He waited for five seconds that should have taken Jones to walk over to the external income at the front door. Nothing. "Jones, report." …Nothing. "Melman, try them on the radio."

"Radio's not getting any reception down here Cap'n."

"Alright, Sergeant Bullock, hook up with third. Check out the topside. Melman. Man this intercom. See if you can raise anyone next door and keep trying Jones until the boys get upstairs."

Bullock was already putting on his J-LIST and grabbing his rifle to join Preston's squad. First Squad and the Chinook Pilots readied themselves to follow squad Three if necessary. The scientists sat in silence, unsure of what to do other than keep their mouths shut. It looked like whatever was going on next door had forced O'Shea's hand. All of a sudden, their internal squabble seemed pointless.

At the top of the stairs, Preston unbolted the door and cracked it open slowly. There, on the ground, not more than fifteen feet away, a pack of Fiends were ripping into the flesh of the dead soldiers. Two of them were fighting over a forearm. Several looked up at the movement in their peripheral vision and spotted Preston. The creatures immediately charged. Preston slammed the door shut and bolted it. The Fiends howled and pounded on the steel. "Now we've stepped in it," he said. "Second squad appears to be slaughtered. The door next to us was pulled shut."

Jacobus said, "Maybe a few got away and are trying to signal us. You know, earlier with the explosion, banging on the pipes."

The men on the stairs looked aghast at the loss of their brothers. Despite the horrific ongoing conflict and the repeated loss of life, no one was truly prepared for this. These men had been trained for, and had fought major insurgencies – insurgencies, which included enemy and even friendly behavior that was at times remarkably barbaric. None of that compared to witnessing your fellow man being hauled down by other humans and torn limb from limb - feasted upon while screaming out their last breath. It created the kind of nightmares that in the long run could send a man to the loony bin.

Bullock asked, "How many you see out there, Corporal?"

Nodding at the eight other men on the stairwell, "More than all of our fingers and toes. A lot more."

"Well, this mission is getting complicated."

"Fucked beyond measure, Sergeant."

"Best go down and tell the Captain."

19 Everyday Occurrences

Private Ken Ridley had nearly caught up with the escapees only a few minutes after his own getaway. A lightning strike had lit them up. The image was still burned into his retina, guiding him in their general direction. He put his back into his paddling.

Doctor Smith, who had grabbed a rowboat with Will, was at the oars and thus facing backwards. He was the first to spot the fleeing guard. "We've got company!" he shouted.

The others turned and stared into the soaking gloom, their rhythm thrown.

"One guy," continued Smith.

Jon said to Nikki, "What do you think?"

"I think he's the only one who got out of there."

"Yeah, but about letting him catch up with us?"

"He's gonna do what he's gonna do. He's probably armed, but I seriously doubt that he intends to threaten us. Nobody wants to be alone out here."

Jon called out to the others, "Let him come. We'll see what he wants."

"Fuck that!" said Miller.

Will piped in, "What are you going to do, David, hit him with your paddle?"

"Fuck that guy. He can fucking get eaten with the rest of them."

Ken called out, "I can hear you. I'm only fifty yards away."

"Good! Fuck you!"

Nikki said, "You should paddle somewhere else, soldier. It doesn't seem you're wanted."

"Paddle where?"

"To fucking hell, asshole!" yelled Miller.

Ken pulled close enough to become a shadow, his flashlight feebly cutting through the rain. His voice rose to a pleading level, "I didn't agree with Deighton. I thought what he was doing to you guys was terrible."

"Bullshit!" yelled Miller.

"I swear! If I didn't think I would get shot, I would have let you out. A lot of others were talking about it."

"But you didn't did you?" said Will.

"You left us in there to die," said mousy Ingrid.

"I'm sorry. I'm so sorry. Please let me stay with you."

No one said anything else so it was assumed, without objection, that Ken would continue paddling with them. Their boats were becoming heavy with the accumulating rain. They'd have to find shore soon or risk getting swamped.

The rain was coming down in huge black sheets. The sound as it churned the water was almost deafening. Nikki felt rather than saw the ground as the canoe slid over the rocky bottom at the edge of some kind of landing. "We'll have to risk pulling out here."

They turned the water out and then dragged their boats ashore. With one uncoordinated effort, they all tipped them over, each couple pulling their shivering bodies underneath. Ken considered asking Will and Smith if he could join them under their rowboat, but knew the answer already. Feeling miserable and awash with guilt over both leaving the castle door open and then these people, he credited them with not beating him to death, then decided that they were probably too tired and cold anyway. He'd have to watch his back in the morning.

Jon and Nikki huddled under the pitch-blackness of the canoe and tried to ignore the drumming of the rain on the hull. To add more misery to the situation (not that it really mattered to their shivering soaking wet bodies) small streams of water ran under them on their way to the lake. Jon pulled Nikki to him, spooning her for warmth. She didn't resist; instead pushing her backside into him. He tried to cover as much of her body as he could. She pulled his arm around her tight, interlacing her fingers with his and pressing his hand to her rising and falling stomach.

Her breath was hot and surprisingly sweet as it rose to his nostrils, and to Jon's astonishment, he felt himself getting erect. Nikki had to feel it too; her thigh was pressed against his groin. He tried to adjust himself away from her, but she pulled him back.

"It's okay. Stay. You're warm."

To his dismay, his erection became even stronger. The situation was absurd. He was stunned at the sudden awakening of his libido.

"I, I'm sorry...I..."

Nikki found the pressure coming from Jon's groin a pleasant surprise. Here she was, having just survived another harrowing escape, lying under a canoe on a soaking wet pebble beach, the rain so loud she couldn't hear herself breathe, and she was suddenly contemplating having sex with this guy.

They lay holding each other like that for several minutes. Jon tried to remain still, wishing away his excitement and then she pushed into him even harder.

He almost had to yell into her ear to be heard, "Are you? Do you want..."

Nikki said, "Hell with it."

"What?"

She turned her face to him. "I said, hell with it."

She began to unbuckle her belt and unzip her fly. It was pitch black, but her actions were clear enough. He could feel her movements and he started to do the same, quickly releasing his straining lower half from the grip of the leather riding pants. Nikki shoved her pants over her hips and spooned back into him, and just like that, he drove himself inside her. She grabbed his hip and pulled him in tight and he found his hand cupping her strong stomach muscles as she pushed onto him. It was quick and they moved with ferocity, discharging tremendous amounts of stress. At the last moment, Jon had a flash of clarity, the risk of an unintended pregnancy overcoming his animal urge, and he pulled away leaving them both hanging with the fierce exhaustiveness of the act, the moment incomplete. The lack of a crescendo left their nerves pulsing for more, but they said nothing. They pulled their pants back on in silence, words being too messy to fill the new odd void. She stayed with her back to him, but allowed a small gap to exist in the space between.

Despite the awkwardness of the moment, the noise, the miserable wetness and hardness of the ground, Jon felt a minute of peace for the first time in seven months and he used it to fall asleep. In her mind, Nikki shook her head at her compulsiveness. Some things about her would never change. She lay awake for a little while, reminiscing over other reckless exploits and then she shrugged, letting the sound of the drumming rain carry her away. As sleep took her, she pushed herself back into him. Jon reflexively held her tight.

It was light out when Jon woke to the feel of Nikki's hand over his mouth and her whispering in his ear, "I just heard a light scream and a scuffle." When his eyes focused, she took her hand off and looked over her shoulder. The canoe was naturally tilted to one side creating a smaller gap behind her. Jon looked past her shoulder, but could only see gravel and forest debris. He grabbed one edge of the canoe and with a nod from Nikki they flipped it over. They stood and looked around quickly at their surroundings, their backs to each other. At almost the same moment Smith and Will climbed out from under the rowboat and Ken from under his canoe. It was sunrise but the light was diffused with continued overcast and light drizzle. There was a gurgling gasp from under David and Ingrid's canoe. Ken was closest and noticed a trail of blood seeping out from beneath. He drew his sidearm and cocked the hammer. Jon and Nikki grabbed their paddles, the others followed suit.

Using hand signals, Jon indicated to Ken that he would flip the canoe over and that Ken should have his weapon ready. The others crept closer and raised their paddles and oars. Jon stepped to one end of the canoe, took a deep breath, and as quickly as he could, flipped it over while positioning his paddle to fend off any attack.

Ingrid was alone. Her eyes were wide with fright, the last of her life escaping out of a huge bite in her shoulder. Her face was bitten, her nose and lips were completely missing and her body shook with cold and shock. Everyone was momentarily too horrified to move and that's when David, or what had been David, made its move.

With an inhuman scream, it ran out of the bush and latched itself to Ken's back. David-the-Fiend's face was covered in Ingrid's blood and it growled with gleeful malevolence as it gnashed its teeth into Ken's neck and shoulders. Ken's gun arm swung up and he pulled the trigger randomly while screaming with fright. The first bullet found Doctor Smith's throat, severing his spine and dropping the professor like a brain-punched cow. Everyone else hit the deck. Bullets shot off into the woods and sky until Ken bent his elbow back and jammed the gun into the socket of infected David's right eye, blowing his infected brain across the shiny wet rocks.

The whole event took maybe five-seconds. Two people were dead and two others were either going to die or turn with infection. This was common. This was every day. The population of the United States had been cut in half in seven months due to compounded five-second moments like this.

Ken stepped away from the brain-splattered corpse and sat down limply on crossed legs. He held his shoulder with one hand and with the other, his now deafened and powder-burned ear. As the survivors came off the adrenaline Ken stared at the gun in his lap with a surprised look, like the thing was talking to him, saying, you know what to do. Ingrid sputtered an unintelligible bloody word and then her eyes went blank.

First Jon, then Nikki, then Will stood. They checked themselves for blood splatters and then all looked to Ken. What was there to say? It was yet another mind-boggling tragedy that for these people was now just matter-of-fact. David had clearly become infected from having a Fiend hiss right into the open wound on his scalp. He had turned in the night and made his breakfast out of Ingrid.

Ken pulled his bloody hand away from his shoulder and stared at it. "So I guess that's that. It's hard to survive this thing, you know? I mean the whole thing, not just the infection, the collapse of the world and everything."

The three others just looked at him. Will finally said, "What's your name?"

"Ken, Ken Ridley. I'm twenty-four and I was really good at shooting pool, playing Xbox and I was a ski instructor for a few years. I was a bad soldier."

"I'm sorry, Ken."

"I'm not. Living's not so fun anymore anyway." He stood, leaving the pistol on the ground. "I'm going to walk that way now. Good-bye, okay? Sorry for what I did to you, you know, back there." He absently brushed off the seat of his pants and began to slowly walk into the woods.

The others looked at the gun on the ground, but no one moved. Finally Nikki said, "Fine, I'll do it." She picked up the gun, aimed at Ken's back and fired. The bullet pierced the top of his wounded shoulder, sending up a small spray of blood. Ken stumbled but then stood again keeping his back turned.

"Fuck," said Nikki. "I'm sorry, Ken."

"It's okay. I'll just stand instead. You can – "

The second bullet hit him square in the back. He dropped to his knees and fell forward dead.

Nikki handed the gun to Jon and said, "Next time it's your turn."

20 Dungeon

Jones and Copper waited for the air to clear and then both crawled forward from opposite sides of the room. Copper only had a knife, but a knife was a handy thing in close quarter combat with an uninfected person. At least he assumed the person was uninfected. Fiends had lost their ability to process language. Man, were his ears ringing. They heard the intercom come alive again. "Hello, can anyone hear me there? This is Specialist Alexander Melman of the Seventy-Fifth Rangers. Can anyone hear me?"

"*Fuckukukuk youououoouu,*" came lilting down the hall.

When the two Rangers got themselves on either side of the hall entrance they stopped. Jones took a quick peek around the corner and looked down the hall. He gave the all-clear signal to Copper, who then signaled that he would crawl in first, Jones covering him. Copper got on his belly and started to worm his way forward. Jones pointed the machine gun around the corner and watched for the slightest movement.

"*One, two, three, six, which one surprises the fufufucking dicks? Fufufufuck yooooouuuuyouyou, fufuckers,*" came down the hall, followed by the gentle click of a shutting door.

Copper got to the first door and put his ear to it. There seemed to be no sound beyond, but to be sure, he lifted his arm and tapped the wood lightly with the tip of his knife, hopefully giving the impression that he was standing there rather than lying on the floor. No hail of bullets came through the hollow core door. He listened again, decided the room was empty and slithered forward to the next one, going through the same routine - empty. When he reached the entrance to the communal bathroom he could smell water and a hint of mildew coming from under the crack. He could also smell something else; something that he'd only smelled once before in Chad and that he didn't want to smell ever again. It was the distinct odor of blood mixed with urine and feces. It was the smell of fear, the smell of pain, the smell of torture. While he was distracted by the memory, the door opened behind him. He turned and got a brief glimpse of a man in a rumpled army uniform with a kerchief tied around his head. He held a filth-covered baby, no, a little demon out in front him like some type of talisman. Its black eyes were positively huge. Copper was suddenly filled with terror. His muscles locked up. A buzzing noise filled every inch of his mind like he'd become ensnared in a cloud of locusts. He could see himself on the floor, then his hand gripping the knife – he couldn't control it – he watched as his own hand raised the knife to his throat, the sound of his days old beard scraping against the blade, then it was cutting. He wanted to scream, but couldn't.

The man said in a half possessed voice, "*Scary, isn't it?*"

At the same moment, Jones let off a burst from the M240, with a round hitting the assailant in the shoulder and spinning him back into the room.

Suddenly Copper had his mind back. He pulled the knife away that had started to cut into his own neck, warm blood soaking into his collar. His heart raced and he was vaguely aware of Jones charging up next to him, firing into the open door. He caught the briefest glimpse of the assailant's head disappearing in an explosion of brains and bone, followed by the destruction of the demon infant. Jones then turned and kicked in the remaining doors, finding them all empty until he came back to the communal bathroom. When he opened that one, both men's faces twisted into a grimace. Copper pulled himself up and they stepped into a dungeon from hell.

With her hands tied to a fire sprinkler pipe above her head, a naked woman hung with her chin resting on what was left of her chest. She had been badly mauled, as if by a wild animal. Her breast tissue was mostly chewed off and there were obvious human bite marks all over her body. Blood, piss and shit, mingled on the floor at her feet. To her right, two women and a man were shackled naked to a handicapped rail inside an open toilet stall. They all burst into involuntary tears at the sight of the Rangers.

"Jesus," muttered Jones.

"For serious?" asked Copper who took a shaky step toward the hanging woman.

"No. Don't!" yelled one of the women.

Copper stopped and just then a huge male Fiend, also naked, came charging out of a shower stall, surprising both of them.

The thing let out a piercing scream and launched itself at Copper. Its teeth snapped in front of Copper's gas mask just as it was yanked back off its feet crashing to the floor. It writhed in fury, trying to pull a metal collar off its neck.

Jones fired a fusillade of bullets into the thing, hammering it into the floor. It had been chained so that it could only reach as far as the victim hanging from the sprinkler pipe.

The woman shackled in the stall cried out again, "Get away from her! Get away from her!"

Suddenly, the naked, chewed up girl, snapped awake and faced the soldiers with infected eyes. She gnashed at Copper, and again teeth clacked together only inches from his face. He nearly slipped on the feculence at her feet as he reeled back.

Jones lifted his gun and put one round through her head.

The people who were tied up burst into further tears and wails, the relief of rescue overcoming every other emotion.

"I've seen some chron shit, but this is some fucking jacked up chron shit," noted Copper, his Newark inner-city Italian/Indonesian roots wrapping his words with personal comfort.

A search of headband boy's headless body came up with a key to the handcuffs. As they released them, the victims all hugged Jones and Copper without conscious notion of their nakedness. The soldiers were at once proud of saving these people and utterly repulsed by their wretchedness.

"The baby?" asked one of the women. "Tell me you killed it?"

Jones looked at Copper and then tried to soften his stance, his body language offering bad news. "I'm sorry, I'm pretty sure I did."

The woman burst into tears of relief.

—

The trapped and separated Rangers and scientists explained their respective situations to each other over the intercom. O'Shea decided to call in another air strike of nerve gas over their position. Problem one solved. Problem two was the civilians, now cleaned up, clothed and fed, but without hazmat suits. They were also suffering from the extreme psychological effects of their captivity. There was no way to continue on the mission with these people in tow and not have them affect the situation with what would obviously be special needs.

Captain O'Shea conferred with Ottawa via the bunker system's satellite relay and it was decided that they would have to leave these people behind. The bunkers were secure with plenty of fuel, food and water. Jones and Copper would seal off the rooms that held the leftover carnage. A psychologist would be made available to the victims via the satellite system and they were repeatedly reassured that the team would try to pick them up upon their return from Florida.

All three of the victims found themselves repeatedly falling into fits of tears. Jones and Copper provided them with scrounged up blankets, pulling the doors shut behind the carnage. Copper privately hoped that they wouldn't completely lose it (like so many of his buddies with PTSD had) and off themselves while they waited in solitude. He couldn't imagine being tied up naked to be fed to one of those things, watching the horror and knowing you would be next. Shit, if he was honest with himself, after the tore-up chron shit he'd seen over the past few years, he needed some serious mind magic too. It was only his fierce loyalty to Jones and Ghost – well Ghost is all ate up now idnit? – that kept Copper going. If Jones bought it, Copper would probably step up and fade to black, be done with the whole fucking badong shit storm.

"The man with the baby was one of us," said the woman who had yelled out the warning about the charging Fiend.

"That was your friend?" asked Jones.

Her companion continued for her, "Carl. At first, when we'd taken refuge in the fort, there weren't that many Fiends around, but when the city was lost, they sorta spread out, you know, hunting for healthy folks. We got caught flat-footed trying to scrounge up some food from a vending machine in one of the hangers. There were nine of us and maybe twenty of them. When it was over and we'd killed them off, there was a baby still alive. It was different."

"Saw that," said Copper.

"We think it was born like that. And… it could totally control our minds."

"Me too," said Copper, feeling the fresh wound on his neck. "Like my own body attacked me."

Jones looked at Copper with fresh eyes. "Wait. You sayin' that that thing was in your head? Controlled you?"

"Nearly made me cut my own neck."

"Carl was its favorite," said the woman. "The baby made a kind of pet out of him."

Jones was incredulous. "How's a baby make you a pet?"

The woman's face squished up. She paused, wiping tears off her cheeks. "Yesterday there were three more of us. They were able to pull the bar from the wall on their side. We're pretty sure they got away." False hope filled her eyes.

Copper and Jones chose not to say anything. Why make it worse for these folks? But she knew. She let her head hang down and burst into muffled sobs followed by the second woman who had not spoken a word, just sat there catatonic.

Copper touched the sobbing woman's shoulder, "You a strong lady, lady. You take care of these two. They needs a strong lady."

The soldiers gave as much comfort and reassurance to the civilians as they could and then made their way up the stairs. Next door, the rest of the platoon stood by, suited up - ready to go. They'd gotten the word ten minutes prior that the airstrip had been gassed, and a return loop by Lieutenant Reese in her F-22 confirmed several dozen Deadheads on the tarmac, no further activity. To her private dismay, a quick pass over the fenced in tank depot revealed nothing but motionless wreckage.

The Rangers waited five minutes more to be sure that nothing outside was breathing, and opened the doors. The pilots ran for the Chinooks to start the liftoff sequence while a perimeter was temporarily setup to protect them.

Everyone tried not to look at the gruesome mess that was spread out across the tarmac. They were especially mindful of the torn up uniforms of their comrades. O'Shea and Melman collected the dog tags that they could find.

Up to this point Aaron Burnbaum and Christy Tsue had not seen any of the horror that the others had seen. Both scientists had been evacuated before the fall of Atlanta and had missed out on the gory details of a nation gone mad. What they had seen had been on TV or on autopsy tables, sanitized and fit for 'consumption'. Their first encounter with the real thing had both of them nearly puking in their suits.

Everyone wanted a breath of fresh air, but the Chinooks themselves were coated in nerve agent, and unless they could figure out a way to wash them off completely, they were all doomed to keep their hazmat suits on until they were safely on the ground again. The sun was just coming up as the helicopters rose into the sky. The massive storm that had brushed over them in the night had moved far to the north leaving the horizon dark and ominous.

21 The Lake

There were several houses along the lakeshore that could be seen through the mist. At one point the sky had even cleared enough for Jon, Nikki and Will to look back toward the castle and the town. The shoreline was crawling with Fiends all walking in one direction – north. The three survivors had decided to take one canoe, the craft being quieter in the water than a rowboat and less likely to attract attention.

Will explained that he lived on the lake, his house being over on Dead River Road. As the three survivors pushed off, leaving behind four more dead Americans, Nikki asked, "Can you find it if we stay out in the middle, hide in this mist?"

"I think so. Flagstaff's a big lake. There's a lot of little islands and one big one in the middle. I wonder... I bet it's pretty well covered in game, God knows we've got fish. We could get some gear together, you know, do the survivor thing. I hunt. You guys hunt? I bet we could make it work for a good while."

Nikki said, "Let's call it a fallback. We need to keep our eyes on the prize. Canada."

Will nodded at the teaming shore, "I wouldn't be surprised if we were cut off from Canada by now."

They paddled in silence for maybe a mile, the shore occasionally popping into sight as the mist ebbed and flowed.

Will finally spoke. "This is it."

Using his paddle to steer, he turned the canoe toward shore. As the trees and then lower scrub came into focus, it looked peaceful enough. The rain had stopped and a few birds chirped to the change in weather. There were houses, but they were more separated than the ones closer to town.

Will said, "They should all be empty. As far as I know, everyone from the surrounding area had either evacuated or thrown in their lot with Deighton."

As they got closer to shore, a flock of Cormorants shot out from a tree and circled over them to make sure they were not marauding humans before returning to their nests.

Will named his neighbor's houses, "Bennett got out a month ago. Carpenter, don't know, Jensen stayed - sent the wife and kids to Idaho where her parents were. He's either dead or a demon after last night's mess. You remember him - he was the one in the orange hunting vest who handled old Mrs. Tanner like a bag of trash." Will flipped off Jensen's house and said, "Good riddance, you bastard." He pointed at the house closest to them, "My next door neighbors, the Costas'… don't know - Steven, Liz, two kids. And that one there is my place."

It was modest looking, comfortable, and like most of the newer houses, it had a big picture window. A small covered motorboat was tied to the dock, nothing else outside other than a barbecue and a couple of Adirondack chairs. The landscaping was pretty much nature's call. They let the canoe glide up to the side of the dock and Will hopped out, holding it for the others. They pulled it out of the water and set it on the dock.

Jon said, nodding at the motorboat, "Before we go any further. That thing gassed up? Key's in it?

"Gassed. Keys are in the house."

"Well let's get the cover off her and get her turned toward the lake in case we need to make a dash for it. Trust me when I say, Nikki and I have experience with that one."

They pulled the cover off to reveal a perfectly restored 1940 Chris Craft Barrel Back. The wood shone glossy like new, every piece of chrome, facet and bit of upholstery had been lovingly cared for.

Will noted, "I don't have a wife. Tess here has gotten all of my devotion."

When they got it turned around, the Marine in Nikki took charge, "Okay, we stay in a group. Jon, I don't know how you feel about continuing to carry that pistol, I can take it if you like. I wasn't serious about you having to shoot the next one."

Jon smiled, "You're not getting my new gun. I'm good with the gun. I just wish I still had my riot helmet."

Nikki grabbed two of the canoe paddles and handed one to Will, then took the gun from Jon and handed him a paddle. "You're so-so with a gun. We walk the perimeter and then we enter the house. Agreed?"

Jon smiled with sarcasm in his eyes. Nikki stepped forward. "One other thing," she said. "If we come upon one of the things alone, you two try to take it out with the paddles. Gunshots just bring more of them."

"That's a fun plan," said Jon. "Can I have the gun back?"

"No"

They moved around the property and found nothing. The clouds were breaking and it was developing into a gorgeous day.

Will said, "It's surreal, isn't it? How nature continues on its timeless schedule? The planet would thrive if we weren't here."

Neither Nikki nor Jon chose to respond to the obvious statement. When they felt secure about the outside, they moved to the front door. Will said, "It's unlocked. No one locks their doors around here."

They stepped into a great-room, which made up the bulk of the interior. It was a comfortable, masculine space, with a wood stove and a small kitchen. Will wasn't kidding about the hunting; several local species had been preserved and were on display. There was also a horrible smell. A few flies flew about the room; many more were piled dead along the windowsills; a growing theme in abandoned homes. The source of the smell was obvious. Assorted breakfast food was spread out on the counter, quite putrefied.

Jon whispered, "Another thing I've seen a lot. Folks getting their meals interrupted."

Will shrugged and whispered, "Planned to clean up when I got home." He opened a door next to the kitchen, revealing an empty toilet/laundry. He stepped toward the only other door, paddle raised, "Just one bedroom," and kicked it open. Nothing. Empty. The three of them stepped in to find an unmade bed, clothes on the floor, piled on a chair. Will peeked into the bathroom and smiled with relief. Raising his voice to normal, he said, "Well that's it. You've had the tour. Sorry about the smell. When I left to go deal with the Deighton situation I didn't exactly expect to get locked up."

"What about a bath?" Nikki asked with longing.

"There won't be any water pressure. Without electricity, the pump for the well is useless. No hot water either. I've got a diesel back-up but it's noisy as hell."

"Not to be a drag," said Jon, "and I know it suddenly feels like a normal day. And God knows we need one of those. But shouldn't we gather what we can and get the heck out of here?"

"Bubble popper," said Nikki.

Will gave Nikki a gentle pat on the shoulder, "Have at my clothes. Pick what you think might work for you and then grab some things for me and Jon."

"Lots of socks and underwear," said Jon. Off Will's sour face he said, "Yes, I'm happy to wear your underwear. I've been without for too long – leather riding pants, not so fun."

Will scrunched his nose and shrugged. "You're welcome to use it." He steered Jon back toward the kitchen. "Why don't you work on gathering food? I'll pull together a few backpacks, tents, camp stove, flashlights and whatnot and crack open my gun safe."

"You wouldn't happen to have any cholesterol medication?" asked Jon. "I haven't taken mine since I ran out in Charleston."

"No. Why? You think you might actually live long enough to die of heart disease?"

"It could happen."

The three of them worked quickly, laying a great pile of gear on the center of the great-room floor. Will had a variety of bachelor-friendly processed food, which Jon crammed indiscriminately into a backpack. Nikki, having found a new heavy leather coat for herself, packed an assortment of durable looking clothes while Will packed everything else.

When they were done, they looked at the pile, contemplating the next step. Will said, "Oh, I almost forgot." From a desk drawer, he pulled out a hand crank radio. "This should come in handy, even picks up shortwave." He stuffed it in his pack. "Okay, weapons." Hefting each he said, "Standard shotgun, Winchester pump-action, 12 gage, twenty five rounds of buck, ten slugs, twenty of bird, not that the bird will do much, but we can use it to hunt. This lever action is my deer gun, though I've shot moose with it too - Savage 99, .30 caliber, fifty rounds. And finally my dirty secret..."

Nikki finished for him, "The SCAR L special forces assault rifle, 5.56 NATO round. Love the gun. Standard issue for me. I'll take it."

"Okay, sure." said Will, not really thrilled about giving up his baby. "I've got two extra 30 round magazines and about a hundred loose rounds."

Jon said, "I guess I'll take the shotgun. It's what I'm used to, and contrary to Nikki's opinion, I'm okay with a pistol as well." He picked up a 9mm Smith & Wesson and strapped on the holster, which included pockets for three more magazines.

The birds were still chirping as they walked down to the dock. The Chris Craft had three seats up front and a second row behind where they tossed the gear.

Will felt his pockets and said, "Eh, forgot the key. Be right back." As he walked up to the house, the birds suddenly stopped chirping and then the insects stopped buzzing. The silence was nearly deafening.

"Oh shit," said Jon with resignation.

Nikki said, "Will, hurry."

Instead, Will slowed his gate as they all listened.

The forest suddenly erupted with sound. The cormorants burst out of their tree, and a slamming screen door echoed from the Costas house next door. The voice of a man hollering gibberish bounced among the leaves. This was followed by high panicked screams from a woman and two children.

Will's pace froze to petrified stillness as he tried to get a sense of what was happening. His gun was behind him, the key in the house in front of him.

Flashing past the trees that led to his driveway, a woman and her kids, a young boy and a girl, came running into view screaming in terror. The woman saw Will and angled toward him. Nikki got on a knee and was about to drop them all with the SCAR when she heard the woman yell out, "Will! Help us!" Beyond her, was the distinct scream and howl of Fiends. There were lots of them.

Will took a few steps toward the fleeing family, "Run faster Elizabeth!"

As she ran, Elizabeth pointed back. "Hundreds of them. They chased Steven. I think they killed my Steven!" She and the children got to Will and she grabbed his jacket in horror and desperation.

Jon racked the shotgun and ran up to Will shoving him at the house, "Get the fucking key!"

Will snapped out of it and ran into the house just as a horde of charging Fiends appeared at the driveway. Jon grabbed both of the kids and ran toward the dock. Nikki immediately started shooting in quick bursts of three, taking out the first Fiends but not even slowing the pack.

Elizabeth looked at the dock and freedom then turned to the house and screamed, "Will!"

Will stepped back out of the house, looked at the onslaught and tossed Elizabeth the keys.

Nikki shot two Fiends that were running for Will, but there were so many. He was tackled under a gang of ten.

Elizabeth ran for her life.

Jon got the kids in the back of the boat and untied it.

Nikki kept shooting until she clicked on an empty chamber. She grabbed her next full clip and that's when two fast and wiry ones tackled Elizabeth. They were quickly followed by at least ten more. With sharp rocks, sticks and knives, they split her open like a sack of giblets, tearing her insides out and tossing them amongst themselves in an orgiastic display.

Throwing the tarp over the children to hide their eyes from the horror, Jon jumped back off the boat firing the shotgun, over and over until he emptied the magazine. "We need that key!" He dropped the shotgun and pulled out the Smith & Wesson.

Both he and Nikki stepped forward firing evenly and with precision, either mowing down or backing the monsters up. When they reached what was left of Elizabeth, Jon snatched the key out of her twisted fingers and they backed up while still firing. They ran out of ammo as they got to the boat and jumped. Nikki threw the tarp off the bawling children and snatched up the lever action deer rifle and kept shooting as Jon turned the key. The momentum of their jump caused the boat to slowly drift away from the dock, but the engine wouldn't catch. One Fiend leaped into the water and managed to get a hand on the side of the boat. Nikki brought her gunstock down hard and crushed its fingers to ruin. A blow to the head pushed it under water and she kept shooting. The engine turned and turned, the battery weak from not starting.

Jon yelled at it, "Come on, come on, come on, dammit!" and suddenly it fired up. He threw the throttle forward and they were away.

The children looked back at the shore with a mixture of terror and astonishment. In a matter of minutes they had lost both of their parents in the most violent way imaginable and now found themselves amongst strangers, racing across a lake in a motorboat.

The boy quietly spoke up, "You have to go slower."

Jon turned and said, "What?"

The boy said louder, "There's lots of shallow spots. You'll hit bottom."

Jon pulled back on the throttle and then pulled it back all the way to idle. The boat coasted to a stop. The girl was crying, shivering, her teeth chattering with shock.

The boy wiped away his tears and said, "It's a shallow lake. Not a lot of power boats."

Jon said, "What's your name?"

"Teddy Costas. My sister's name is Amanda. We saw you paddle past our house. My dad was going to walk over and let you know that we were there... We, we saw the bad people outside. They must have followed you along the shore while you were paddling. He said to my mom to take us out the driveway and run to Mr. Parker's house and he ran out the back toward the water to make them chase him."

Nikki asked, "So he might have made it to the water?"

"My dad's a good swimmer."

Jon moved the throttle forward and turned the boat around. The shore was teaming with Fiends. The girl, Amanda started to become hysterical and Nikki did her best to comfort her.

Steven Costas sat on the shore of what his family had dubbed, Getaway Island, a small place that they would row to for picnics on pretty days. He had easily out swum the few Fiends who managed a feeble dog paddle. The lake was actually part of a river, and near his house it narrowed and picked up speed. As he swam from shore, the current had slowly swept him away from the battle at Will's house, making it impossible for him to get back to help.

He cursed himself over and over for his foolishness. They'd had all the time in the world to evacuate to Canada. He had assumed that there would be food riots and fights over housing and fuel, and there had been some of that, but mostly his radio told of the good; the cooperation and coming together of community. A majority had remained steadfast in their determination to maintain the rule of law. He should have gone. His family would have been safe. He pounded his leg in frustration and despair.

When his boy spotted him ashore, new tears poured down his face. His daughter stood and gripped the side of the boat with stolid longing. But where was Elizabeth? Maybe she was hurt and lying down. Of course that was it. If the children were safe, then so was his wife.

Dressed in high-tech looking leather clothes, the man driving the boat was young and strong looking. There was a young woman onboard, holding an assault weapon and dressed in an oversized leather coat and jeans. Both of these people looked exhausted. Steven said a quick prayer of thanks and waded out into the river, grabbing the bow as the boat inched in. His children tried to charge into his extended embrace, but were stopped by the man.

Jon said, "Wait! Sir, have you been bitten? Have you come into close contact with any of the infected?"

Steven replied, "Thank the Lord, no. I outran and out swam them. Where is my wife Elizabeth?"

Amanda choked up anew and said, "Daddy."

The children stepped forward into his embrace. A scan of the man and woman's eyes told Steven all he needed or wanted to know about his wife. As the man let go of the bow, Jon hopped off to hold it steady in the shallow water. They gave the distraught family a few minutes to mourn, then Nikki spoke up. "I'm sorry, but we need to find a safe place and set up some shelter before the end of the day. We have enough gear and provisions to keep all of us alive for several days, even a couple of weeks, but a safe place is another story."

"Big Island," said Steven, clearing his throat, "It's in the center of the lake."

Nikki said, "That's the place Will was talking about."

Steven took a deep breath and wiped his tears. "There was a rumor that one of the local parish's set up a settlement there. If it's true... well I hope they'll welcome us. They're uh... they've got a slightly different perspective on things than most folks."

"Meaning?" Jon asked.

"Judge for yourself. Given the circumstances, I can't imagine that we won't be welcome."

22 Chicken Farm

The pilots for the Chinooks could see from miles away that Orlando still burned. A modern burning city was like a tire dump fire; there were so many plastic and rubber products and synthetic construction materials that the fuel just lasted and lasted. The rural areas didn't make out much better. The haze became thick as they passed the wildfires that continued to consume the better part of Central Florida.

The breadth of the destruction was overwhelming. The observer's minds simply couldn't catalogue so much devastation. Mile after mile of forest, field, and town was scorched black. Great swirls of ash moved in the wind. The decision to nuke central Florida had been one of final desperation.

O'Shea turned to Susan and nodded at the blackened land below. "Neutron bombs. Made in China. Supposed to be clean – kills the body, leaves the buildings, no radiation after just a few days. Unfortunately the initial explosions started those wild fires. Mixed with the drought down here...."

"Yes, I remember the uproar." Susan sat back and chose to close her eyes instead.

When Operation Bugbagger reached Happyland Farms, they gave the whole area a wide lazy circle. There were no guarantees, but a hovering helicopter would generally bring out any Fiends hiding below.

Specialist Jones gripped the handle of the mini-gun mounted on the window in front of him, his finger a millisecond away from pulling the trigger on any movement. The place seemed to be empty so O'Shea gave the go-ahead for the Chinook carrying the Hummer and its single squad led by Cavanaugh to set down while the other craft continued to circle, ready to offer cover fire if necessary.

The farm was located on the southern edge of Lake Okeechobee and consisted of several large modern barns, an office/residence, outbuildings and a large grain silo. The place was already overgrown. Weeds stood as tall as a man, and vines crept up the buildings, offering natural camouflage.

Cavanaugh's squad deployed their Humvee and made various figure-eights around the compound. While one man tracked the area with the roof mounted fifty-caliber, the others kept their HKs pointed out in every direction. If there was a horde of Fiends present, this maneuver was sure to coax the monsters out. The only thing to move was a startled flight of pheasant.

After the second Chinook landed, O'Shea directed everyone to stand clear of the helicopters and carefully remove their hazmat gear. Cavanaugh's squad would remain geared up and begin the tedious job of scrubbing down both the helicopters and any gear that might have come into contact with nerve agent. They were fortunate that the farm had its own water tower. They'd have plenty of gravity fed H2O.

The lucky ones who got to step out of their suits, were greeted by a warm balmy breeze and the buzzing of insects. Susan's skin felt like a sponge as is soaked up the moist air. "Okay, then. My team is looking for live chickens as well as feedstock for testing. Captain O'Shea, can you have some men check the barns?"

O'Shea deployed Preston's squad for that mission while Bullock, O'Shea, Jones and Copper escorted the scientists.

They began with the main office building, a Victorian era gingerbread house.

At the entrance they found the front door locked. O'Shea nodded at Bullock, "Sergeant, a key please."

Bullock lifted his big combat boot and with a swift and practiced kick, smashed the door open, breaking the deadbolt and the old wood that surrounded it. The three other soldiers pointed their guns inside.

O'Shea said, "Okay, teams of two. Jones you're with me. Science stays outside."

The building, though built in the late nineteenth century, had been significantly remodeled. The interior was furnished with modern office equipment, comfortable furniture and halogen lighting. The houseplants that graced the main foyer had died for the most part, but several hearty species were climbing up the walls. A sign above the reception desk read: Happyland – The Future of Poultry.

After checking every nook and cranny, the soldiers dubbed the place clean. There were no signs of chaos or a quick exit. The former employees simply didn't show up to work one day.

Bullock stepped back outside, "It's all good."

Susan brushed past him, "Thank you, Sergeant. Now would you mind escorting Doctor's Tran and Warner. We're looking for a feed storage building and any laboratory equipment."

Bullock looked at O'Shea for permission.

"You heard the lady."

The four men headed off while Christie Tsue, Aaron and Rick Decker followed Susan inside, Susan saying, "Okay, we need to track down any paperwork: bills, work orders, etcetera, anything to do with feedstock or antibiotics. You know what to do."

Thinking that Happyland Farms was probably never very happy, Preston and his squad approached their first chicken barn with wonder at the size of the operation. The doors as well as the windows had been boarded up from the outside. That alone, put them on immediate alert.

Preston stopped, "You hear that, Cowboy?"

There was a dull buzzing sound coming from inside the barn. It was at once a low hum and a high pitch while remaining steady in tone.

Cowboy asked, "What the hell does that?"

"Sounds like maybe insects, lots of insects. Only way to find out is open the door." He turned to his specialists, "Rand, Jacobus, open the door."

The two men gave their corporal a skeptical look, but went to work trying to pry the wood planking off with their kukri knives. The rest of the squad fell back with their weapons pointed in support.

The planks made loud creaking and popping noises as the nails were pried out, and the soldiers carelessly tossed them in a pile as they worked. The noise got the attention of O'Shea who radioed Preston. "What's the racket, Corporal?"

Preston toggled his mic, "Got something making noise in one of these barns, Cap."

"Coming to you."

Having left Copper with Susan and her team, O'Shea arrived just as Rand and Jacobus were nearly done. "Hell of a sound you found here, Corporal."

"Ain't stopped since we started, sir."

When the last plank was off, the specialists positioned themselves so they could run once they pulled the doors open.

O'Shea pointed his HK with the others, "Okay, men. Let's see what we got."

Rand and Jacobus yanked the doors open and spun around with their own guns pointed. It was almost pitch black inside, but the atmosphere seemed to be alive with motion, like a snowy TV screen, but dark. Suddenly a vast wave of flies poured out of the door. The whole squad was startled and Cowboy let off a three round burst in a panic.

Preston immediately scolded the soldier, "Bitch? What's wrong with your ass?"

"Sorry! I'm sorry. Fuck."

"Shouldn't be giving guns to no aidmen anyway."

"Keep sharp!" snapped O'Shea.

The air cleared. Dim light poured through cracks in the boarded up windows, filling the space with crisscrossed shadows.

The soldiers cautiously stepped into the gloom. Feathers coated every corner of the floor and thousands of flies still flew and crawled on every surface. It was the ultimate chicken massacre. Thousands of cages stacked one on top of the other lined the walls and made rows down the center of the building. In front of each row was a long thin feed tray. A small hole in the front of each cage would let an individual bird stick its head out and eat. Chickens, or what was left of them, were partially or wholly pulled through the wire of their cages. All had been reduced to feathers and bone. There were very dead humans as well. Most leaned against a post or a wall or simply laid on the feather and bone covered floor. They were badly decomposed, the bulk of the flesh long ago consumed by maggots.

In the center of it all, like a pathetic wolf caught in the most simple of steel traps, was a live Fiend. It was staring at them with the hungry look that every man in the platoon had seen all too often - insatiable, ravenous. It was an emaciated male, dressed in giant coveralls and trapped up to the waist in a tangle of wire cages.

"Clearly, this dumb motherfucker was one fat bitch," said Preston. He yelled at the monster, "Got yo ass all snagged up in them cages, huh? Appetite get the best of you, motherfucker?"

The exposed parts of its body were covered in puss-oozing sores that attracted hundreds of egg laying flies. Maggots chewed at exposed wounds while flies surrounded the creature's eyes, ears and mouth. It licked around its lips with a great sucking sweep, pulling in tens of the black buzzing things then chewing and licking up more. Then it hissed at the new flesh in the room and reached weakly for better vittles.

O'Shea raised his rifle and put a round between its eyes.

Cowboy said, "Shit. For once I wish I had my fucking gas mask. This place fucking stinks."

In the mansion Copper finally got his nerve up and spoke to Susan. He'd been wanting to ever since they'd boarded the Chinooks, but hadn't had the chance. "Beg pardon, ma'am."

Susan stopped rifling through a file drawer and turned to the soldier. "Yes?"

"Um. Back there. At Jackson. Down in the bunker. Me and Jones." His voice trailed off as he tried to think of the right words.

"Yes?"

Copper sighed deeply. "There was a baby down there, ma'am, that didn't look like any baby I ever seen. It, uh, it was controlling those people."

Susan leaned against a desk. "I'm sorry you're not making sense."

Copper explained the whole scenario. When he was done he showed her the cut on his neck. "Almost made me kill myself."

"So let me get this straight – A demon baby took over all of those people's minds and made one of them torture the others. And it took over your mind too?"

"That sums it up pretty well, ma'am."

"I'm not sure how to respond to that, soldier."

"Me either, but I thought you should know."

Susan turned back to the file drawer. "Well, I'll think about it."

"Yes, ma'am." Copper gave her a slight bow and backed out the door.

Tran and Warner found the jackpot in one of the outbuildings. It housed a very clean and very hi-tech looking laboratory. A side room held rows of chicken cages that were cleaner and larger than the ones in the barn, but also filled with the remains of dead birds.

Warner opened a walk-in refrigerator. The shelves were stocked with boxes of antibiotics, growth hormones and countless other drugs. He said, "Wow. This is way beyond chicken farming."

Tran looked among the labels and then waved around the rest of the space, "Look at this gear; DNA sampling, gene splicing. These people were hardcore. I'd say they were redesigning the chicken."

"Redesigning the chicken?" asked Bullock. He and Jones had just walked back into the room having made sure the rest of the building was clear.

"Better get Susan over here, Sergeant. We've got to start sorting through this stuff. Oh, and see if they've caught any live birds. If not, we'll work with these dead ones."

Within an hour the CDC team had set up its own temporary lab. Several live chickens were found in the rafters of another barn that shared a wall with a feed storage building. The tenacious birds had pecked a hole in the adjoining wall and had found a lifetime supply of food. A hole in the ceiling had provided a puddle of fresh water on the floor every time that it rained.

Though there was no further sign of infected humans, the Rangers took proper precautions and set up lookouts on the water tower. Cavanaugh's squad continued to clean the helicopters as well as the Humvee. Removing nerve agent was a detail-oriented task and the crew informed O'Shea that it would probably take twenty-four hours or more. An auxiliary diesel generator was found and the pilots, Warrant Officers Axelman and Frick, made themselves useful getting it online. The fuel tank was empty so they used some of the spare diesel that they'd brought for the Humvee.

It was near dark when they started the thing up. As the generator coughed to life, all of the exterior lights blinked and then blazed into life. The whole farm was lit up like a grand ball.

"Jesus H. Christ," yelled Frick as he hit the kill switch.

Bullock broke in on the group call frequency, screaming through the men's radios, "What the hell was that?"

"Uh, Standby, Sergeant." Axelman retraced the cables that were connected to the genie, yanking them up from the thin layer of dirt and debris that covered them until he found a second set of cables branching off from the first."

"Report, God damn it!" yelled Bullock.

The cables led to a small exterior closet attached to the side of the building. They opened the door and found a large breaker box inside.

"Shit," said Frick. He keyed his mic. "Apparently the back-up geni has its own breaker but it's also tied to the main. We didn't see it, Sergeant."

"Well, can you get us power without lighting up the whole fucking neighborhood?"

Frick slapped the main breaker switch off and said, "Yes, Sergeant."

By nine in the evening, the scientists were well into breaking down the chicken DNA and sorting through and uploading whatever seemed pertinent on the Happyland servers. Much of the work was now left up to the assorted machinery that they had brought with them. Shifts were decided upon and Tran was lucky enough to bunk out on the first watch. The scientists chose to sleep in the main house - a couple of the executive offices had sleeper sofas. The Rangers found a bunkhouse intended for itinerant workers.

23 Salvation

The Big Island was indeed occupied. The moment that Jon pulled the Chris Craft up to a small dock occupied by a few other boats a militia of sorts took the new arrivals into quick custody. With their options literally down to none, Jon and Nikki chose not argue, and along with Steven and his children, they were escorted to a storage building where they were strip searched to confirm that they had not been bitten. They were then left in the same building for twenty-four hours of quarantine before anyone would even bother to speak with them. Other than the gentle request to respect the need for quarantine, pleas for information were met with silence from their guards. They were provided with meals and that was all. To say that Jon and Nikki were uncomfortable with this procedure, given their recent turn as Fiend bait, was an extreme understatement.

On the evening of the following day, after it was confirmed that none of them were infected, the Right Reverend Horatio "Buzz" Calder visited. He was a large man in his early sixties, sporting a Santa Clause beard and shoulder length white hair. He entered the building with a pitcher of instant lemonade and introduced himself. His demeanor was actually rather jolly and that seemed to set everyone at ease. "Please accept our congregation's apologies for the inconveniences you've experienced. I have no doubt that you all have been through some very harrowing times. I'm sure you can appreciate our prudent caution. My name is Reverend Calder - though I am also known by the nickname, Buzz." He smiled at Jon's arched eyebrow. "It's a long story, has to do with my chatty youth, arguing in the name of the Lord." He popped open a folding campstool and sat. "You have found yourself to be guests of the Church of the Revelation in God, Flagstaff Lake, Maine." He smiled and spoke gently to the two children. "I am to understand your mother has joined our Lord in Heaven."

Both children became stricken with the memory of their mother's final moments. Steven put his arms around his kids and whispered, "Yes, she's in heaven."

Amanda said, "The monster people killed her." Tears worked their way down her cheeks and she was soon joined by her brother.

The reverend wiped a tear from his own eye. "Then she is indeed with the Lord, for we know that people of faith, whether they are already risen or slaughtered by the Devil's minions, have taken their rightful place in His Great Kingdom." He turned to call out of the shelter. "Katherine, will you please come in." He turned back to the Costas'. "Others in our congregation have already vouched for you. You are welcome, provided that you adhere to our rules."

A tall blond woman in her forties came through the door. She had obviously been listening closely. Nikki wondered how many others were standing just outside.

The reverend continued, "This craven country has brought God's final judgment upon it. I assume that you agree with that, Steven, and that your children do as well."

Steven glanced at Jon and Nikki, then looked back at the reverend. "Yes, sir."

"Good." He turned to Katherine, "See that Costas' have some lodging. Perhaps the Wanamakers should take them in until we can build a new shelter for them."

"Of course, Reverend." She turned to the huddled family and placed gentle hands on the children's quaking shoulders. "Come with me. We'll get you some clothes and some warm food. What an ordeal you must have had."

As the family headed out the door, Steven Costas turned back to Jon and Nikki. "Thank you. Thank you for saving my children. I shall not forget it."

Jon and Nikki smiled and nodded, both wondering if they would be treated in the same loving manner.

Jon sat up taller and addressed the reverend, "Sir, may I ask how many of you there are?"

"We are seventy-seven souls, well, eighty now for sure. We hail from a small town to the west of here. Several months ago, when it became clear that things were only going to get worse, we chose to seek shelter on this island. I have a shortwave radio and have been able to keep up with events. There is talk of an outbreak near Ottawa. If it's true, it could be mean the end for the fools and sinners up there as well. Don't doubt the meaning of these End Times. There is no geographical escape."

Nikki offered what she hoped was a sincere smile, "So when you say outbreak, you *are* referring to the infection?"

"That is correct."

"So which may I ask is it, Devil's Minions or regular people infected by a horrific disease?"

The reverend smiled back, happily sensing a theological debate, "Only God and Satan truly know the answer to that, my dear. However, it is my understanding that the Seventh Seal, as written in the book of Daniel, has been opened and it is time for the true believers to prepare for the final judgment. The planet will continue to devolve into Armageddon. Billions will die before this world is ruled by His government. This is a cleansing and it must be so."

Jon cocked his brow, but held his tongue.

"You seem perplexed, my son."

"No, sir. Just listening."

The reverend nodded with confidence, his eyes growing brighter, "It is the Great Tribulation. Satan has had his day on this earth. What we are witnessing now is his last futile attempt to claim it fully for himself."

"If that's so," said Nikki, "shouldn't you have been summoned to Heaven already? I mean, from what I've read, the rapture happens and *then* the nasty part comes, not the other way around."

The reverend lowered his voice and leaned toward them. "For the moment, to give comfort in this time of terror, it is soothing to allow those who need it, the thought that they might get swept up and away from this."

Nikki stated flatly, "So you don't buy it either."

The reverend sat back again and raised his voice so that anyone listening outside could here. "You appear to be of Jewish descent. Am I right, my dear?" Nikki was silenced as a sinister grin briefly appeared on the man's face. He turned to Jon. "Are you a Christian, my son?"

"There are all kinds of Christians, Reverend. What denomination are you?"

The reverend hummed lightly to himself – what to do with these people? His visage shifted back to warm benevolence and he stood and folded up his stool. "I'll ask you to stay here while I consult with the congregation. In the meantime, I'll have some further refreshment sent in."

"Um, excuse me," said Nikki. Fear was crushed by the sound of threat in her voice. "We came here for safety, just like you."

The reverend turned. "Yes, and we must do what is necessary for the safety of all." With that, he stepped out and closed the door. They heard it latch from the other side.

Nikki stood and looked at Jon, saying loudly so to be heard outside, "I'm not fucking doing this again. I will not be someone else's prisoner."

"You're not going to get an argument from me."

Night fell with no further news of their fate. They were, however, fed well. With little to do but catch up on desperately need rest, they chose to sleep. For warmth and a feeling of protection, they pulled the bedding off their individual cots, gathered it together and lay down with their backs pressed against each other. It was a fitful sleep at best, each aware of the other's wakefulness, yet unwilling to break the night's silence with unanswerable questions.

At dawn, a light breakfast was brought to them. Nikki asked the boy who delivered the food about an opportunity to bathe, but the boy just blushed and quickly left.

Finally Katherine returned. She stood very tall with a curious combination of dourness mixed with an almost angelic thousand-yard stare. She wouldn't make direct eye contact, choosing instead to speak toward their mouths. "You've been invited to morning prayer. You may use the communal bath. Fresh clothes will be provided while yours are washed and repaired."

24 Bug Out

At 2am Susan, carrying a laptop under her arm, walked into the upstairs office that Tran was crashed in and shook him awake.

Tran grunted, "Ten more minutes."

"We've got bad news."

Tran sat up, suddenly wide awake, then blinking as Susan turned on a bedside lamp. She opened the laptop and brought up an area map of Ottawa. "There's been an outbreak in Chelsea. It's an Ottawa suburb."

"Oh no."

"They fire bombed it."

"What?"

"Incendiaries. And the town next door, Old Chelsea. The two towns shared the same water system. Zero tolerance. We're finally at Zero tolerance. Estimates are fifteen thousand dead."

"This come over the satlink?"

"Ten minutes ago, from the director herself. We were told that the second we get a match, we haul ass back north. CDC's moving to Quebec City. They can't risk that Ottawa has been compromised. They're setting us up with a temp-lab in Martha's Vineyard of all places until the move to Quebec is complete. Looks like your migration theory is the only plausible one. Anyone caught not boiling water gets quarantined."

Tran sighed and got off the bed. "I don't even know what to say. You going to lay down?"

"Can't. We need all hands."

Tran nodded, tucking in his shirt.

She looked at the bed, "Well maybe ten minutes. I'm not much use exhausted, right?"

Tran closed her laptop, set it on a chair, and gently pushed Susan toward the bed. "I'll wake you in twenty."

She nodded and yawned. "FYI, this computer's pretty much full. Aaron's using the other one to keep uploading data. Happyland Farms was into some serious science."

"More than messing with feedstocks?"

"There's notes down there about bioengineering the birds to be staff resistant, stuff like that, but they also had forced evolution experiments going on - rapid maturation, muscle enhancement – all sorts of things - I'm pretty sure that the lead scientist was Mitchell."

"Mitchell? As in Oscar mix-human-DNA-with-name-a-plant-or-animal Mitchell?"

"The same. This was no ordinary chicken farm. It was a research facility for one of the big national outfits up in Georgia."

Copper and Jones sat atop the water tower keeping watch. Both men scanned the horizon with thermal binoculars. The image was like looking at a black and white negative, the heat signatures of various objects making for crystal clear differentiation.

Copper whined, "Now why in the F.U.C.K didn't we have these fucking things when we were down in that bandong dungeon of horrors?"

"'Cause there's only two pair for the whole platoon? Cause the pilots like havin' 'em all to their selves? Cause the army's a cheap ass – hold on. I got contact. Bearing one eight five degrees – shee-yte, it's a boatload of the motherfuckers."

Copper spun around and focused his glasses on Jones' angle. "Uh oh, bad night. I count four klicks out."

"Bitches are running. Not fast, but running." Jones keyed his mic. "Sarge, come in."

Bullock came on line, "Go for Bullock."

"We got incoming. Looks like a whole mess of them Shitfobs. Coming from due South. Estimate… half hour out."

"Keep an eye out. Will advise."

"Roger that."

They could hear the rest of the troops come alive as Bullock passed the word to O'Shea and orders filtered out.

Jones kept looking through the binoculars and spoke to Copper out of the side of his mouth. "I'm guessing at least a hundred, probably more."

"Yeah, at least." Copper spun around and scanned behind them again. He suddenly sucked air in through his teeth. "Bad, bad, bad, bad. Not good."

"What?"

"Whole pack comin' down the highway, one-six degrees. I count maybe twenty."

Jones spun around. "Got'em. Two klicks. Fuck if they ain't runnin' too."

O'Shea decided to confront the smaller band head on. He didn't have a large enough force to confront both groups at once. He called on Cavanaugh's squad to abandon the nerve agent clean up and instead make the assault in the newly cleaned Humvee.

Bullock was searching with his own binoculars. "Cap, we could also wind up the dirty bird. Attack the larger group with the mini-gun. Keep the clean heli, 'case we still need to bug out."

O'Shea gave it a moment's consideration. "Hmm, okay, get Frick suited up and in the air, just one to work the gun. I want to keep the main force together."

With this new order, the pilot for the still contaminated Chinook, Warrant Officer Frick, went through the start-up procedure while PFC Deeter pulled on the last of his JLIST gear.

Jones and Copper watched from the silo as Cavanaugh's team raced out to the North, confirmed that the smaller group of humans were infected, then laid into them with everything they had. The gunfire and grenade explosions echoed off the various farm buildings. It was a turkey shoot.

The Chinook's engines throttled up just as the gunfire from Cavanaugh's assault was dying down. The other mass coming from the South heard all of this and typical of the infected, broke into a sprint toward the farm.

Jones radioed, "We got a banzai charge, Cap. A couple hundred, I'd guess. They're all sprinting. Ten minutes, max!"

O'Shea was looking through his own standard binoculars now. The moonlight more than lit up the charging Fiends. "I see them. You and Copper get your asses down here."

Frick's Chinook wasn't sounding right. A whining sound mixed with snapping loud electrical arcs echoed off the building walls. White smoke poured out of one of the engines. The RPMs dropped rapidly and the blades slowed down.

Frick clicked his mic. "Engine's er wet, Cap."

O'Shea swore at the sky and looked again through his glasses. The Fiends would overwhelm them. They simply didn't have enough firepower to kill that many people quickly enough. He'd been through it before.

Bullock said, "They got the drop on us, sir."

"That's it then." He keyed his mic, "Bug out. Bug out! Everything on Chinook one. Cavanaugh, get back over here and give us a two hundred-meter buffer. Frick, keep trying. Get that thing in the air."

Frick's voice buzzed in O'Shea's ear. "That's a no go, Cap. I told them not to aim the hose directly into intake manifold. Killed it for now. It's got to dry out."

O'Shea looked at Bullock who shrugged. "Never seen a battle plan go as planned, Cap."

O'Shea keyed his mic, "Axelman, get Chinook one wound up now. We fly in five."

Cavanaugh's Humvee came roaring back through the farm, charging southeast. The bug out call was simple enough and had been pre-arranged. The soldiers who weren't shooting fell in with the CDC. They had important gear to move.

Aaron Burnbaum cursed as he stubbed his toe on a table leg. He and Warner nearly dropped the centrifuge they were carrying. Tran, Susan, Christy Tsue and Rick Decker formed a chain with Cowboy Johnston and Corporal Melman and a few other Rangers to get their gear to the Chinook. As the turbines wound up, the new echo of Cavanaugh's assault on the southern threat broke into their rhythm. It was going to be close.

25 The Rite Is Wrong

The Church was fashioned out of a portable greenhouse. The residents clearly had an artist among them: Various scenes from Christ's life were painted across the walls. When the sun shone, the whole structure appeared like a giant stained glass window. It was full of stern-faced ruddy Yankees who stood with a stoic posture that nevertheless failed to hide the fear that gripped them. They held themselves as if against an approaching tidal wave, death by violent deluge inevitable. As the intruders were led in, some offered hard stares, while others would only look at the floor as though filled with shame. Jon and Nikki were guided to sit in the front pew. They could feel the eyes of the congregation searching their backs, seeking answers - angst-filled curiosity boring into them. The walls were full of slogans sewn onto colorful, almost cheerful banners: *God Hates Fags, God Hates Jews, God Hates The Criminal Left Wing, God Hates Wetbacks, God Hates Adulterers, God Hates the USA.*

Jon whispered, "I know who these people are now. This church has been spreading under different names over the past decade or so. They protest against Jews and gays in front of synagogues and universities. Tell them God hates them, then offer salvation. Started a big riot in New York a few years ago, praying for our soldiers to die overseas."

"I remember that."

The reverend walked out from behind the altar and stepped up onto a raised platform. He invited everyone to rise and sing a hymn. The gathered voices were beautiful and strong and contradicted all of the venom that screamed back from the walls. When the hymn was finished, the reverend asked everyone to sit.

"Good Morning." He paused and looked around at the familiar faces and settled on the Costas Family. "We are blessed today, for our congregation has grown. To my right we have Steven Costas and his beautiful children Teddy and Amanda."

The congregation spoke as one, "Welcome."

"We also have guests - Jonathan Washington, a newspaper man and Nicole (he paused) Rosen."

The second response of welcome was more subdued. The people seated in the next pew over, stole glances at Nikki as though she had just stepped off a spaceship.

The reverend continued, "Mr. Washington and Miss Rosen were quite heroic yesterday, saving the lives of Steven, Teddy and Amanda. It is with both sadness and joy that we must note that Elizabeth Costas is now as one with the Lord. We regret that she was taken from us with her children still so close to the womb, but also celebrate that she has risen during this time of earthly travail and now lives with our Lord in Heaven."

There was a congregational Amen.

"There will be a service for Elizabeth this afternoon at one." He paused and gazed out upon his flock with a gentle smile. "I would like to open this morning's observance with an acknowledgement of our mission." He cast his eye about the room and settled on a pudgy nine-year-old boy. "Jerry Halverstrom, will you please step before the congregation and deliver the Church's word?"

The boy looked wide-eyed at the reverend and then turned to his parents who murmured encouraging words, his father prodding him to go up. The room was silent as the people waited for the dark-haired boy to stand and tentatively walk up to the altar. The reverend put his hand on the child's shoulder and turned him toward the audience. "Do not fear, Jerry. God will help guide your words."

The boy had brilliant blue eyes, and as he cast them upon Jon and Nikki he was momentarily struck dumb. The reverend leaned down and whispered into his ear. "We... We know," The boy remained dumbstruck, so the reverend whispered again "We...know that the...path..."

Jerry picked up the words, his high voice rising in tenor as he spoke. "The path of life is fraught with peril. That this particular existence is designed to offer us unlimited opportunities for both good and evil." He spoke with the cadence of automata, reciting by rote. "We also know that the Lord's promise of salvation doesn't rest on a tally of good deeds outweighing bad. There is no bank of deposits and withdrawals." The boy paused and thought, struggling to find the words. The reverend prompted, "Being...." Jerry blurted forth, "Being saved, being born again to serve Christ is about one thing, acknowledging that Jesus paid the..." The reverend whispered again, "Ultimate." Jerry burst out with the rest, "Ultimate penalty for our sins. He died and was risen so that we may live."

"That's right. Wonderful," said the reverend. "Now some would say that all that is required to join Him as a child of God is to acknowledged this sacrifice, ask for his forgiveness and he'll take you into his mighty heart."

The reverend paused and looked at Jon and Nikki to make sure that they were following. For both of them, it was like a spotlight had been shined on their faces.

The reverend put a firm hand on the boy's shoulder. "But that would be a mistake. Wouldn't it, Jerry?" The boy nodded, wincing at the pressure. "Who does God hate?"

Jerry responded with a full throated, "GAYS!"

"That's right. Who else?"

"JEWS!"

The reverend put a hand to his ear, "Uh huh, and?"

The congregation joined in. "FORNICATORS!"

"And?"

"MUSLIMS!"

"How about this vile country and its faggot-loving army? – May the devil enjoy feasting on their souls."

"YEAH!"

"God hates all of those who ignore his message."

There were shouts of Amen and Hallelujah.

Nikki turned to Jon, "Right. I'm outta here."

"Right behind you."

They stood and marched past the surprised congregants, avoiding eye contact as they went. A big man with red hair, who had been sitting in the rear, stood along with three others and followed as Jon and Nikki stepped out the door.

The big man's name was Ben Watson, and despite his girth, his movement was jackrabbit quick. He stepped outside and swiftly caught up. "Stop." Jon and Nikki turned and Nikki naturally fell into a defensive posture.

"Can't have you wanderin' where you like now, can we?"

"What the fuck is wrong with you people?" Nikki yelled, hoping that the people inside could hear her as well. "The world is going to shit and you teach children to preach that bullshit?" She took a step closer to Watson who flinched. The men around him readied themselves for violence. "I've gunned down fanatical scum like you and not given it another thought."

The reverend stepped through the door, followed by Katherine. "I think that's all the talk we'll have like that." He bored his dark eyes into Nikki's. "I remind you that you are a guest on this island."

"Screw you, you fucked up bigot."

Calder cocked his head as though he had been lightly slapped. He closed his eyes for a moment and inhaled deeply. "I invite you to return inside so that we may proceed."

"I don't think so, Buzz," said Jon.

"It's not a request Mr. Washington..."

"I know you." Jon seethed. "Media-loving whores who have one narcissistic goal – get on TV and piss people off."

The reverend gave an amused chuckle and with an impish look, invited Watson and the others to join in his mirth. "I don't know how you've come to that conclusion, Jon. You are the only media here, and I assure you that we have no intention to provoke you. This is just an ordinary day for us, the only provocation being right now. Now please step back inside or I will be forced to ask Mr. Watson to lock you back up."

"That's not happening," said Nikki, taking another heavy step forward. "And I will tear the throat out of the first fool to lay a hand on us."

They could hear the congregation chattering to each other inside now and then Steven Costas stepped outside with Teddy and Amanda in tow. "Everything alright here?"

Jon gently pulled Nikki back. "It's a big island. Give us our gear. We'll make ourselves scarce."

"That's really not an option," said Calder, who was wishing that it was. He didn't want to kill these people, but to protect his flock... "We have strict rules of concealment here. The risk is too high that you'll give us away."

Steven spoke again, "I have a suggestion. If I may, Reverend?"

Calder acknowledged him, silently offering the floor.

Steven tried to make his voice sound as optimistic as possible. "We let them stay here. In the village. They can work for the communal good. But for now, skip the services." He gave a nearly imperceptible wink to Jon and Nikki. "We can't exactly expect a newspaper man and a Jewish woman to accept the church's teachings in one day can we?"

Calder mulled this for a moment while glancing past Jon and Nikki at the storage shed/lock-up and then finally said,

"As a temporary solution, I can live with it. For a short while - until we can find a more permanent one."

Steven turned to Jon and Nikki, "Will that work for you? It's not like you can safely leave. You wouldn't make it a day out there now."

Jon gave Nikki a look indicating that the final choice was hers. She looked away, studying the morning sunlight as it twinkled across the lagoon, and finally nodded, "As a temporary solution."

Reverend Calder puffed up his broad chest and said, "I have a mass to complete. Katherine please escort Miss Rosen to the women's dorm. Mr. Watson will show Mr. Washington the men's. Mr. Watson, you will place a detail with each of our guests. They are not to be out of our sight for even a moment. Clear?"

"Very clear, Reverend."

Nikki said, "I sleep in my own tent. I did all of the communal living I could ever hate while I was a Marine, defending you and your right to spout vial bullshit."

"A Marine? Interesting. No, I'm afraid we couldn't allow you to sleep alone. It quite simply isn't fair or right for a single woman to be away from the safety of her sisters."

Nikki looked at Jon for support and then back to the reverend. "Um, I'm not sure you're getting me. I will not sleep in a dorm. This is not negotiable or temporary, capice?"

Jon interjected, "Uh, why don't we do this - Nikki can sleep in her own tent and so can I, but we'll set them up next to your dorms, women's and men's respectively?" Before the reverend could answer, Jon continued, "Do you really want your single, young parishioners bunking with us anyway?"

Calder seemed to appreciate this move in the game and nodded an acknowledgment at Jon. "You have a point." He looked at Nikki with fresh eyes. "For now, you have your own tents."

"Thank you, Mr. Calder," said Jon.

The reverend beamed a crocodile smile, "You will be expected to labor with the rest of us."

"Of course."

"And Mr. Washington…. It's Reverend Calder."

At mealtime, Jon and Nikki sat in the mess hall at their own table. The paneling was adorned with the same messages that screamed from the church walls, and they found themselves hunching over their food, the oppressiveness of the space pushing down on them. They received a lot of stares, particularly from the children, but no one offered conversation. That part was a relief. They put their heads close and used hushed tones.

Nikki said, "This isn't going to work."

"I know."

"I'm not saying that we get off this rock. I agree that we're dead if we do, but we've got to convince them to let us go to the East Side. Carve out our own camp. They're not using it. It's not like we'd make ourselves known."

"Obviously."

"I just can't be around this shit."

Jon glanced at the Costas' who were sitting with a group on the other side of the room. He could see the false niceties emanating from Steven's face as he nodded politely, listening to them speak. "I don't think the Costas' are ready to sign up for it either. Maybe we can talk to Steven, get him to convince Calder that the five of us should have our own spot."

A woman stood and spoke quietly to her husband and child. "It's our Christian duty, Robert. We have a responsibility to reach out to these people and save them from themselves." The husband frowned and stood as well, lifting his three-year-old daughter into his arms. The woman picked up their food trays and the three people stepped over to Nikki and Jon's table.

The woman asked, "May we join you?"

Jon said, "Um, of course."

"I'm Martha Brown. This is my husband Robert, our daughter Melissa."

The husband nodded a hello and Melissa buried her head in her dad's side.

"Jon Washington."

"Nikki."

Martha offered Nikki a smile that hid a bad taste in her mouth. Robert, his tongue working a thick Maine accent, asked, "So where're you two from, then?"

Jon said, "Well, neither one of us is really from anywhere. I'm a roving reporter, though I kept an apartment in Atlanta. Nikki's just discharged out of the Marines." He then filled the pregnant pause that followed. "So you're from Maine as well?"

Martha smiled, "Oh, yes. We all are. Same town pretty much. When the call to get out was given, the reverend rightly assumed that it would turn into a den of iniquity up north. We started laying out and provisioning the island back in January, just in case."

Her husband said, "Never thought the demons would get all the way up here. Good folk around here. Pretty far away from the cities, don't ya know?"

Jon said, "Well, the primary food supply went north. If you're a meat eater, you follow the meat."

Martha put her hand to her chest, "Oh my. I guess so."

Robert said, "Saw some video on television at the barber shop, before we came here. Cannibals they said."

"Robert," admonished his wife.

Melissa spoke up, "Mommy, what's cannobles?"

"It's just another word for the demon people, honey."

Nikki, unwilling to indulge these people's fantasies, put down her fork and looked at the pretty little girl, "They are people who have succumbed to a horrible disease. They still need to eat, but they don't know how to make food anymore so they…"

"Please don't." Martha interrupted. She turned to her husband and child. "I think maybe we're finished with dinner, hmm? Let's clean up and get into the kitchen. It's the Brown family's turn at KP duty." They stood and Martha turned back to Nikki and Jon, "May God bless you and find mercy on your poor souls."

Nikki and Jon had been assigned KP as well. When dinner was over, they found themselves washing a mountain of dishes with the Brown family. There was also a young couple, perhaps nineteen or twenty years old and suffering from hormonal fireworks. It was clear that they hadn't been married very long. At one point Nikki walked in on them kissing in the pantry. "Sorry," she said and started to turn around.

"Wait?" asked the boy. "Can I ask you a question?" Nikki stopped. "Are you really a Jew? 'Cause, uh, 'cause uh. Aren't you supposed to have horns?"

Nikki tried to keep her jaw from dropping. "You're serious aren't you? What's your name?"

"Ham Unger."

She smiled and shook her head. "Well, Ham Unger, they only come out on the full moon. If you like, on the next one, I'll show you."

Both of the young people seemed to grow pale.

Nikki chuckled to herself, "Let me offer you children some advice. Grow up fast or I promise that your incredible ignorance will get you killed."

Darkness over early summer Maine didn't arrive until late in the evening. The extra light let everyone get in a few hours of simple relaxation, either reading or playing games, but when the night did come, it was bedtime. The whole village turned in at once. Fires were doused, lanterns turned off. No point in advertising their presence, even if they were mostly hidden.

Reluctantly, Nikki said good night to Jon, giving his arm a squeeze. It was strange for them both. They hadn't had a night apart in the short time they'd known each other. They'd quickly grown used to each other's company.

After washing up at the men's communal bath, Jon nodded goodnights to various people as he was escorted to the male dorm. His tent was set up next to the larger more permanent tent that housed the single men. He didn't bother saying goodnight to his guards and crawled inside the shelter. He undressed and pulled the sleeping bag around him. The night quickly cooled down, and a damp chill moved in from the lake and he was grateful for Will Parker's cozy down sleeping bag. He thought of the brave man with the Red Sox cap and his horrible end. Then fell into his nightly loop of nightmares.

26 Mind Fuck

Cavanaugh hating fighting with his J-LIST gear on. Still, he took careful aim with his HK, and despite the ma deuce punching orange flame through the air above his head, he unshakingly brought down one Fiend after another with simple precision. The fifty-cal tracers looked like laser beams spraying through the ranks of the crazed humans and even with his night vision turned down to avoid flash burns on his eyes, he could make out the horrid sight of human bodies exploding into pieces with each bull's-eye.

Several of the Fiends were children and a part of Cavanaugh still cringed at their little bodies being mowed down without mercy. He had to remind himself that it *was* a mercy - then he saw the infants – "Oh shit," he said to no one in particular, "there's at least two females carrying babies." Then there was a buzzing, and his head started filling with imagery: sights and sounds of battle, grunts and screams and horrible smells. It got stronger and stronger so that he became completely disoriented and suddenly he could see his own Humvee in the distance - his peripheral vision was surrounded by running Fiends. Then Peabody, who was driving, yelled out, "What is that? What's going on?"

Andrews abruptly stopped firing the fifty-cal and the other soldiers held their hands to their heads, squeezing their eyes shut.

"Drive! Fucking back up!" Cavanaugh screamed at Peabody.

Peabody slammed the transmission in reverse and stepped on the gas. The Humvee fishtailed in a huge circle as Peabody randomly steered, barely able to concentrate. Then suddenly they were driving nearly sideways in an irrigation ditch. When Peabody corrected his steering in the wrong direction, the big truck flipped, tumbling over several times, crushing Andrews who had been standing up through the roof - The fifty-cal smashed to pieces. The truck flipped back onto its wheels and slammed to a wet halt in the swampy ditch. The four men left inside were battered and dazed. Cavanaugh shook Peabody who was unconscious, his head leaning against the wheel. Then he heard the approaching Fiends. The crazed assault on his senses was gone for the moment and he had the presence of mind to tap his mic, "Squad one under full assau…" - Suddenly he was yanked through the open door by two of the beasts. The creatures snarled and ripped at his clothes, and then just as suddenly stopped. They fell away from him, shaking into convulsions. More Fiends climbed over their comrades and grabbed him, slobbering teeth gnashing, trying to get a lock on him, and then they spit, as if trying to get a horrible taste out of their mouths and within seconds they also fell away, shaking and vomiting – Of course! His hazmat suit was still covered with sticky bits of Novichok. In the Ranger's haste to clean the Chinooks, Squad One had given little thought to the contamination on their suits. The other soldiers were experiencing the same thing: The Deadheads that touched them were twisting in agony, vomiting and dying. Cavanaugh had never really taken in how lethal the stuff really was and he looked at his arms in amazement.

Watching their brothers and sisters die horrific deaths, seemed to give the infected pause and they backed up, still circling the Humvee but aware that somehow it was killing them if they got too close.

The sound of the Chinook spinning up, floated across the field. O'Shea had been calling repeatedly over the radio and only now had Cavanaugh realized it. He turned to Gomez who was seated behind Peabody who was groggily coming to, "Pull him back there with you. And jump behind the wheel." He clicked his mic, "We're okay, Cap." He saw the machine gunner's crumpled body lying face down in the water. "Strike that. We lost Andrews." Several infected had tried to bury their teeth in the dead man's body and had died the same horrible way as the others. A huge Fiend armed with a machete held its arms up in the air and the infected fell silent. Then almost as one, the Fiends parted to reveal three small children, toddlers really – but not – instead they looked like imps from Cavanaugh's worst nightmares – huge intelligent eyes. They stood on long steady legs; the legs of a predator, feline, but also goat like - and they stared at him.

O'Shea's voice barked over the radio, "I'm not hearing anymore shooting. Status?"

"Shit," said Cavanaugh to himself. He unholstered his pistol and – in a blink, his sense of place and purpose was wiped free. One of the imps leaped forward like a monkey, hopping back and forth amongst the Fiends to finally land in the open arms of the machete holder. It smiled a row a shark sharp teeth and moved steadily up and down with excitement. The other soldiers in the Humvee started moaning in delirious fright. Cavanaugh mindlessly stepped back inside the truck, sat down, and pulled a grenade off the webbing on his chest. The men could see what he was doing but were powerless to stop it. Cavanaugh's hand shook while one part of his mind fought for some control, his teeth gritted, a groan of frustration pouring from his lips. He struggled for a moment longer and then lost the battle – his finger pulled the pin. The Fiends backed away and watched without passion as the truck exploded.

With the rest of the infected following, the machete wielder set the young imp down and started charging for the farm again.

Back at the farm, O'Shea and Bullock watched in dismay as Cavanaugh's Humvee burst into a fireball. Bullock yelled out, "Okay, that's it. Everyone onboard."

Tran was the last one out of the lab. He ran to the Chinook with two Pelican cases full of gear. Jones was strapping himself in behind his window-mounted mini-gun and nodded at him as he ran up the loading ramp. The rotor blades were at full power and the prop wash raised a huge cloud of dust and bits of straw around them.

Bullock turned to O'Shea, "Had to turn on the lights." He and O'Shea glanced at Susan who was yelling at Aaron about something. Then she ran back off the helicopter.

"Where the hell is she going?" O'Shea unbuckled his harness. Tran got up to follow Susan. "Sit down, Mr. Tran!"

Tran sat as O'Shea jumped off the helicopter. Susan ran as fast as she could toward the big Victorian. "Ms. Chancellor, get back on the helicopter! Susan!"

"The notes, all the notes!" She yelled back and kept running.

"Jesus fucking Christ!" O'Shea looked to his left – the damn things were getting close. He realized that his only weapon was his sidearm.

As Susan ran inside the house, Quentin O'Shea had to decide for the umpteenth time in his career whether or not to be a hero. Fifty yards away, the first of the Deadheads came around a building. In the back of his mind he noted how thin they looked. Starvation was setting in. He'd file that away for his action report. They saw him and started to run faster. He screamed at the house, "Susan, get out now! It's too late! Get out!"

Just then she opened a window on the second floor and yelled, "Catch!" She tossed her laptop computer down to him and he caught it. "Save us, Quentin. Save us all. Run!"

O'Shea pulled his sidearm and was startled when the Fiends closest to him were shot to pieces. Jones had opened up with the Chinook's mini-gun. He hesitated another moment.

"Run!" she yelled, before ducking back inside.

He looked at the laptop, then at the charging Fiends and ran. He ran in a way he hadn't run since he was a little boy, charging up the stairs from his family's dark basement, the open slats in the steps just perfect for clawed fingers to reach through and pull him back down into the dampness. He didn't feel his feet touch the ground as he dashed for the Chinook, twisting his arm around over his head, indicating that Axelman should lift off. He dove for the ramp just as the machine broke with the earth and was pulled inside by Copper and Bullock.

When the bird was fifty feet in the air it turned lazily toward the farmhouse. They could see that the house was surrounded. Fiends smashed in the windows and poured through the door. Suddenly a second floor window opened above the porch roof and Susan climbed out slamming the window behind her. She deftly climbed up to the next level of roof just as a Fiend crashed through the glass. Jones lit up the porch roof with the mini. Empty brass casings rained down on the Fiends below as the monsters reached up in futility for the hovering feast.

Axelman's voice came over the helicopters internal speakers, "We are saving that woman. Recovery team, lower the hoist."

Copper and Jacobus quickly unhitched and deployed the cable hoist harness. Jones kept a withering fire onto the porch roof, ultimately demolishing it, but also lighting the house on fire. The old Victorian had multiple steep roofs. Susan had climbed to the highest peak she could scramble to. She stood on a gutter and hugged the shingles.

Copper threw the harness on as quickly as he could, latched himself to the hoist and gave Jacobus the thumbs down as he leaned out the door.

Axelman lowered the huge helicopter as low as he dared, not wanting to blow Susan off the roof.

The wash from the blades acted like a bellows on the flames and the house was being quickly engulfed. As Susan was buffeted by the wind and nearly knocked from the rooftop, the scientist in her couldn't stop observing her environment. To her astonishment, she watched two infected assault a wounded one, biting off small chunks of the injured one's arms. As far as she knew, no one had observed a fully infected person feast on another. Perhaps if the things were starving, then anything edible was up for grabs. As she considered the ramifications of that notion she was suddenly startled by a small child climbing, no, hopping up onto the roof with her. Though devoutly atheistic, Susan said a small prayer before the tiny devil entered her mind and filled it with horror. For seconds that seemed like minutes, she shared her consciousness with what could only be described as pure evil. Somewhere inside the labyrinth that was her gray matter, in the place she kept her consciousness, she was aware of her heart seizing up. Just as suddenly it all stopped, like a black pillowcase being ripped off her head. Loud explosions from a pistol fired near her ear. She looked up to find Copper dangling in front of her. At the same moment two particularly tenacious Fiends leapt onto the roof with them. "Jump, lady! Jump!"

Susan jumped into Copper's spread eagle arms and legs and he wrapped them around her while throwing a kick into the face of the nearest ghoul. The creature's head snapped back, clearing a sightline for Copper to make eye contact with the Fiend behind it. What he saw gave him gooseflesh. The thing was huge. Drool poured from its mouth as it gnashed its filthy teeth.

The Fiend smiled thinking, *I will hack it and reach inside it and gleefully watch it scream and die.*

The eye contact was broken as the Chinook banked away, the hoist starting to rise just in time to deny the monster a machete full of Copper's thigh.

Copper snapped out of his reverie and realized that he was crushing Susan to him. "Jesus, lady. You are one bandong, loco, crazy-ass lady, lady. I told you about the babies. Now you know."

Susan smiled weakly, her freshly restarted heart doing its best to pound a hole through her chest. Her sense of smell was in high gear and she breathed in the delicious aroma of the Ranger's healthy sweat. In another few seconds they were pulled back inside.

Aaron Burnbaum screamed at her with tears brimming his eyes, "I had backed it all up! It was all backed up, you fucking woman!"

"What?" Susan gasped.

He opened a briefcase, which cradled two portable hard drives, "I tried to tell you it was all in here, but you ran out the door!"

"Well, shit," was all that Susan could say.

27 River Battle

In the morning, Jon & Nikki drank their coffee alone in the canteen while a soaring hymn ended the early service. When they stepped outside they were joined by Steven Costas who walked with a brick of a man wearing overalls. He wore a wide brimmed hat over grey streaked black curly hair and sported a huge bushy black beard. "Mornin'. Name's Alan Garber. I'll be escorting you to the fields to report for crop management. Mr. Costas, as I was saying, you have my condolences for your loss. A little work in the fields will do you good."

They were led along a path that worked its way into the interior of the island and found themselves falling in with other parishioners heading in the same direction. Jon and Nikki's re-acquaintance after just one night apart was making them feel oddly self-conscious. As the path narrowed, they're hands brushed once and they awkwardly held themselves apart so it wouldn't happen again. Jon was surprised at both of them and decided that they must be suffering from some kind of juvenile-lust-itis. He chuckled out loud.

"What?" she asked under her breath.

"Nothing."

They fell back a bit from Garber and Steven quietly asked them, "How you two holding up?"

Jon whispered, "We need to persuade them to let us settle on the East Side."

Nikki said, "What about you? You can't want your kids to stay exposed to..."

A tall woman strode past them carrying a compound hunting bow. She had a quiver of arrows strapped across her back. When she was past, Steven said, "We've been through this kind of thing before. Their mom and I have home-schooled them from the start. We'll get along."

Jon said, "Still, we've been thinking that maybe you should join us."

"They're not going to let us do that."

Nikki whispered harshly, "They're going to have to let us do that. I'm not going to give them the option."

Several people turned. Garber said, "There a problem?"

"No problem," said Jon. "Just a rough night of sleep."

Big Ben Watson suddenly hurried past them and caught up to the tall woman with the bow. He stopped her and whispered into her ear. She clutched her bow tighter, turned around and jogged back the way she'd come. Watson then walked back toward Nikki and Jon. "Alan, I need to talk with Miss Rosen."

"Suit yourself, Ben. Want me to wait?"

"Nope. Go ahead. Minor security thing is all."

Jon stood fast next to Nikki. Steven hesitated, and then continued to fall in with Garber. Watson looked at Jon. "Go ahead, Mr. Washington, follow Mr. Garber. This regards Miss Rosen's military knowledge."

Nikki grabbed Jon's arm. "No, he's practically as well schooled in this war as I am. What's your situation?"

Watson gave her a frustrated scowl and then led them slightly off the path. "We have a small situation and could use a professional military opinion."

"Okay."

"If you'd follow me."

They double-timed it to catch up with Lukei, whose six-foot tall frame gave her a long stride. They passed back through the main village - The Lord's Village, as a small sign stated - and then worked their way out to the fortified edge of the island where sharpened stakes protected the shore.

As the forest thinned, they crawled out to a sentry's blind. This morning's lookout was Ham Unger, the young man who believed in horns. He nodded a greeting, gave Nikki a double-take, and then pointed to the opposite shore.

Standing amongst the reeds, hip deep at the edge of the river, were two female Fiends, one of them holding a baby. They were identical twins, perhaps thirty years old, tall and skinny. Their clothes were rags, their skin covered in thick grime. They were sniffing at the air, breathing in big lungfuls of it. The baby's head was tucked into the shoulder of the one who carried it.

Watching this, the people in the blind realized that they could all smell the aroma of cooking food on the air.

Nikki asked Ham, "I assume they haven't seen you."

"No, ma'am."

"Have you spotted any others?"

"No, ma'am."

"How long have they been there?"

"About fifteen-minutes. I seen 'em come out of the woods. Just kept walkin' closer, sniffing the air. The baby looks like its alive. They hadn't et it or nothin'."

Ben asked, "So do we let Lukei try to kill them?"

Nikki looked at Lukei, "Even if you get a heart shot on one, the other will give out a call to hunt. If there are any others in earshot... What kind of shot are you?"

"Almost never miss, if I'm standing. Not sure about crouched in this blind."

Ben said, "Should we wait? Hope they walk away?"

Ham asked, "What about the baby?"

Jon said, "The baby could only be infected too. They won't walk away. The damn things are single minded. They know there's food on the island. They probably won't leave until something else distracts them."

Nikki said, "If we ignore them, others may see them, come over here and smell our camp as well."

Ben said, "So we let Lukei take the shot?"

She looked at Lukei. "I don't think we can take the chance."

Jon said, "We distract them. Take a boat up the river here. Get them to follow us down the shore in the opposite direction. When we're far enough away, we close in and shoot."

Ben said, "That's good, but it might be quicker to just row out and shoot them right there."

Nikki smiled, "Guys, either of those solutions gets the things screaming the alarm before we ever get near it."

"So what's your idea?"

"I get close and kill them as quickly and silently as I can. We go up shore and tie a rope around my waist. I float down while swimming to the opposite side. They won't see me until I come around that bend and by then it's too late. I draw them out into the water a bit, stand up and club them to death. After that, you can reel me back over to this side."

"That's nuts," said Jon.

"It's a classic assault. The art of surprise. It's exactly the kind of thing I might have done in Africa."

"It's still nuts."

None of them spoke about what to do with the infant.

They stood upriver, on the North Side of the island at the edge of the sharpened stick defense. Nikki was ready to go. She was armed with a heavy hand-carved club and Ben's hunting knife. She had stripped down to her wifebeater-T and had taken off her combat boots. A length of nylon rope was tied around her waist. She had asked for some Vaseline and greased down exposed skin to ward off the chill in the water; no sense in getting to the other side just to have her muscles freeze up. Also, her skin would be slippery and hard to grab onto.

Jon paced nervously behind her as Ben coiled the rope again after giving it one wrap around a thin tree trunk to get some leverage when it was time to pull her back across.

Jon said, "I should do this. Believe it or not, I've already done it - fought in the water while holding a club and a knife. It's hard."

She smiled at him warmly.

He smiled back weakly and said, "I'm serious."

Ignoring him, Nikki began to climb over the smooth slippery stones that made up the shore on their side. Jon whispered loudly at her, "They let female Marines do commando work?"

Nikki kept walking and the swift current pressed against her legs. "Actually, the Force Recon guys do most of the commando work. No females yet. But Marines are all commandos in once sense or another." She launched herself into the water and was quickly swept downstream.

Ben played out the line as fast as he could while Nikki swam with all her might.

Jon watched slack jawed as she disappeared around the bend. Then he turned and ran along the forested path that led back to the blind.

Nikki was surprised at how cold the water was; it was shocking and her breath came in short gasps. The speed of the river was also greater than she'd anticipated and her muscles became quickly fatigued. To make matters worse, Jon was right; swimming with a club and knife was goddamn hard.

She was coming up on the spot where the Fiends stood and she knew she wasn't going to make it. In another moment she would pass the things, dangling in the wide open, bait on a hook.

She dropped the club to swim harder, passed the reeds that had blocked her from view, then swore at herself as the monsters caught sight of her and began to moan. Then the baby looked up – what the...? She made eye contact with it

– huge black irises, pointy ears. Its mouth gaped open, displaying a line of razor sharp teeth – like a smiling piranha. Nikki's head filled with the image of herself struggling in the water. She could smell strong body odor and her stomach contracted as though from intense hunger. Then her mouth filled with saliva. It was utterly disorienting. Suddenly, she was jerked to a stop as the line played out to its end. The river water poured over her head, temporarily taking her out of the baby's eyesight. Her head cleared, but she had to fight to stay on the surface.

Up river, Ben cringed at his bright red palms. The rope had shot through his grasp and burned until the line snapped taught. He couldn't see Nikki, but he could tell things had gone wrong. The knot on the tree trunk held, but it also tightened and was not going to come loose by hand. He cursed as he felt for his knife and then remembered that Nikki had it. The weight on the rope was too great and he couldn't pull her back alone. Where the heck had Washington gone?

The infant Fiend looked at the struggling thing in the water and felt its mouth flush with saliva. It was already old enough to put together that dinner was dangling right there in the water. *Finally!* Thought the sister holding the infant. She was beginning to doubt the skills of the baby, when *finally it steered it toward this place and its smells and then like a gift, a Fresh One was delivered right in front of it. Now it had to just get to it. The wet was bad. The wet sucked Others down.* Hunger won over the remote spec of rationality left in the demented humans and they began to call out with hungry glee, wading out further into the river. The infant, no more than a month old, struggled; its fear of water causing it to reach back for the land.

Nikki found herself staring at them from only fifteen feet away. She could see drool pouring out of the closer one's ravenous mouth while it contemplated launching itself at her. Then she made eye contact with the baby again and her mind exploded with visions of horror, dread and fear. She was utterly incapacitated; the water gushed over her face, freeing her once more from the mental invasion.

The Fiends had enough wits to judge the current and figure out that they would be swept downstream before they could get to her so they waded their way up the shore a bit. That's when Jon came crashing into the blind, scanning the water and seeing Nikki's predicament.

He yelled, "Nikki, cut the rope!" The baby looked right at him – "What?" It was in his head. The baby was in his head, and suddenly he felt compelled to swim toward the Fiends, offer himself up as a meal. It was an overwhelming sensation. Unable to control his body, he stepped through the branches of the blind and he started to wade out.

Nikki was struggling under the strain of swimming against the pull of the rope and the rush of the water. The Fiends screamed with heated excitement - a fat meal so close. Suddenly, one was silenced as an arrow pierced its neck. Lukei had stood up and aimed her arrow true. The stricken creature fell into the water and was swept away. A second arrow pierced the shoulder of the baby carrier. The Fiend clutched itself, gasping, instinctively grabbing the arrow and breaking the shaft off at the point of entry. Then it lost its footing, falling into the river, dashing the infant's skull across a semi-submersed boulder.

Jon's head was instantly cleared. He watched the monster get carried toward Nikki and he yelled up river, "Cut the rope, Ben. She's gonna drown. Cut it!"

Ben had been doing just that with the sharpened edge of a rock. The nylon was tough and he groaned inwardly with anxiety after hearing Jon's distress; worse was the scream of the demon. He hacked furiously at where the rope wrapped around the tree and it finally snapped. Then Ben watched in frustration as the still tied knot snagged on a partially submerged tree branch in the middle of the river.

As the Fiend was about to float past Nikki, it reached out with a clawed hand and latched on to the rope while the other still held onto the dead infant. With bloody receding gums surrounding crooked yellow teeth, it smiled with ferocious triumph. Its eyes cast about her neck and shoulders, choosing the best place to bite. Then it said it out loud, *"Fresh!"*

Nikki faintly registered her bladder involuntarily releasing and the water momentarily becoming warm around her crotch and waist. Had the thing just spoken? She yelled out a battle cry and jammed her knife directly into one of the creature's bloodshot infected eyes.

Though the Fiend was instantly killed, its clenched fist tightened even harder around the rope in a death-bound reflex.

Nikki tried to pull the knife back out, but it was firmly lodged in the skull and to her horror, the current forced the dead Fiend to bump into her while it bled. She kept her head turned away and kicked with growing fatigue to stay above it all, but it was a losing battle. She was going to drown or swallow infected blood. The knot around her waist wasn't going to come loose and she needed her arms to keep her head above water.

"Oh God. Oh Fuck. You've got to be kidding me." She gasped. The infant bobbed up directly in front of her face, unconscious, but with a beating heart squirting blood out of a deep gash on its skull. Nikki tasted iron as she heaved back from the big sightless eyes, the small pointed teeth.

Then suddenly Jon was there. He had swum out with Lukei's knife in hand. He grabbed the rope next to Nikki's torso and sliced it clean, leaving the dead Fiend to continue to hold the snagged line within its death grip. The infant submerged once more, not to be seen.

As Jon and Nikki floated away, they looked into each other's eyes and gave each other a fierce hug.

Jon said, "Don't do that again."

She repeatedly spat an iron and coppery taste from her mouth. "That one spoke. It said, Fresh. I heard it. The baby. Did you see it? It wasn't human. It was in my head."

"Mine too. Just like a soldier told me it was."

As they slowly floated away, they both glanced back toward the island. Lukei, Ben and Ham were pushing a canoe into the water, Ben sitting down with the paddle, being pushed out of the shallows. Finally Jon said, "I know what you're thinking, but we've got nothing and we're surrounded by infected. We wouldn't stand a chance. We have to go back."

With reluctance, they turned and swam against the current.

28 The Vineyard

After several hours over open water, which included a carrier-based mid-flight refueling, the surviving members of Operation Henhouse had found themselves off the coast of Norfolk Virginia, relieved to land on the USS Iwo Jima. The Navy carrier was on a reconnaissance mission, probing the Southern states to determine the number of infected along the Atlantic coast. The scientists and Army Rangers got hot showers, hot food and a good night's rest. Though the information and samples that they were carrying were critical to the survival of their species, their species needed sleep in order to continue to function.

The following morning, after another hot meal, they were sent to once again board their Chinook. As the team was guided across the busy flight deck, they noted that the big ship had moved to within a few thousand yards of the city/naval base. It was just another example of the bedlam that had ruined the richest nation on Earth. From the vantage point of the Iwo's flight deck, nothing but blackened wreckage greeted the eye. But for a few foraging infected, the streets were nearly deserted. Then they saw movement along the docks of the shipyard. Gunshots echoed out from the shore.

"Good God, will you look at that?" barked Decker.

Thirty or more people were running toward the end of a pier. A huge mob of infected was hot on their heals.

A voice spoke over the Iwo's loud speakers, "Condition three, condition three. Boats away, boats away."

A moment later, two of the carrier's big tenders could be spotted on the water, moving out from under the blind spot caused by the flight deck. They were racing for the pier. The survivors had a good head start and a cheer erupted across the big ship as the sailors watched them dive off the end, swimming with everything they had.

The scientists found themselves gawking and cheering as well. Susan, in particular, screamed at the top of her lungs, "Come on! Swim! Swim, you people!"

When it looked like the last healthy person had jumped, the air was filled with what sounded like a giant sewing machine - The ship's Phalanx system Gatling gun blazed a hot trail of tracers toward the pier. The structure and the infected on it appeared to disintegrate under the hail of 20mm high-explosive incendiaries.

Despite the show, there was no time for dilly dallying. O'Shea yelled for everyone to board the Chinook.

As a playground for the politically well connected, the Vineyard had been one of the first places in the US to be secured against infection. Travel to the island was strictly controlled and only residents and their invited guests were allowed to stay. As a matter of practicality, the island could only sustain a certain number of people. Worldwide, food commerce and distribution was at a standstill. On the small island, most arable land had been quickly converted to agricultural purposes. The fishing fleet had become the lifeblood of the island during the dark hours of February, March and early April, when food could not be grown in the hard winter soil. In addition to the harbor at Edgartown, the municipal airport had been taken over by the Navy; the Seabees extending the runways to accept even the largest of aircraft.

The inhabitants shared the island with a brigade of Marines. Except for the few who had convinced themselves that they were above all of this, the comforts that the military brought in terms of supplies and strong backs were gladly accepted. When money had become worthless, even the doubting holdouts stepped up to the plate, converting their expansive lawns into furrowed rows for assorted crops. Given the chaos that reigned on the mainland, the island was a happy and well-organized place. The residents of their sister island of Nantucket were not so lucky: The contagion had taken hold over there when a boatload of infected had drifted ashore. Only hungry Fiends roamed its picturesque beaches and cobblestoned streets – but that was about to change. For the Marines on Martha's Vineyard, Nantucket would be a test case for the invasion of Connecticut and Rhode Island.

As the Chinook carrying the Rangers and scientists made its approach for landing, they watched a very busy island preparing for the first step in the re-taking of America. In the distance to their right, they could make out the hazy shape of what was once the whaling capital of the United States. Axelman spoke over the PA system, "Brace yourselves, everyone. I asked them to let us land first, but the Navy has its schedule. Please shield your eyes from the right hand side of the aircraft." The occupants did as instructed and then a bright flash, bright as a noonday sun filled the windows of the helicopter. After waiting for a moment, they turned to look outside as a mushroom cloud rose up over Nantucket in all its horrid splendor.

"Brace, brace, brace!"

The shockwave hit the helicopter and it tilted to its left as though pushed sideways by a gentle god. Both Axelman and Frick held tight to the controls and wrestled the machine back on course.

"Once again neutron bombs are being dropped on America," said Susan with shaken nerves.

"Good riddance," said Decker, nodding toward the afterglow, which still lit up the small island.

O'Shea rubbed his palms together, "In a couple of days the Marines will do a full beach assault over there. Mop up any irradiated stragglers."

Upon landing, the scientists were brought to a teleconferencing room where a large screen was lit up with the image of the Director of the CDC, Barbara Louis-Gelding. Discarding any niceties, she got right to the point. "Tell me you've found it."

Susan stood at the front of her team. "We believe so, Director. The farm was, in reality, a huge R&D lab. We only had a short time, but a preliminary DNA sequencing seems to be a match. There's a lot to isolating this thing. A vaccine..." Her voice trailed off and her head filled with the vision of a mind-grabbing imp hopping across a rooftop.

"Well, that's something," said Gelding, filling the sudden silence. "I'm sorry to say that there's been another outbreak, just north of Ottawa. Another town has been burned. The healthy population up here is in near riot. Even if the military can pull off their re-invasion, it will mean nothing if there are continued outbreaks behind our lines. There's no time for rest. You and your team will begin work there right away. Though we are still in the throws of yet another move, you should have the equipment you need to begin. In short order, all of resources of our country's joint disease control operations will be at your disposal. The moment we are resettled, we will send for you. In the meantime, you'll of course do your very best."

"Ma'am, there's more to it. They seem to be breeding."

"Excuse me?"

Susan's colleagues looked at her with curious glances.

"Some kind of mutation. I don't know. I saw... felt it too. One of the Rangers did also. Two different places. Fort Jackson and in Florida."

"I'm not sure I understand," said the director.

"Neither do I. There was something human... but not human down there. They...They're having babies.... Some kind of rapid evolution. They have the ability to get inside your head – I mean like ESP. It sounds crazy and it's hard to explain, and I don't have any proof, but a Ranger named Copigliani can confirm it."

Gelding paused in thought. She let a whole minute go by and finally said, "Our plate is overflowing. We need to keep our eye on what we know and what we have. We have samples and data collected by you. Focus on that."

"Yes, ma'am."

"Good. And Susan? You and your team get some sleep. I know you've been through hell."

The video chat ended. Susan turned to her team. "You heard the lady."

They did their best to ignore the twist that Susan had thrown in. They confirmed without a doubt that the FND-z bacterium had been originated at Happyland Farms, but the nasty little bug resisted all efforts to break its defenses. For now, until they could really drill down on it, it appeared that the thing was going to keep mutating, defeating their every step. Seven frustrating days later, the call came for them to pack up for Quebec. They were escorted to the airfield where a Black Hawk helicopter waited. This time there would be no Rangers. The dirty work was done. The special ops soldiers needed to be coordinated into the land assault.

Meanwhile, at several airfields across Eastern Canada a different set of aircraft were being refueled and loaded for the continued assault on New England. The ordinance was mixed: neutron bombs for the major cities, chemical weapons for the towns. Rural areas were being saturated with incendiaries with the hope of starting massive firestorms. Three days earlier, conventional bombs were used to wipe out the last bridges across the Hudson - from the Saint Lawrence River, past Lake Champlain, and all the way down to Manhattan, millions of infected had entered the kill zone.

There were some who protested. Burning the forests of New England meant killing countless defenseless animals. Their opinion was noted and ignored.

29 Dirty Water

Nikki and Jon found it ironic that while they were once again in quarantine they were allowed to sleep in the same structure together. When it was time to turn in, he started to pull the mattresses off the cots to put them on the floor next to each other.

Nikki said, "No. I don't think that's a good idea. If I'm infected, I can't be breathing on you."

"It's not contagious like that until much later. After the fever breaks."

"Jon," she admonished. "We're sleeping on separate beds."

He shrugged an agreement and pushed his cot mattress back into place.

They both lay down and stared at the dark void above them. The single candle that they had been allotted provided enough light to eat by, but they had blown it out to conserve it for the next day or however many days they would be stuck in this room. Now it was pitch black, so dark as to be disorienting and Jon found himself feeling a sensation like he was floating. He decided to enjoy it and let it envelope his sore, tired, body. It was sort of like laying down on a gliding magic carpet and he imagined himself floating across a desert on a cool star-filled night, billions of light pricks shining through the void. As he let his mind drift with the pleasure of it, he was pulled back to the present as Nikki's breathing changed to a soft, almost, snore. It did occur to him that if Nikki had become infected that she might turn in the night. That she might roll over, leap off her bed and bite a chunk out of him. To his surprise, between his exhaustion and his growing affection for this brave woman, he didn't seem to care.

Some time later, he awoke from a half sleep to the sound of Nikki finishing using the toilet (a bucket hidden behind a simple sheet curtain). She returned to her cot, her feet shuffling so as not to stub a toe, and climbed back under the blankets with a sigh.

He said, "Hey. You okay?"

"I woke you. Sorry."

"No. I was awake. Sleep's not much fun if nightmares are your escape from nightmares. How're you feelin'?"

"You mean, do I feel ill? Certain loss of faculties? Building unreasonable anger?"

"Something like that."

"I feel fine. Just sore - bone sore. Maybe a bit of a scratchy throat but, I'm hoarse from all that yelling."

"Hmm. We're not out of the woods yet."

"No, but I think we're okay. I think I would know."

"Nobody knows until it's too late."

"I think I know. Try to go back to sleep."

"Okay. You too."

When Jon awoke again, the dim light of dawn penetrated through the thin lines in the building's siding. Nikki was awake. She was still lying on her cot and she quietly coughed into her blanket. He sat up and looked at her. Her back was turned to him and he could hear a wheeze in her breathing. He instinctively looked around for some kind of defensive weapon and then cursed under his breath, noting that any weapon in quarantine was of course prohibited.

Nikki turned over upon hearing the curse, and their eyes met. Hers were bloodshot and her face with flush with fever. She coughed again, then said, "Good morning."

"How long have you been like this?"

"Couple hours maybe. I still think I'm just fine though. I would have woken you if I felt worse."

"You have a fever."

"How do you know that?"

"Your face is flush with it."

"Shit. And.... I'm really thirsty..."

Jon poured her some water from a pitcher that sat by the door for easy refilling. She accepted the steel cup and drank deeply.

They were both silent for a while. Finally, Nikki said, "If it looks like I'm going over to the dark side, you have my permission to smother me with a pillow. In the meantime we better request some rope so you can tie me to this cot."

With the addition of Amanda and Teddy Costas, there were seven children under the age of 12 on the island. Though they had their fair share of chores as well as daily schooling, they were also given a certain amount of free time to simply play and be kids. The only rule was that they were to remain on the paths of the interior portions of the island. They were not to play along the shore and risk being seen. The Western shore was completely off limits. Voices were to be kept low as sound carries well over water. If a child became too loud, there would be no playtime for a week. This punishment seemed to keep the danger in check.

The whole island was a potential playground, but the kids had found a favorite spot in a small spring-fed inlet, set well away from the shore. It was covered by thick-leaved trees and surrounded by low shrubbery, which made for natural cover. For the kids, the bushes stood in for a fort, a cave or any other structure that their imaginations decided upon that day. The inlet also had the added bonus of being a nesting spot for a huge flock of songbirds. The kids spent hours watching these gentle creatures building nests and going through mating rituals. Much of the material for the nests seemed to come from the feathers of other birds. It was particularly exciting to see them in aerial combat, fighting to steal each other's found feathers.

On the morning that Nikki was tied down and sweating on her cot, nine-year-old Jerry Halverstrom was cupping water from the inlet to quench his thirst. All of the kids were flush from a vigorous game of tag but chose to drink from the two canteens that they had brought with them. Jerry didn't like sharing a canteen. He was horribly afraid of germs.

Teddy Costas shook his head at the kid, "Halverstrom, you have to drink the disinfected water. There could be parasites here."

Jerry ignored this contradiction in his phobia, stating, "I've been drinking from this lake since I was a little boy. My dad does too. Look, it's as clear as melted ice. You can see all the rocks and leaves several feet down, even little fishes." Just then a bird dropping landed in the water nearby and made a small splash. The children squealed with laughter and then choked themselves off at the sudden burst of noise.

Teddy said, "So you like drinking bird shit."

There was a gasp from the other kids at the use of such a powerful word. Sally Jenkins, the group tattle-tale piped in, "Teddy Costas, you said a bad word. I'm telling Ms. Katherine so you don't go to hell."

"You say anything to Ms. Katherine and *you'll* be swimming in bird shit."

The children gasped again and Sally nearly burst into tears.

Amanda Costas stepped in, "Teddy, you better say you're sorry."

"Why?"

"Say you're sorry or *I'll* tell Ms. Katherine."

"What's the big deal? The world is going to *shit* and you stupid jerks are worried about a word that means poop?"

The children were stunned into silence. Jerry Halverstrom burst out in a nervous giggle. These same children who had been taught to yell out "God hates Faggots" at various street rallies, felt themselves feeling profound collective embarrassment.

Teddy turned back to Jerry, "Don't drink the water, you dumb fat jackass. You're going to make yourself sick."

Some of the kids laughed at this, others remained in silence. They were both nervous and amazed at how bold Teddy was. Nobody in the whole congregation ever spoke like that.

With the situation getting personal, Jerry stood up in anger. "Who you calling fat, Mr. Skinny Chicken Legs?"

"I'm just saying we boil our water for a reason. You want to get sick, drink up."

By nightfall Nikki was sweating in a deep fever. Jon had done his best to tie the rope so that it wouldn't chafe her wrists or ankles, but in her fitful sleep, with her body twisting in delirious pain, the bindings inevitably abraded her skin.

Hannah, the congregation's nurse, had passed Jon a bottle of aspirin and some of the congregation's precious stash of antibiotics. She had approached the door dressed in a makeshift trash-bag-surgical gown and mask, which was burned as soon as she had completed her mission. There was little to do but wait.

For the time being, Jon was able to convince the congregation not to burn down the shed with him and Nikki in it. He had little doubt that if she succumbed, the two of them would be roasted alive.

The antibiotics would have no effect if the infection was Cain's, but if it was anything else, the community felt it owed it to Nikki to volunteer its minor stock of pills. Jon watched with growing apprehension as her delirium increased. She barked out nonsensical sentences and shuddered and shivered with a kind of pain that the aspirin seemed to have no effect on. He continually flashed on his grandmother's fevered hours and her final change when she became suddenly aware again, her eyes sharply focused with that wolfish grin crossing her face. He desperately didn't want to see that face appear on Nikki's lovely visage. In Jon's eyes, even in her sweaty, grimy, fever, Nikki was beautiful. The flush in her cheeks only added to the allure; at least until his gaze rested on her mouth. Her lips were gray and cracked from dehydration. She could no longer hold a cup to drink so he soaked a washcloth in fresh water and squeezed what he could onto her tongue, trying not to choke her. It was in those moments, when she responded to the water, swallowing and opening her mouth for more, that Jon was reassured. For now she was still with him and he could put aside thoughts of having to smother her with a pillow held firmly on her face.

As the night wore on, Nikki had moments of peaceful rest and Jon would find himself nodding off as well, only to awaken again when she made a soft whimper or moan. For too long now, he had held up, been brave and strong in the face of danger, sympathetic but merciless in his complicity with mass euthanasia, remaining nonplused in moments of sheer tragedy, and faithfully reporting it all so that the world might know. Now, in this moment of relative tranquility, on an island inhabited by yet another group of delusional people, he broke down. He curled into a fetal position on the thin cot mattress and let a flood of pent up tears soak into his pillow. He cried with a silent open mouth, the strain of it cramping his neck and shoulders. Then he sobbed so hard that he exhausted himself, and in his exhaustion he fell asleep - a deep and trouble-free sleep where there were neither nightmares nor night sweats or any dreams at all. He slept as though in a coma, forgetting about his disease-riddled friend, lying tied to a cot only a few feet away.

When he woke, dawn filtered through the cracks, casting the room in gray dim light. At first he was confused by his surroundings, not recognizing this world, and then it all flooded back and he closed his eyes with disappointment. He could hear Nikki breathing softly and he gazed over at the cot. She was laying still, just the rise and fall of her chest to indicate life. His gaze shifted to her neck and he watched as her thick carotid artery gently pulsed under the skin. He stood and looked closer. Her color had returned almost to normal. He leaned in to within two feet of the cot and looked at her peaceful face - then suddenly her eyes flashed open and he gave out an involuntary yelp as he fell back on his butt.

"Oh?" she blurted.

Jon's eyes grew wide and he said, "Are you, you?"

"I am."

"Jesus, what a night."

"I have to pee."

"I'll untie you."

30 Release

It was determined by Hannah, the congregation's nurse, that Nikki was not a victim of the Devil (which was obvious since she wasn't trying to eat other people) and that Jon was safe as well. As such, Nikki was invited to stay in the storage shed for another night or two while she was on the mend. It was deemed appropriate that Jon should settle back into his tent in order to maintain propriety.

The reverend stopped by bearing vitamin C pills and handed them to Nikki. "From my own personal supply. Help you get better quicker."

Nikki was standing now. "I'm a bit confused, Buzz. Yesterday, I was the enemy. I know I helped out, but that was as much for me and Jon as any of you. Why so nice?"

"No souls are unreadable, child. Say what you will, but you did a selfless thing. The people are grateful."

"Well, if that's true, then you'll agree to let us move to the East Side."

Calder smiled and ignored the question. "Mr. Washington, if you'll join me. I'll make sure you're settled once again in your own space."

Jon stood and instinctively leaned in to give Nikki a kiss on the cheek. She briefly hesitated at the gesture and then offered her cheek for an air kiss. Jon looked at her for an awkward second before turning to follow the reverend out.

"Wait," she called.

He stopped and turned back to her.

She smiled weakly. "I didn't get infected, right?"

"Right."

"Then this is probably safe." She took him into her arms, kissed him gently on the mouth. When they parted, she looked into his eyes and said, "Thank you."

He smiled, gave her lips another quick peck and turned back for the door. "I'll see you later." When he stepped out, the reverend turned and poked his head back inside, "The door will be unlocked. You may of course use the ladies washroom again."

That night, after a long day working in the fields, Jon found himself bone tired and staring at the ceiling of his tent while falling pine needles pattered upon the roof. For the first time in nearly a year, he wished that he had something to read, something to occupy his wandering mind and especially distract him from thoughts of Nikki. He had to admit that he was building strong feelings for her. As far as her feelings for him... he was still trying to decipher that kiss. Was it just appreciation or was it more? Heck, he knew he was appreciated. He suspected that her military training let her put such feelings in check. It was only recently that women had finally achieved near equality in combat roles. Such gains required a certain sacrifice of the heart in order to maintain professionalism and efficiency. So he was startled when he heard the zipper on his tent part a few inches and Nikki's familiar breathing enter the space. For a split second he became alert to the notion that she had succumbed to the disease after all and was looking for dinner, but then she said, "You there? Can I come in?"

"Uh, of course."

She finished unzipping and crawled in while he slid over to make room for her. "Did I wake you? Give you a scare?"

"More of a startle. I was awake."

It was so dark that he could barely register her silhouette as she turned and zipped the tent closed. She said, "I missed you." He felt his heart flutter and he told himself, I guess that answers that question. "I was thinking about you too."

She had brought her sleeping bag and unrolled it next to his. "It's cold." She lay down and he pulled her chilly body next to him, her back spooning against his front.

"Better?" he asked.

"Much."

"How are you feeling?"

"Surprisingly good."

They lay like that in silence for a while, but for Jon it was difficult to be comfortable. Her body felt very good and quickly warmed next to his. They fit together like they were cast in the same die. Listening to her breathing he could detect a change in its rhythm. Rather than getting more relaxed it seemed to increase slightly in pace. He let his hand rested on her hard, flat belly. The contours of her stomach muscles stiffened and then softened again, relaxing with the rise and fall of her diaphragm.

She whispered, "I was kind of hoping you might want to give me another one."

"Another what?"

"One of these." She turned her face and kissed his mouth. It was deeper this time, long and slow and their lips parted in order to explore more.

Slowly he could feel himself become hard against her. Here they were again, he told himself, the intensity of survival bringing out their most primal instincts. But maybe not. This felt like something more.

She turned further toward him and he felt her warm sweet breath against his cheek. His hand slid up her torso, brushing her breasts as he cupped the side of her face, kissing her softly and then more urgently as she kissed back. His chest filled with warmth, heavy with it, and his scalp lit up with tingling sensations as her tongue flicked about, teasing his lips. His hand moved back down and found one of her full and firm breasts, the nipple pressed back against his thumb and she let out a soft moan of pleasure. He was getting crushed inside his pants, and he reached down to adjust things, making Nikki giggle.

"What?"

"I don't know. Don't ask me to explain."

She turned, placed her hand flat on his belly and slid it down inside his shorts, gripping the firmness of him with gentle strength. He gasped at the touch, the long hibernating sense-memories kicking into gear. They kissed harder, tongues urgently exploring.

Her lips found his ear and neck, sending shivers down his spine and she whispered, "Female Marines have time released birth control implanted under the skin." She put his hand on her arm. "If you touch my shoulder right here you'll feel a little bump."

He rubbed gently on the spot. Sure enough, there was a centimeter long tube under her skin; almost like a pencil lead had been broken off there. He could barely concentrate on this information as she continued to stroke him with her other hand. Still, he could hear in her voice that she wanted him to confirm it back to her. "Okay, I feel it."

She said, "I want you to make love to me again." She kept stroking him.

With the 'okay go' switch flipped, Jon needed no further instruction. He yanked at her T-shirt, fumbling with one hand in the dark, and she released him in order to shrug herself out it. She had intentionally left her bra out of the equation and he found himself teasing her breasts with his mouth. She gasped and pressed her pubic bone against him, grinding with expanded urgency. She pulled his T-shirt over his head and breathed on his body while pulling in his scent.

"For someone who doesn't get to bath much, you sure smell good."

"You too."

They continued to kiss as he unbuttoned and unzipped her pants. She kicked them off with another light giggle, then held his face to her neck, letting him take in her scent, moving his head down between her breasts. With the tip of his tongue he could feel the downy peach fuzz that covered her skin.

She pulled off Jon's shorts next and didn't hesitate to place him inside her mouth. He threw his head back and gasped as he was taken away, his heart pounding, his breathing short and quick.

Then suddenly it wasn't enough. He wanted to feel her body pressed to his. He needed to kiss her again. He reached down and gently took her by the shoulders, laying her over on her back, kissing her deeply. With a quick tug he had her panties off. He marveled at the softness of her pubic hair and he could feel her expand as he slid his fingers across her wetness. She groaned as he brushed her swollen skin, parting her soft folds with ease as his fingers gently explored. She grabbed his neck with one hand and pulled him back to face her, kissing him again as he slowly pressed against her.

"Hi," he whispered in her ear.

"Hi," she said back.

"This is nice."

"Very."

"My heart is pounding."

"So is mine. Can't you feel it beating against yours?"

"Yes."

"Jon?"

"Uh huh?"

"Don't pull out like before, okay? I want... I need you, the essence of you, to be with me afterwards. Okay?"

"Okay. I mean, you did say you had that thing under your skin."

"Just making sure you got it."

"I got it."

Then he slid inside her. They both groaned and Nikki grabbed his buttocks, pulling him in deeper. "Oh my God that feels good."

When it was passed and the spasms that rocked them repeatedly had ceased, Jon breathed out and let some of his weight rest on top of her. She reached out for his sleeping bag and pulled it over them, warding off the chill. They listened to each other's breathing.

Finally, she said, "Thank you."

"Thank *you.*" Jon kissed her neck, felt her pulse, and pondered this new development in their relationship. He decided he needed to confirm what it was by blurting out, "I like you."

"What are you, fifteen…? I like you too."

"I'm feeling a bit like a teenager," then he ground his remaining hardness inside her.

She let out a feigned gasp of surprise. "Sir? You require more?"

"Not counting our mad moment the other night, it's been at least a year. Hell yes, more."

They made love for hours; sometimes with urgency and other moments with tenderness while whispering fond words and feeling happy thoughts, tasting and smelling and sensing and listening as their hearts grew in contentment, and finally they slept - way past dawn, past the church service, past the time to labor in the fields.

When they finally poked their heads out of the tent, Reverend Calder was sitting outside on his folding campstool, Katherine standing at his shoulder. Several children watched from afar and giggled amongst themselves with wonder and embarrassment. Many other congregants stood in stoic silence, arms crossed, judgment written across their faces.

Calder said, "We've conferred upon your request. We think it's best that you move to the East side. You will be given two weeks provisions. You'll sort the rest out yourselves. When the crops come in, we will share what we can."

It was agreed that they would offer each other information on any unusual happenings, but that any other communication would be strictly limited. The community that had settled this island had carved out a space for themselves in these End Times to avoid the severe moral decline that Jon and Nikki represented. A line was drawn on a topographical map. They were not to cross it.

As they humped their gear out of the village, Nikki said to Jon, "If I had known it would be that easy, I'd have jumped your bones the first night we were here."

PART FOUR

THE CRUCIBLE

31 Broken Fever

A week had passed. Nikki and Jon lay in their tent enjoying the moonlit leafy shadows that moved gently across the ceiling. They were blissfully unaware of the bombing campaign, which had begun far to the south. Instead, they were exhausted from another marathon round of sexual gymnastics. They held hands as their bodies cooled down, their heartbeats returning to normal.

Nikki said, "I think it's the roof."

"Hmm?"

"I want a different roof."

"Are we being cryptic or is this a new guessing game?"

She turned on her side to face him. "I can't keep doing this."

"This? You mean us?"

"No, not us. The roof. It's too close. I want a different roof." She regarded the tent. "These things have always made me feel claustrophobic."

Jon listened to the loons serenade the night air, then said, "You want to build a lean-to? A log cabin?"

"I want to live in a house or at least an apartment. I want to be able to go to the grocery store, stream a movie, see a play. Would you believe that I've never been to a play? Go to the gym, buy clothes – you know, live life as we knew it – or at least the way I want to know it. How I planned it after my discharge."

"Okay. I can understand that."

"I want a real roof over my head. I don't want to hide out on some island in the middle of nowhere with a bunch of religious whackos and the constant threat of some crazed cannibal floating ashore, ready to tear my throat out."

"I hear you."

"I want to make love in a real bed or in the kitchen or the back yard for that matter."

Jon nodded with some enthusiasm.

"I've just spent three years of my life in Central Asian and African wars. It was a shit-storm over there almost as bad as this. I come home with the hope of a normal life and instead get to watch the worst calamity ever to befall man. I'm tired, Jon. I'm tired of fighting."

Jon was at a loss for words. His instinct was to offer solutions. He'd read a book once that said that women, when they downloaded like this, were just looking for comfort and acknowledgement, not fixes. But his man-brain couldn't help itself. "Hon, from what we've heard, Canada is no picnic right now either. Housing is a premium with multiple families sharing one house or apartment, petty crime, food shortages – I doubt there's very many plays. I know what you want, but I'm pretty sure it doesn't exist right now. Add to that the millions of those Things between here and there and we've pretty much found paradise right where you're lying."

"Are you always so realistically negative?"

"I'm sorry, but that's our reality, Hon."

Nikki let out a poof of air and a sigh. "You're making me sleepy. And don't call me Hon. You sound like a diner waitress."

"Okay. So let's go to sleep - Honey."

"You're making me sleepy is an expression, knucklehead. It means I don't want to hear what you've got to say."

"I was just pointing out that we've got it pretty good – considering..."

"You're right. But next time I bring it up, I expect you to fantasize about it with me. If I can't have it, at least I can pretend we're heading that way."

"Okay. You wanna talk about a delicious steak dinner at my favorite Atlanta restaurant?"

"No. Talking about food just makes me depressed. I like the log cabin idea though. We'll need to borrow a saw or two."

"Sure. How hard can it be?"

"Kiss me. I'm going to sleep."

Jon gave her a deep kiss, which she returned, and they cuddled up for the night. Loons continued to sing out across the dark lake, backed up by crickets and frogs - all of them offering up a call to mate.

"Listen to all of that," whispered Jon.

"I'm listening."

"Life goes on."

"Always has. Goodnight, Jon."

"Goodnight, Nikki."

Jerry Halverstrom was a very sick boy. The nine year old, who didn't listen to the curse-riddled advice of Teddy Costas, had continued to drink from the pool that the Tree Swallows were nesting over. His mother fretted over him and Nurse Hannah grew concerned as the boy's fever rose to death-defying heights. Aspirin had no effect and they had no ice-water to lay him in. It was decided that they would carry him down to the lake and place his raging hot body in the cool water there.

His parents sat in the water with him, cradling their boy on their laps, cooling his face and lips with a damp rag. It seemed to have a positive effect and the adults visibly relaxed as the boy's raving nonsensical statements abated. The brightness of the full moon shimmered across a lake, alive with night songs and the adults let their heads bow, sleepiness mixed with the lapping of the water calming them all after such a fright.

An owl called out a questioning hoot, waking Mrs. Halverstrom from the subconscious stroking of her son's fevered head. "Perhaps it's enough time in the water," she whispered.

The child's shivers and moans had subsided and he seemed to rest in peace for the first time in many hours.

Hannah and Mr. Halverstrom stood up and helped the mother with her boy. As the three adults stopped to look down at him, the boy's eyes flashed open and he stared from one concerned face to the other.

His mouth split into a gaping grin and his mother smiled back, but with a question on her brow. Her boy had never smiled like that. It was somehow… Fiendish looking.

Nurse Hannah's head cocked as she sought understanding in the boy's abrupt transformation, and then her eyes met his and her blood ran cold. Her legs locked in place as though the earth itself had grabbed her ankles and her bowels opened up, sending a cascade of filth down her legs.

"Good Lord, woman! What's gotten into you?" barked Mr. Halverstrom.

"Jerry?" questioned Mrs. Halverstrom. And that's when her son bit her. She gasped and tried to pull away, but the boy had a lock on the meat of her upper arm and she screamed as her husband tried to pull the boy off. Nurse Hannah joined too and suddenly all three were rapidly bitten as the child, now a Fiend, tried to feast on them all. The father, in excruciating pain, fell to the ground as the eighty-pound beast bit off part of his ear and then latched onto his cheek. Without even thinking about it, the man took hold of a river rock and began to pound the boy's skull.

The mother screamed at the murdering of her son and fell upon her husband, clawing at his hands as he continued to beat his nine-year-old's head to a pulp.

Nurse Hannah pulled the distraught woman back and received a scratch to the face for her efforts.

The boy lay face down on the rock and pebble-strewn shore, his head caved in, blood and brains seeping out into the water. The mother sat in horror at the sight and the father regained his wits, sitting up, aghast at what he'd done.

The nurse, blood coursing down her face and dripping down her bitten arm, just stared at the nightmare before her and then she cried. The realization of her plight washed over her like a wet blanket of dread. She was a dead woman, doomed to become a monster. Her chance for salvation was over. She would become one of *Them*, the un-saveable, spawn of Lucifer.

The father put two and two together pretty fast as well. He looked at his son and wife and then at the distraught nurse. He said to his wife, "They mustn't know. Our boy was not a minion of the devil. They mustn't know." With that, he picked the rock back up and smashed it across Nurse Hannah's skull. The woman stood stunned for a moment and then sank to her knees. Mr. Halverstrom followed with another blow, and his wife flinched at the dull wet cracking sound of shattering living bone. One more thwack finished the deed and the nurse's worries were over forever.

More rocks were displaced around the bodies of Nurse Hannah and the dead boy, further evidence of a struggle. The shocked parents washed their wounds and talked of the bear that had swum ashore, surprising them all as they had tried to reduce their son's fever. The hungry beast had attacked them voraciously before the father had scared it off with a thumb jammed into the eye. The congregation would be none the wiser and the legacy of their son, an angel now with Jesus, would be intact.

The parents were quickly convinced of their lie and in moments it had become their truth. A bear had done this. They would go back and report the incident and get on with grieving for their son.

32 Boiling Point

The night before Jerry Halverstrom had his infected head caved in by his now very infected father, the Halverstrom family had been at KP duty – it was their turn to help prepare the night's communal meal. Jerry, who at that point was suffering from a severe runny nose, a sore throat and the beginnings of a fever, was placed in front of the soup pot and told to stir. The boy found that sipping from the pot as he stirred helped sooth his throat. The soup was set on simmer to keep it from overcooking, and so through the simple act of non-sanitary meal preparation, the FND-z bacterium was introduced to that night's soup du jour – beef barley. The mega-shot of nutrients and just the right amount of heat sent the nasty germs into a fit of reproduction. Billions of dividing cells settled into a microscopic feeding frenzy. Nearly the entire congregation enjoyed the soup that night.

As a neighborly gesture and a chance for the congregation to once again offer them salvation, it had been decided that Jon and Nikki should be invited to the burial. Deciding that it would make relations with the neighbors worse to ignore a little boy's memorial, Jon and Nikki agreed to come. So on the morning of the funeral, they had coffee, grabbed their guns and trundled off toward the main camp to enjoy some better food at what was supposed to be a prayer breakfast before the ceremony.

About six hundred yards from the settlement they came upon Ham Unger digging the second of two graves by himself while Ben Watson, the militia leader, approached hauling the canvas wrapped bodies of Nurse Hannah and Jerry Halverstrom on a makeshift cart. Watson was assisted by Teddy Costas who put the weight of his eleven-year-old body behind one of the wheels.

Jon called out, "Morning, there. Where's the rest of your help? No procession?"

Ben stopped pushing. "Seems a flu has hit pretty much the whole congregation. Had to skip the breakfast, some cold vittles is all if you're hungry."

Nikki put her hand in front of Jon and they both stopped. "Flu? What kind of flu?"

"You know, headache, sore throat, fever, the works."

"How can you be sure it's the flu?"

"I guess we can't, but it's not that demon virus."

Jon asked, "How do you know that?"

"Cause the only folks around here that have been near any demons is you two, and you seem pretty fine. Nikki, you came down with a little something, but you're okay now, right? There's still other diseases in this world."

Jon said, "Who else is healthy?"

Ham stuck his head out of the grave. "My wife Kelly and Katherine, the reverend's assistant. They're both tending to the sick. The two babies seem fine."

"That's it?" Nikki asked.

Teddy said, "My dad and my sister are okay. Lots of folks weren't making sense though. Some couldn't speak right at all. My dad kept us inside all day yesterday".

"What do you mean they couldn't speak right?"

"Fever talk," said Teddy. "Jerry Halverstrom had the same kind of thing before his parents took him to the water to cool him down."

"You don't know that," said Ben. "Don't talk out of turn. There's adults speaking here."

"I do too know it. Their house is next to ours. I could hear Jerry calling out, not making sense. It woke us all up. I saw it when Nurse Hannah came out with Jerry's mom and dad and helped carry him."

Nikki turned to Ben. "We were told that the boy and the nurse died from a bear mauling."

"That's what they said."

"Have you looked at the bodies?"

Ben glanced at the wheelbarrow, "Yup. Pretty nasty." The bodies were wrapped in old canvas in lieu of coffins. It wasn't a fancy way to send off the departed, but it made sense given the thin resources of the community.

"Besides moving them on that cart, did you handle the bodies? Get near any blood?"

"Nope. Lukei did that. She washed them and wrapped them as well as she could."

Jon asked, "So where's Lukei?"

"Sick like the rest of them."

Suddenly, the air crackled with a shrill scream of a woman in terror, sending solitary birds flapping haphazardly into the morning sky.

Ham launched himself out of the grave. "That's Kelly!" He ran as fast as he could back toward the camp.

"Ham, wait!" yelled Nikki. "Shit." She looked at Teddy. "Stay put. And if anyone comes running back this way, including us, you run away until they've verbally convinced you that they aren't sick or bitten."

Several human howls echoed through the woods. Jon, unconsciously felt the Smith & Wesson holstered to his hip.

"Jesus wept!" cried Ben. He picked up his shotgun and the three of them ran off.

Teddy found himself trembling with uncontrollable shaking. The primal, uncontrollable part of his nervous system remembered running from the Fiends - hearing his mother being torn to bits. It took all he had to move his legs and climb into the shallower of the two graves. His eyes stared over the dirt mound back toward camp and then they rested on the bodies lying in the wheelbarrow. As tunnel vision overtook him, his sight blurred with welled-up tears.

Ham intercepted Kelly as she was running through brambles, her skin immune to the reach and scratch of branches and twigs. Blood poured down her face where her right cheek had been and she screamed at being held fast by a husband unrecognized. Ham yelled in her face to make her stop and look at him. Her huge eyes filled up with recognition, but her face remained rigid with terror. She could only point back the way she came and then scream again at the sight of Jon, Nikki and Ben running toward them.

"It's okay, it's okay!" Ham attempted to sooth.

The three others stopped in their tracks at the sight of the poor woman.

"Oh no." said Ben. "Oh my Lord no."

Her speech was thick and slurred from her wound, but Kelly blurted out, "The wrevren bhit meee. He khilled Khathlerine. Others. Khilling. Khilling the bhabiess. Coming." Then she stopped and felt her own face, the jagged edges flapped about under her fingertips and she burst into tears.

Ben turned to Jon and Nikki. "What do we do?"

Jon said, "Ham, your wife is infected. You have to step away from her."

"What?" asked the young new husband. Kelly appeared even more stricken and looked back and forth between them.

"I'm sorry. There's nothing you can do for her. You have to carefully clean that blood off or you will get infected too. Her breath is not contagious yet, but when the fever is done it will be."

"What? No!" Hamm's eyes scanned all over his bride as though she had become strange to him.

Nikki tugged on Jon's sleeve and said, "Jon, we should go. There isn't time for this."

Kelly's tears came in earnest and she fell to her knees in fear and agony, her young husband holding her tight.

Nikki grabbed Jon's arm, pulling him away from the scene. "Listen. We know how it ends. We have to go, now! Ben, you can follow us or go your own way. Your community is either dead or infected."

Jon said, "We have to go back and get the boy."

The crack of breaking twigs, thundering feet and deranged human voices echoed through the forest. Fiends were coming. They had to run.

Nikki flipped off the safety on her SCAR. Jon un-holstered his pistol and slapped Ben on the back. No more time for talk. They ran.

Ham sat with his stricken wife and listened as the Fiends grew closer.

"Gho," she said.

"I, I can't."

"Gho or yhou'll dhie."

"Can't."

"Jusht end iht fhor me." She reached out for a heavy piece of tree limb lying on the forest floor. "Uhse this."

"I can't."

"Plhease."

But it was too late anyway. The Reverend, or what had once been the reverend, appeared, standing on a granite boulder above them. The jolly Saint Nick was now an obese monster - its once white beard smeared with blood and bits of flesh. Other former congregants quickly joined it. Their mouths and hands were covered in gore.

The flight instinct took over Ham's legs and he turned to run, only to be cut off by Big Alan Garber, now a Fiend, who grabbed him by the throat. With one swift jerk of his muscled fist, he tore the young newlywed's larynx partially from his neck.

The reverend threw his obese weight on top of Kelly, who cried out in fear. Several others held her down. The reverend got his face close to hers and sniffed her wound, sniffed her gasping breath and then turned his face away. She wasn't fresh any longer; the infection had already taken hold. The instinct to kill and gorge was replaced by an instinct to preserve, if only by not killing the host. Kelly would live. She would lose her mind, and if she didn't die of a secondary infection due to her horrific wound, she would join the legions of other Fiends - only to die of starvation on a lonely island in Maine.

33 The Wall

Jon, Nikki and Ben were quickly back to the gravesite. At first they thought that Teddy had run, but then found him in a fetal position at the bottom of the shallow grave, thumb in his mouth. Nikki, who had only in the past few days let her heart feel open again, felt it suddenly slam shut. Jon was almost overwhelmed with this horrible turn of events. For a week they had found solace. For a week they had found happiness. For a week, they could almost let go of the horror that surrounded them.

Both of these people, these strong people, who had survived when so many others hadn't, looked at the terrified boy and became nearly catatonic as well. Fear and exhaustion left them with a paralysis of indecision - the primal part of them wanting to crawl in there with him.

Then Ben spoke up. As a paramedic he had seen lots of folks with too much pain or trauma to process, move into a default mode of submission. Some folks let themselves float along, letting others decide life or death for them. Others simply gave up the ghost once and for all. Ben was a master at snapping people out of such temporary weakness. It was this personality trait that got him the militia leader job.

"Eye's on me!" he hissed. "You, boy with your thumb in your mouth, get up! Quit being a baby and get out of that hole!"

Jon and Nikki snapped out of it.

Jon chimed in, "Teddy, we have to move now."

Teddy stirred and looked up at them.

"At-a-boy" said Ben, and he reached into the hole and grabbed the boy's jacket yanking him up. Teddy reached out and Jon and Nikki grabbed hold as well. They didn't have to say more. They could hear the Fiends crashing through the woods.

Ben said, "We've got to somehow circle around to the boats. They're all stocked with gear in the event of an emergency evacuation. I say we run north; the river side of the lake and let the current sweep us back down toward the boat inlet."

"What about my dad and Amanda?" asked Teddy.

They all hesitated. Nikki moved to speak but was interrupted by Ben. "If we're lucky, we'll see 'em at the dock or on the water. Everyone knows to go to the boats if demons come ashore."

They all assumed that the lie appeased the boy. No one wanted to contemplate telling him that the rest of his family was gone as well. They underestimated him: "Don't call them demons." Billy said. "It's regular people infected with a disease. I have to save my dad and sister." With that he started running back toward the camp.

Jon grabbed a fistful of his jacket and hauled him back. "Not that way." Jon paused, letting the Fiends in the woods echo his statement. "They'll kill you as sure as they'll kill the rest of us."

Tears filled the boy's eyes and his mouth twisted from anger to hatred. Then just as quickly the anguish was replaced by resolve. He wiped his eyes, listened to the movement among the trees and turned, getting his bearings. "I know the best way. Follow me."

Jon let him run. He, Nikki and Ben followed as best they could.

They reached a natural granite wall that subdivided much of the eastern part of the island and had been used as the demarcation line between the settlement and Jon and

Nikki's space. It had natural steps cut into it, offering purchase for small trees and damp mossy outcroppings. The peak was perhaps forty feet high, making it impractical to take the long way around.

Teddy was already halfway up when the others reached the base. They all began to climb at different points. It was slick going and Jon found himself at a steep dead-end when only half way up.

Teddy reached the top and looked down on them. He loudly whispered to Jon, "Can't make it from there."

Jon let out a quiet, "Fuck". And started back down.

The Fiend's whoops and shrieks echoed off the rocks and bounced among the trees. It was impossible to tell how far away they might be. As Jon reached the forest floor again, Nikki and Ben made it to the top and joined Teddy watching Jon search for a better route.

"There," Nikki whispered loudly and pointed. "That's the way I used."

"Oh, Lord," said Ben. He pointed into the woods below. The Fiends were charging right for Jon. Nikki shouldered the SCAR, aimed and fired. A chunk of tree flew off next to a Fiend's head. The deranged human didn't even flinch. It had spotted Jon on the lower rocks and started to run even faster. Others saw this and ran harder too.

"Jon, climb!" screamed Nikki. She fired again and this time she gut shot what had once been Alan Garber. The burly giant doubled over and then looked up, snarling at the people on top of the wall.

Jon found himself slipping on the rocks and he painfully fell to a lower ledge, bruising his thigh - Like a late night encounter with fear in a lonely parking lot, Jon's arms and legs tumbled about like stricken fingers on jangling car keys. He told himself to calm down and breathe, pay attention to his climb. Then a hand slapped against his foot providing him with a fresh dose of adrenaline. He suddenly leaped up the cliff-side, hop-scotching like a mountain goat.

Ben said a quick prayer and shot the Fiend that was trying to duplicate Jon's effort. The poor former congregant bounced back down to the forest floor with a sickening crunch.

Nikki put out a hand and pulled Jon up the last few feet. He bent over, his hands on his knees and breathed hard toward the ground. "Just give me a sec."

Nikki slapped him on the ass. "Too bad."

They turned and ran.

Teddy was in the lead again, but then he got winded as well and had to slow down. Nikki's Marine training was doing right by her and she forged ahead of the group, the rest following as best they could.

A little farther on, Nikki spied an inlet, the river portion of the lake meandering by in the distance. "It's straight ahead." She charged forward and ran into the inlet startling what seemed like hundreds of small birds. They burst into the air and flitted about in a chirping panic.

"Wait. Don't go in that water!" yelled Teddy.

Nikki turned. "Why? The river's right there."

The rest of the group caught up and stopped at the water's edge.

"That's the place where Jerry Halverstrom was drinking from. I tried to stop him, but he wouldn't. He didn't like the camp water and he hated sharing a canteen."

Nikki lifted her hands from the water and looked at it dripping off her fingertips. "What are you saying?"

Teddy caught his breath. "I'm not sure, but he drank that water. Lot's a birds pooped in it. He got sick".

Jon said, "Maybe you should get out of the water, Nikki."

Nikki waded back to shore, careful not to splash. "You think the water is passing the disease?"

"I've always thought that," said Jon. "I just didn't know how. Maybe it's in the bird poop. Why not?"

"Come on, this way," said Teddy and they followed him along a deer path to the water's edge. They looked around to make sure they weren't being followed and then jumped in. The current naturally swept around the island, carrying them along the shore and then down the channel to where Nikki and the Fiend had had their fight.

The dead Fiend was still there, the top of its head still breaking the water, its bloated body bobbing in the current. They had to swim hard to stay close to the island lest they be swept out into the larger lake.

The camp's boat inlet was hidden among tall reeds at the southwest tip of the island and it was there that the current met the larger side of the lake and slowed down. They swam until they found the opening to the small channel and then they set their feet down in the thick silty muck.

A cool breeze had built up, bending the reeds around them, rubbing the stalks together, and creating a peaceful sound that countered their reality. It said, relax and rest, let the day's stress roll off your shoulders. The idea that the shore was potentially crawling with deadly infected seemed to almost make a mockery of nature's tranquil side. The rubbing reeds also masked the small group's own sounds, helping them to sneak forward, but also making it impossible to hear what might be around the next bend.

34 Safe Harbor

As they drew close to the beachhead, they stopped. By unspoken agreement, they would rest a moment before walking back into the cauldron. It was a chance to listen and observe as well as work up more nerve. Nikki and Jon kept an ear and eye out while Ben closed his eyes and whispered a quiet prayer. Teddy started trembling - the water was cold. Nikki pulled him close and wrapped her arms around the boy.

When three minutes passed, Ben opened his eyes. "Okay, shall we do this?"

Nikki released Teddy and gently held his face in her hands. "We can't go wandering about looking for them. If they made it, they've likely already left. Hopefully they aren't paddling back to shore somewhere else in search of you."

"I understand. Let's go."

They found it easier to swim, even in three feet of water, rather than to try to walk in the mud, but eventually they had no choice. When the reeds thinned out they could see the small rocky beach where the boats were tied up, none of them missing. Teddy let out a defeated sigh.

The congregation had a few rowboats and canoes and two powerboats. Will Parker's boat was there too. No one needed to explain to Teddy that his dad and sister hadn't gotten away. The boy simply let silent tears stream down his cheeks while he bravely moved forward. All three adults felt compelled to lay a reassuring hand on him.

The village lay just beyond the shore. Nikki held up her hand and they all stopped to listen. The birds and insects had once again become still; the woods filled with the sounds of walking death. Fiendish grunts bounced among the buildings, but from the water side of the boats, it wasn't obvious where the sounds were coming from. She put her hand down and they continued to wade forward slowly.

The two boats that were worth their trouble were Will Parker's Chris Craft and the pride of the congregation, a Bayliner deck boat, sporting an enclosed head.

Ben pointed at the Bayliner and whispered, "Got the keys in it."

Without a word, they all crept up the stern swim platform and silently climbed onboard. With their heads above the waterline they could see onto the shore – and those on the shore could see them. At least twenty-five former parishioners were feeding on almost unrecognizable, bloody red meat. The victims had likely been running for the boats when they were brought down. The monsters turned almost as one at the new movement.

"Oh, shit!" Nikki leveled the SCAR and started firing at the same moment the Fiends stood up to charge. Ben ran to the helm and twisted the keys. The engine fired right up and he slammed the gearshift into reverse. Mud and silty brown water churned under the propeller, but the boat wasn't going anywhere – it was still tied off at the bow! The line pulled taught, causing the Bayliner to fishtail back and forth in its struggle to break free.

Beneath their feet they heard a girl's muffled scream. "Amanda!" yelled Teddy who threw open the door to the head. There, crouched into a corner was Amanda Costas, tears and terror filling her eyes. Teddy jumped into the space with his sister and slammed the door shut.

As the Fiends hit the shallow water, Jon ran forward, firing his pistol. The dock line was pulled too tight to untie. Nikki ran forward and brought down the congregation's building engineer, young George Mickelson, just before he launched himself at Jon. They kept shooting until empty, too many, no time to reload. Killer animals grabbed onto the front railing. Jon & Nikki kicked at their hands, their faces, trying not to trip, Nikki struggling as the lightweight rifle offered little heft in its new role as club. Suddenly a strong fist clamped around the stock and she found herself in a tug of war with the former Lukei Jansen. The big blond Fiend snarled and laughed with delight at the competition.

Ben picked up his shotgun, pumping and firing while tears poured down his face, his former friends and neighbors dying under his own hand. He fired until he ran out of shells and then charged forward with his knife. He reached between Jon and Nikki and hacked at the dock line. The Fiends were coming at the boat from the sides now – it was almost too late – then the rope's final strands snapped. The engine was still in full reverse and the boat charged backwards away from the shore. Jon had to grab Nikki by the arm to keep her from pitching over the bow as she gave a sharp final tug on the SCAR, yanking it out of the Fiend Lukei's hands and leaving the creature floundering in the deeper water.

Without someone at the helm, the Bayliner started to turn in a wide circle, pointing itself back toward the shore. Ben stumbled back and threw the throttle into neutral. Then he flipped the wheel around and slammed the big engine into full forward. The propeller slid right over Lukei the Fiend, churning the water red.

Ben drove out of the little reed-filled harbor and onto the lake, only stopping when he had them a hundred yards from shore, in deeper water, nothing trying to kill him.

Nikki pulled on the door to the head but it was latched from the inside. "Teddy, Amanda. We got away. It's safe. Can you open the door?"

Teddy opened the door and stood protectively in front of Amanda. "My sister's not sick and she said my dad got away. He ran to where your camp is".

Nikki looked at Jon then Ben. Ben said, "I guess we best drive over there". He steered the boat toward the eastern end of the island.

Nikki turned back to the children, "Amanda, how do you feel?"

The fear stricken girl clung behind her brother and shivered.

Jon kneeled at the door as well. "Honey, are you shivering 'cause you're scared or because you feel sick?"

Amanda spoke into her brother's shirt, "Scared".

Teddy spoke for her, "She said that everybody tried to get her and Dad. They had to run in separate directions and he told her to hide in here."

Amanda spoke up, "My daddy said he was going to find you guys for help."

Nikki nodded, "Well, if it's like it was last time, we'll find your father right there."

As the boat got closer to Jon and Nikki's corner of the island, they saw Steven Costas in a tree near the shore kicking at several Fiends on the rocks below. One was the reverend himself. Nikki aimed the SCAR, then hesitated as she recognized Martha and Robert Brown, the couple who with their daughter Melissa, had joined Nikki and Jon at dinner their first night.

Both Fiends hissed and laughed at the occupants of the boat with wide, hungry eyes. Nikki and Jon pulled their triggers.

The reverend stood alone now. He laughed with wild Fiendish glee and then ran at the approaching boat. Nikki's bullet hit him square between the eyes.

Ben, wiped away a continuing flow of hot tears as he let the boat coast toward the shore. Just before touching the rocks he shifted into reverse for a moment to stop the momentum and put it in neutral.

Steven climbed down from the tree while still keeping an eye over his shoulder. He smiled, waving at his kids with the nonchalance of a man suffering from mild shock.

"Daddy!" yelled Amanda.

"That's twice you folks have saved me and my kids. God has clearly sent you to be our guardian angels. Ben, I'm glad to see you made it. Any others?" Steven turned again at the sound of more crashing footsteps in the woods.

"No. Better hop aboard, Steven," said Jon.

Steven quickly waded out and jumped on. His children shot forward and clung to him as Ben backed up and the pulled away from the island.

Everyone sat in silence as the boat moved slowly over the flat windless water. Finally Jon spoke up, "Guess we better take inventory of what we got on this thing."

Ben wiped away his tears and said in a lifeless tone, "Provisions for twelve people, ten days. Check it every week m'self. Make sure the water's fresh. Just checked yesterday."

"Okay. So where do we go from here?"

"Emergency spot is the other large island on the lake. We call it Two Harbors. Well-protected anchorage. Just a little too small and too close to land to set up the church there. It'll be fine for us. Fishing's good. There's still plenty of summer left to grow some food." He nodded at the coolers that held the provisions. "Got seeds in there. Probably some berries on the island."

This suggestion was accepted with continued silence until Ben said, "It happened so fast. One moment we were burying young Jerry Halverstrom and Hannah, next thing... Wasn't supposed to happen to us. Lord was on our side. Reverend said so. Gotta fight the good fight."

Nikki said, "I'm sorry, Ben. It's happened to all of us".

"Reverend said they were demons. Said we were supposed to get lifted up to heaven, be by the Lord's side - 'till the Reverend took it back. You suppose God was angry that the Reverend took it back?"

No one answered, then Teddy Costas spoke up, "I don't think it has anything to do with God, Mr. Watson. Everyone can catch a cold from somebody else. This cold just turns people into monsters."

"You blaspheming, son?"

"No, sir. I'm just trying to help you see it another way."

Ben looked at Steven Costas, "Steven, I'd appreciate it if you'd keep your son in check. We don't need to upset the Lord anymore than he already is."

Steven put a hand on his son's back, "Why don't we just sit back and let Mr. Watson drive?"

"But, Dad. I'm just-"

"That's enough, Son," Steven said gently.

The boy crossed his arms and sulked his head into his chest. He was tired of being talked down to, tired of adults thinking they knew better. Teddy knew exactly what was going on in the world and he swore to himself that he would protect his family from it with every bone in his body.

It was a glorious summer day. They were in no hurry and Ben wanted to conserve fuel, so he let the engine run just above idle. The boat coasted, leaving a gentle wake. As a breeze brushed across the water, the sunlight shimmered on it, offering the illusion of countless jewels. The maples and oaks joined in with a chorus of leafy friction.

In the rear of the boat, Jon settled down next to Nikki and put his arm around her shoulders. She leaned into him and rested her head, letting her rifle slide to the floor.

"I'm tired, Jon, bone tired".

"Me too. I don't think the human body was meant to make so much adrenaline in such a short time."

"Even in combat, we got breaks".

"We'll rest some on this new island. No need to rush back into the storm."

"Hmm. From what we've been through so far, I'm quite convinced that the storm is still coming to us". Nikki had a cut on her finger. The blood was just coagulating. Jon took her hand and kissed the wound. She pulled it away. "Don't do that. You don't know."

He gave her a slight pout. "You didn't catch it, Nick. If you did, we'd both be running mad across the countryside."

Two Harbors was made up of a large inlet on the western side of the island, and a smaller one mirroring it on the eastern side. A narrow rocky beach connected the two wooded islands north and south, with the southern woods protecting the bulk of the island from view of the mainland.

It was decided that they would build their fire pit on the beach, close to the southern woods. Ben would set up his camp there as well. The Costas family built their camp inside the tree line of the North Islet. Jon and Nikki set up their shelter in a small opening in the forest on the South Side rimmed with dense bunches of ferns and padded by a thick carpet of pine needles. They agreed to gather on the beach for their meals and otherwise tend to themselves for now. Like anywhere on the lake, the water was fairly brimming with bass and fat delicious catfish. Fishing would be a simple matter of casting a lure or dropping a hooked worm. It occurred to Jon that if Fiends succeeded in taking over the world, the waterborne, and birds and insects would be the only creatures sharing the planet with them.

The artificial lifestyle that these six people carved out for themselves lasted for nine hours. As night fell, the weather stayed unusually warm, and everyone found themselves laying down on top of their sleeping bags.

The great northern forests of New England that had been re-sewing themselves into the landscape since the end of the Nineteenth Century. After 72 hours of steady incendiary bombing, those dense forests crackled into the greatest inferno the modern world had ever seen.

Only the big cities and their miles of concrete were spared the cleansing by fire. The repopulation of the United States would have to begin somewhere. It was deemed logical and practical to begin in the cities and let settlers spread back out into rural areas as they became tenable again. For the cities and larger towns, it meant the administration of chemotherapy mixed with large doses of radiation. Everything else: thousands of burgs, villages, parishes, RFDs and watering holes, were being scoured to ash and bone.

It was an all-or-nothing gamble, not unlike the fight against a spreading cancer; annihilation, with the hope that what remained was strong enough to live on.

35 Inferno

Admiral Remrick was aware of the importance of the CDC scientist's mission; yet he had chosen to send them to Quebec on a slower moving, relatively low flying Black Hawk helicopter. His methodology was simple: A helicopter would safely drop the scientist right outside the door to their new lab. He could have instead given up his personal Gulfstream Jet for the task, but time would have been lost transferring gear to a ground vehicle with a longish drive upon arrival, and frankly, it would be a cold day in hell before he was going to give up the Von Fest (named after his great-great granddaddy, a hard charging Prussian cavalry officer). Unfortunately, he didn't account for the overwhelming effect that the firebombing of seven of the original thirteen colonies would have on atmospherics.

To create this inferno, the US and Canadian air forces, and their allies, had bided their time. They won their debate with the politicians and pushed off D-Day for three days while they waited for a cloudless and unseasonably warm Nor'easter to buildup. With the help of the warm wind, their job was made that much easier.

For Jon, Nikki, Steven, Teddy, Amanda and Ben, it began with the sound of what seemed like a distant freight train backed by the illusion of a midnight sunrise coming from the wrong direction: west.

The roar of the flames arrived so quickly that they barely had time to grab their guns and clothes and run to Ben's beach camp. They stood together in awe as a rain of firefly-like embers announced the front edge of the conflagration. The hot bits of floating wood spun about in violent circles as air was sucked from the East, only to crash into the western breeze like a wave rebuilding on a beach. The effect was to replenish the flames with fresh oxygen while a vast cloud of smoke blotted out the stars like a great black blanket sweeping across the sky.

Then the trees of the North Islet began catching flame. The pines lit up like gasoline soaked torches, exploding one after another and scattering their embers like wind shattered dandelions. The weak and the dead foliage toppled, dragging the fire to their neighbors, while heavy showers of embers set the ground cover alight.

Jon yelled out, "Into the water!"

No one needed more coaxing than that. They grabbed stones to fill their pockets and then held on to bigger rocks to weigh them down. They waded as a tight group out into the western lagoon until the taller men could only breathe with their heads tilted back. Jon and Nikki stood close to each other, while Steven and Ben held the children. Frequently, they had to douse their faces as hot bits of flotsam landed on the water, sizzling and throwing up tiny spouts of steam. With each movement of their heads, the roar in their ears alternated from dull and water-filtered to blazing and fierce. Searing gases swirled, bringing tears to their eyes and forcing their lungs into harsh fits of coughing.

Jon yelled to no one in particular, "What the fuck else could happen?" He began to think that his ceaseless optimism; that they could survive no matter what, was really just foolishness built on a string of luckyish circumstances. Their gear and provisions were being returned to the elements while their ammo reserves cooked off in their shelters like firecrackers on Chinese New Year. The core of the forest glowed like a great iron forge and they knew that there would be nothing left to salvage. Even Ben's shelter on the beach glowed with kinetic reduction.

The Bayliner lit up next and the acrid concoction of cooking fiberglass and melting vinyl swirled through the air. The toxic fumes occasionally overwhelmed them, causing hacking convulsions and the brief inhalation of water mixed with ash and floating charcoal. Then the boat's dock line burned through, letting the fire ship adrift, spinning its way toward them. They watched with astonishment as the molten plastic dripped and poured off the boat's gunnels, sending jets of white and black smoke out of the water.

Jon said, "On three, everyone hold their breath and duck". He counted out the seconds, dragging the last one out, "Threeee, Now!"

They plunged their heads under water and crouched as the boat floated by above them, the dripping plastic making *zip, zip, zip* sounds as it hit the water.

When it was safely passed and the children were kicking their father and Ben with the panic of lungs depleted, they raised their heads only to be met with the distinct sound of a helicopter, a very powerful sounding helicopter, somewhere above.

This night sky was no place for a helicopter. As the flames reached hundreds, even thousands of feet into the atmosphere, their sparks and embers reached ever higher and mixed with great black clouds of smoke. In a swirling and violent cauldron of super heated air, burning mountaintops gave rise to even higher sheets of flame and this concoction boiled and twisted until it reached several kilometers, all the way up into the troposphere.

Chief Winters and his co-pilot Warrant Officer Poole were well trained to fly in zero visibility conditions, but the thermal gusts pushed their aircraft around like it was just another of the billions of hot glowing embers. They desperately fought the controls while agreeing to search for a safe place to put down. The Black Hawk had a maximum ceiling of 19,000 feet, and as such there was no cabin pressure system to provide a safe escape to a higher altitude. Too toxic to bother taking along for the rest of the trip, the scientist's had left their hazmat gear back in Florida. As the craft violently heaved up and down, the scientists and pilots found themselves choking for air and gagging back vomit. They needed to put down in a clear space now or they would all pass out and die a fiery death.

With ground penetrating radar and night vision equipped helmets, the pilots could peer through the smoke onto the ocean of fire below and found that the land directly beneath them was interrupted by a large lake.

Winters chose an area near a burning island with two lagoons. As he brought the craft into a hover – hover being a relative term - the wind blasted in fierce twists, and despite their advanced optics, the smoke and embers reduced the pilot's sight to near zero. Winters hoped and prayed that the nearer lagoon might be shallow enough to set down in.

It was then that Admiral Remrick's second error in judgment bubbled up to the surface: As the theater commander for the Southern New England portion of the re-invasion, the Admiral had personally intervened on the pilot choice for this mission. He overrode the Army Colonel under him in charge of Army AirCav Operations, and insisted on Winters and Poole. As Army National Guardsmen, these pilots had not yet seen any actual combat missions. Both had been slated for Pakistan, but had been kept home when the pandemic broke out of Miami. Even then, the two pilots had been held in reserve. Other than ferrying refugees, they had limited experience with anything out of the ordinary. As far as Remrick was concerned, ferrying a handful of scientists a few hundred miles was pretty routine. He needed experienced combat pilots for the invasion. The team's original pilots, Axelman and Frick, who had flown in every kind of crazy situation possible, were kept behind for just that mission.

As he descended, Captain Winters did have the presence of mind to order his co-pilot to send out a May Day over the radio. Unfortunately, they were in the middle of nowhere, descending into a densely forested area. Though the range of their radio was as much as 600 miles, that distance could only be achieved at a greater altitude than their current position and required more normal atmospherics. The radio was also designed to work with a directional satellite relay, but the density of smoke, flame, ash and embers made that ability moot. Lieutenant Poole was calling out, but nobody was listening.

Using the Black Hawk's internal PA system, Winters calmly asked the scientists to open one of the side doors and to be ready to jump if necessary.

Below all of this the tiny group in the water watched the Black Hawk descend right on top of them. Jon Washington found himself yelling out, "You've got to be fucking kidding me!"

They all screamed in unison with no time to get out of the way.

As Winters hovered over what he guessed might be three feet above water, a last gust pushed the aircraft sideways, dipping one wheel into the lake. The effect was as if a giant hand had grabbed the wheel and yanked down with a sharp tug. The helicopter heaved over on a tilt, blades driving into the lake, and then crashed face first into the rocky shore, rotors shattering, scattering composite bits and pieces hundreds of yards. The craft came to rest upside down, its broken tail hanging in the lagoon.

Winters had been killed instantly, the angle of the crash perfectly lining up the windshield and avionics with several large boulders. Poole was a mess, but breathing. The scientists in back found themselves in various forms of disarray, hanging haphazardly, still strapped into their seats.

A piece of shattered rotor had skipped off a rock and ricocheted through the open door, killing William Warner, whose head was nearly severed off - the ten pound ball of bone, brain and flesh dangling by only a few tendons. Like a freshly slaughtered goat, his corpse bled out all over the ceiling. Rick Decker held his shoulder and screamed in pain.

Outside, the initial blaze had used up the bulk of the island's more volatile fuel, and the fire had settled down to a steady, less threatening rhythm. Jon, Nikki and company looked on in astonished relief that they hadn't been crushed.

Nikki said, "We have to help them."

Inside the copter, Robert Tran was the first to unbuckle his flight harness. He tumbled to the blood soaked ceiling and helped Susan, then got Aaron and Christy free. Decker was a different story. He threw his head back and forth while gritting his teeth in pain. There was no visual evidence of injury, but the man was clearly overwhelmed with something. As a group, they propped him up as best they could, unbuckled him and lowered him to the ceiling.

Decker grunted out, "I broke my shoulder or something."

Tran crawled forward toward the pilots, a quick glance telling him all he needed to know about Winters. Poole groaned through a bloody, smashed face. Tran unbuckled the man's harness, using his own body to cushion the pilot's fall. The army flyer barely acknowledged the change in position. Then something caught Tran's eye - movement outside the window. It was human. His first thought was that they'd landed in a nest of Fiends.

"There's someone moving out there. Maybe more than one."

Everyone forgot Decker and Poole's pain and spun around looking outside. Tran grabbed Poole's 9mm Pistol out of his survival vest and chambered a round. Then a person outside spoke up. It was a woman, "Hey! Anyone alive in there? You're leaking fuel!"

Susan took immediate command. "Out. Everybody out! Grab the samples and notes!"

Robert threw open the door facing the island and found himself looking at an odd assortment of people. The woman was wearing a heavy leather coat, her hair tucked under a rolled bandana. A man with a scruffy beard stood waist deep next to her, dressed in motorcycle racing gear. Beyond them were two more men and a couple of kids.

Tran didn't waste a second. He shoved a Pelican case at them. "Take this!"

Nikki said, "No time. You gotta get out!"

Tran ignored her, grabbing another case from Christy and shoving it at them, "And this".

The far side of the helicopter suddenly caught fire and so did the water around it. Aaron barreled past, clutching his briefcase to his chest, and wading away as fast as he could. Christy and Susan hopped out next, each carrying a piece of gear. Decker stepped out, bravely holding another Pelican case with his good arm. Then Tran grabbed a hold of Poole, sliding him across the bloody ceiling toward the door, brushing past Warner's severed head.

Jon yelled, "Come on man!" as Nikki herded the rest away from the burning hulk.

Tran jumped out and with Jon's help, heaved Poole into the water just as the helicopter became fully engulfed. Tran couldn't believe that in the middle of all of this, in a part of the country that was supposedly ruled by Fiends, that they had descended amongst a bunch of survivors. Then the helicopter exploded and they all ducked underwater as hot debris crashed down all around them.

36 Decision Time

They huddled in the water as a group while they waited for the fire to die down enough to move to the beach. Lieutenant Poole died within minutes of being dragged from the helicopter. They removed his survival vest, weighted his flight suit down with stones, and let him slip under the surface. Ben Watson offered some appropriate funereal words and included his congregation back on the Big Island in the eulogy.

Susan, originally trained as an MD, determined that Decker was suffering from an anterior dislocated shoulder. "Rick, you're probably hurting less now. Those are your endorphins at work. It would be better if you were lying down, but we can do this standing. It'll just hurt a bit more."

"Hurts a lot now," said Decker through gritted teeth.

"Well, sorry in advance." She turned to Jon, "Will you stand behind Rick, Mr…?"

"Washington. Of course."

She grabbed Tran and pulled him close. "I need strong arms for this." She put his hands onto Decker with her own, "Here goes. Slowly bend the elbow ninety degrees like so and hold it across his belly. Good. Now with your right hand, hold his shoulder stationary. Mr. Washington, keep pressure on the back side of the shoulder."

Decker huskily whispered, "Okay, that hurts more."

Susan stepped back out of the way. "Now, Robert, you're going to keep the elbow bent and open the arm as though you're opening a door. Ready? Now slowly, slowly."

Tran twisted Decker's arm out and away from his body. Decker howled in agony.

Susan said, "If it worked, you should feel relief."

Decker gritted his teeth, "Didn't work, didn't work."

Robert looked helpless. "Sorry, man. Sorry."

"Robert, close and open the door again. Keep it real slow"

Robert did as instructed and then yelped, "I felt it!"

Decker sighed with relief and carefully took his arm back from Tran.

Susan said, "Good, now Rick, slide your hand in between the buttons of your jacket like Napoleon and let it rest. Robert, is there some pain medication in that survival vest?"

As Jon participated, he noted how fully distracted everyone was with the procedure. The world was burning down around them and the small group was fixated on a dislocated shoulder.

Tran searched the vest, which had auto inflated when Poole had hit the water. There was a small radio, various signaling devices, flashlight, water dye/shark repellant - which got a few smiles of amusement - and assorted other small utilities. The emergency food and water rations noted that it could be stretched into a five-day supply for one person. There was a basic first aid kit and a compact foil blanket.

Tran gave Decker two ibuprofen. They would husband the rest.

Surprisingly, given the nature of their meeting, there was little chitchat. Perhaps all of them had witnessed so many things out of the ordinary, that this was just one more instance; no more worthy of comment than any other fantastical moment during these hysteria filled months. They also knew something else – they were a long way from being done with it.

When the fierce flames had reduced the island's timber to a low and even blaze, they waded back to shore and warmed themselves by the fire burning at the edge of the southern woods. Noxious gases had them all breaking into coughing fits and they mostly breathed through their wet shirts.

When the flames died down further, Susan explained who she and her fellow scientists were and their mission. Nikki and Jon offered a few words on their history, as did Steven for his family. Ben kept to himself.

Aaron spoke up, "You think we could get somebody on that radio?"

Nikki recognized the model, "Standard military issue, waterproof, good for maybe five miles depending on what ground you're on." Her instinct and training subconsciously directed her speech toward Susan. As the lead government scientist, she was sort of the default leader for all of them. "We're best off keeping the battery fresh until we find ourselves in a situation where we might use it. I'm a recently decommissioned, well, actually re-commissioned Marine, ma'am, that's why I'm offering my opinion."

"Call me Susan. It's good to know that we have your skills among us, Nikki." She looked at the others. "Anyone with an opinion on how to get ourselves out of this, is welcome to speak up. As far as we know, we are all that's human between here and Canada. Any idea how far we are from the border?"

Ben said, "About a hundred and sixty miles to Quebec. Border's closer of course, but the new wall is across the Saint Lawrence."

"That's better than I hoped. There will be a search and rescue operation. Our absence has, I'm sure, already been noted."

Nikki looked down at the ash-coated water then returned her gaze to Susan. "Forgive my pessimism, Ma'am, er, Susan, but I can say from experience, that unless they've got an idea of where you went down, we're but a few specks in a sea of burnt trees. In Sudan, if a plane went down and the whereabouts was sketchy, just as often as not, the JEM or ICU would nab our pilots before we could find them."

"So what are you saying?"

"Don't count on a ride. We don't know how many infected may have survived this fire, but we'd be smart not to draw too much attention to ourselves. We keep a low profile; try to walk out of here. We find a highway - a hundred and sixty miles is a seven, eight day hump on a flat road."

Ben said, "Route 201 is just east of here. Probably take us a day, day and a-half's walk to get to the Moscow dam. Firebreak's not far. Leads right to it. Dam's right next to 201. The other way is to follow the Dead River north, but that's iffy country. There'd be a lotta places we'd have to swim for it. Can't say how long it would take."

Jon said, "What happened to not drawing attention to ourselves? We've been avoiding the highways. The Fiends are all bunched up there."

Nikki said, "It's a matter of weighing odds. I think this fire has changed that equation. Besides, we're more likely to get spotted by friendlies walking on the highway. We take the woods, assuming the fire dies down, and we're exposed for another week, probably two with little chance of being rescued. Heck, on the highway maybe we'll find a working car or two."

They looked at their food situation and found that their catch of the day lay burnt and black on the rocks near Ben's camp. It was still edible and would at least provide dinner. The rest of the food cash had been consumed in the boat fire. They would share the pilot's survival rations in the morning before they headed out, and hope that the town of Moscow could provide something for the rest of the trip. Assuming that the huge forest fire surrounding them had moved on and would allow for foot travel, they would begin their journey at first light. For clothes, they had what was on their backs. There would be no blankets or shelter for the night. They had four weapons between them: Poole's Beretta with a spare clip of ammo, Jon's Smith & Wesson with two clips, Nikki's SCAR L with a second 30-round magazine taped to the one mounted to the gun, and finally Ben's Remington twelve-gage with five slugs and six rounds of buckshot.

As the evening wore on and the fires cooled off, they were able to speak without yelling over the din. They brought each other up to date on their various adventures while roiling clouds of smoke reflected the marching inferno's orange light as far as the eye could see. When it came time to turn in, they agreed that they would lie as a group on the one gravely portion of the rocky beach and snuggle up for warmth. The pilot's emergency foil blanket was laid over the children in an attempt to deflect the now cooling breeze.

By four AM a steady drizzle began to fall. It was still dark, but the growing dampness precluded further sleep. Ben, Jon and Tran stepped into the now smoldering tree line and grabbed various pieces of still glowing wood. They built a fire up near their camp and the group stayed warm as best they could around its flames.

When dawn finally broke, everyone was eager to move and get their blood flowing. They shared the pilot's rations, taking the edge off their hunger. Since Ben knew the route to Moscow, he naturally took charge. "The mainland shore is just south of this here island. It's maybe seventy-five yards away. Unfortunately, we'll have to swim it. From there, we work our way south along the shore. There should be a boat ramp after a way, and there'll be a road leadin' inland. That road hooks up with a larger one that crosses the firebreak. From there it's hilly country, but a fairly straight path to the Moscow Dam."

"So we're talking how far?" asked Nikki.

"Roughly fifteen-miles as the crow flies. Maybe seven, eight hours - maybe."

"Fifteen miles of hilly country will feel like twice that."

"Well then, we better get a move on," said Susan.

The scientists had broken down their lab equipment so that all they needed to carry was two sample cases and a smaller briefcase holding their data, backed up on two portable hard-drives. Though painful to leave behind, the rest of the equipment would hopefully be replaced in Canada.

When they got to the island's shore and faced the mainland across the water, Teddy Costas tried to be helpful, noting, "It doesn't really matter that we're going to get wet swimming." He looked at the sky. "This drizzle's gonna turn to rain." Most of them nodded politely at the boy as they waded out into the lake. Teddy pushed his voice to sound stronger than he felt. "The one good thing about the rain is that it doused the flames."

His father put a loving hand on his boy's shoulder, and while holding his daughter's hand they waded out with the rest. Amanda turned to her brother and said in a low voice, "It's gonna be okay, Teddy. Don't be afraid."

He looked at his sister as though she was mental, and chose to ignore her. They were eleven people in the middle of a burned down nowhere, with no real way to call for help, no food, no shelter, a handful of weapons and the potential for lots of virulently crazy people trying to eat them. Everyone was terrified out of their wits.

They were greeted on shore by voluminous thick steam and white smoke rising steadily from the burned down forest. While Steven helped his children, Jon knelt in the shallow inlet filling their water bag. He had cut a slit in the top of Poole's lifejacket and filled the volume with water instead. When it was nearly full, he stood and put it on like a yoke. It would be all of their water until they found the next fresh source. Then he thought about the flock of birds back in Teddy's inlet - and dropped in a few of the dead pilot's water purification tablets.

Lining up single file, they had barely taken ten steps when they all pulled up short. There was a mass just beyond the tree line, a pile of human remains, burned nearly beyond recognition; limbs and faces were twisted into various forms of agony. Amanda hid her eyes against her daddy's shirt while Teddy glanced, but only out of the corner of his eye.

Ben said, "It's God's providence." He looked at the scientists, "You folks could have just as well landed on this shore and been devoured instead."

Aaron quipped. "If we'd landed on this shore, we'd have been fricasseed like this infected bunch."

"Don't doubt the way of the Lord, son. It were His hand that kept your helicopter from landing right on top of us. His hand that brought you to us to help guide the way. He has a purpose for us all."

Aaron smiled and cocked his head, pointing a finger into Ben's chest, "Let's just get something straight. It was you and your ilk that helped get us into this mess. Mumbo jumbo about demons and the devil, Armageddon and what not. It's types like you that deny what's right in front of your own eyes, keeping people ignorant, helping to spread this thing."

"Suit yourself, friend. But I think it's you who are blind to your own good fortune."

"Friend? Listen, jackass, if the *Lord* wanted us home, we would have landed there safely last night and gotten back to work trying to find a cure for this thing."

Susan broke in. "All right, all right, enough! Concentrate on the task at hand. We survived this fire. These infected didn't. That doesn't mean others aren't out there." She gave Aaron an admonishing look and said, "Mr. Watson, please lead on."

Aaron let himself fall to the back of the group, muttering under his breath, "Merciful deity, my ass."

Ben took point followed by Tran. Nikki and Jon took up the rear; the more likely point of attack if they were followed. Both ends of their single file line were covered by their handful of weapons. They looked extraordinarily weak given the circumstances. They might as well have been a band of lost settlers in the middle of Apache territory. The depths of the foggy forest could be hiding dozens of eyes.

37 The Traffic Team

The CDC scientist's absence was noticed immediately. No more than an hour after the loss of communication, Director Louis-Gelding was scrambling to put together a search mission. Her people, the six people on this earth with the key to a potential cure for this horror, were down in that hell somewhere with all of their samples and data with them.

One helicopter was offered up for the mission. The major general leading the Northern Command could spare nothing more. He had other "immediate" issues taking priority over the "chance" of a cure. There was an invasion to still mount as well as numerous outbreaks within Canada to either contain or destroy. The armed services were already stretched beyond their ability to function efficiently.

The slapped together SAR (search and rescue team) wasn't military, not even paramilitary private contractors. They were a pair of civilian volunteers: Toronto's most popular weather and traffic gal, Kelly Stormberg (originally Stromberg, but how could she resist?) aka - Kelly Storm and her pilot Samantha McNeil (a hotshot who had cut her teeth flying stunts for "Hollywood North" Vancouver). They had signed up for aerial reconnaissance work, tracking down concentrations of infected and were prepped for takeoff on yet another search and report mission, when a last minute order drafted them to go find some poor bastard eggheads who had lost their way.

Defoliated by fire or not, Central Maine was a huge area of mostly forested land. Sam McNeil gave their odds at a million to one. Kelly was more of an optimist; she put it at half that. They had a general notion of the Black Hawk's flight plan: pretty much a straight shot from The Vineyard to the big French-Canadian city, with a third of the flight taking place over the Atlantic. Assuming that the Black Hawk had made it to shore, the scientists would have crossed somewhere just south of Portland; approximately two hundred and fifty miles as the crow flies from Quebec. Their Eurocopter AStar had a range of five hundred and ninety-one miles; enough for the trip down and back with a little fuel to spare. They drew a grid on a map, with the idea of moving south to the sea and then turning back north to Quebec - like mowing a giant lawn in the sky. They'd have to land and refuel each time, but even with that, they could make five, maybe six trips in a fourteen-hour period, give or take. Thank God for long summer days. They were given seventy-two hours. After that they were to return to recon duty.

Their bird was equipped with all of the latest gadgets. It could broadcast everything from major weather events, to tire factory fires, to multi-vehicle pileups and car chases. Prior to the pandemic, they figured they'd pretty much covered it all, even a stint in Alberta on Antelope migration back in '09.

They had fully integrated, high-definition, gyro-stabilized, camera systems (front and tail), a customized aerial microwave antenna, infrared cameras, HD and SD monitors and digital scanners, even internally mounted talent cameras and lighting. The external cameras would be especially helpful; they arranged for their signal to broadcast back to the Canadian Broadcasting Company (CBC) Quebec, where two young volunteers would sit and pore over the footage. This way, even if the two in the helicopter missed something, there would be two more pairs of eyes back home looking at every frame. One search helicopter would become the equivalent of perhaps two. It was that caveat that kept Director Louis-Gelding's mouth shut rather than her demanding more and still getting nothing.

A second mission to Florida was of course out of the question. They were on the eve of D-Day minus one. There would be no Ranger platoon with two Chinook helicopters available. If her people were alive, she had to find them. To her profound frustration, even drafting a fixed wing private pilot to pitch in was out of the question. All aviation fuel was directed to the war effort. Traffic Maven and Stunt Girl were it.

Storm and McNeil would leave from the CDC headquarters itself and then vector south in the direction of Biddeford, Maine. The poor visibility that would normally keep another helicopter grounded was not a problem for their AStar. The infrared cameras would actually help them separate the wheat from the chaff as it were. Of course the freshly burned and burning forests would offer innumerable hot spots, but they would still be able to pick out human movement.

To the weather woman and her pilot's frustration, they picked up lots of human movement as they flew south. The massive bombing campaign had surely killed thousands of Fiends, probably tens of thousands, but what they observed below was truly disheartening. New England was still filled with infected. With the exception of a distinctive arm wave or some other thinking man's signal, there was no way to distinguish between a Fiend and the healthy. They saw no such signal.

The eleven refugees found the initial going pretty easy. Once they had made their way along the shore to the boat launch ramp, it was a simple walk - to begin with; the dirt road was well maintained. But as they moved into denser woods the true value of burning the forests of New England became obvious; even the most basic path was littered with fallen trees, many of which were still smoldering despite a steady drizzle. The seven or eight hour walk seemed a fanciful concept as they skirted the debris, climbing over and under and working their way around while getting coated with damp charcoal and ash. This was looking like an epic walk for fifteen miles of progress. When they finally reached a paved road, the challenge became even greater; the fire had been so hot that it melted the asphalt. Fallen trees were glued to the ground and the terrain resembled hardened lava. To make matters worse, as the ground fog became even denser, their visibility was shortened to perhaps twenty-five yards. The dying forest dropped constant debris as weakened limbs and ashen leaves rained to the ground. Each sound was a jolt as the party reacted to the potential charge of voracious death. To top it off, they were all hungry, as expressed thoroughly by Amanda to her father, "Daddy. My tummy hurts and my legs are tired."

"I know Sweetie, but you have to keep being strong. Daddy will give you a piggyback in a little awhile."

Aaron quipped, "I'll take a piggy back when you're finished."

Everyone chuckled at this until Nikki spoke up. "Okay, folks. I know we're all a bit punch-drunk, but let's keep ourselves quiet and alert."

"It would do to tighten up a bit too," said Jon, "We don't want to get too spread out. Strays make easy targets."

The single file shrunk up after that and they continued to listen to the sounds of the forest, occasionally getting spooked and unconsciously reaching out to make contact with the person in front.

They stopped every mile or so to take a breather and sip some water, until three hours later when they reached the firebreak. This zone of low scrub was perhaps 50 meters wide and though it offered the southern forest a reprieve from a fire from the North or visa-versa, the nature of the fire bombing campaign insured that both sides of the border were equally destroyed. Nevertheless, the path itself was relatively free of fallen debris; the low grasses and shrubs had burned but didn't act as an obstruction. Nikki decided to show the team a different pace of walking, one that had found efficiency with foot travelers over the eons and long success for marathoners; they would run-walk-run.

"In this scrub we can make an eighteen minute mile by jogging for thirty-seconds followed by walking for sixty then jogging for thirty more and so on. We'll take a break every mile."

Ben said, "Twelve miles or so from here to the Moscow dam."

"That's four to five hours," added Tran. He looked at Teddy and then Amanda.

Teddy whispered to his sister. "I've seen you run around for ten hours straight when you're excited about something." He glanced at his father. "Dad's already pretty pooped from carrying you for the last mile. You can do this. I know it."

Amanda turned to her father. "Daddy, are you tired?"

"I'm okay, Doll."

"I can make it on my own. I've got stronger legs than Teddy." Teddy started to challenge that notion, then realized that he'd won his argument.

Nikki said, "Okay, Amanda sets the pace with me out front. Mr. Tran, you take the rear with Jon."

They hadn't even made the first mile before Nikki quickly held up a hand to halt them. Twenty yards in front of them was a paved road running north/south. In the middle of the road was a loan Fiend kneeling amongst a small herd of deer. The deer were all dead, their body positions suggesting that they were cooked alive. The Fiend, a skinny looking middle aged male covered in several nasty burns itself, was tearing into the roasted flank of a young buck with the edge of a sharp hunk of rock. A dozen crows stood nearby. One was brave enough to hop forward and stick its beak in at the fresh kill before the Fiend barked at it like a jackal.

Ben stepped to the front of the group and leveled his shotgun.

"No," whispered Nikki, pushing the barrel down, "Fire that thing... Who knows how many are out there."

Everyone glanced at the misty woods without taking an eye off the Fiend. The wounded creature looked up and hissed at the sound of Nikki's voice, then feverishly dove back into its meal, pulling off a hunk with its teeth and chewing loudly with a lip smacking open mouth.

Jon said, "Clearly it's more interested in that dead deer than us. I say we cut off some meat ourselves and skirt our way around the thing. It looks like it's in pretty bad shape. Its left leg looks mostly cooked too." Jon realized that he was reducing the infected man to the level of some asexual alien creature. "I bet he can barely walk, much less run."

They steered a wide path around the savage looking man. Tran, Nikki and Jon kept their guns trained on it, while Steven, Ben and Christie cut off thigh meat from two of the dead animals. The meat had been baked as though in an oven and came away from the bone with the ease of a rotisserie chicken. The Fiend continued to ignore them as it feasted away. Jog-walk-jog was suddenly energized with more incentive.

When they had put at least a mile between them and the Fiend, the small band stopped again and ate. Despite the way it had come off the bone, the meat was lean and a bit tough to chew. No one complained. Even the children gorged themselves. None of them had had red meat of any kind in some time.

With bellies full, they continued on. The firebreak revealed all manner of burned animals that had run to it for refuge. Using the foil blanket for a cache, they collected more meat to provision themselves for later. There were several human remains as well. Everyone prayed or hoped in their own way, that they had been infected people and not the healthy.

The food gave everyone new strength. The only person having trouble was Rick Decker. His shoulder was back in its socket, but the ligaments were still bruised. For him, each landing on his right foot in particular was an agonizing jolt.

They stopped at a brook for water. It was coated in ash and floating bits of charcoal and other debris, but by spreading the ashes way from the surface they were able to get to it. Crouching and kneeling over the water, they looked like apes on the veldt, repeatedly looking up, glancing around. They refilled the lifejacket/canteen and decontaminated it with the last of the pilot's emergency water treatment pills and moved on.

After five hours, they reached a clearing with a view of the Kennebec River and the northwest side of Moscow. The bulk of the village was obscured by burned forest, but a small hydroelectric dam stood out below. It had a single generator building, which appeared to be still intact on the far side of the river. The river continued to flow through the dam's sluice and they could hear the sound of the generator working all by its diligent self. High-tension wires led out from it, north and south, and Nikki and Jon found their thoughts racing back to their incarceration and escape from the fools back in Stratton.

Ben said, "Beyond the tree line over there is the Canada Road. Moscow village is just down to the right, Bingham just south of them. There's a fair amount of folks that lived in Bingham. No telling about demons, but Lord knows they had their fair share of sinners. Canada Road follows the Kennebec for a fair piece up to The Forks anyway, then away from water. Next town up the way from here is Caratunk. Mother-in-law lives in Caratunk." As he said this he spit on the ground.

Aaron not being able to help himself from sticking it to the Jesus lover, said, "Demons and sinners aside, we should check the town for some staples, right?"

They all looked to Susan who found herself in charge again. "Well, clearly we are not going to walk to Canada with our current food supply as it is. It would be good to find some sort of portable shelter or at least some blankets. Of course a working motor vehicle or two wouldn't hurt."

They could see the road pretty well. It was clogged with burned abandoned cars and trucks. The final push out of the country had turned into the greatest gridlock in history. For most people it was easier to walk.

Decker said, "No way we're going to be driving up that road, even if we find a working anything."

Nikki spoke up, "May I make a suggestion, Ma'am?"

"Susan."

"Sorry, Susan. The generating plant or whatever it is over there seems like a good place to rest up. We could probably break in and use it for shelter. It's far enough back from anything to be able to keep an eye out for an ambush. I say we go over there, make ourselves at home. Then Jon and I, and maybe Ben, can scout out the town and see what we see."

Susan looked at the others. "Anyone got a problem with that idea?" No one spoke up. "It's settled then. Lead on Nikki."

38 Home Sweet Home

The dam's transformer building had a large sign on the door explaining the dangers of the high voltage within and was backed up by the sound of a steady hum. There was also a thick brass padlock on a heavy hasp. They couldn't shoot it off. The noise would be like ringing a dinner bell. They tried a nearby rock first, but the banging made a loud metal echo after each beat and they all winced while looking around like frightened rabbits. The lock was built to discourage just this kind of assault and after several tries the rock just broke apart in Jon's hands. There was nothing lying around for leverage and so they all stared at the door with defeated frustration.

Susan said, "Maybe we go with plan B."

"Which is?" asked Aaron, his voice trembling with accusation.

"That house over by the road didn't burn. Maybe there's food. It's not near any other houses. It's certainly shelter."

The rain had picked up in intensity and the group looked pretty miserable. Amanda shivered against her father. Teddy made it look like he was trying to warm her from the other side, but really he was just trying to warm himself.

Nikki said, "Houses are hard to defend. Lots of ways to break in."

They took a vote and agreed to check out the house. The dammed up river behind it and the open road in front of it, had allowed its roof to avoid the storm of embers that had laid waste to the few other buildings they could see.

Nikki, Jon and Ben went first with the rest of the group hanging back a hundred feet or so. The dam was narrow and therefore more easily defended. Should things go south, the plan was to run there and make a stand.

If one avoided looking at the decimation that surrounded it, the house was charming enough in a weather-stained sort of way. It was a simple two-story affair with the upper level mostly devoted to a steeply sloped galvanized steel roof. It had a separate garage that had burned. There was no evidence of a car inside. There was a much abused lawn tractor parked in the center of the front lawn and a laundry line was fixed between two posts on the side.

The windows appeared to be intact and the scouts were feeling hopeful until they reached the front. The door stood wide open. Certainly an invitation to any infected taking shelter. Nikki went in first, followed by Jon, then Ben. The men followed Nikki's lead on how to clear a room. Jon was happily surprised that house clearing was second nature to him. It was common sense, really – enter cautiously.

It was a small house with a simple layout, living room, den, kitchen, dining and lavatory. Judging from the photos of generations of families that lined the central hall, it was a grandparent's house. A framed crocheted "Home Sweet Home" completed the picture. Jon ducked as a fly made a beeline toward his face and then continued out the door.

When Nikki took the first step to go upstairs, it gave out a tremendous creek and they all winced, pointing their weapons at the landing above. No mad drooling grandmas came rushing from any doors. They stayed in a line as they moved up, their guns covering the upper banister, the spaces between the spindles offering them a view of all of the doors; two were closed, one was open. They chose the open door first and Nikki stepped back almost immediately with revulsion on her face.

"Christ, I'll never get used to that."

Jon looked past her and saw the remains of a blood bath on a queen size bed. It was difficult to make out the details of the gruesome scene; primarily dried blood and mixed up bones. Two skulls with part of their faces and most of their grey hair intact, said grandma and grandpa were long digested by now. Even the flies had finished their work, with only a scattered few buzzing about – the bulk of them were piled on the windowsills, dead from starvation.

A check of the other rooms found nothing more than a second bedroom, sewing room, bath and an attic space of sorts. The Fiends had come and gone. Ben found a note on the dresser of the master bedroom.

Darling Ones,

Your Grampy and I have chosen to go with God. We know that in his mercy he will forgive us the sin of taking our own lives. We are too old to run from this holocaust and prefer to remember the world as it was before.

Know that we love you all so very much and we pray that you will have time left on this earth to enjoy the wonders that it can still offer. May you remain safe and sound. Should that not be possible, know that we will be waiting for you on the other side. May the world know peace once more.

Love,

Grammy

On the floor an empty bottle of sleeping pills and two empty pints of whiskey showed the choice of exit. They closed the bedroom door, giving the couple back their tomb. A check of the kitchen revealed a working refrigerator stocked with mold-covered vegetables and assorted pickled condiments. The cabinets were thinly but evenly stocked with canned foods, rice and dried pasta. There was plenty to eat. Apparently, the healthy who had rushed past this place in their urgency to get out, had given it no thought.

Ben fetched the rest of the group while Jon and Nikki took lookout, pulling down the window shades and closing the front door. Just for the heck of it, he picked up the telephone to see if there was a dial tone. It was an odd sensation to pick up a phone and hear nothing on the line. The hunk of plastic, which had always represented life at the other end, was just a dead thing now, like the town, like the whole country. It made him sad and he wished that he hadn't touched it.

They ate well to the point of bloated bellies and then everyone decided to make camp in the living room. The upstairs and its terrible tale kept them all downstairs anyway. Only the people on watch would use the rooms up there, the view being better. Though there was daylight left, it was decided that it would be prudent, given their exhaustion, that they sleep in the house for one night. There was no knowing where or when they would find shelter like this again. The adults took turns on watch. Two would sit in the windows upstairs that faced up and down the road. It would change every two hours so there would be no chance of someone nodding off.

The night came and went without incident, and, in the early dawn hours, they all gathered for breakfast. Christy and Tran decided on a contest: who could make the tastiest breakfast treat with the limited ingredients on hand? It was agreed that Christy's Bisquick muffins with diced cornichon pickles and raisins were surprisingly good. Tran's rice cakes with ketchup… not so much.

With the meal complete, they forced themselves back to reality.

"Obviously a vehicle or two would be very helpful," said Aaron. "Without the competition from other desperate drivers, we might be able to weave our way around a lot of the mess out there."

"I hate to break it to you, buddy," said Decker, "but did you look at the offerings on the lot? Fireball dominoes seems to have put the transportation option off the table."

"Don't be such a pessimist, Rick. We could still find something, just like we found this house."

Susan, choosing to ignore this exchange said, "It couldn't hurt to have some more clothes."

Tran paced the room. "Well, the clothes in this house might fit a few of us, but if we assume that there's no transportation option, and we're going to be on the road for several days, we could use some camping gear, back packs to carry food, tents, cook stove."

Aaron rolled his eyes, "Since we're apparently indulging in fantasy, let's just head on over to Camping World. I'm sure every Maine town has one."

Ben said, without irony, "Only store around here is down the road in Bingham. General store, but I'm sure it's cleaned out. Good chance of meeting demons in a big town like that."

Jon smiled at Ben's parochialism and said, "We hunt for a car or two, hopefully with full tanks of gas. We find that and we're on our way."

"We could ride bikes," said Teddy.

Jon smiled, "Not a bad idea, sport. If we can't find a powered vehicle, we'll round up some pedals."

"He doesn't like to be called sport," said Amanda. "It's condescending."

Everyone chuckled at this and Jon apologized. "Sorry, Teddy. It's still a good idea."

Jon and Nikki volunteered again for the scouting mission. They decided that Ben and his shotgun were put to better use protecting the house and the others. Tran would join them instead.

A search of the house turned up no further guns. Apparently not everyone in Maine packed heat. They did discover that Grampy had been a sword collector. On one wall of the den, a glass display case showed off a wide assortment of blades from different eras. Susan, who dabbled in antiquities, was impressed at the possible value of the objects. Jon was impressed with a Civil War era cavalry saber and strapped its scabbard around his waist. Everyone, including the children, chose to arm themselves. It almost seemed quaint, people walking around with swords, but in reality, given the close combat nature of a Fiend attack, a sword was potentially a damn good weapon.

39 The Scout

Though he knew it made him look like a walking cliché, Tran felt surprisingly more confident with the Japanese Katana strapped to his back. This blade was shorter than a traditional Samurai sword and he decided it was probably used by some kind of Ninja. With the pilot's pistol in one hand and the sword in the other, he felt like he could take down any number of Fiends. "Hey Aaron, check it out. I'm Snake Eyes from GI Joe." His old video-gaming partner looked at him like he'd just stepped off a spaceship.

His feeling of invincibility lasted about twenty-seconds after he, Nikki and Jon departed from the confines of the house and safety in numbers. Being out in the open again was a stomach churning experience. It was as though the very air itself was watching him.

It was still raining outside, but the visibility had improved. The rain had grown heavy overnight, so much so that at one point it sounded like the roof might cave in with the weight of it. The benefit being that it had so thoroughly soaked the still smoldering forests that the fog and smoke had completely dissipated. The storm had finally slacked off some in the pre-dawn hours and had switched over to a steady cold shower as the three scouts made their way outside. The ground was spongy and muddy and they had to move onto the road itself in order to walk with ease. The homes left and right were burned to their foundations and the air was filled with the smell of damp charcoal, burned plastic and ozone. As most were heated with propane, many of the houses were literally blown to pieces. Some of the big high-pressure tanks had been installed too close. They had exploded with remarkable power, littering the road with assorted debris.

The scouts observed no useable vehicles, the abandoned and wrecked ones instead blending in with the old rusted hulks that were already part of the landscape.

"No bikes, either," said Tran.

"Probably lots of people took Teddy's thought to heart," said Jon. "Bicycle's actually a really good idea."

"Why don't you two shut it now?" hissed Nikki. "Pay attention."

A little further on, they found the elementary school saved from the inferno by its vast playing fields. A banner hung above the front door with a red cross painted on it and the words Aid Station.

Tran said, "Seems like we'd find some supplies in there."

Nikki quipped, "Seems like we'd find a bunch of infected in there."

Jon whispered from where he was walking on the opposite side of the street, "The town's dead. The infected have moved on."

"Yeah? So why are you whispering?"

The drop-off circle in front of the school was strewn with bits of clothing, bags, and discarded suitcases. They stepped past this debris, keeping an eye out for useful items to pick up on the way back out. The front door was closed but unlocked. When they stepped inside they were greeted by a vision of unfolding catastrophe. The main corridor was littered with personal items: temporary beds, suitcases, clothes, toys, camping gear, everything a person on the run might need to survive, as well as a huge assortment of the mundane and not so useful. It was all abandoned. There were no bodies, blood or any evidence of struggle. It was just left behind. There was also trash - heaps of it. The smell was overwhelming. They cautiously explored further and found that the toilets were overflowing and inoperable. A classroom had become the new toilet with buckets and trashcans of human waste left full and stewing in the closed up room. Clearly, the refugees had been terrified to go outdoors.

"God. The smell. It's overwhelming," said Tran.

"Guess they have a Camping World after all," said Nikki.

"Why did they leave their stuff?" asked Jon. "If Ben were here, he'd swear it was the rapture." He and Nikki shared a smile.

Tran picked up a rolled sleeping bag and looked it over. "When the Army made its final exit, they were escorting every bus they could get their hands on. They were packed to the breaking point with people. No room for stuff like this."

They wandered the halls and looked in on more classrooms filled with abandoned possessions. The walls of course, were adorned with the typical décor of an elementary school: history posters, math problems, art, awards and the like. It was a cheerful building in what appeared to be a rather dreary town. Of course the town being burnt to the ground didn't help sell the place very well. Nevertheless, the community clearly cared about its kids. There was pride in here, a sense of self-respect. They had offered it up as a place of refuge for friend and stranger alike. Now it sat empty, free from the fire, but a testament to the shear panic of the evacuation.

Jon said, "There must be a cafeteria. With the electricity still running, I bet the refrigerators are working too."

They continued to the back of the school where they found the entrance to the gymnasium. There were three sets of double doors designed to open out in the event of an emergency. They were ominously tied shut.

"That can't mean anything good," said Nikki

Tran stepped over to one of the doors and listened, knocked and said, "Hello?"

"Robert. What are you doing?" whispered Jon.

"I'm seeing if there's anybody in there."

"Why would there be anybody in there? They tied the doors shut."

"You remember Titanic? Not enough lifeboats. The rich folks locked the poor folks down below so they could have them to themselves."

"You think the Army left people behind, locked up?" Nikki asked skeptically.

"Only one way to find out." Tran grabbed his sword out of its sheath –

"No!" yelled Nikki and Jon.

- and sliced through the ropes.

"Why would you do that?" blurted out Jon, stepping back from the doors.

"I didn't hear anybody answering, did you? An infected person would have been pounding on the door the moment I knocked. We need to find out what all of our options are. Right?"

Nikki hefted her SCAR and pointed it at the door. "Listen, doctor dickhead – don't make decisions for us. We talk before we make choices like that."

"Fine. Sorry."

Jon pointed his pistol and so did Robert as he pulled the door open. A waft of rot and decay washed over them as yet another horror show was revealed. The gym had been set up as a temporary medical center. It was now just one more orgy of murder and mayhem. Many of the cots had eaten victims on them. Many were empty. There were other corpses in wheelchairs. Several leaned against the walls or lay on the floor, undoubtedly infected, as evidenced by their intact bodies.

"Holy…" Jon was stunned. "They locked them in together."

It took everything It had not to show itself. To wait –wait for the Fresh Ones to step inside. It's stomach gurgled in delirious anticipation and It thought for a moment that the sound of it had given It away. It squeezed Its eyes shut in frustration, held Its breath for just a little longer. Just a few feet, that's all. Step inside a few feet so It could have a fat juicy meal. Then It snapped open Its eyes as It heard more steps.

"Likely died from dehydration," said Tran, pulling his shirt up over his face. He was immediately knocked to the floor by a male Fiend that had been hiding up against the wall. His pistol and sword went scattering across the waxed hardwood as he instinctively balled up into a fetal position.

Jon ran in and grabbed the creature by its filthy, greasy hair, trying to hold its head and snapping teeth away from Tran's exposed neck. He couldn't risk a shot - had to drop the gun to hold on – the thing shaking its head, trying to break free - rail thin, completely naked, screeching and gnashing with manic delight.

Nikki screamed, "Step away and I'll shoot it! Step away and I'll shoot it!"

The Fiend suddenly glanced over its shoulder and flipped itself around, causing Jon to lose his grip. Before he could push it away, it bit down on the top of his head.

For Jon, it was one of several slow motion moments in his life: taking the folk's VW for an illegal joy ride, losing control and flying off an embankment into a shallow river - The time he jammed a carving knife into his thumb - When he lit his face on fire with his first flaming shot of 151, his roommate laughing, throwing a wet bar towel on his head. He could feel the pressure of teeth clamping down on his skull - didn't register the pain yet. Rather, the skin of his forehead felt stretched. There was an almost popping sound as it was breeched and the blood started flowing down, rancid breath surrounding his face - the odor of this thing enveloping him in disease and decay. He missed his riot helmet a lot - and then he knew he was dead.

To his surprise, he felt resignation. It didn't stop him from kicking and punching and then finally shoving the thing off, but he accepted this twist with almost emotionless alacrity. Nikki shot the anorexic thing nearly in half with a full-auto burst from the SCAR.

Tran rolled up off the floor bawling, "I'm sorry, I'm sorry."

Nikki shoved him back down and screamed spittle in his face. "Motherfucker you killed my best friend!" He kept saying sorry in wide-eyed astonishment, and she kicked him in the legs, his hands covering his face. "You cavalier piece of shit. There's no room left for stupid pricks like you." She pointed her assault rifle at Tran's heaving chest. The horrified man made no effort to defend himself, threw his hands back in subjugation.

"I'm not dead yet," said Jon, while feeling the tattered ridges of the bite - looking at the blood on his hand.

That stopped Nikki cold, and she let her finger off the trigger. She turned and looked at this man who had become her lover and friend. Tears welled in her piercing gray eyes. "Shit, Jon. Not you."

Then his resignation wore off and the full weight of the loss shook him, dismay filling his heart. This wasn't right. This wasn't the plan. He was supposed to spend quality time with this person, this daredevil, this strong brainy woman. Best friend. It's true. God damn it! He had been falling in love with her.

She took a step toward him and he held out his bloody hand, warding her off. "No, don't come closer."

Tran slowly picked himself up, tears swelling his eyes. "Mr. Washington. I'm so sorry, sir. I-"

"Stop. What's done is done. I don't have time. Fuck, it was liable to happen at some point." He focused on Nikki, "I've got maybe fifteen hours of usefulness. I help you guys get geared up and on the road, then cover you from behind.

When I start with... When I get the fever, I..." He cleared his throat and wiped the blood away from his eyes with his sleeve. He pointed to his pistol lying on the floor. "I put that in my mouth and end it. Go see my grandmother. Apologize for killing her."

40 Suicide

Through constantly seeping tears, Nikki bandaged Jon's head. He held himself away from her, only letting her touch his head – while wearing gloves - wanting so badly to hold her - wondering if he let himself become one of the monsters, if he'd have any memories at all. Tran stood off to one side and shook with rage at himself. After the tenth, I'm sorry speech, Jon gently asked him to stop again. "Learn from your mistake, Mr. Tran. There are few chances to survive them now."

They finished exploring the school and found no other surprises. In the cafeteria, a walk-in freezer/refrigerator was stocked to the roof. Clearly, when the people running the aid station decided it was time to bug out, they did it in a hurry. Any relief they might have felt over finding the food was erased by Jon's plight.

They walked a mile or so farther south on the Canada Road and didn't see another soul, just burned, or partially burned, structures and endless, ominous, defoliated black forest. The three scouts returned to the house and reported their tale. The disapproval of Tran's rashness didn't need to be restated, it oozed through the air. Tran found himself standing aside, his opinion no longer valued. The group took another vote and decided that they would all walk down to the school together. From there they would gather supplies and food before setting out on the next leg north. Ben estimated sixteen miles to Caratunk.

Everyone kept giving Jon sideways glances. It wasn't out of mistrust; they all knew how long it took for the disease to take hold; it was pure rubbernecking – morbid curiosity getting the best of them, as much fascination as there was sympathy. They were in the presence of a guy who but for a bullet in the brain, would in a few short hours, lose his identity and devolve into a man eating psycho. For Steven and the kids it was adaptation to more loss – surreal in the wait, knowing what lay ahead. For Ben, it was about doubt. The label of demon was not so easily cast now.

For Nikki it was simply devastating. Her reaction was born of experience. As a war vet, she had lost many friends in combat. An old switch turned on in her head; the same switch that turned on for Bob back at the mansion. It said that Jon was already gone and she needed to brick over the hole - make it solid, impenetrable. On the outside, the manifestation was simple; she ignored her friend like he wasn't there. She wouldn't even look at him, and she sure as shit wasn't going to befriend any of these other people. She allowed herself a single moment of gratitude; acknowledging at least to herself, that during her time with Jon, she had re-discovered some of her self-worth. After her return from Africa, she had just wandered, couldn't hold down a job and even flirted with heroin (she still had the connections). Thank God she hadn't succumbed to it. At one point, she'd become so destitute that she'd sell her rare O Negative blood to eat. She told herself that she was going to make it through this thing, no matter what. To do it, she had to steel herself against the loss.

Jon immediately felt the change in her, and it hurt. He didn't need to be babied, coddled with explanation, but he needed his friend to at least offer a face of sympathy. She was practically cold to the touch. When he did just that, reached out to touch her sleeve, she gently pulled it away. "Don't."

"I don't want to feel this from you."

"I don't either. But you've got to let me stay focused. I have people to get home safe." She still wouldn't look at him as she aimlessly pawed through discarded camping gear.

He nodded - It wasn't rejection, it was coping. She was now the sole combatant. It was a revelation to him that he had turned out to be a natural warrior, that he would be missed for that as well. "I understand." He started to walk away and then stopped. "If you think about it, we don't really know each other."

She felt her eyes grow hot and moist and she kept her back to him. "I know you. I'm sorry."

McNeil and Storm where on day two, flight number eight, when they spotted the ruined Black Hawk. Actually, they didn't spot it, one of the volunteers back at the CBC watching the video feed did. They got a call to turn around and investigate and found themselves hovering over a small lake island, split by a causeway beach.

Sam set the bird down on the rocky shore between the north and south tree lines and let the engine wind down. As they climbed out, Kelly grabbed a short-barreled shotgun and slung it over her shoulder. There were the remains of a campsite, a burned and partially submerged motorboat in the lagoon, and debris scattered across the rocks to the North - the two searcher's hearts pumped with an immediate sense of failure. A human hand, still ensconced in its flight glove, was lying near the shore, the bloody stump covered with ants.

Something else caught Kelly's eye, "Sam, look there." Piled neatly near the south tree line was the scientist's discarded gear.

"Someone survived this thing." She stepped up to the middle of the beach. "Hello? Anybody here? We're looking for a group of CDC scientists!"

"Uh, Kel, if they were here, you don't think they might have heard us land?"

"Don't be a bitch, bitch. What if they're injured?"

So team Storm and McNeil wasted precious time stumbling through the island's burnt forests in search of injured scientists.

Meanwhile, the survivors over in Moscow were putting together the last of their newly found gear. Nikki walked past the gymnasium and found Susan and Tran assembling some basic first aid items. It was surreal to see these two scientists almost nonchalantly packing a rucksack amid such horrible carnage. Tran wouldn't make eye contact with Nikki. His mortification over the incident in this very room set his stomach rumbling with anxiety and regret.

Staring at an IV pole, its drip line leading to a butchered corpse, Nikki found herself with some un-solidified notion tickling the back of her brain, and she unconsciously picked at the fresh scab on her finger; the wound Jon had kissed when they were back on the boat.

Susan interrupted the thought saying, "That should cover us. We've even got antibiotics."

There it was again, just on the threshold of Nikki's forethoughts.

The group assembled in front of the school with Ben ready to lead them up the road. It was agreed that Jon would hang back, just in sight, and then after a couple of hours or so fall back further and then stop. It didn't need to be said that they all hoped that he would then quickly kill himself before he got the fever and lost his ability for rational thought. In the event that her friend came racing up the road foaming at the mouth, Nikki would take up the rear and keep an eye out.

Everyone offered Jon awkward goodbyes, no one touching him, Steven holding his sobbing little girl back from hugging the man. They then all walked ahead a hundred paces or so and gave Jon and Nikki some privacy.

She said, "When you do it, don't point the gun at your temple. You may not have the gun lined up perfectly and you'll just shoot the front of your face off. It could take a while to die from that. Put the gun in your mouth and aim up at the roof. You're guaranteed to scramble your brains that way. Please don't let yourself succumb to the fever. I don't want to have to shoot you running after us."

"See, I'm still learning about you," said Jon, hurt choking his voice. "You're a suicide expert."

This stopped her short and she turned to him making eye contact for the first time since the moments after he was bitten. Her eyes hardened. "Don't – do - that. It's hard enough contemplating the rest of this without you."

Jon looked chastened. "Well, could you at least say goodbye?"

Her eyes softened slightly, "Goodbye, Jon. You're a good man." He looked at her with hope, wanting to hear more. She finally said, "I felt something. I really did. Now let me go."

Jon started backing up slowly while still looking at her. "Goodbye, Nikki."

She turned her back to him, walking away. The tingling picked up again in the back of her mind. She was missing something. It was right there, at the edge of her consciousness, yet at the same time, something seemed to be willing her to keep it in the shadows – don't face it, it's not true. Jon snapped her out of her reverie. "I'll make sure you're still in earshot when I do it. That way you can be certain."

She didn't turn. Just kept walking, whispering quietly to herself, "Goodbye, Jon." She started a slow jog to catch up with the group.

For an hour and a half they trudged north up the Canada Road. Jon let himself slowly fall back, and for much of the time he was out of sight beyond a bend or below a hill. On the occasional straightaway he could be made out as a small speck on a rise and then finally Nikki could see him no more.

The group continued on for another half-an-hour, paused to sip some water, take a bite of bread, and kept on moving. Nikki tried to steel herself against her building sadness, and let herself fall back a few yards from the others, her vision clouding over, her pace becoming disjointed. She wiped the tears away in mild frustration and shook the drops from the tips of her fingers. She focused on a stray drop as it nestled in the cut on her finger. The one Jon had kissed. She had worried about her blood in his in his mouth, but that was silly. They'd shared a lot more than blood... and that's when it all came to her in one giant rush.

"Stop!" She called to the others, holding up her hand.

The group involuntarily crouched and spun around looking in all directions, certain that they were under assault. Nikki ran forward to Susan.

"I think I'm immune."

"Excuse me?" she asked, nerves rattled to the edge.

"I survived the infection. I'm sure of it."

"What the fuck are you talking about?" swore Aaron, who was just about ready to fall over and die from this steady diet of fear.

Nikki looked at Ben, "Ben, tell them. You saw me sick and then I got better."

"It's true. She got sick and then got better. Don't know what else she's talking about."

Nikki grabbed Ben by his jacket. "The fight with the Fiend in the river. I swallowed some of its blood, the baby's too. I didn't admit it, but it happened."

"Hold on a second," said Tran. "You ingested blood from an infected person, became sick and then got better?"

"Yes! That's what I'm saying. I must be immune."

Susan looked at Ben. "You're certain that this person was infected?"

"It was a demon all right. No doubt of that."

"Well, that's remarkable," said Susan. "We know of no case of immunity."

"It happened, I swear."

Decker said, "What if you didn't get the blood in your mouth? You said this fight happened in a river? Water up here is chilly, liable to knock your immune system down if you exhaust yourself in it. What if you just caught a cold?"

"That's what I've always assumed. Like you said, nobody is immune, but I know I got the blood in my mouth. I'll never forget the coppery taste." She turned and started back south. "Come on. There's no time."

"Where are you going?" called Susan.

"To save, Jon. You've got to do a blood transfusion."

"What?"

She called over her shoulder, "I've got O neg blood. I used to have to volunteer for the Marine Corp Blood drive every fifty days." She stopped, "In Southern Sudan we were doing exchange transfusions for Malaria on a regular basis. Come on."

"But...-"

"You're CDC for Christ sake. You know what I'm talking about. Get your asses moving! We can't let him shoot himself!"

Nikki picked up her fast walk to a jog, then dumped her pack and began running a sprint. The others followed tentatively at first, the scientists conferring.

"Could it work?" asked Christy

Aaron blurted, "What about getting back to Canada? We've got the original bacterium in these sample cases!"

Susan said, "We're not going to make it to Canada without her. Dump everything but the samples and the hard drives and run. If she is immune, we've jumped light years ahead in the ability to fight this thing. Hell, if she's immune, nothing can happen to hurt that woman. Move!"

They all dropped their packs on the ground and ran after Nikki.

41 Cold Steel

Sam got the AStar wound up again while Kelly called in their findings, certain of survivors. Whether they were still alive was unknown. The searchers would proceed to zigzag east to west while working their way north. The scientists couldn't have gotten too far in two and a half days. Storm and McNeil patted each other on the back; their needle in the haystack had enlarged to size of a twig.

Of course they couldn't know that they were making the wrong choice. They naturally assumed that the refugees would have chosen to move north, not considering their need to travel south first to get to the Canada Road. The AStar's new search pattern kept them north of the town of Moscow, towards which the refugees, even now, were returning.

Despite the Army's desperate need for reconnaissance, with the discovery of the downed Black Hawk, Director Louis-Gelding was able to get an extension on Sam and Kelly's mission. They would have an additional forty-eight hours before they were to be peeled off for urgent information gathering.

Jon sat down with his back to a thick tree that stood alone from its charred sisters in the nearby forest. It had survived the inferno and stood green and radiant against a world of blackened sticks and damp ash. He had chosen a piece of high ground in order to observe anything coming from the South. His body felt tired and he knew it wasn't from the walk. Unlike his comrades further up the road, he was carrying no gear. He had a half full canteen, that he was gulping from. He finished off the water and wanted more, the notion of which, filled him with dread. The first symptom had arrived. He tried to imagine the changes occurring inside of him, his body's hopeless defenses beginning their valiant last fight. It occurred to him as he shook the last drops onto his lips, that it was a nearly pointless act. But thirst was thirst and the cool water felt good as it soothed his fiercely parched throat.

He un-holstered his Smith & Wesson, felt its cool steel in the palm of his hand, the weight of it, the cross hatching on the wood clad grip, and his heart began to pound. It was the same intense feeling he got just before he had to step on stage to give a lecture – the fear of public speaking surprisingly similar to the fear of certain death. He utilized the calming technique that he'd developed for such situations: putting his fingers on his wrist, feeling his pulse and willing his heart rate to go down while taking slow, steady, deep breaths. As he counted back from one hundred, the panic slowly subsided and he concentrated once again on the gun. Without racking the slide, he experimented with placing the barrel in his mouth and managed to tap his lower teeth, giving himself a sharp stab of pain and scraped the roof of his mouth as he pulled the gun back out. He chuckled through watery eyes, thinking that suicide by bullet to the head was supposed to be a painless affair. Then despair slowed his heartbeat further as he took stock of it all, the life that he'd led: He had never really loved, though he knew that had changed with Nikki. By the time he was eleven, he knew he wanted to be a reporter. He'd wanted nothing more. Focusing on that task at the expense of nearly everything else. His true love was the out-of-town assignment, the thrill of foreign travel, submerging himself in other cultures. He had friends, but they were really more acquaintances at the various way stations of his life. He'd never had a confidant, a soul brother, someone to spill his guts to – well maybe Granny Washington. His gut spilling snuck into his writing instead – editorializing - something that his editors had put up with because his reporting was so good. He had built a following at the Atlanta Daily Mail and he had been offered national syndication just before Cain's broke out. His last assignment was a test of that new position. He felt that he'd done well with his final reports. He'd hung on longer than any of the others, the bigger and better known reporters having long bugged out when the shit truly hit the fan.

He scanned the horizon. His position offered him the ability to see a couple of miles. Nothing was coming his way so he took a deep breath and thought to himself, no time like the present. As his heart began to rev up again, he chambered a round and looked at the dark metal tool. The forty-five-caliber bullet inside would likely take the top of his head off. He'd be just one more horrid sight in a country overflowing with them. He smelled the gun's barrel, taking in its oily, bittersweet metal scent, and then slipped it carefully into his mouth, this time avoiding tapping his teeth. He thought of his grandmother before she had turned and he dearly hoped that she would be waiting for him on the other side. Then he heard footsteps. Running footsteps. They were coming from the North. He slipped the gun out of his mouth, tapping his top teeth hard, adding more tears to his eyes, and he swore. He squeezed his blurred eyes shut in frustration. Damn it. His friends must have been attacked. Now the Fiends were coming his way.

He pulled his legs to his chest and crouched on the balls of his feet while trying to blink his vision clear. When he judged that the first Fiend was no more than twenty-feet away, he hopped up, whipped his arm around the tree and fired.

Nikki pulled up short and skidded to a stunned halt. She had heard sonic boom as the bullet wiz past her ear. She bent over breathing hard while looking with incredulity at her friend. "That's - how - you treat someone - who's trying - to save - your life?"

Jon dropped the gun. "Oh my God, did I hit you?"

"No. Good thing you're a shitty shot."

He could see the rest of the group down the road, still running, but slowing their pace. "Are you being chased?"

"No." She stood up stretching her lungs with a deep breath. "I'm trying to help you."

"What? How?"

She walked up to him and kissed him full on the mouth before he could react and pull back. She then picked up his pistol and turned the stunned man around back toward Moscow. "Come on. I'll explain while we jog. We've still got time."

As they came around the bend in the road, revealing the dam and the beginning of the ruined town, everyone remained skeptical of Nikki's idea, including Jon.

Nikki countered, "You know that the Army perfected exchange transfusions for severe malaria, particularly for those suffering Cerebral Malaria."

Susan said, "They're not even remotely similar diseases. Malaria is caused by a parasite."

Decker, the team's blood analyst jumped in, "She may have something, though. Like Malaria, the FND-z bacterium rides on red blood cells, right? So swapping out Jon's blood with Nikki's not only removes a lot of the bacteria, but it also replaces the diseased conduit with one that should theoretically already have antibodies ready to fight off the infection."

"What he said," nodded Nikki.

Teddy said, "Wait. So you're talking about taking out Jon's blood and replacing it with Nikki's?"

"Exactly," said Nikki.

"Gross," said Amanda, making a face.

"So what do *you* do for blood, Nikki?" asked Teddy.

Christy got on board, her voice rising with excitement. This was what she did. This was stuff she understood. It wasn't running in sheer terror through an unknown countryside. "We hope that there is a stock of O negative in the aid station's blood bank. If there's no O, Nikki, there's no way you can donate and not die."

That's when Ben noticed that the front door of the house they had taken shelter in the night before. It was open. "I remember closing that."

They all followed his look. The day was gray and overcast. The inside of the house was dark. The shotgun hallway bisected the first floor, leading straight to the back. This gave the adolescent male Fiend plenty of room to build up a full head of steam as it charged out the front door, fierce eyes locked directly on Amanda Costas.

Ben, who had unconsciously lowered his shotgun to hip-height, was surprised when his finger pulled the trigger. The un-aimed blast went wide right, but a couple of pellets of buckshot hit the Fiend in the shoulder, spinning it slightly and throwing off its angle of charge. It was just enough to give a screaming Amanda Costas time to run the other way.

As the thing passed him, Steven Costas yanked out his Persian scimitar and hacked at the creature, giving it a wide gash across the back. The monster barely flinched, its sole focus remaining on the little girl.

Jon stuck out a leg and tripped it and then blew the top half of its head off with the Smith & Wesson.

As the shocked group checked themselves for blood splatters, they were suddenly jarred by Amanda's renewed screaming. She had run to the wooded far side of the road, only to be met by four more Fiends scrambling through the burned underbrush. It was a classic ambush in the style of wolves: One flushed out the prey and the others chased it down. They went for the smallest and easiest to capture.

This pack had been working together for a while. Not one of them was older than eighteen.

Nikki aimed, but had to release the trigger, the Fiends right on top of the girl. Amanda had her legs swiped out from under her and she fell hard, tumbling and scraping on the rough asphalt, her breath knocked free, cutting off her scream. The snarling, shrieking, things grabbed her up like a rag doll and started running back into the woods. The group of survivors charged after them, running as fast as they could.

Jon and Steven ran the fastest, both men holding their swords at their sides. Then more Fiends were coming through the woods. They could hear their whoops and howls echoing through the burned trees. Nikki fell to one knee and started firing, taking careful aim with each shot. Ben stopped as well and sprayed buckshot at three that were coming from the right. Then the Fiends stopped. A higher whoop was heard above the others and the second group of Fiends turned and ran back into the denser foliage.

Jon and Steven had almost caught up with the three who were running with the struggling little girl when the monsters simply dropped her and kept running. Steven threw his sword aside and dove to the ground, pulling his baby into his chest. The child's sobs were only broken by the deep breaths needed to make more. Jon stood above them, his sword and pistol ready for a second assault, but the Fiends kept retreating into the woods. A hasty inspection revealed that the girl was unbitten, but her many abrasions made it difficult to tell for sure.

"Dad...Daddy...Daddy. I don't want to be out here anymore. I...I...want mommy. I...I...want to go home."

"I know, Baby. I know."

Jon remained focused, saying, "Steven, we gotta get back on the road, back to the school." He picked up Steven's sword while the man stood, still holding his daughter.

The group fast-walked the rest of the way, this time without the distraction of medical debate. Everyone felt eyes watching them, the hairs standing up on the backs of their necks, their eyes dilated, providing maximum visual information.

It stood with Its pack, hidden in the tree line, watching. Having already saved these Others from the great fire, making them stand hip deep in the much feared lake while the world burned around them, It had stopped the struggle for the little Fresh One; too many Others were dying. There was plenty of food to be found in the forest. The fire had killed many creatures, making them easier to eat than a raw Fresh One. There was no hurry. It could sense from the infant Other that It carried, that more Others were coming from the South. It would wait until there were reinforcements.

A skinny male looked at this female Other that led them, the one that held the baby with the big eyes, and tightened its muscles with frustration. The infant Other had entered its mind once more – *controlling It through the one that led them. Made it stop chasing. Drop its squealing prize. It had it. Had the little Fresh One, its thick young skin smelling so good, the sex of it calling to its loins. It and the Others that had grabbed the Fresh One would have played with it until dark and then finally feasted on its sweet flesh. Then the infant Other made them drop it. It looked with hatred at the infant Other. Its mouth filled with bile as it followed the female that led them back into the deeper wood.*

42 Barricade

Before doing anything else, they had to sweep the school again. Mercifully, it was still empty. They gathered once more in the school's panic ridden foyer. "All right," said Nikki. "This place is too big and we are too few to defend it. We set up shop in the cafeteria. The blood's there and so is the food. We tie the doors shut, make sure the windows are locked."

"Lock the windows?" barked Decker, "You think glass is going to stop these motherfuckers?"

"We cover the windows and work in the kitchen, staying out of sight."

"How long does a blood exchange take?" asked Teddy.

Susan looked at the still shaken group. "It'll be a few hours. We have to set things up and then it has to be done incrementally, small amounts, a few minutes at a time."

"No offense, Jon," said Aaron, "but this is a crazy waste of time. We'd be most of the way to our next stop by now. Instead, we've locked ourselves into this place where we know there's infected outside. With all of that shooting, who knows how many others might be drawn here. If Nikki is immune - great. We can test her blood when we get back to Canada. Find out what makes her tic."

"I agree with you," said Jon, "You've lost valuable time. I don't matter a bit compared to the knowledge that you guys are carrying. We should just turn back around and keep you moving."

Aaron gave a satisfied nod, scanning his fellow scientist for back-up. The group as a whole seemed unsure how to proceed.

"Look, my feelings for Jon aside," said Nikki, "we were kidding ourselves. There's no way we were going to walk up that road and survive. That last assault should be proof enough."

Tran said, "I gotta agree with Nikki. We know that they, the Army, are out looking for us. We've got all we need here. I say we go up to the roof and lay out an SOS with some of these sleeping bags and whatnot. We can write CDC right next to it."

"That's a good idea," said Nikki. "I'm glad I didn't shoot you, Mr. Tran."

"Feeling's mutual, Ms. Rosen."

They found the roof access via a ladder in a janitorial storeroom. Tran and Ben dragged up the brightest colored sleeping bags they could find and started laying out the signal, holding it down with textbooks. The rest of the group started settling in. First they confirmed that there was O negative stored in the refrigerator; unfortunately, there wasn't enough for Nikki to get a full transfusion. The result would be a partial transfusion for her. They'd have to top Jon up with A (his blood type) once they'd taken what they could from Nikki.

Decker, Christy and Susan set up the transfusion space, culling their equipment from the overwhelmingly rancid gymnasium. Nikki, Jon, Aaron, Steven and the kids went to work covering the cafeteria windows with sheets of craft paper and then pulling the blinds so that everyone could move in and out of the kitchen without being observed. They then turned over all of the tables and chairs and shoved them in front of the windows, piling them as high as they could, creating a tangled obstacle course of sorts. If the Fiends wanted in through the windows, they would be slowed down, becoming easier targets. There was one problem that was unsolvable: their minimal supply of ammunition; they'd used up half their reserves. A concerted attack would result in eventual overwhelming odds.

Ben had decided to remain on the roof to keep the first watch. He was uncomfortable with all of these folks anyway. His people were gone, and he found himself adrift in his own backyard. Staying focused on a mission was the only thing that kept him from deep depression. His faith had been deeply shaken, and he found that sitting on the roof with that big sky overhead gave him the time and the space to confront his merciless god.

Nikki realized that she had dumped the pilot's radio with the rest of her gear up the road. She cursed her haste and thoughtlessness. It was dumb things like that that got people killed. Everyone tried to offer forgiveness with the exception of Aaron, who just about had a fit. It was Susan who reminded him that they had all dumped their gear in haste. "It could have been any one of us."

"Bullshit!" yelled Aaron, "She started running off with practically no explanation! What were we supposed to do?"

Everyone chose to ignore this melt down, cutting the man some slack, despite his annoying whine. After all, they were frightened out of their wits too. The anxiety was overwhelming, even for the most resolute among them.

They had one logistical problem: the janitor's room with the roof ladder was over near the gymnasium at the opposite end of the school. If there was a break in and they had to seal themselves inside the cafeteria, the person on the roof would be cut off. A solution didn't present itself and they decided that there were only so many contingencies that they could handle. They had a blood exchange to do, with no time left to waste.

Nikki and Jon were guided to lie down on separate cots. As the catheters were inserted, great care was taken to avoid exposure to Jon's blood. They figured he had about nine hours left, tops, before he would start experiencing the fever. Of course he had been running around after Fiends, barricading the cafeteria - no way to calculate if the extra exercise had any negative effect, shortening the window. The one hope they held onto was the time it took for the bacteria to actually enter the nervous system. It was the last step in the infectious assault, when the brain began to be permanently altered. If they could arrest some of the onslaught by removing Jon's infected red cells, perhaps what was left of his own immune reaction would jump in along with Nikki's, giving him even more time. The whole concept was throwing spaghetti on the wall to see what would stick, so they strapped Jon to the cot in the likely event that nothing did. Nikki promised that this time, she would be the one to end it if he succumbed.

While they finished prepping, Aaron calmed himself by pedantically waxing on for the laymen in the room. "This process is also used to help patients with sickle cell anemia; where malformed red blood cells block blood vessels, cutting off the nutrient supply and damaging internal organs. Interestingly, sickle cell, so called for the C shaped red blood cells that are the hallmark of the disease, is an evolutionary reaction to malaria, which, as you probably know, is a tropical and subtropical disease. That's why…"-

"Burnbaum," said Decker, "Give it a rest. Find a correlation between FND-z and malaria in your own head and save us the headache."

"Preposterous," said Aaron, "FND-z is a straight case of genetic manipulation resulting in a bacteria. The two are mutually exclusive. I'm not one for smoking dope, Rick, but when you're done, why don't you pass me the pipe."

"Aaron, I'll happily shove it right up your pompous ass."

"Alright, alright," said Susan, "Let's focus on the task before us."

It was decided that Steven would be excused from any further duty. His kids were quite rightly terrified to be out of his presence, even for a moment. After determining that Amanda's scrapes were just that - scrapes, the family was allowed to huddle in a tent set up in the cafeteria. Steven found himself reading *Black Beauty* out loud to them by flashlight, and he was secretly grateful to be taken away by the narrator-horse's tail of trial, tribulation and human goodwill.

Ben saw the first movement just before the change in watch. He and Tran had set up a blind on the top of the gymnasium; the high point of the school's roof system. With an air-conditioning unit on one side of him and an easy-up with a green tarp laid out over some lawn chairs on the other, he figured he was pretty well hidden and hoped that a passing Fiend wouldn't notice his perch. So it was very disconcerting that one stepped out of the burned tree line and stared straight at him. It was yet another youth; a female this time and he could see it was pregnant. He watched its eyes scan the base of the school, searching for a way to get to him. Fortunately there were no exterior ladders, the architects knowing full well the curiosity of children and the liability issues thereof. Then another female stepped out of the woods. It was carrying an infant child. Something didn't look quite right with the baby and Ben lifted a pair of binoculars to his eyes. The baby turned and looked straight at him. Its eyes were huge and glowed at him like a hungry jungle cat. It had pointy overly large ears that turned and focused on him as well. Suddenly his mind's eye saw his own image, perched atop the school. His senses became overloaded with sights, sounds, and smells. He could feel the arms of a woman holding him, a scratchy sweater against his side, and he dropped the binoculars with an involuntary scream.

It glanced at the female next to It - the Other that had the belly. It would soon have a baby Other slide out of its fuck hole just like the one in its own arms. The females acknowledged the big screaming Fresh One on the roof, yearning to bite its fat fresh tongue, taste the blood gushing forth. Its breasts ached and it looked down on the infant Other. It had to make it feed so the ache would go away. While the Fresh One screamed on the roof, It lifted the dirty sweater above Its breast and coaxed the infant Other's mouth to the swollen teat. The small one took Its focus off the Fresh One, which then immediately stopped screaming and started sobbing instead. The mother was able to make the connection that the Small One had this affect on the Fresh Ones, and it loved to observe them fall into confusion. It was frustrating that this one was out of reach, but more Others were close or on the way. It and the Other standing next to It would find a way in. They always did.

The male with the spiteful feelings stood behind the female that held the infant and stroked itself, thinking that it wanted to bend her over and.... *It hated the infant Other. It hated the way it showed its sharp teeth and cackled as it made It eat the worst parts: the gristle and tendons, sometimes just dirt and sticks. It had broken several teeth on small rocks and Its mouth and jaw always ached, always a reminder of its tormentor. It hated when the infant was in its head. It waited and waited for the female Other that led them to put the infant Other down, turn her back. It would smother it, fuck it and bite its throat out. Oh how It longed to bite the throat out of the little one who enjoyed making It suffer so. But the female Other that led them never put the infant down. The infant wouldn't let her.*

As Tran came up through the roof hatch, he saw that Ben was holding his head and crying softly. The Fiends switched their gaze to the new piece of meat. Tran saw them at once and instinctively ducked out of sight. He whispered, "Ben...Ben, what the fuck?"

Ben glanced at Tran. "Don't come up here. The devil will try to steal your soul."

Tran took another glance. More began to appear through the trees, all stopping and looking up at the roof, then the building as a whole. The bulk of the building was probably only fourteen feet tall, the gym maybe twenty. It was too tall to climb up on, but with a little innovation a human would easily discover a way to overcome fourteen feet. Tran hoped that they weren't smart enough to sort that out.

Almost as one, the group of Fiends looked to their left toward the South. Tran looked too and was dismayed to see more Fiends coming up the road. There were dozens of them.

"Ben. Look at me. Pull yourself together!" Ben stopped crying and looked at Tran, focusing only on Tran. "I don't think the blind is working. We're surrounded. I think you should come down, get out of sight and maybe they'll go away."

"They ain't goin'."

"How can you know? Come on. Come down."

"Had one stand vigil outside our house for three days till we finally broke and ran, trying to get to the church. Thing drank the water right out of our birdbath when it got thirsty. Tackled my wife, Clare. I couldn't stop. There were more. Had to keep runnin'."

"I'm sorry."

"Sheriff Hill freed her of the possession." He looked at the sky. "Clare, I best come see you soon. Can't put it off anymore, God forgive me."

Tran didn't know what to do. He felt totally exposed - all those eyes watching him. They had approached in silence, but now a chorus of screeches, wails, and laughter was building and the assault on his ears was more than he could bear. He needed to get off of this roof.

Ben saw his hesitation, said, "I'm fine up here. You go back down and arrange a relay. Someone pokes their head up every few minutes or so and I'll give 'em the news."

"I guess that's okay."

"Go down now, before they try to steal your soul too. I've got God on my side. The two of us will fight this together." Ben popped up for a quick scan using only his peripheral vision, his mind cataloging shapes, avoiding anything that might be another one of the devil children. He didn't want to make eye contact with another one again and he quickly popped down.

Tran hustled back to the cafeteria. The sounds coming from the outside had been enough to inform everyone about the deteriorating situation. Their moment of lighter breathing was crushed as the weight of claustrophobia filled the room. On the positive side, the blood exchange was nearly complete. Nikki had the last of the stored O negative hooked up to her while Jon had moved on to the A.

Tran asked, "How are you guys feeling?"

"Other than a sore arm, I don't feel much different," said Jon.

"Same for me," said Nikki. "Maybe a bit tired."

Decker said, "In another hour or so, you should feel pretty good. You can get up and walk around. Well, not you, Jon. You'll obviously have to remain strapped down until we're sure you're out of the woods."

"I don't know if we've got another hour," said Tran. "There's so many of them out there."

They worked out a relay system: Tran would stand below the roof hatch and occasionally pop up to check with Ben. Christy would sit at a bend in the corridor between the janitor closet and the cafeteria, and Aaron would hang out by the cafeteria door. The others would try to nap for a few hours and then they'd switch. The children asked to be involved in the relay part and tried to treat it like a game.

The rest of the day passed this way; the continuing arrival of more infected. By dusk the refugees had lost count; the infected standing well back from the building. Experience had taught their leader that Fresh Ones sitting on roofs invariably meant guns.

The refugees ate their meals on an individual level. With appetites almost non-existent, eating was a job, solely for energy. At eight o'clock, Jon began showing signs of a fever. It had been eleven-and-a-half hours since he'd been bitten, and as some had feared, the vigorous exercise seemed to have sped up the process. Nikki had been up and around for a while, but only went as far as the cafeteria entrance to participate in the relay. Now she paced the room to the point of distraction.

Jon watched her worried movements and finally said, "You're making me dizzy. Maybe you should read a book or something."

"Sorry." She sat and noticed her leg bouncing until she firmly put a hand on it.

The Fiendish howls, shrieks and laughter continued to fill the air and they sat in stony silence, trapped with it, their nerves under constant assault.

When Jon's temperature reached one-o-five, he began to toss his head with delirium. Decker packed frozen pieces of meat around the man, trying to keep the fever at a safe level. He refrained from giving him aspirin; hoping that this time, the fever was a sign of the body's defenses winning. They would monitor his temperature and remove the meat when it reached one hundred four.

By ten o'clock Jon's fever had come down to one-oh-two on its own and he opened his eyes with some clarity.

Decker asked, "Do you know your name?"

"Jon Washington. I'm a reporter stuck in an elementary school cafeteria and I'm waiting to be eaten alive."

At eleven o'clock Jon was suddenly, violently, projectile vomiting. He turned his head away from his friends to keep the potentially lethal liquid from them and heaved until yellow bile was all that he could produce. He was left exhausted and covered with chills as the temperature took hold again.

Susan said, "I haven't seen this. Its possible that he is suffering from a secondary bug - from the transfusion perhaps. We can't be sure of the validity of the blood that was in that fridge."

"Oh for Christ sake," said Decker, parting Jon's sweaty head bandage with a latex gloved hand. "Look at this. The bite's getting all infected."

Christy said, "There's Vancomycin with the other antibiotics. We know it won't stop FND-z, but…"

"I say we try it," said Decker, "Who knows? If Nikki's blood is giving the little bastards a fight they can't handle, maybe a shot of the hard stuff will do them in; along with whatever else has got him. We've got to put him on saline anyway or he'll die from dehydration."

Nikki broke in, "Jon, you still with us?"

Jon nodded through pain and discomfort. "Hurt all over."

An hour later, the howling outside stopped, the silence sudden and unnerving. A minute later, Aaron poked his head in the door, his eyes affright, his fists clenching and unclenching. "The word from the roof is that the infected are closing in." His tenor became that of a frightened boy. "They seemed to be waiting for total dark. There was a moon, but clouds came and made it go away."

Nikki let out a long breath. "I'm going up to have a look. You guys should do whatever you have to do." She nodded at Jon. "It's not like any Cain's that I've seen."

"She's right," said Susan, "He'd be incoherent by now, bordering on coma."

Nikki passed Teddy at the bend in the corridor and patted him on the shoulder. "You're doing a good job, Marine." When she got to the janitor's room and began climbing the ladder, Tran whispered, "We're fucked."

A breeze blew drying ash through the air as she climbed through the hatch, and she found herself squinting to avoid it. She could just make out Ben, who briefly pointed a powerful flashlight at the field behind the school. The beam caught the motion of several bodies running toward the school then disappearing from sight as they fell in next to the building.

Ben said, "They've been doing that for five minutes now. I've lost count how many. There's no point in shooting. I wouldn't hit the dirt if I was aiming at it. Afraid the time has come. Come at last."

Nikki hefted the SCAR and quietly walked to the side of the roof and peered over the edge. What she saw made her new blood run cold. There was a dark mass of moving limbs and torsos. They were building a human pyramid. It was chaotic, but they were intentionally using each other to make a ramp of sorts.

"Shit!" She fired a few rounds into the pack and started running back toward the hatch. "Ben! They're climbing up. Get the fuck over here! We've got to lock this door!"

The air was suddenly filled with cries and hollers. The monsters started hopping up on the roof near the front entry behind her. Nikki spun and shot one, but there were five more running in earnest, some tripping over and destroying the SOS made from sleeping-bags. More popped up on the roof from several different points. They would be overrun in seconds.

"Ben!"

She saw Tran climbing up out of the corner of her eye, shoved him back, "Get back down there!"

Ben spread his arms and yelled out, "Come to me!" And they did, vectoring right for him. He blasted one in the face, re-racked and winged another in the arm. He looked hard at Nikki and for a moment she was mesmerized by the intensity of his gaze, almost as if his eyes somehow got closer to her. "You are an Archangel sent by Him!" he yelled. Then, as he was about to be tackled, he put the shotgun under his own chin.

The shot coincided with Nikki slamming the hatch down.

"What about Ben?" yelled Tran.

"He's with his God now."

Nikki locked off the hatch and flinched at the sound of pounding fists. They heard glass breaking as they stepped out of the janitor's room. A rock shattered a window down the hall, followed by another. Teddy squealed in fright.

"Run!"

They careened past rows of lockers. A classroom door swung open and Nikki slammed it back into the entering Fiend's face. They made it back to the cafeteria with the sound of shattering glass echoing down the halls.

"Ben?" asked Steven, pulling his son through the door.

"Gone," said Tran as he and Steven pulled the doors shut, tying them together with the same heavy rope that had held the gymnasium doors.

43 Assault

Storm and McNeil were at their wit's end. They'd covered and recovered the area that any northbound people on foot could make it to. Outside the unlikely event that the scientists marched directly through the dense burned forests, they'd covered every road and expanded it as time went on. They saw lots of Fiends, but no signs of people holed up against them. There were no reports of any cars making it to the border in the last two days. The Armed Forces were in full assault, having progressed twenty miles across the fertile Saint Lawrence flatlands before getting bogged down in some of the larger towns and villages. The battle for Saint-Georges was sucking up a huge amount of equipment and personnel. Despite new tactics designed to bait and ambush the infected, just as often the soldiers found themselves being ambushed – and now there was some kind of mind control/ESP thing happening that was throwing the whole operation on its head. There were refugees; people who had managed to seal themselves off from attack, but they were extremely few and there was no word of the scientists. The only option the searchers had left was to keep covering the same territory or assume that the scientists had met a gruesome end. The odds of that were looking extremely likely. They had landed for the night at a forward air operations base near Sainte Marie where they could refuel, eat, and crash-out in the back of the helicopter for a few hours. They managed to get an Air Force mechanic to look at their bird, and discovered a nearly unserviceable fuel filter. The thing had been a ticking time bomb and could have resulted in a stall mid-flight.

While stuffing their mouths with a hot meal at the base's mess, they poured over their maps again.

Kelly pointed to a line, "So what about this fire break south of the lake?"

"The fire would have stopped anyone from going that way."

"Yeah, but the rain."

"But why go south?"

"Look, if you follow it west it takes you over toward Stratton and the 27 north, but they would have had to climb these mountains to get there. Go the other way, it ends up at this place, Moscow. They could take the 201 from there."

"We've been all over the 27 and the 201."

"Maybe they're holed up. Still south of the lake."

"Well, Stratton is a no go. If they went that way, we know they're dead." Sam yawned and stretched her limbs. "I guess we could check out Moscow. Maybe they made it there and then got trapped. All I know is that if I don't get some sleep I'm liable to fly us into a hillside tomorrow."

"I know what you mean. I think my elbows are permanently locked from holding up binoculars."

They finished their meal, headed back to their bird and stretched out on camp pads in back, falling asleep in minutes.

The assault on the cafeteria was immediate and intense. The moment that Aaron and Steven had the doors tied shut they were forcefully rattled and yanked from the other side. At the same time a barrage of rocks smashed through the windows, billowing the roller shades and careening off the furniture. Tran, Nikki and Decker took up a defensive position behind the built-in steam table. Everyone else moved into the windowless kitchen where the only other entrance was a large steel delivery door in the back.

To everyone's dismay, Jon had fallen into a coma. His body lay still, his breath shallow, an IV still hanging from his arm. Christy nodded toward Jon, steeling herself against the racket outside, "Sort of wish I could trade places with him."

Steven drew his sword and walked to the cafeteria door.

"Daddy, no! Don't go!" cried Amanda.

"I can better protect you with this out there, Darling."

Steven stepped out into the cacophony while Teddy drew his own sword and threw a comforting arm over his sister. The children made eye contact with Aaron, who was trembling with fear next to the walk-in refrigerator, dialing up the temperature. "Don't want to freeze to death if we have to duck in here."

Susan and Christy looked at each other, trying to get psyched up. Susan said, "This is nuts." They drew their swords and stepped out into the lunchroom.

Nikki turned her head at the new people coming from the kitchen and yelled, "Get back in there! If we have to run through that door, you'll just get in the way." She turned around again as Tran fired at a Fiend that had launched itself half way through a window. Tran's shot missed it by three feet, blowing out another window instead. Nikki dropped the thing with a headshot, leaving it hanging on the sill.

She turned back to Steven as he herded the others back through the door, "Unhook that big industrial stove. Shove it near the door. We'll block it with that."

Decker fired at another Fiend smashing its way through. Then suddenly the entire wall of windows was under assault. The blinds were being ripped down, human bodies poured through as the safety glass harmlessly crumbled into pebble sized pieces. The tumbled furniture was an obstacle, but barely.

Nikki dropped one attacker after another while Tran and Decker did their best to do the same. The strength of the assault was astounding. Clearly these creatures were hungry beyond their last shred of self-preservation. Nikki slapped in her last clip of ammo; thirty more rounds. Decker took the top off a female's head with the last round from Jon's pistol, then pulled his sword. Tran used up the pilot's second clip and pulled his sword as well.

Nikki aimed at a female then held up. The creature was pregnant; probably eight or more months. Her stomach was positively huge. She fell through the window onto the tangled furniture and then looked up with pure menace in her eyes. She shoved a chair out of her way and pushed forward through the tumbled furniture, a line of drool pouring from the corner of her mouth.

A large cleaver slipped between the tied up double doors. The Fiends on the other side were using it as a saw against the rope.

"That's it," said Nikki. "Into the kitchen." Thank God it was a one-way door and not the double-hinged kind. She locked it with its flimsy latch, only to find Steven and Aaron still unhooking the gas line from the big industrial stove. *Why didn't I think to have it ready to go?*

"No time!" cried Decker, grabbing the end of a steel prep station and dragging it toward the door. A Fiend pressed its face against the porthole window. Christy, Susan and Tran jumped in with Decker, jamming the table up against the rattling slab of wood. Then the porthole was smashed out with a fist-sized stone. A Fiend stuck its face in the hole with a laugh and got a mouthful of Tran's blade for its effort. More Fiends replaced their wounded comrade, avoiding Tran's jabs, while bashing themselves against the door and hitting it with rocks, clubs, a fire extinguisher.

As Jon remained comatose, blissfully unaware, Steven finally got the gas line free. While Susan and Decker continued to hold the table, everyone else, including the kids, started shoving the stove. The steel feet on the heavy machine scraped across the ceramic tiles in loud screeching protests.

When they were close, they flipped the table against the door, effectively creating another door made of steel, and then pushed the stove against that. The pounding on the other side was only slightly muffled as they paused and stepped back to take a breath.

Finally, Susan said, "Let's push whatever else we can against it too."

Two hours passed as the infected kept up a steady beat on the door; the sound driving the healthy to the edge of madness. They had all found a place to sit or curl up, trapped with their own nightmarish thoughts. Steven, with the help of Christy, did what he could to comfort his children.

Aaron abruptly stood and started furiously pacing the room. He squeezed his fists and let out huge sighs as he brushed past people without a thought for their personal space.

Finally, Susan said, "Enough! Aaron, sit down."

"Can't."

"You can and you will."

"Nope. Sorry. It's this or I go mad and run out that back door."

"You try and open that door and Nikki has permission to shoot you."

"Yeah? Well, fuck you too, Susan! I've had enough of your bossy bullshit."

"I *am* you're boss. And you'll not speak to me that way!"

"Guys, guys," Tran admonished.

Decker said, "There you go again, Susan."

Susan stood and silenced Decker with a look that said shut it or die then turned to Aaron. "Mr. Burnbaum! I repeat. You will not speak to me in that tone. Is that clear?"

Aaron stopped pacing and stepped right up to her. "Eat me, you fucking narcissistic, brown-nosing, job-suck-up, research-hack, work-thief, especially Robert's, as well as anybody else's good ideas, cunt."

With the exception of the pounding outside, the room went silent. Aaron resumed his pacing, but more quietly.

Tran finally said, "I don't think you steal my work, Susan."

Susan ignored this, gathered herself and said, "Guess what, Aaron? You're fired."

Aaron chuckled at this and then started laughing out loud. "That's ripe. That's fucking perfect, Susan. Susan Chancellor, big shot at the CDC. You delusional whore! In case you didn't notice, I don't give a fuck about a job right now. I want to go outside and run my ass off all the way Canada, but I've got enough wits left to know that that's insane. So again, fuck you!"

Everyone remained respectfully quiet, which was surreal, given the horror trying to break through the door. Finally Aaron said, "How come I'm fired for yelling at you when Decker does it all the time?"

"Because, Decker has been calling me a commie brown-noser ever since I inherited his annoyingly conservative but brilliant ass from the last administration. You, on the other hand, are supposedly my personal assistant... And bottom line, nobody calls me a cunt."

Aaron looked at the floor. "That was probably going too far."

"Far enough that you're still fired."

Suddenly, Jon's eyes flashed open and he stared around the room, seemingly without comprehension.

"Shit!" said Decker, who saw him first and stepped back brandishing his sword. Nikki slapped a hand on his wrist to prevent him from thoughtlessly slashing.

They all looked at Jon, who blinked and swirled his tongue around thickly inside his mouth. His turned his head to the group and his eyes focused. "Is somebody trying to get in?"

Nikki cracked a smile and fell on her knees next to him, pulling him into a hug.

Jon continued, "What the hell's going on?"

"Welcome to the last refuge," said Nikki, kissing his cheeks. "I'm so glad you're alive." She turned to the others. "Can we untie him?"

Decker said, "If he's not trying to kill us now, he will if we don't."

Nikki started unbinding his arms. "We're surrounded. We've sealed ourselves as best we can in the kitchen. I've got three rounds left for the SCAR. We're out of ammo for the pistols."

"Sounds familiar."

She said, "Ben's dead."

He slowly sat up. "Hmm. Sorry to hear that."

Aaron added, "I've turned up the temperature for the coolant in the walk–in refrigerator. If it comes to it, we can seal ourselves in there."

Jon nodded slowly, thinking about that. "We're sort of like a Russian doll. We keep squeezing into tighter and tighter spaces." He licked his teeth and made a face. "I'd kill for a toothbrush."

This got some smiles and he let Nikki steady him. He rubbed his wrists where the bindings had been. "I'm kinda thirsty."

Christy handed him a glass of water while Decker slipped on a pair of latex gloves to remove the IV.

Jon frowned at the tap water, but drank it anyway. He looked back at Aaron, "Seriously though, Aaron. I don't think the air supply in the walk-in would keep us alive for very long. Better to keep the food fresh. We may need it if we have to wait this out for a stretch."

"I hadn't thought of that," said Susan. "Aaron, turn it back down."

Aaron scowled, but did as he was told.

Susan continued, "Its good to have you back, Mr. Washington. I'm afraid we can't be certain that you aren't somehow still contagious so I suggest we all keep up proper precautions. Nikki, I suppose you're excepted."

Christy refilled Jon's glass again and he drank the water slowly while nodding at the door, "Annoying, huh?"

"Tell us about it," said Teddy.

Everyone cracked another smile, but it was quickly buried again under the continued assault. The door was solid oak and built to code with a three-hour burn time, but it was still only made of wood. The refugees couldn't see it, but the Fiends were gradually demolishing the barrier. Ever so slowly a pile of splinters and shards was building on the floor of the other side.

44 Heavies

Storm and McNeil way overslept. They'd driven themselves to exhaustion with their hunt. The racket that was the comings and goings of a busy airfield didn't stir either one of them. When they finally woke, it was only because an airman banged on the helicopter door, yelling that they needed the space for other aircraft.

The two women noted each other's greasy hair and rank smelling clothes and decided that the folks they were looking for had it far worse. They would forgo a shower, but talked the airman into letting them grab some quick grub.

As they stepped out into the soft morning light, the full buzz of this sector's air campaign came to life. The small commuter airport was maxed out with helicopters and cargo planes as well as a handful of F-35B jump jets.

As the two women made their way to the mess tent, they noted the combat support hospital and cringed at its ominous presence. In addition to mending wounded soldiers with accident-related battlefield injuries, combat support hospitals had been converted to a dual role, one that no American hospital had ever filled before: The mobile lifesaving post was also a de facto euthanasia station. A soldier or civilian who had been bitten or had in some other way become infected, was brought to the hospital to receive a more humanitarian ending than would otherwise be possible.

In the beginning, when the outbreak had already reached epidemic proportions, the authorities had simply locked up the victims. Upon fully succumbing to the disease, the infected continued to be fed like livestock. It was thought that if a cure could be found, that the victims would one day be repatriated to society. As light-weight criminals, and then even more scurrilous types were cleared out of prisons to make room for the ever growing numbers of diseased, the nation's scientists finally weighed in, explaining that the damage was irreversible and the practice, pointless. After the fierce debate that ensued in Congress, and also the media, the prisons were gassed and euthanasia stations were created instead. Narcotics, barbiturates, and anesthetic gases were deemed too complicated to administer for the mass killing of so very many. What was needed was a quick, mechanical, coup de grace that was relatively clean. After some trial and error, it was decided that it could be best achieved by "helping" the patient lay face down on what was more or less a massage table, and utilizing a captive bolt (also known as a cattle stunner). A pistol variant, originally used by veterinarians in the field, was found to be most effective. A retractable steel bolt was fired into the base of the neck, destroying the spinal connection and thereby creating near instant and certainly painless death. Naturally, the reactions the victims had to this ending, varied widely. Most people recognized that they were doomed and did 'go gentle into that good night'. There were, however, those who weren't so eager to cooperate. For them, the Heavy Squad was created. Typically made up of a team of nine soldiers, preferably heavily built, they wore a variation of a shark suit under hockey pads and a full riot helmet with gas mask. It was the Heavies job to haul the poor struggling bastards into the Heavy Room where force was applied and the result was just the same.

There was a crematorium attached to each euthanasia station (thankfully far from the mess tent) and with remorseless consistency, it burned the dead, day and night. For those who worked around these facilities, the sheer volume of rendered, sweet-smelling, human meat could only be scrubbed from the senses through consistent familiarity or menthol cream smeared under the nose. The smoke would drift up in thick gray volumes, and on a cloudless day it could blot out the cheeriness of the sun for miles. To bring some comfort to these circumstances the hospital set up loudspeakers throughout the enterprise. It was somebody's clever idea to play the *Going Home* score from the soundtrack of the 1973 dystopian film, *Soylent Green*. Beethoven and Tchaikovsky played in an endless loop, the soaring strings blending with the smoke, dulling the senses. With these rudimentary techniques, it was hoped that taste, smell and hearing, for those who labored in such places, would become numb to the constant parade of death.

Needless to say, the battlefield tactics of the infected, as simple as they were, often left even the most resolute combat unit paralyzed with fear. With the knowledge that a light wound involving an exchange of fluids or even a close inhalation of breath meant sure death, combat effectiveness was often driven to near zero.

It was Storm and McNeil's bad luck that they walked to the mess tent as a load of "wounded" was being "escorted" to the euthanasia station. One soldier with two fingers chewed off and a catastrophic bite in his left calf, nevertheless fought with the strength of a badger as the Heavies steered him to the Heavy Room. The man screamed out, "No! I won't let you! Just let me go! I'd rather become one of them!"

The more docile wounded who were shuffling toward the Ending Room looked on in horror at this display. One broke loose and started running only to meet up with the electric fence that funneled everyone toward the tent. The jolt was enough to knock the man unconscious and his body spasmed on the ground for a moment before two more Heavies lifted him up and carried him off to the Heavy Room.

Sam said, "You know what? I'm not so hungry after all. What do you say we grab some instant coffee and a snack bar and get up in the air?"

"I'm not sure I could even get that down, after seeing that. Promise if I get infected you'll just shoot me in the head right there and then."

"Ditto."

Their bird was all gassed up. With forced looks of determination, they buckled in and wound up for another day of near impossible odds.

At 3:00 A.M. the Fiends at the kitchen door had stopped their assault. Even an infected human needs its sleep. The refugees inside got two hours of respite, only to be jolted awake again at five when the battering began with renewed vigor.

They forced themselves to choke down an early breakfast and went over their limited options.

Susan began with, "Every day that we stay in here is another day that we aren't able to work on a cure."

"That's a helpful thought, Susan," said Decker with deep sarcasm.

"Mr. Decker, you best even your tone."

"Don't be an idiot," he shot back with exhaustion.

She chose to ignore this and looked pointedly at Nikki and Jon. "We have one advantage. You two are immune and therefore might be able to create a diversion, draw the infected in one direction, while we go the other."

Jon said, "It's still a long way to Canada."

Susan turned to the rest, "Any other ideas?"

The group was silent until the unmistakable sound of splitting wood filled the room. They all looked at the blocked door. The sound got louder as the wood was broken to pieces. Suddenly a hand appeared through the gap between the steel prep table and the doorframe.

Aaron fell back into a corner, "Oh my God, they're through!"

Jon pulled his sword, stepped around the piled appliances and slashed at the hand. The fingers fell to the floor like tree trimmings. A scream of anguish came from the other side of the barrier as the rest of the hand was withdrawn. Everyone else pulled their swords.

Suddenly, the prep table jolted back an inch. "Come on everyone," yelled Jon, "Push back!"

They did so with all they had, closing the gap again and keeping pressure on the kitchen equipment. There was a slam as though a Fiend had hit it with a running start and the table moved back another inch only to be shoved back by the group.

Tran stated the obvious that they could keep doing this forever and was answered by Aaron who screamed, "I told you we should have gotten the walk-in ready."

"And what? It's not like we can lock it from the inside," shot Decker.

"We tie it shut."

"We'll still die of asphyxiation. Moron."

"Better than getting eaten alive."

Decker looked at the fridge, "He makes a good point."

There was another jolt and they shoved back again.

Christy said, "What if they're all in there? You know, the other side of this barricade? We haven't heard a single bang on the back door. What if it's wide open out there, and we make a run for it?"

"To where?" asked Nikki.

"The only place they can't seem to go very far, the water. I saw a rowboat tied near the dam. If we can make it there…"

Jon said, "Its maybe a quarter mile back up the road. That's a long run in the open. Especially with the kids."

The infected heaved again on the other side of the barrier. Nikki said, "I think Christy's got the only idea."

45 The End

Before the hopelessness of their situation had set in, they had pre-loaded fresh backpacks with food and medical gear. The hard drives and samples were still in their cases. The group grimly strapped the packs on. Amanda and Teddy would carry nothing.

With his sword drawn, Jon cracked the back door and peered outside. Dawn had barely arrived. A thick cloud cover diffused the light into shades of gray. The only sign of infected was three dead by the wall that Nikki had shot from the roof. He opened the door a bit more and stuck his head all the way outside. As they kept their weight against the kitchen equipment, the refugees watched him with growing anxiety, their packs on, their muscles tensed to run.

The playing fields were empty so Jon stepped all the way outside. Not a Fiend in sight. He could hear their continued barrage echoing from within the building. The way for now, looked clear. He poked his head back inside. "Okay."

The group single-filed it out the door as quickly and quietly as they could. Jon took the point with Nikki in the rear. Without a word, they shuffled past the cafeteria and angled toward the road. They were spotted almost immediately.

Nikki looked back and saw Fiends pouring out of the windows. "Run!" She turned, dropped to one knee and shot three with the SCAR's last bullets, then tossed the gun and pulled her sword, running to catch up with the others.

Steven and the kids were falling behind and she caught up with them first. She bent down in front of Amanda. "On my back, now!"

The little girl jumped and clung to Nikki's neck as they picked up speed again. The road seemed to last forever until finally the house by the dam came into view. A bird's-eye-view showed a huge mass of Fiends slowly catching up with them. They ran past the house and angled toward the dam. Aaron dropped his pack and burst ahead. Jon and Steven lifted Teddy off the ground and ran with the boy between them. Aaron disappeared over the top of the earthen wall that made up the bulk of the dam and then they heard him yell "FUCK!"

They all caught up and saw Aaron below with a hopeless look on his face. The beached rowboat had a huge hole in its floor. It was little more than a rotting hulk.

Nikki looked behind them and shoved people toward the water. "Go! Out! Out in the water!" Everyone jumped into the lake and began swimming away from the dam. The Fiends poured over the top and crashed into the water as well. The group shrugged off their packs and swam for their lives. Nikki and Jon stopped in waist-high water and turned to face the onslaught with their swords. They slashed and cut, hacked and punched, managing to slow the Fiend momentum. Seeing others slashed down, the infected tried to give wide berth to the two blade holders while becoming enraged as their prey were quickly swimming out of range.

The infant Other watched all of this with childish pleasure. It could feel all of the heartbeats of what it now felt to be extensions of its own self, its children, and reveled in the sensation of one of those heartbeats suddenly coming to a stop, the victim of one of the Fresh One's blades. It stretched its long hocked lower limbs and directed its mother to step forward. The infant would enter the minds of the Fresh Ones and make them stop, make them come to it so that all of the Others could feast.

The Other who hated the infant with every cell in its body, watched the female leader step forward while holding Its nemesis tight. Both of them were distracted. It could smell its chance.

A helicopter's thumping blades echoed faintly across the water and then the sound grew louder until it eclipsed the shouts and growls of the Fiends.

Storm and McNeil had followed the Canada Road south directly toward Moscow. What they saw at the dam sent their hearts to pounding.

"Holy shit! Look at those people!" Kelly put her binoculars to her eyes. "If it's them, there's more than just the scientists."

Sam swung the AStar off the line of the road and aimed straight for the dam. "Kel, grab the shotgun and open the side door."

Kelly unbuckled herself and climbed into the rear. "I count ten healthy."

The AStar could only hold six, including the two of them, maybe seven with one kid. Both women thought, how are we going to deal with that?

Sam put the bird into a hover while Kelly slid open the door, cocked and shouldered the shotgun, and fired over and over into the crowd of Fiends. Sam brought the helicopter lower, hovering inches above the water and then slowly side slipped until she was close to the group that was swimming.

The group was collectively stunned at this last-second rescue, and watched in wonder as the helicopter lowered itself toward them. Nikki was the only one who knew the truth of the situation. That it would be only a partial rescue. It was obvious to her that the helicopter couldn't take them all.

The infant Other put its great muddy brown eyes on the fleeing Fresh Ones and gathered as many of them into its mind as it could.

A collective buzzing entered the refugee's heads. Those that weren't looking toward shore saw their comrades do so and followed their gaze. Upon seeing the infant, they were also sucked into its mental grasp. Nikki felt a sense of calm take over her whole being. She could smell the comfort of mother's milk and she was faintly aware of her heart rate falling. This was true for all of them. A part of Nikki knew exactly what was going on. She'd been in this place before – the memory of it faint, familiar, water all around, a foreboding presence, doom. She knew it meant the death of her, but there was nothing to be done. There was only the entity that filled her mind and the smell of the mother's milk.

The people in the deeper water found it difficult to swim and they turned as one back to shore. Even Sam and Kelly were mesmerized; Sam keeping the bird mindlessly steady while Kelly laid down her gun and simply stared. The Fiends stopped attacking, instead, slowly waded back toward the shore, inviting their feast to come join them on dry land.

That's when It, the tormented Other, the Other that had been treated like a plaything for the amusement of the little one with big ears and eyes, the sharp pointy teeth - that's when It felt the hold of the little fucker let go – just enough, just enough to raise its blade... The tormented Fiend hacked down on its insufferable nemesis with fiendish glee, plunging the butcher's knife into the mother for good measure....

The spell was gone. Friend and foe looked upon each other with startled recognition. The Fiend nearest Nikki lunged forward, tackling her into the water. Jon, who had only just snapped out of it enough to remember he was holding a sword, was also tackled. Suddenly they were engulfed in a melee of punches, kicks, head-butts and bites. The only thing they could do was to try to swim down, but the water was too shallow for escape. Robert Tran stepped in, swinging his sword with furious intent. "NO YOU FUCKING DON'T!" He brought the legendary sharpness of the Japanese blade across one screaming Fiend's face, rendering its lower jaw to flapping skin and teeth. He hacked at the monsters with only one thought in mind – these people are not going to die!

Kelly yelled out, "Are you the CDC folks!" The swimmers nodded affirmative as they dog-paddled. She went with cold logic and continued, "One kid can come! Then four of you!"

The swimmers pushed Amanda onto the hovering landing skid and she quickly climbed aboard, turned and screamed with her arms out, "Daddy!"

Kelly held the girl, "Four more. Only four!"

Steven held on to Teddy and they looked at each other with understanding. They would sacrifice themselves for the baby girl.

Aaron, who didn't give a single thought to another scenario, jumped aboard next.

Decker looked at his two female companions and said, "Go!"

Susan said, "We should both stay. Nikki is the priority."

"Get on the fucking helicopter, Susan!"

She looked at the others holding back the horde with their swords, closed her eyes for a moment, then gave him a kiss on the cheek and followed Christy onboard. Decker shoved the pack with the hard drives into Susan's hands.

Kelly yelled, "One more!"

Decker looked at Steven who nodded with a smile and they shoved Teddy on board.

The boy screamed and reached out to his dad while Kelly held him to her chest. She yelled, "We'll be back as soon as we can!"

Sam pulled on the collective and the helicopter rose back up. With a twist of the cyclic, the bird banked away from the battle below.

Nikki had broken free, gasped for air, then hacked at the Fiends above Jon until he too got his head back above water. He took in a huge lungful of air and then screamed out a bellow of rage, lacerating anything in front of him with the saber. Nikki and Tran continued to hack and stab as they all back pedaled into deeper water, finally freeing themselves enough to swim away and move out with Decker and Steven.

Nikki said, "Robert, are you bit?"

"Don't think so."

"No blood in the mouth? No bloody water?"

"No, Ma'am."

Jon said, "Well I'm fucking bit and I can't swim with this fucking leather on and this fucking sword."

They paused and dog-paddled as they dropped their weapons and struggled out of their jackets. Jon had a nasty bite on his forearm and his head bandage had come off revealing the red bite-shaped wound. The Fiends watched from the shore to see which way they would go. There weren't a lot of options. The lake had no islands. The right shore hugged the Canada Road. The left shore hugged the burned forest. The group slowly swam north, trying to conserve their energy. To their frustration, the infected split their forces, with half walking up the road and the other half crossing the dam to follow them from the other side.

After fifteen minutes of hopeless swimming, Jon and Nikki had somewhat separated themselves from Decker, Tran and Steven.

Jon said, "I think we're finally done." He got closer to her, getting her attention, then nodded at the Fiends on the shore.

She said, "It doesn't look good."

"Thank you anyway."

"For what?"

"Saving my life for a few more hours. Keeping me human. Besides, I'd rather drown with you than shoot my brains out."

"That might be the craziest statement I've ever heard. What a world we've found ourselves in."

"How did you figure you were immune?"

"When you kissed that cut on my finger a few days ago, I was afraid for you... Infected blood... I swallowed a lot in that river. I couldn't admit it to myself. I'm so sorry."

"No reason to be."

"I almost didn't. Something in me didn't want to own up to it. That I'd gotten sick, that I had gotten the disease."

"I wouldn't have wanted to admit it either."

The effort to swim was becoming exhausting. Their breath was getting labored and it was becoming a struggle to keep even their mouths above water. They swam for a while, just breathing through their noses.

She finally spoke again. "Before he died, Ben said I was an Archangel."

"Ben was a fundamentalist wacko."

"That's true, but it doesn't negate that something special happened to me, and because of that, to you too."

"That's true, it doesn't. I'm cold. Aren't you cold? This water's fucking freezing."

"Yes, but listen. What if we have a higher purpose? You know because of this?"

He looked around them and nodded at the teeming shore, "I think our purpose now, is to finally be done, Nik."

"No. I don't believe that. All of this didn't happen so we could drown."

"So you're getting religion on me, now?"

She slowed her swimming and looked at him square in the eyes. "I'm going to tell you something that I've never told anyone, not even my own parents."

He looked at her with curious anticipation.

Her words came from someplace deep, had to break through a lifetime of fear, finally coming out strong, and full of courage. "Jon... I love you."

He was taken aback. Hadn't expected this. He glanced at the three other swimmers. They seemed to be in a world apart. His mind swayed with this knowledge and he almost forgot how to dog paddle. Then he smiled. "Really?"

"Really."

"But when you left me for dead, you were so... mean to me..."

"It hurt too much to be any other way."

He tried to look deeply in her eyes, preparing himself to say the words back.

She laughed at him, pushing him away. "Stop. Don't even think of saying it back with that goofy grin on your face."

"What grin?"

"Just... keep it to yourself. When you're ready, maybe you'll say it. Not like this. Not now." She smiled and gave him a quick kiss.

"Well shoot. Now I don't know what to say."

She looked at the sky and then briefly closed her eyes. "Say you want to live."

"I do. I very much want to live."

Just then, Storm and McNeil's AStar swooped around a hilltop and down over the lake.

"And so you will."

They watched the logo-splattered chopper come down into a hover. The three men behind them let out loud whoops of joy, waving and splashing each other in celebration.

Jon pulled Nikki to him and gave her a quick deep kiss. Then he looked into her eyes, and with deep sincerity, said, "I love you too."

AUTHOR'S NOTE

I hope you enjoyed this dastardly adventure If you simply can't get enough, the second book in the Of Sudden Origin universe: *Children of Fiends* is waiting for you to read.

Please don't hesitate to add a review to this book's Amazon page. Just type the following into your browser:
Amazon.com/dp/asin/B00KH89CU4
I've provided the soil and the seed - reviews are the sun and water to make it grow.

You can also jump over to my website to learn more about me and join my email list: www.cchaseharwood.com

Cheers,
C. Chase Harwood